Shared
Blood

THE SENSE OF BELONGING SERIES
BOOK 1

BRENDA BENNING

Shared Blood
Copyright © 2024 by Brenda Benning

ISBN: 979-8895311448 (sc)
ISBN: 979-8895311455 (e)

WRITERS'
BRANDING

Writers' Branding
(877) 608-6550
www.writersbranding.com
media@writersbranding.com

Special thanks to the Eastern Shore of Maryland for providing the inspiration and environment for me to pursue this dream. And for those who helped us along the way, especially Gee and Susan.

Disclaimer

This is a work of fiction. All characters, names, places, and descriptions are strictly a product of the author's imagination and used solely in a fictitious way. Any resemblance to a real person or situation is purely coincidental. Any trademarked name, place, or otherwise referenced are not a reflection of the holder of the trademark and are used without permission and do not reflect on said owner.

Contents

Chapter 1

"Ash, We did it!! Can you believe it? College graduates!" Aja gushed as she adjusted her black cap, the gold tassel dangling in her face.

Ashley nodded and smiled, hugging her twin sister tightly against her. Aja didn't know it yet, but her plans would be separating them for the first time in their lives. But now wasn't the time to bring it up. She would enjoy the next few weeks before she dropped the bomb her sister was least expecting.

"I'm so proud of you guys!" Lundyn and Sally Jo came up behind Ashley. She turned and gave Lundyn a hug and then moved to Sally Jo. As she pulled away, she noticed Jacob behind them, waiting his turn with a goofy smirk on his face.

Ashley moved away from the girls and reached around Sally Jo to her brother. "Why are you hiding behind your sister?" she asked with her eyebrow raised.

Jacob smiled and shrugged. He pulled her into a hug. "I'm proud of you, babe. Well, actually *us* I guess." He chuckled in her ear making her giggle from the vibration.

Ashley had met Jacob almost two years ago when she and her sister transferred to the University of Minnesota. Ashley had taken the last two years to focus on elementary education, like her mom always wanted to do. Shaking the sad thoughts from her mind, she looked back at her sister who was now surrounded by the other two women who had come to congratulate them.

Lundyn Carter and Sally Jo Hughes were best friends who happened to be as close as sisters. They weren't even related but acted as close as she and her twin did. Ashley always thought it was fun to hang out with them, although she didn't get many chances. She saw Sally Jo more often because Sally Jo was her boyfriend's sister, but where Sally Jo was, Lundyn wasn't far behind.

Lundyn had gotten married a few months back and Sally Jo's boyfriend also moved from Boston to Minneapolis around the same time. Since then, Sally Jo had been around her parents' house less. Sally Jo had a drop-dead gorgeous boyfriend, so she probably had to keep him away from prying eyes too. But Ashley had seen them together and he clearly only had eyes for her. They were engaged now, but Sally Jo said she was hoping for a sneak away trip somewhere tropical to get married, nothing like what Lundyn had or tradition dictates.

Both Sally Jo and Lundyn were grad students in English literature. They had attended the University of Minnesota for their undergraduate work as well.

Ashley looked over at her sister again. She sighed softly. She didn't know how to tell her sister what her plans were, but she knew she couldn't keep it to herself for very much longer. They were so close they could almost read each other's minds by now. Ashley was actually glad for the distraction of graduation. She was amazed Aja hadn't been clued in already considering Ashley's mood lately.

As if she sensed Ashley's anxiety, Aja moved toward her and grabbed Ashley's arm. She looped hers through Ashley's and leaned close. "I know, I wish they were here too. But let's celebrate, ok? Sam's meeting us by the entrance." Aja leaned her forehead against her sister's and sighed.

Ashley nodded and gave her sister a small smile, grateful that Aja had misinterpreted her melancholy mood for missing their parents and not her impending departure.

"Pictures!" Sally Jo yelled from only a few feet away, making Ashley jump and then laugh.

Shaking her head, she pulled Aja to the side and grabbed hold of Jacob's arm with her free one. Sally Jo and Lundyn both took out their phones and snapped a couple of pictures.

Aja spotted one of her friends from class and ran off to chat with her. Ashley turned back to Jacob. "So, what are the plans for the rest of the day?" she asked him.

Jacob shrugged. "No clue. I think Gran Marion had some dinner plans for everyone, right Lundyn?" He glanced over at Lundyn who nodded.

"Actually, Ashley, I was wondering if I could talk to you for a second," Lundyn said, looking at Jacob and then Ashley.

"Sure. What's up?" Ashley glanced over at Jacob and then back to Lundyn, wondering what she would need to talk to Ashley about, or if she wanted Jacob to leave.

Lundyn smiled softly. "I was actually wondering if I could use your final paper on Toni Morrison's 'The Bluest Eye' for one of the freshman classes I am teaching this summer. I just want to show an example of how to use the text to write papers and yours turned out wonderfully."

Ashley was shocked. She had forgotten that Lundyn was the teaching assistant in her African American lit class

3

last winter. It turned out to be one of her favorite classes and she had only taken it because she needed a higher-level literature class for her graduation requirement. Lundyn had met with her once or twice to talk about her essay because Ashley had a lot of difficulty with the text. It was complicated by Ashley's own sense of identity and where she belonged, not only because of her skin color. Her sense of family had been so disjointed from an early age.

"I guess so, but I struggled so much with that paper. Why do you think it will be helpful?" She tipped her head slightly to the side as she watched Lundyn.

Nodding, Lundyn smiled. "You did, but the end result was so well written. It will be helpful for students to see how they can connect with the text and apply it in different ways in their papers. *And* if I recall you did get the highest grade in the class on that paper." She raised her eyebrows at Ashley, who blushed a little at the compliment. "Prof Collins was disappointed when I reminded her you were an El Ed major, not English," Lundyn added with a wink.

"That's really sweet. But I don't think I could do that many papers in every class! You guys love to write." Ashley laughed and Lundyn just smiled and nodded as Aja reappeared by her side.

"So, should we go find Sam, Ash? I would like to get a couple pictures with him too. Without him, who knows where we would have ended up!" Aja took hold of Ashley's arm, dragging her to the front of the building. They had congregated outside, and Ashley wondered why Sam didn't just meet them there too. She waved goodbye to Lundyn and Sally Jo. Jacob threw her a kiss and a wink then mouthed "See you later" with a huge grin on his face.

Ashley turned back to her sister and lightly shook off her hand so she didn't feel like she would be pulled down. She was enjoying this side of her usually quiet and shy sister. Aja was the thinker of the two. She would contemplate things for a long time before acting, while Ashley would jump right in. She had a motto of "Why not?" or "What's the worst that could happen?" She figured that's why she loved Sally Jo so much. They were so similar. Thankfully Jacob was more like her than Aja. Then again, they probably wouldn't have lasted as long as they had if he was. She loved her twin and would die for her, but she didn't want a partner in life who was just like Aja. She wanted adventure and to live life to the fullest without regrets. She wondered if her mom ever had regrets, besides not being able to go to college. She silently promised her mom a long time ago that she would live her life in a way that she wouldn't regret anything. And that's just what her plan was—but she still had to tell Aja.

Ashley knew that their early life and how they came to live with their uncle was why she's the way she was. It was likely why Aja was the way she was as well, she figured. Ashley didn't want regrets like her mom who never got to fulfill her dreams while Aja wanted to make sure everything was going to be ok before she jumped in. Sam raised them since they were barely five years old and while Aja liked the overprotective role that he played Ashley felt suffocated a lot of the time. She tried to be understanding since it was his sister who was killed, but she still felt like he was too protective of her and her sister.

Before she knew it, Ashley was engulfed in a suffocating bear hug by her uncle. His huge arms and body could easily squeeze the life out of her. It wasn't that he was fat or anything, but his work required him to continue to work out even at his age so he could run after bad guys and stuff like that. He was tall and muscular and had freakishly long arms—which she reminded him of daily.

"Ok, ok, you're going to literally kill me if you don't let me go," Ashley complained, as she pushed away from her uncle.

Sam chuckled as he let her go. "I am so proud of both of you! I am impressed with everything you have had to overcome and to come out where you are now, I am just so proud to be your uncle."

Aja reached up and touched his cheek. "You know we couldn't have done it without you, Sam," she said with a smile.

Ashley snorted. "You know that's exactly what he was looking for, right?" She put her hands on her hips and raised her eyebrows at her uncle.

Sam laughed his deep rumbly laugh that had always been comforting to Ashley. "Is that so wrong? I mean I should get a tiny bit of the credit for raising you two right and making sure you did your homework and all that." He pulled Aja closer to him and planted a kiss on her head, now empty of her cap.

"Sure sure, whatever you say old man," Ashley said with a smile and a wave of her hand.

Sam laughed again. "So, are we headed to Gran Marion's mystical café for food?" he asked, looking between the girls. His brown eyes were filled with something she couldn't quite figure out. Pride maybe? His salt and pepper hair was barely moving in the light breeze, but then again the tight curls prevented that. His light brown skin looked darker against his pressed white shirt.

Ashley looked at her sister. She knew what she wanted to do, but Aja looked more uncertain. "Aja? What do you want to do?"

Gran Marion was Lundyn's grandmother. Ashley figured the reason Aja was hesitating was because Lundyn was now married to Ryan, Aja and Sam's coworker. Aja liked to keep her worlds separated, which annoyed Ashley. It was too much work to make sure you kept your work friends away from your school friends and so on. Ashley didn't want to pressure Aja into doing what she wanted either, even if Ashley would be disappointed having to go home instead of socializing. She felt their accomplishments should be celebrated, and what better way to do that than with friends and good food?

Finally, Aja shrugged. "Ok, for a little while."

Ashley wanted to fist pump in the air but resisted. She didn't want Aja to feel bad. So instead, she smiled and nodded. "I'll let Jacob know that we'll be there." She leaned over and gave her uncle a kiss on the cheek and then headed off to find Jacob.

Jacob's and Lundyn's families had a long and complicated history that Ashley wasn't even a hundred percent sure of. But even though Gran Marion was Lundyn's grandmother, she treated Sally Jo and her family as her family as well. Some day she might try to understand it all, but at the moment she just cared about finding her boyfriend and getting some food. She'd heard that Gran is the most fantastic cook around—at least Sally Jo doesn't stop talking about her desserts, not that she's ever shared so Ashley could try them.

The early afternoon sun was starting to hang a little lower in the near cloudless sky. The temperature was perfect at seventy-four degrees. Ashley wished they could have had the ceremony outside, but for some reason they couldn't. Plus, it would have been quite a production to move the huge crowd to the outdoors. Right after the ceremony though everyone spilled outside to enjoy the beautiful weather.

Ashley found Jacob talking to a group of guys he hung out with from the baseball team. Jacob didn't play like his sister, but he knew a few of the players from high school. She always wondered why he never played, especially since Sally Jo was such an amazing softball player.

Sneaking up behind him, Ashley tucked her arms under his and around his waist. He jumped slightly and then looked over his shoulder and grinned at her. Jacob wasn't short, but Ashley's height and heels made them only a couple inches different.

Pulling her around to his front, Jacob kissed her nose. "I think I like you this tall," he said with a wink.

Ashley giggled and nodded. "I could get used to being tall I think, as long as I'm not taller than my guy, whoever that is or will be." Her playful smile didn't go unnoticed by her boyfriend who feigned shock and hurt.

Jacob grabbed his chest and dramatically groaned. "Oh, my sweet Ash, are you leaving me? Replacing me with someone younger already?"

"Hmm, not yet, but you never know," she teased and leaned in to kiss his cheek. "Come on, I'm hungry. I might actually get to try one of Gran Marion's brownies if we beat your sister there!"

Jacob laughed. "Good point." He waved to his friends, and they headed back arm in arm to where Ashley had left Aja and Sam.

As they neared Sam and her sister, Jacob leaned over and whispered in her ear. "Have you told Aja yet, Ash?"

She felt his eyes on hers as she shook her head. Ashley couldn't hold his gaze. She felt so guilty for keeping her secret. Jacob already knew about it and fully supported her decision. But they both knew it would be a difficult conversation with her twin sister. He offered to be there with her when they talked, but Ashley said she had to do it herself. She just had to find the right time. But when was it a good time to break this kind of news to her sister?

Sam held out his hand to Jacob as he and Ashley reached them. Jacob took it, giving the older man a firm shake. Ashley and Aja exchanged smiles, and the group made their way to the parking lot. Jacob still lived at his parents' place in Bellbrook Springs, which was north of where school was located, so he had driven separately. Ashley, Aja, and Sam had come from the southern end of the Twin Cities area and Sam and Aja would likely head back to their place after lunch while Ashley stayed a while longer with Jacob.

Sam and Aja followed Jacob's car out of the parking lot and through the Minneapolis streets to the highway. Ashley and Jacob were quiet for most of the ride, Ashley still lost in her thoughts. She looked over as Jacob took her hand in his and squeezed it lightly.

"Hey, you ok?" he asked his baby blue eyes filled with concern.

Ashley nodded and turned back to the window. "I'm just worried about how Aja will react to my news." She leaned her head against the seat back and stared at the passing buildings and then eventually houses on the side of the highway.

She had actually started to love it here. She wasn't a huge fan of the winters, but the change in seasons and especially the fall was amazing in Minnesota. Before moving here, they had lived in a few different places, but always a big city for Sam's work. They had lived in Florida for a while but didn't even make it to the ocean. Sam was just too busy with work to take a day off to go to the beach, not that she was a big fan of the beach, but it would be fun to see the ocean and spend a day there. He also kept their circle of friends and acquaintances small for safety he always said.

Ashley's thoughts drifted to her parents. Her mom had died when she was just five years old. She had held her mom's hand while she passed away, which is something no little girl should ever have to go through. Her dad had held the gun that took her mom away from her forever. She would never forgive him, even though he had tried to reach out from prison on multiple occasions. Her tears and her sister's cries would be forever engrained in her soul. The loss of her mom was far more impactful than losing her father.

When she was a teenager, she had no one to talk to about boy problems or her first period or anything else moms and daughters were supposed to talk about. She had Aja, but they were going through it together. Sam didn't understand and tried to get women in their lives who could be role models and support for the "girly things" as he called it. To his credit he did a really good job surrounding them with the right people. But none was her mom.

Thankfully, Sam understood the need for African American women to be present in their lives. He kept his nappy hair short and had no clue about how to manage a little girl's tight curls, let alone two of them. From little on, Aja liked her hair in tight braids, neat and tidy and off her face. Ashley was the opposite. She liked it free and bouncing all over. It made for a difficult process when it was time to sort it and try to pick through it, but she didn't care.

Once Ashley got closer to adulthood, she realized the brilliance of her sister and having her hair braided, needing little to no maintenance for weeks. So, she began trying different styles. Her favorite became crochet braids. But she quickly found that these were much heavier than just braiding in extra hair. Aja loved her box braids because she always added a new color to the ends. She had added a pretty burgundy color to match their U of MN gopher colors for graduation. Aja had also added a couple of strings of gold ribbon in a few to get the gold and maroon school colors.

Ashley had just gone with simple braids starting at her hairline and all coming together at the crown of her head. Then the braids were brought together in a tight bun on top. Low maintenance and pretty, she told the stylist. Ashley had to admit the girl nailed it.

The crunching of the gravel brought Ashley out of her daydream and she straightened up in her seat. Jacob looked at her and grinned.

"Did you have a nice nap?"

Ashley looked over at him and swatted his shoulder. "I wasn't sleeping." She let out a soft sigh and added, "just thinking."

Jacob nodded in understanding and parked next to his sister's little blue Corolla. He nudged Ashley and tipped his head toward the building in front of them. "Sally Jo is already here. She probably broke every speed limit and vehicle safety suggestion to get here before everyone else. We better hurry if we want any dessert."

Chuckling, Ashley nodded, and they made their way out of the car. She couldn't help but notice the similarities in the siblings' cars. Jacob's car was a little newer and a different color, but she found it cute that they drove the same kind of car. Jacob had to finally let go of his grandfather's old Pontiac. It hurt him so much that he couldn't even bring himself to find another car, so Sally Jo helped—and found him the same car. That old Pontiac still sits on the side of his parents' garage, hoping to be restored again someday.

Aja came bouncing up next to Ashley and grabbed her arm with her hand. Ashley raised her eyebrows at her sister. She was never this bubbly and excited. Aja was the quiet one of the two while Ashley was the social butterfly, as Sam always said. He stopped short of calling Aja the well-behaved one though. Both girls were good students and stayed out of trouble for the most part.

"What has you all giddy and weird, Aja?" she asked, studying her twin suspiciously.

Aja shrugged. "I'm just so excited to be moving on to the next big thing. Aren't you, Ash? I mean, school is done, we have degrees, and now the big new jobs. I'm just excited to finally be an adult." Aja's hazel eyes were bright and shining and the sun made them pop against her caramel-colored skin.

"I guess, but we both have grad school still." She leaned close to her sister's ear and whispered, "And besides I heard adulting isn't all it's cracked up to be."

Aja giggled next to her and pulled her toward the café. Sam and Jacob had already gone inside. As the girls opened the door, the noise and sweet smell of sugar assaulted their noses. Ashley also noticed the group of people in the small space. Lundyn was next to her husband Ryan, who worked with Sam and Aja. Sally Jo was next to her boyfriend, well, fiancé now, with a brownie in each hand, making Ashley laugh. She spotted Jacob's parents and his brother with his family. Jacob was standing next to his sister-in-law who was holding one of the twin girls they had last winter. She briefly glanced around for the other baby, spotting her in Lundyn's aunt's arms.

Ashley felt herself being pulled toward the counter, where Gran Marion had set up a ridiculously large buffet with so much food. It didn't go unnoticed that the desserts were far more abundant than the dinner food. She glanced again at Sally Jo. She wondered if the girl had eyes somewhere and she would charge at Ashley if she dared to take a brownie. But she had been dying to try them for so long that she decided it was worth the risk and slowly made her way to the dessert table, watching Sally Jo out of the corner of her eye with caution.

"You can help yourself, Gran made her an entire batch all to herself, so you should be safe," a whisper came from next to her, making Ashley jump.

She turned and grinned at Lundyn who was laughing. Lundyn patted her on the shoulder. "It's ok. I understand. Even Ryan is afraid of getting between Sally Jo and her brownies." She smiled and nudged Ashley toward the enormous plate of brownies. Still, she hesitated. She had heard Sally Jo's temper when she was hanging out with Jacob at their parents' house. It was scary. So, if a big bad FBI guy like Ryan was afraid of her, Ashley didn't stand a chance.

Giggling, Lundyn picked up a small plate and put three brownies on the plate and handed it to Ashley. She leaned in close and said in a low voice, "Here. Take them and go that way. I'll block her view." Ashley looked up and giggled at Lundyn's smiling face. She took the plate and made her way over to Jacob and his family. She couldn't help but glance at Sally Jo, who somehow managed to catch her eye as she moved away.

Ashley quickly moved to Jacob's side and turned her back to Sally Jo. Jacob laughed next to her and picked up one of the brownies on her plate. She shot him a glare as she picked one up and took a bite. The chocolate literally melted in her mouth. She couldn't believe the flavor that erupted in her mouth. It was just a brownie—right? She didn't even notice her eyes had closed until Jacob leaned over and whispered in her ear.

"Good, huh?" he said with a smirk.

Ashley's eyes flew open. "Oh my god! No wonder she guards these with her life! I would too. These are amazing!" She had never gushed over food, but these were so delicious, even for someone who wasn't big on sweets.

Jacob looked down at her with a knowing smile. "Yep. That's why Gran Marion always makes Sally Jo her own. She wouldn't share otherwise. And even then, Gran Marion has to threaten her to leave the rest for everyone else or she won't make her any more special batches just for her. My sister and sharing just don't go well together." He snorted as he watched his sister scowl at him.

How did she hear him? Ashley couldn't help but wonder. But she knew if it were her, she would have a hard time sharing these too. She glanced at the counter and was relieved to see there were still more brownies on the plate. She caught herself sighing in relief and then chuckled at the ridiculousness of it all.

Papa Jasper, Lundyn's grandfather, called everyone's attention to the counter and led a short prayer. He thanked everyone for coming to celebrate at their place and then led the line for food. They had closed the café for today's celebration, so they were the only ones there. She felt slightly uncomfortable but then remembered that Jacob and his family were like family to them, and she relaxed a little. This was for Jacob more than her and her sister, but it was the only family celebration she would have. She shook off the sadness that was trying to creep back in over the lack of family connections she had.

Jacob took hold of her hand, and she looked up into his concerned eyes. "Are you sure you're ok, Ash? You seem a little out of sorts today."

She smiled and squeezed his hand back. "I'm good. Let's get some food. I've been dying to try *the* Gran Marion's famous cooking."

Chapter 2

Ashley sat on a lounging chair by the pool, soaking in the warm June sunshine. Her eyes were closed and covered by sunglasses. She had intended to read, but decided against it, enjoying the cloudless day and heat of the early summer sun instead. She found she preferred the Minnesota summer sun over the Florida summer sun—the heat difference being roughly fifteen degrees on any given day. The humidity could be stifling here, but it wasn't constant like it was in Florida. There were only a few truly humid days in a Minnesota summer compared to continuous months in the southern states.

Cold droplets of water spraying on her bare stomach shocked her eyes open wide as she looked up at a grinning Jacob, shaking his wet shaggy hair out on her like a dog. She screamed as she scrambled to her feet, nearly knocking Jacob backwards into the pool.

"Are you crazy?" she yelled at him. He wasn't fazed however and grabbed hold of her arms, crossing them in front of her as he twirled her around pinning her back against his chest. It took her a second to realize his goal and she quickly lifted her arms and slid out of his grasp and ran the opposite direction, laughing as he chased her.

The pool area outside the condominium where Sam and the twins lived wasn't huge and it didn't take long for

Jacob to catch up and cage her in between his body and the fence. Thankfully the younger kids weren't out of school yet, so it was empty except for the two of them. Aja was working with Sam and Ashley hadn't started her summer job, and she hadn't told Aja why yet—or that she really didn't even have a job for the summer. It was the first time in her life she had lied to her sister.

"Now what, Ash? I got you cornered." His blue eyes danced in amusement as he waited for her to answer.

Ashley shrugged. "I'm actually kinda hungry. How about lunch?" she smiled innocently at him, batting her eyelashes.

Jacob chuckled. "Really? Or are you just trying to get me to let you go so you can push me in instead?" He took a tiny step away from her and crossed his arms over his bare chest.

"What? Why would you think such a thing about me?" Ashley spread her hand across her chest in shock. "Seriously, Jacob. You really need to work on your trust issues." She did an exaggerated flip of her hair over her shoulder.

"Oh, I trust you completely. And that means I *trust* that I know exactly what is going through your mind and I *trust* that my instincts are never wrong." His smug look made Ashley want to push him into the pool anyway, but she resisted knowing he would catch her and bring her in with him.

"Ok, ok. I won't do anything. Let's just go get food," she said as she slipped out of his reach and headed back to the chair to grab her things.

Jacob followed and grabbed a towel from the other chair. "So, when are you going to drop the bomb on Aja,

Ash? You're running out of time. The fourth is going to be here before you know it and I would hate for you guys to fight right before you leave and then feel guilty. She's going to need time to accept it, hopefully before you go." Jacob's voice was soft and gentle.

Ashley knew everything he said was true and she didn't need to be reminded time was running out. She just couldn't find the right opportunity. It was already the second week of June, three weeks since graduation. She let out a deep sigh. "I know. I just don't even know how to bring it up. She's literally going to kill me, Jacob."

She stood and lifted her head to the sky and closed her eyes again. She felt Jacob come up behind her and wrap her in his towel with him. He was still wet, but she didn't mind. Her swimsuit was dry and offered a little buffer between his cold wet body and hers, still warm from the sun. She leaned into him and sighed again. She was going to miss this.

"You know she won't kill you. Lock you in a tower like Rapunzel so you can't leave? Maybe." She didn't have to turn and look at him to know his lips were turned up in the all too familiar lopsided smile she loved so much.

She was quiet for a few minutes just soaking in his warmth. She opened her eyes and squinted at the brightness. It really was a beautiful day.

"I guess I could talk to her tonight. We are supposed to have dinner just the two of us." Her voice was quiet, not wanting to say more. But she knew Jacob understood. It was their mom's birthday, and they decided a few years ago when they were in high school that they would celebrate this day together every year, just the two of them. No matter where they went in life, they would always come together on this day. It was also the reason why Ashley's plans wouldn't take effect until after the fourth of July. Their mom's birthday and the fourth were the two times a year that there was no fighting between their parents. These were the only happy memories Ashley had of her family as a foursome.

Jacob pushed her gently forward and she turned to face him. "Are you sure you don't want me to be there?" He pulled a stray braid away from her face and tucked it behind her ear.

Ashley shook her head. "No. I need to do this on my own. I just hope she understands and doesn't get Sam involved. He'll just shut us out and I won't get any answers. I need answers, Jacob." She leaned back into him for support as he wrapped his arms around her.

"Ok, but I *will* be here if you need me." He paused for a second and then asked, "Does she know about the report yet?"

"No and I am not telling her that part. Hopefully I can get some information before I tell her that part. If she knows, she'll just run to Sam and tell him. She thinks the guy walks on water, I swear." She grunted and took in a deep breath of air, listening to Jacob's even breathing and rhythmic heartbeat beneath her ear.

Jacob chuckled. "Well, there is the whole 'FBI team leader is your uncle' thing, Ash. So maybe he could help."

She looked up sharply and glared at Jacob. "Did you not hear anything I just said? He will take this away and I won't get any answers, Jacob! He will shut us out and won't tell us anything he finds out. I'm not giving him control of this. Not this time. I mean it's not like it's some dangerous mission I am going on or something. I'm just looking for someone and asking questions." She shrugged her shoulders gently and then leaned back into her boyfriend's chest.

Jacob rubbed her back in slow gentle circles. "Ok, I get it. But I am still going out there to help, Ash. As soon as I finish helping Papa Jasper train in a couple of new high school kids to take over the summer inventory at the feed store. Then I will be able to stay as long as you need me to." He looked down into her eyes now looking back at him.

She nodded with a smile. "I hope you do. I am going to need some emotional support. And hopefully it will only be for a couple of months. But I am prepared if it's longer. Let's go get dressed and get food." She pulled away from Jacob and picked up her bag with the rest of her things.

They made their way upstairs to the condo and quickly changed and headed right back out to get pizza, Ashley's favorite comfort food since becoming a Minnesotan. Greasy thin crust pizza from Carbone's was the ultimate in her opinion. Living in a southern suburb of the Twin Cities had its advantages. One of them was the abundance of food places nearby. Carbone's was just a ten-minute walk from the condo and with the weather so nice, they opted to walk instead of drive. Within just a few minutes' further walk, they could choose from a number of other options.

As they walked into the small little pizza shop, Ashley breathed in the garlic and pizza sauce smell. It was just what she was looking for. She knew Aja would prefer Italian food later so there was no worry about doubling up on her pizza for the day. Besides, Aja didn't care much for pizza.

Jacob ordered at the counter and then they headed for one of the few tables. Most of the restaurant's business was takeout so their seating was pretty limited. Once in a while it was nice to sit here and eat though, and today was one of those days. Ashley was grateful she and Jacob had similar tastes in pizza toppings. He liked anything and she had only a handful of things she absolutely wouldn't eat on a pizza. It made ordering and eating together easy.

Everything about their relationship seemed easy, she thought. They complimented each other and although Ashley was very outgoing, Jacob wasn't a wallflower like Aja. He liked to go out and have fun too, but he was also the voice of reason when it was time to leave. Sometimes if she went out without him, she would regret not going home sooner. He knew how to read her, and she knew he had her back no matter what. It was the first time she let a guy get as close to her as he had.

But it wasn't always like that. She thought back to when they first met. He didn't know her very well and kept asking her out. They had joined a couple of study groups together before getting to know each other and they hit it off quickly. But Ashley wasn't keen on sharing too much about herself and stayed pretty isolated. She wasn't sure yet about how long they would stay in Minnesota, and she hated having ties she had to break when they moved again.

Jacob was relentless. He came to her one day, cornered her in the hallway outside the one class they had together and told her he wanted to take her out and he wouldn't be rejected again—since she had said no at least five times. She couldn't avoid him anymore. It wasn't that she didn't find him interesting or attractive. She just didn't want to get close to anyone. Ashley had laughed and finally agreed to go out on a date with him. It didn't take long for her to discover how much they were alike and how much she really liked him. He seemed to reciprocate, and she quickly gave in to being his girlfriend, hoping Sam would keep them there until after she graduated so she could decide for herself if she moved again or not.

Luckily that's exactly what happened and here they were. She looked over at him with his loosely curled dark blond hair falling in his bright blue eyes. She reached over and moved it away from his eyes so she could see them better.

Jacob tilted his head slightly and studied her. "What are you thinking about?" His smile was what always made her feel safe and comfortable.

She returned his smile with her own and shrugged one shoulder. "Just the first time you begged me to go out with you and how desperate and irresistible you were." She set her chin on her folded hands propped up by her elbows.

Jacob let out a laugh. "Yeah, desperate." Then he thought for a second and grinned wider. "Yep, I was desperate. I couldn't figure out why you wouldn't go out with me. I mean, look at all this?" He waved his hands in front of his body and leaned back in his chair, making her giggle loudly.

"You're ridiculous, you know that?" Ashley said with a huge grin on her face. She was honestly so grateful for Jacob. He had been an unconditional support while she figured out what to do with the information she'd discovered a few months ago. She knew she couldn't take it to Aja, and she didn't have any female friends whom she trusted enough to go to.

Their pizza and drinks arrived, and Ashley smiled up in thanks at the person making the delivery. He nodded his response with a small smile and headed back over to the register. Ashley eyed the pizza hungrily as Jacob took a plate and lifted the cheesy goodness from the pan and then set it in front of her. He chuckled as he watched her.

"You would think you haven't eaten in weeks, Ash. Just pick it up and eat it already, don't drool all over it," he joked as he made himself a plate.

She refrained from moaning as she took a bite. Nothing compared to the extra cheesiness of this pizza in her mind. You didn't have to ask for extra cheese, they just always made it that way.

Before long the entire pizza was nearly gone, and Ashley looked over at Jacob with a grin. "I'm going to miss this place." She leaned back in her seat and looked around the small restaurant.

Jacob nodded. "It's only for a little while, Ash. And then we'll be back and hopefully have some answers for you. I'll be right beside you. I just wish you could wait a couple more weeks before you go so that I could be with you the whole time." His eyes held worry, as he took her hand across the table.

"I know, but I feel like I need to get going on this. And if I have to stay longer, I can get registered for fall classes and not miss any education time either." She met his gaze and smiled sadly. "It'll be ok though, right Jacob? This is all going to work out in the end?"

Jacob squeezed her hand tightly and put his other one on top of their joined hands. "Yes, Ash. It's all going to work out. I know this will all be figured out and your questions will be answered." He leaned forward and lowered his voice as he added, "and then we can get a place together when we get back, ok?"

Her eyes widened. "Really? You think we are ready for that big of a step, Jacob?"

"I know we are, Ashley. I'm ready now, but we have to get you the answers you are looking for first." His gaze bore into her as she swallowed hard.

She hadn't ever really thought seriously about moving in with Jacob. She knew he wanted to move out of his parents' place, but he was still looking for that perfect job. She didn't realize how serious he was about it until this moment. So much depended on what she found when she left Minnesota, and she knew she couldn't ask him to stay away from here with her indefinitely. His family was too close-knit for him to be ok being far away from them all.

"There are still so many things to figure out though, Jacob. Can we wait to see what this summer brings before we agree to that?" The look in his eyes, made her quickly add, "It's not that I don't want to be with you! I just want to know that we will still be in the same state when this is all said and done. Ok?"

Jacob sighed and dropped his hands from hers, leaning back in his chair. He dragged a hand through his unruly curls and nodded. She couldn't help but smile at his hair flopping as he nodded his head. It had grown longer, and she loved it. He had always kept it shorter because he didn't like dealing with the curls, but since she mentioned how much she liked it, he decided to try it longer and found it easier than he thought to maintain. He also found the wash and go look suited him well.

"I know, Ash. I just don't want to think about the possibility of losing you. And there isn't anything for me here, so if we stay out there, I am good with that too."

Ashley looked up in surprise. "I thought you wanted to stay here forever."

"No, not really. I only said that because that's where you would be. Ashley, I am happy wherever you are. I mean that. If you find you want to stay out there, I will find work there. I don't have ties here except my family. And there are planes for a reason." He grabbed her hands again and grinned that special grin just for her.

She smiled back and nodded. "Ok. Then we wait and see what happens." She leaned forward and he met her halfway in a quick kiss. "I'm so glad you will be beside me on this journey. If I can't have Aja next to me, you're the next best thing." She winked at him, making him shake his head.

"I know I should be offended, but I'm ok with that," he said with a smile and a shrug. "Let's get going. I want to take advantage of the pool as long as we can before the monsters get out of school."

As the afternoon wore on, Ashley was getting more and more nervous about dinner. She and Jacob stayed by the pool most of that time and when they finally went inside, his cheeks were bright red with sunburn. She giggled at him when he complained.

"It's just not fair. You just get more and more golden brown while I get red." He pointed his finger at her nose and scowled. "Not fair." He gingerly rubbed after sun lotion on his nose and shoulders and then went to get changed. He stood outside the bathroom door and looked back at Ashley. "Last chance for backup tonight," he said, trying to lighten her mood a little.

Ashley just looked at him and smiled, although it likely looked strained. She had to do this; she knew it was time.

It was probably long overdue, but she had to do it now. She only had a couple weeks before she was supposed to leave, and Aja needed to know. Jacob was right. Aja might be upset, but she needed time to come around before Ashley had to leave or it would be bad between them. Ashley couldn't handle her sister being mad at her.

Even worse than Ashley leaving was the lie she had to tell to convince her sister why she was leaving. The real reason would have to wait, but she needed a story to convince her sister it was all good and part of her bigger plan for her teaching future.

After Jacob left, Ashley laid down on her bed and stared at the clock on the nightstand, watching the time slowly tick by. She had heard from her sister that she would be home around five so they could make their dinner reservation at a small Italian place downtown. Neither had tried it before and since Italian was their mom's favorite, they tried to find a new place every year. This place was suggested by one of Aja's coworkers.

Ashley must have drifted off to sleep while she waited because the next thing she knew, Aja was standing over her with her hands on her hips and a smile on her face.

"You don't look ready to go, Ash. Why are you sleeping? Rough day?" Aja asked with a glint in her eye, knowing Ashley was hanging out with her boyfriend by the pool all day.

Rubbing her eyes, Ashley sat up and looked at the clock. "Ugh, sorry. Too much sun, I guess. Let me go change quick and we can go." She darted off to the bathroom, grabbing her dress off the hanger on the door as she passed. She stood in front of the mirror in the bathroom, trying to give herself a pep talk about tonight. She thought about trying to have a script ready, but she was never good at memorizing anything, and it would probably get all jumbled up. The best way was to just let it come naturally and hope she said the right words.

She quickly applied a little mascara and then headed out to meet her sister, who was sitting at the island looking at her phone. Aja looked up as Ashley entered the room. She smiled and asked, "Ready?"

Ashley nodded and slipped on her sandals, fixing the back as she balanced on first one foot then the other. "You driving or me?"

Aja gave her a side look and huffed out her response. Ashley smiled at the expected reaction. Aja was a control freak and insisted on driving everywhere they went—especially since Ashley had more speeding tickets and drove much faster than Aja liked.

Ashley laughed loudly. "I was kidding. I know you don't have a 'death wish'." She made exaggerated air quotes with her fingers to her sister who rolled her eyes so dramatically her eyeballs nearly disappeared under her eyelids, making Ashley snort.

"Come on smarty pants," Aja said as she opened the door. "Sam's working late tonight, some new case or something." She said as she turned and made sure the door locked behind them.

Ashley just nodded and waited for her sister to do her mental checklist before they could leave. She sighed softly, knowing she was going to miss all these silly little things her sister did.

Aja glanced over. "You alright?"

"Yep," Ashley answered and then turned to head down the hall to the parking lot. They had one spot in the underground parking, but that was reserved for Sam's vehicle. Ashley and Aja shared one car so they could save money. They tended to go to school at the same time and when Aja worked, she rode with Sam anyway. So, there wasn't a need for them to each have one.

The drive was quicker than Ashley thought it would be and before long they were sitting at a cozy little Italian place in downtown St. Paul, not far from the arena where the professional hockey team played. All their food was homemade and cooked from scratch. They had heard about this place before, but this was their first visit. They were seated almost immediately, and Ashley picked up a menu. A waiter set down two glasses of water with lemons in them and then stepped away.

"What was mom's favorite again? We should get one order of that and then split something else that neither of us have tried before," Ashley suggested as she studied the menu. "There's so much here though."

Aja nodded behind her menu. "That sounds good. I need to try something new anyway. I think mom liked the chicken parm or baked manicotti. But I can never remember if that was her favorite or mine." She looked up and gave Ashley a grin.

Setting her menu down, Ashley laughed at her sister. "*You* like the parm, mom liked pasta. And I do not want parm, sorry, sis. How about baked mostaccioli? And then you can get your parm. Mostaccioli is a good compromise—and it's yummy."

Aja closed her menu and set it at the edge of the table. "Deal."

They placed their orders and then started to talk about their day. Ashley let Aja talk first, trying to find the right words to tell her about her plans. She didn't hear what Aja was saying since she was so lost in her own thoughts—and fear of what this would do to the two of them. They had been inseparable since they were born. They were each other's support through their difficult childhood and relied on each other for almost everything emotionally. This would be the first time they would be apart from each other for longer than a matter of hours.

"Ash, what's on your mind? You are off somewhere else and not even listening to me. What's going on?" Aja leaned forward in her seat and studied her sister.

Ashley met her sister's gaze and felt her fear rise in her throat. She took a gulp of water and swallowed it past the lump firmly planted there. "Aja, I have something to tell you and please don't hate me." She felt herself pleading quietly. "I am going to be leaving for a little while. For grad school."

Aja gasped. "What are you talking about, Ash? Leaving? Where? Why? I don't understand." Her eyes darted back and forth across Ashley's face; complete confusion clouded her eyes.

Ashley finally looked up and met her sister's eyes filling with tears and worry. "I'm sorry." She took a deep breath and focused on the story she needed to tell, to convince her sister this was planned. The lie that she hoped wouldn't destroy her friendship with her twin forever. "I'm going to look at a school out east for my master's in elementary education."

Chapter 3

Ashley rolled over in her bed and glared at the alarm clock beeping loudly at her. With a groan, she turned it off and then threw the covers over her head. Today was the day, the moment of truth. Would she actually be able to leave her sister and uncle behind and tackle this mystery on her own? For a brief second, she doubted she could. But then the memory of that report popped back into her mind, and she bit her teeth together and pursed her lips. *No, I have to do this. It's not an option,* she told herself firmly.

After scolding herself on the inside, she threw off the blankets and made her way to the bathroom quietly. It was only six in the morning, and they had stayed up late the night before to watch fireworks over the state capital. They sat at a park high above the city skyline and had a perfect view of the colorful explosions.

Aja had forgiven her, but it took her a solid week to get over it and talk to her. Ashley expected it. And she also knew it wasn't that her sister was mad, but that they were never apart, and she was scared—and Ashley had to admit she was a little afraid to be alone too. She had always had her sister next to her, through everything. In the end, Aja knew she was firm in her decision and there wasn't anything she could do to change her sister's mind.

The conversation with Sam was a lot harder than she expected. He was not on board with her decision and was genuinely angry that she didn't talk to him first. Even though he was mad, she also detected some fear in his eyes. She knew his fear was different than Aja's. Sam's was for her safety, while Aja was afraid of being without her. But there wasn't anything for him to be afraid of. She would be safe and where she was going was a little town where there wouldn't be any danger. *I mean, who even hears about scary stuff in small towns? Isn't that why people are drawn to them anyway?* Ashley knew she was rationalizing, and any place can hold danger, but she wasn't worried.

Eventually, Sam came around but not after insisting she get a decent car. He decided he would pay for it so she wouldn't use public transportation or Ubers or taxis. So, the last couple of weeks had been busy, planning and getting everything that she might need. She had a place she could rent for the first month or two that was close to the campus if she chose to accept it. Hopefully she could still stay there if she wasn't a student—because she wasn't planning on enrolling right away, something she didn't share with her sister or uncle.

After she showered and got dressed, Ashley moved back into her room. The condo they had was an end unit with three bedrooms and two bathrooms. It was perfect for the three of them. Their rooms weren't huge, but they offered privacy for each of them. She sighed as she moved back into her small space, now filled with boxes. She had decided not to take everything and keep the space the same as much as possible. Even though she didn't plan to stay in Maryland long, she had to at least make it look like she was planning on being there two years for school.

She had bought some new bedding for the trip and boxed up a lot of her clothes. Most of the winter stuff she was leaving since her research showed her that winter wasn't really a thing on the Eastern Shore. Well not like Minnesota anyway, she thought with a smile. She moved to her closet and opened it to see what she had left. Her winter coats and boots, those can stay. She had a few scarves and hats that stayed on the shelf. The rest of her sweaters and hoodies could stay. She had packed a few of each and a lighter coat. She secretly hoped she would be back home before Christmas, but she couldn't be sure so she packed what she thought she would need to get through some cooler months.

Aja came up behind her and wrapped her arms around Ashley's waist. "I can't believe you are actually doing this, Ash. What am I going to do without you here?" She could hear the sadness in Aja's voice and knew if she turned around, she would see tears and would probably cry herself. All the resolve in the world would crumble if she allowed herself to be sad.

Leaning back against her sister's embrace, Ashley sighed. "I know," she whispered. "But I will be back as much as I can. And who knows, maybe I won't even like it there. I hear it gets really humid and hot." She tried to sound hopeful, secretly knowing she would be back sooner than her sister knew. She hated lying to Aja, but knew it had to be like this for at least a little while.

Aja snorted and moved to turn Ashley around. "Right. You'll have the ocean and the millions of beaches. You are going to love it. Maybe I will come out there too." Aja shrugged and Ashley felt a sudden panic rise in her chest.

Aja would ruin her plans if she came out to join her. Ashley's lies would be exposed, and Aja would call Sam in, and they would whisk her away so fast, she wouldn't even know what happened. No, Aja couldn't come out there.

Trying to laugh it off, Ashley shrugged. "Maybe but you have it made here with Sam and the job."

"Yeah, but I could go work at Langley. That would be an experience! Hmm, I might have to think a little more seriously about that." Aja tapped her lips with her finger as if thinking seriously about the idea.

"Well, how about you come and visit me and then we can see if I even like it and then you can see if you like it and then who knows," she rambled. Ashley knew she was talking fast, but she was nervous. And she hated lying to her sister. Hopefully she would be able to wrap up this thing out there quickly and then come back before anyone got any weird ideas about following her.

Aja shrugged. "We'll see. When is Jacob coming?"

Ashley and Jacob had decided that he would drive out there with her and then fly back, since no one wanted Ashley to drive that far by herself. She was grateful for his offering because she was nervous about driving by herself. "I think around eight. We wanted to get going at a decent time to hopefully avoid too much leftover holiday traffic." She glanced around the space again and sighed. Even with leaving a lot of stuff behind, she still had a lot to pack.

She found that a lot of places were fully furnished in the area due to the number of tourists that visit every summer. The Airbnb business was booming with all the beaches and close proximity to the ocean. Ashley wasn't ever a beach person, so she wasn't sure what to expect, but she would have to at least make a couple trips to the ocean. She had to admit she was most excited about that.

"Let's go get breakfast and then once he gets here, we can load up your car." Aja moved away from Ashley and headed for the door. She turned and rested her hand on the door frame, her eyes looking around the room, finally landing on Ashley. "This is going to suck big time, Ash."

Ashley nodded. "I know. But we will be ok, AJ. Nothing can keep us apart." She shot her sister a smile as Aja scowled at the nickname.

Growing up no one could say her name right and would pronounce it as "A-Jah" and Ashley would laugh and started to call her AJ. She knew it irritated her sister that people would stress the "J" when it actually just sounded like the continent "Asia". Eventually they would correct people and say just that—it's pronounced like the continent, just spelled differently.

"Come get breakfast when you're ready, brat," she said and left the room, leaving Ashley biting her cheek to keep from giggling at her sister's annoyance.

Ashley glanced around her room one more time and sighed. *This is going to be harder than I thought,* she mused. She stacked a few boxes against one wall and cleared most of the middle of the room. Once satisfied with her organization, she moved to the door. She started down the hall and heard voices. As she entered the small kitchen, she saw more people than she expected in the tiny space.

Jacob was there with Sally Jo and Lundyn. Sam was in the small, attached dining room and Ryan was leaning up against the wall behind Lundyn. They rarely went anywhere without the other it seemed. Ashley raised her brows at the group.

"What is all this? Don't you all have to work or something?" she asked with a grin, secretly happy they had come to send her off.

Jacob moved to stand next to her and wrapped an arm around her shoulders. "I think everyone is just looking for an excuse to skip work," he said as he winked at her.

"*Actually*, we don't have to work since it is the officially recognized holiday for the fourth, since it was Sunday yesterday," Aja corrected.

Ashley laughed at her sister. Aja was always so serious. "Well, whatever. I'm glad you are all here."

Sally Jo cleared her throat and moved a step ahead of the group, holding something in her hands. "So," she dragged out the single word, "Gran Marion heard a rumor that you loved her brownies, *almost* as much as I do, so she made a special batch for you for your trip." She held out a container with one hand and then put her other hand on her chest and added, "And I swear I did not eat any because if I did, she wouldn't give me mine later." She chuckled as Ashley took the container.

"Uh, do I need to count them to make sure, Sally Jo?" Jacob asked quickly, attempting to take the container from Ashley.

Ashley moved and covered the container with her hands, turning away from Jacob. "No way, you don't get to touch!" She slapped his outstretched hand, drawing laughter from around the room.

Jacob rubbed his hand dramatically as if he were a scolded child. But his smile gave away the humor he felt in the whole situation.

"Seriously, you'd think these things were laced with some addictive drug or something," Ryan said with a chuckle. "Hey, Sam, do you think we should bring in one of the narc dogs to check them out?"

Sally Jo and Ashley screamed, "No!" at the same time, making them all laugh again.

"I think Sally Jo has met her match when it comes to Gran's brownies," Lundyn chuckled, leaning into Ryan behind her.

Aja moved to the cabinets and pulled out plates and glasses. "Let's eat before it all gets cold so you two can get on your way." She attempted to sound happy, but Ashley knew she was hurting deep down. Maybe not even very deep down.

The group made their way through the little buffet line of eggs, sausages, and waffles. Ashley swore she heard Lundyn mumble something about pancakes, but she wasn't sure what that was about.

"Aja, did you make all this?" Ashley asked.

Aja shook her head. "No Sam actually did most of it. I just did clean up—like normal." She winked at her uncle who shot her a scowl in return.

Ashley glanced over at her uncle, who hadn't spoken to her much the last couple of weeks. She wasn't sure if he was worried about her or disappointed, but he wasn't a man of many words anyway, so she tried to shrug it off. She just hoped he didn't figure out what she was really doing, at least until she got her answers.

Sam looked over and gave her a small smile and then turned back to something in his hand that she couldn't see. Jacob gave her a little nudge and they moved to the line for food. The group gathered in the small dining room and living room space to eat. The condo wasn't huge, but even with this size group, they managed to fill the two rooms without feeling crowded. And without walls, it was easy to have conversations.

It didn't take long for the food to be finished and everyone to begin moving on to the rest of their day. As the space emptied out, just Sam, Aja, Ashley, and Jacob were left. Aja sighed and started to clean the dishes. Ashley bumped her shoulder lightly and Aja shifted a little to allow her room to help.

"You know it's going to be ok, right?" Ashley asked her sister quietly. She heard Sam and Jacob talking quietly in the living room and she could only imagine what Sam was threatening him with.

Aja shrugged. "I guess I know that. But we have never been this far apart. I have always had you by my side. I'd be lying if I said I wasn't a little scared."

Ashley set the plate that she had been washing back in the water and turned to her sister. Grabbing her shoulders, she looked into the same hazel eyes as hers and smiled. "We are one, Aja. Wherever you are I am and wherever I am you are. We have FaceTime, the phone, and even mail. We will still see each other and talk all the time. Heck we might even talk more. I promise. We will be ok. And I'll be back before we even realize I left." She tried to smile, but it was strained. And it was mirrored back at her through her twin's eyes.

Aja pulled her into a tight hug and sighed deeply. "I know. But I am going to miss you so much, Ash."

Ashley felt a tiny sob escape her sister and she held on tighter. She felt a pang of guilt eat at her chest as she thought about the secret she couldn't share just yet. She hoped she could soon because she would need her sister once this was figured out.

"I love you, Aja." She pulled away and wiped her own tears from her cheeks.

"I love you, too, Ash. Forever and back, three times," Aja said with a grin, remembering her mom's words every night before bed when they were little.

"Forever and back, three times," Ashley repeated and hugged her sister tight one more time.

They finished cleaning the kitchen and then moved to start loading boxes into Ashley's car. Sam and Jacob helped, but Sam didn't do too much moving, claiming he had a sore back, and his age just didn't help. The girls laughed at him, knowing he was probably in better shape than all of them combined, if that was possible to measure.

It didn't take long, and Jacob moved to throw his bag and suitcase into the car as well. Sam pulled Ashley into a tight hug and whispered, "You behave and be careful, Ashley girl. I am just a phone call away and I have friends everywhere. If you need anything, call, you hear me?" His voice was gruff and full of emotion, but Ashley didn't miss the small hint of threat about her safety. She knew his arm's reach was long, and she hoped he didn't have anyone watching her. That could really mess up her plans.

She pushed the feeling away and smiled at her uncle. "You know we aren't little girls anymore, right, Sam? People might wonder why you would refer to your adult nieces as 'little girls'." She stepped back out of his embrace and crossed her arms.

Sam snorted. "You will always be my little girls. You will forever be my pride and joy and everything your mama wanted for you I will give you. Just be safe so I can fulfill that promise to my sister."

It didn't go unnoticed that Sam didn't mention their father. In his eyes, he stole Sam's sister from him, and he was as good as dead to Sam now. Hopefully he would "stay locked up forever" he would often say.

By the time they were finally loaded and ready to get on the road it was almost nine-thirty. Ashley didn't care too much about the time since she knew it was more important to spend these last few moments with her sister and uncle. She waved one more time before climbing into the driver's seat of her little white Nissan Rogue. Her uncle thought it was funny since she was "going rogue" from the family. She didn't think it was so funny, but the car was nice, and the room was perfect for just her while she was out east. She was glad her uncle listened to her about feeling safer in a small SUV than a small car, even though gas mileage would be a little bit worse.

Ashley slid into the driver's seat and took a deep breath. Jacob would drive a lot of the way because Ashley knew she would get sleepy pretty quickly, the emotional stress getting to her as she moved further away from home. But she wanted to send the message to her uncle that she was fine and in charge as they drove out of the condo parking lot and headed for the freeway.

She took another deep breath and leaned her head back on the headrest. Jacob took hold of her hand and gave it a squeeze.

"Are you ok?" he asked gently.

Ashley looked over and smiled through her tear-filled eyes. "I hope I am doing the right thing, Jacob." She quickly turned back to the road and tried to stay focused on the future.

Jacob sighed beside her. "I know. This has to be hard. I will be beside you as much as I can, I promise. I know I'm not Aja, but I can still be your replacement other half for a little while," he joked as he held her hand tightly.

"I don't want you to be Aja. Please don't be Aja, ok?" She smiled a genuine smile and squeezed his hand back.

They drove in silence for almost an hour before they reached the Wisconsin border. Crossing the river and entering Wisconsin felt like it was all becoming real, and Ashley started to feel the excitement build inside her again. She was on an adventure that she hoped would bring her something happy, but she knew it could be nothing too. She felt her old carefree mentality come back and she let the air from the open window dry her tears and refresh her spirit. This was going to be a new experience, and she would do everything she could to embrace it, regardless of what might happen—good or bad.

The first rest stop she came to as they moved further into Wisconsin, she stopped to get gas and use the restroom. She wanted to let Jacob drive so she could take in everything around her. Plus, she knew she would get tired as well. She had never been on a road trip before, a true "drive until you drop and see everything you can along the way" kind of road trip.

When they moved around with Sam, they got where they were going as fast as they could and then stayed put. They didn't do many vacations unless it revolved around his work. Ashley didn't blame him though. She understood his work and how important it was, and she also knew it was expensive to raise two kids—especially when you didn't plan on having them. Besides she could travel when they were older, like she was doing now. She was glad Jacob was with her so they could experience this together.

They decided to stop at a travel station called Love's. It was more of a truck stop with a lot of semi-truck parking and inside there were showers and a greasy spoon restaurant, that's what Sam called them anyway. She didn't really understand the term, but the restaurant looked decent enough. Ashley wasn't hungry though, so they just used the restrooms and filled up with gas, snacks, and drinks.

Once they settled back into the car, Jacob turned to Ashley and smiled. "Ready?" he asked.

Ashley nodded emphatically. "I'm ready. Where are we going first?" She didn't care if she made it to Maryland in two days or five. She just wanted to fully experience the road and the states they would go through. She didn't know what she was looking for, but they agreed that if they wanted to stop at something they saw, they would just do it. She had also bought a book with some interesting things each state had to offer.

"I think we just drive and see what we find," Jacob said, looking out the windshield.

Ashley nodded. "Perfect. But I should warn you, I might sleep more than I want to."

"Well, then sleep. It's been a stressful few weeks. If I see something, I'll wake you up. Ok?"

"Ok, deal." She sighed and leaned back against the headrest. "To the adventure ahead!" She pointed her finger out the front and Jacob chuckled at her, starting the vehicle.

Chapter 4

Jacob gently shook Ashley awake and she gradually looked around her. It was dark outside, and they were parked in front of a hotel. She straightened upright in her seat and rubbed her eyes.

"How long did I sleep? I swear it was just three," she said with a yawn.

Jacob laughed. "Yeah, it probably was. You might not sleep tonight either."

"Why are we stopped?" She looked out her window at the brightly lit hotel sign. At least it wasn't one of those shady places with a blinking "vacancy" sign, she thought.

Jacob stretched his arm high above his head, well, at least as high as the roof of the car would allow. "I'm tired and I didn't think it would be a good idea to wake you up and then expect you to drive. You seemed to need the sleep." He glanced around in front of the car.

Her eyes followed his and she saw that the parking lot looked to be about half full. She hoped that meant getting a room would be easy. She turned back to meet his blue eyes and smiled. "Ok. I am fine with whatever. You know I don't have a timeline." She shrugged. "But I can drive if you want. We can just get dinner first and see how we feel." As if on cue, Jacob's stomach let out a deep and angry growl, making her laugh.

"Food it is!" he said sheepishly. "There was a Big Boy restaurant not far from here." He started the car again and looked to see which direction to go in.

"What's a 'Big Boy'?" Ashley asked, scrunching her nose a little. "And where are we anyway?"

Jacob turned back toward her. "We are near Toledo, Ohio. Since you slept, we didn't stop much so we've made pretty good time. Just a gas stop, which we need to do again while we are here, and now food since this morning. And a Big Boy is a place you have to eat at once in your life. We used to stop every chance we got as kids on our family trips. I guess it's a lot like a Perkins."

He pulled out into the street as she leaned back in her seat, watching the lights fly by. It wasn't long and Jacob pulled into another parking lot with a huge sign out in front of a restaurant. The plump boy holding an enormous burger made her giggle a little. *I guess that's where they get the name from,* she thought.

They parked and quickly moved to the entrance. Once inside she realized it was a lot like any family restaurant. She hoped the food tasted as good as the smells that were teasing her nose. They were seated right away, and Ashley couldn't help but notice how dated everything was, but in a charming way, like it was their brand or something. Her attention was drawn away from the space by Jacob clearing his throat.

She raised her eyebrows at him and asked, "What's wrong?"

"Nothing. But we should probably come up with a plan for the rest of the trip. I don't mind driving, but we should stop more. My legs are stiff and my butt hurts," he said with a grin.

"I'm sorry I slept so long, but in all fairness, I did warn you," she said with a point of her finger. "So, let's spend the night here and then head out after breakfast tomorrow. I'll get a couple Monsters and hopefully that will keep me awake a little more."

Jacob nodded slowly. "That's a good plan, but I also think we should look up things and places to stop so we make the most of this road trip. I think the hotels usually advertise stuff to do."

"Ok." She was interrupted by the waiter bringing them glasses of ice water. They quickly placed food orders and then Jacob pulled out his phone. Ashley moved to slide in next to him.

They looked up some different things to do for the rest of the trip and decided to also see what the hotel brochures showed. There were caves they could tour, which could be fun and interesting, she thought. There was also a lot of history to explore as they got closer to the east coast.

The restaurant was pretty empty and it was close to closing time, so their food came out quickly. They ate just as fast, considering it had been more than a few hours since they ate last. Ashley didn't realize how hungry she was when she laughed at Jacob's complaining stomach. By the time they left, it was almost ten. The night air was calm and warm. There was little humidity in the air, so her shorts and tank top were still comfortable.

The night was dark and there were only a few lights along the busy street, which surprised her. They walked to the back of the parking lot away from some of the lights and the clear sky offered a multitude of stars twinkling above them. Ashley leaned back against Jacob and stared up at them. In the Twin Cities or the other big cities that she had lived in there was always too much light pollution to see the stars clearly. But tonight, the sky was perfect, and she didn't think she had ever seen so many stars.

"I hate to be a bummer, but I really need to get some sleep, Ash," Jacob said in a sleepy voice behind her. She chuckled and turned to face him. He smiled down at her and traced her cheek with his finger. "My belly's full now so it won't take long for my brain to quit on me."

She leaned up on her tippy toes and gave him a kiss on his lips. "Ok, sleepyhead. Let's get you a bed to crash in." She was so grateful that he was here with her, and she wished he didn't have to leave her once they got to their destination. But Ashley knew she couldn't be selfish, and he said he would come back after he got his things in order. With a sigh, she moved away from him and headed back to the car.

It didn't take long for Jacob to be sound asleep in the bed while Ashley was wide awake. She had grabbed some brochures from the lobby and was looking through them. There were a lot of historical things to do once they got a little further down the road. She was especially intrigued by the underground railroad tours. She had done a book report in middle school or high school about Harriet Tubman. But the brochures made that look like a weekend activity, not a passing through type of thing. She made a mental note to plan a weekend to do that. If they took a little detour, they could get to the caves in Pennsylvania, which looked fun. It was summer so there would likely be tourists everywhere, but she felt like a tourist now anyway.

Glancing at the alarm clock on the table next to the bed, Ashley saw it was already one in the morning. If she didn't go to bed soon, she would sleep the whole day tomorrow too. She never knew why she slept so easily in the car. Aja was the opposite though. She rarely could fall asleep in the car.

Sam said it probably had to do with the trip they took after their mom died and their dad was arrested. Sam had swooped in and took them to his place a few hours away. Ashley was exhausted from crying and fell asleep almost right away, but Aja seemed to be in shock and didn't sleep for two days. They had only stayed at Sam's place for about two days and then drove further away. He said it was for their safety, but they were little and didn't really know what that meant.

Ashley was only five when Sam whisked them away and she had for a long time thought Sam was protecting them from being arrested like their dad. She thought the police were after them too. When she was older and could better understand, she asked questions. Aja was a listener, not a talker, so Ashley was her mouthpiece growing up.

Sam explained that their dad was a bad guy involved with bad people. Those bad people, who Ashley later learned were into drug dealing and money laundering, could come after the twins in an effort to keep their father from talking in prison or any other kind of nefarious activity. Even now as an adult, she didn't fully understand all of it but knew that Sam was their protector and as long as they stayed close by, he could protect them.

For the first time in her plans, Ashley felt a shudder of fear. It was small, but she felt it. Would she be too far away from Sam to be protected? Would someone still be after her now, this many years later? She gulped thinking of the possibilities. Suddenly she thought about the paper in her bag. Could this whole thing actually be a trap for her?

Ashley shook her head to clear the negative thoughts. *No, you can't fake this stuff, right?* She decided to try to ignore the fear and get some sleep. She quickly used the bathroom and then changed into her pajamas. Standing at the side of the bed, she watched Jacob sleeping, snoring lightly. She smiled, hoping one day this would be their normal.

She climbed under the covers next to Jacob and moved closer to him. He turned in his sleep and she snuggled in closer, wrapping her arm around his torso. Ashley felt a calm wash over her like she hadn't ever felt before. Jacob was her all, she knew that. Thinking about their possible future together brought a smile to her face and sleep came quickly. The negative thoughts and fear from before were long gone and she drifted off to sleep.

After what felt like just a few minutes, light streamed in between the curtains waking Ashley. When she looked over, the bed next to her was empty and the red numbers on the clock showed nine o'clock. She rolled to her back and stretched her arms above her head. She moved away from the blinding stream of light assaulting her tired eyes.

"Hey, you're finally awake," Jacob said coming out of the bathroom. He looked like he had showered and was ready for the day.

Ashley smiled and shrugged. "I feel like I'm on vacation."

Jacob chuckled. He settled on the edge of the bed at her feet. "I was thinking maybe it would be best to get to the Eastern Shore sooner rather than later. Then I can be around while you get settled in your place and all that. I wish I could stay indefinitely, but I only have a week before Papa Jasper needs me back." He dropped his eyes, waiting for her to answer.

Ashley sat up and leaned against the headboard. She slowly nodded her head, thinking about what he had said. He was right. She would be alone in a new place for the first time in her life. She needed to have him there to help her settle and find a place to live while he could. She also knew he needed to get back so he could finish up what Jasper Bell needed him to do at the feed mill so he could come back to her. The sooner the better, she knew he was right.

"Ok, Jake. I know that's the best plan. I am going to be freaking out if I am alone there for too long. I am going to need you close by for a little while." She leaned forward and grabbed his hand. Drawing his eyes to hers.

"I'm sorry. I know you wanted to do the whole road trip experience," he said quietly.

"No, you are right. I forgot we only had a little time before you had to go back." She squeezed his hand tightly in hers. "Besides, the sooner you get back and get your stuff done, the sooner you come back to me, right?"

Jacob finally breathed out a sigh of relief. "Right. Let's get going then. You have a hotel for the first couple nights, right?"

"Yep. The college, Professor Roslin I think is his name, helped me out, with the idea that I could tour their campus and decide if I wanted to enroll. And they said they could help me find longer housing if I need it. My grades helped me out with that." She winked at her boyfriend and who just grinned back.

"Good to be a smart kid, huh?" Jacob said with a laugh. "Ok, so let's get going then. There is a buffet breakfast in the lobby. I can go grab stuff if you want to shower."

Ashley nodded. "Sounds like a good idea." She looked at the clock again and flung the covers off her. "I won't take long."

Jacob headed for the door while she went toward the bathroom. A hot shower and clean clothes would feel good. By the time she came out of the shower, Jacob was sitting at the small desk with his phone in his hand and two plates of food next to him. Ashley noticed two cups of orange juice and one of apple juice, making her smile. She knew he didn't like apple juice and was happy he remembered she did.

She leaned against the desk, bringing his focus to her. "So, what are you doing?" she asked, nodding toward his phone.

He lifted it and showed her the GPS map. "I'm trying to figure out the best way to go. Tolls are killing us right now. I lost track of how much we have spent so far. So, I was trying to see if we could go a more scenic way and pay less in tolls."

Ashley sat on the edge of the bed and took one of the plates. She knew he liked small breakfasts, and she thought he knew she preferred to *eat* at breakfast, meaning waffles, eggs, sausage, all the things.

Jacob looked over at her and smiled, nodding to let her know she had taken the right plate. Ashley felt warmth run through her as she thought about how well they already knew each other.

"Thank you," she said holding her plate up. "So, what have you found?"

"Well, it's about another eight or so hours, without stops. We will have to stop at least once or twice for gas and food. So, if we figure ten hours, we should be good. That means we get into Salisbury, Maryland around—" he looked around her for the clock— "eight tonight, if we leave soon. I found a route that will only cost us a toll to cross the Bay Bridge."

Ashley stopped her hand as it was about to reach her mouth. "Uh, what is the Bay Bridge?" She wasn't afraid of bridges, but she wasn't aware of anything major on their trip, like some historic or famous bridge. Since it required a toll to cross, it must be a big deal.

Jacob smiled mischievously at her. "Oh, I want you to see this for yourself. No googling either." He raised his eyebrows at her and waved his finger at her phone now in her hand.

Ashley popped the piece of waffle into her mouth and shrugged. "Ok. Whatever you say. I'm always up for an adventure." She turned to look at the clock. "But we should probably be going, right?"

"Yep. I can drive if you want to eat. I just got some eggs and bacon, so I am good to go." She hadn't even noticed that his plate was almost empty.

"Ok, but I need to get packed up again." She put a forkful of eggs in her mouth and then set the plate aside so she could get her things back in her bag. She had packed an overnight bag to keep separate from her luggage for just this reason. It was so much easier than pulling everything out to find a clean outfit.

It didn't take long for the two of them to have the room cleared out and be back in the car ready to continue their journey. Ashley settled into her seat with her apple juice nearly gone and her plate of food about half empty.

As Jacob slid in next to her, he looked over and grinned. "Ready?"

"Yep! Let's get the show on the road—literally!" she responded with a grin of her own. Sitting back, she thought again about how normal and comfortable it was with Jacob. They just worked as a couple, she thought. She hadn't ever had that with any other boy before. She looked over at him again, his eyes focused on the road as they pulled out of the parking lot. She let out a tiny sigh of contentment as she thought about the "what ifs" of the future.

They spent a good portion of the next few hours talking about everything from college memories to childhood stories. Ashley was always careful what she told people about her past, at least the one with her parents. She loved Jacob, she knew that, but there were still things that she just didn't talk about. He only knew that her mom died, and her dad was in prison. Jacob didn't know the circumstances of her death or why her dad was in prison. Maybe someday she would feel ok sharing it, but for now she kept it to herself.

So, she stuck to stories with Sam and Aja. She couldn't help a little jealousy sneak its way into her heart when Jacob talked about his family and their close connections to each other. Sure, she and Aja were close, and Sam was a fantastic father figure to them both. But she always wanted her mother. Aja seemed to take to Sam more than Ashley did. She loved him but she yearned for the parents she lost and had a hard time letting that go, even when she thought about the terrible thing her father did. Maybe it was the idea of a father she missed, not her own father.

When she thought about her mom, the memories were fuzzy. Sam never liked to talk about her either, which made it hard to feel a connection to her mom. The only memory she had that was clear was holding her hand and crying. Her mom was trying to talk to her, she figured to try to tell her it would all be ok, but she never knew what she could have said or wanted to say. For a while after, Ashley struggled with guilt, trying to figure out what her mom wanted to tell her. But eventually she concluded it wasn't worth trying to figure out. There was just no way of knowing. When she had mentioned it to Sam, he brushed it aside quickly.

Shaking her head to clear the negative and sad thoughts, her eyes landed on the container Sally Jo had given her from Lundyn's grandmother. She grinned as she remembered Jacob's sister almost grimace handing them over. Ashley reached back and grabbed it. Yeah, sure it was just past breakfast, but so what? She's an adult now, right? She opened the lid and the smell of chocolate hit her nose. Like an addict staring at the temptation in front of her, she reached in and took out two brownies. She handed one to Jacob who lifted his brows at her but didn't have to think twice about the offer. Ashley was still in shock that someone's grandmother would be so kind as to make special treats for her. She could understand if Gran Marion was Jacob's grandmother, since she was his girlfriend. But Gran Marion wasn't related to them at all.

They had stopped for gas a few hours later somewhere in Maryland—finally. Ashley couldn't help but notice how beautiful the landscape was around them. She had read a tiny bit about Maryland and what it had to offer besides the beaches. Where they stopped was in the mountains and the views were gorgeous. Everything was bright green, and the hills and cliffs were never-ending.

It was a couple of hours past noon, and they had decided to stop at a couple of the wayside rests where there were lookout points. Ashley looked out in awe at the beauty surrounding her. It wasn't what she expected when she thought about this adventure. She knew the western-most point of the state was still in the mountains, but she still didn't expect this.

Jacob came up behind her as she looked out over the rolling hills around them. "It's beautiful, isn't it?' he asked, wrapping his arms around her from behind.

Ashley just nodded. She took a deep breath of the fresh and surprisingly cool air. She had heard Maryland was hot and humid all summer long, but where they had stopped it was a comfortable warmth. The sun was shining brightly, and the heat felt good on her skin.

"We should get going. I think there is a welcome center a little ways up we can stop at if you want. They're supposed to have the best views." Jacob's quiet voice behind her made her smile.

"Ok. I just want to take a few pictures." She pulled her phone from the pocket of her shorts and snapped a few pictures. Putting her phone back, she looked out over the hills again. Taking another deep breath, she turned and followed Jacob to the car.

Ashley surprised herself by staying awake for most of the trip. She did nap a little at the beginning, but since they had entered Maryland, she was determined to stay awake. Jacob seemed to know this because he kept the conversations going the entire ride. The stops to take pictures helped too.

As they came over a hill, Ashley gasped, and her eyes widened. "We have to stop here. This is the cutest little town I have ever seen!" She bounced in her seat like a little girl.

Jacob chuckled. "Ok, We can get a late lunch there. I'm getting a little hungry anyway." He looked around for the exit as he changed lanes.

Ashley had forgotten they hadn't eaten yet, so it was a good plan to stop. She watched out the window as the small town built over the hills came into full view. She could imagine what this place looked like covered in a fresh coating of snow, if they got snow here, she wasn't sure. They drove over an old bridge that crossed the river. She could imagine it being used for horses and carriages a long time ago. But she was more interested in her imagination than the facts, she thought with a smile.

There were three churches on one side of town, which was interesting to her for such a small town. But she had heard that religious groups could be territorial about their churches and people. She once heard a story about two churches in Minnesota. They were both Catholic, but one was German and one was Polish. They didn't share well, and the tiny town was split between the two churches. Sure, they were nice to each other, but they did not attend each other's masses. It was deeply frowned upon, she had learned.

Jacob made his way up the hill to what seemed to be the main street through town. It was a gorgeous little city built along the river, and she couldn't wait to get out and walk the streets. She wondered what it would have been like to live in this town during its inception.

They stopped at a small diner and Jacob parked. They made their way inside and were seated right away. It was a weekday and after lunchtime, so it wasn't a huge surprise. Ashley looked over the menu and noticed everything looked like a homecooked meal, from scratch and everything. She couldn't decide what to get and Jacob had already put his menu down.

Ashley scowled at him and looked back at her menu. "How can you decide?" She raised her eyebrows over the menu to look at him.

Jacob shrugged. "I don't know. I just picked."

"Ugh, whatever. I don't know what to choose. Everything looks too good." Ashley flipped the menu to the back and eyed the desserts.

"No, Ash. Food. Besides I saw a little ice cream shop down the street," he bribed, watching her eyes light up.

She waved her hand. "Ok, ok. I'm not used to Gran Marion's homemade cooking though, so I don't know what to get."

Jacob took her menu and pointed to a chicken and pasta dish. "Can't go wrong with pasta, right?" he asked.

"Hm. Maybe." She mulled over the idea. She took the menu back and went to the front. "Also, can't go wrong with breakfast." She grinned at him and set her menu down next to his at the edge of the table.

It didn't take long for their lunch to arrive, and even less time for them to finish eating it. Ashley wanted to get going and stretch her legs before they got back in the car. They quickly paid and then walked down one of the streets. It reminded her a little of Duluth in Minnesota. The streets all seemed to go either up or down a hill. The main street they were on was pretty flat and seemed to cut the hills in half.

Jacob didn't lie, they found the little ice cream shop a few blocks down. There were two little tables set up outside and they faced the river running along the town's edge. Jacob went inside to order, and Ashley made herself comfortable at one of the tables. A woman came walking by pushing a stroller. The toddler was sound asleep, and Ashley couldn't help but smile at the woman. She smiled and nodded back as she walked by. There were a few others walking around on the sidewalks as Ashley just took everything in.

She could imagine herself living in a small town like this someday. Life was slower and safer it seemed. That may be a product of her childhood, but she longed for safety and security. Ashley felt the familiar twinge of longing in her heart as Jacob set down a waffle bowl full of vanilla ice cream, covered in cookie dough bits and chocolate fudge topping.

"So, did I do ok?" Jacob asked with a gleam in his eye.

Ashley rolled her eyes at him. "It's not hard to get me ice cream, but yes, you did very ok," she said with a smile. Her ice cream requirements were simple—vanilla ice cream, chocolate anything and no strawberry, ever. The toppings didn't matter either, she just despised strawberry. She wasn't allergic but had always believed she was for some reason. She avoided the flavor now at all costs though. Even the smell of artificial strawberry flavoring made her gag. Thankfully Jacob wasn't a huge fan of strawberry ice cream either.

"I want to live somewhere like this someday," Ashley said quietly looking out at the street.

"Really?" Jacob asked, clearly surprised by her admission. "I figured you for a big city girl. Lights and entertainment all the time."

Ashley shook her head. "No, I just want calm and peace. Look at all these folks just out for a stroll on a nice summer day. No worries or fears." She let out a soft sigh.

When she turned back to face Jacob, she noticed a strange look on his face. "What?" she asked.

Jacob studied her for a second and then shrugged, turning back to his ice cream. "Nothing. You just surprise me sometimes."

"That should be a good thing, right? I mean if we don't surprise each other anymore, life would get boring," she said with a grin.

"I guess you're right," Jacob said, as he met her eyes again. He turned his eyes to roam the street as well. "It is definitely peaceful, isn't it?"

"M'hm," Ashley said as she faced the river again. A lazy boat was floating down the river with a couple of people in it. She watched as it just seemed to float with little interaction from the small crew on board. They just seemed to sit back and enjoy themselves as well.

She turned and looked up at one of the hills. She pointed up to a rocky ledge overlooking the river above them. "That's where I would build my house."

Jacob turned to follow her finger and laughed. "I'm not sure that's a great idea Ash. But maybe a little ways back would be ok to build on." He turned back to her and smiled at her scowl.

"You are such a killjoy, you know that." She took her last bite of ice cream and wiped her mouth with her napkin. "Shall we?"

They both stood and joined hands as they met on one side of the table. They took their time walking back to the car. As they headed out of town, Jacob filled up with gas again and then they got back on the highway. Ashley fell sound asleep for another two or so hours until Jacob was shaking her awake.

"Ashley, get your camera out. You are not going to want to miss this," he said with excitement in his voice.

She groaned as she rubbed her eyes and looked around. All she saw was traffic in front and behind them. They were nearly at a complete stop. Grumbling, she asked, "Why do I have to wake up? I could sleep through this. We do have cars and traffic like this in the Cities, Jacob."

Jacob chuckled next to her and pointed his finger to his left. She followed and then the cars around suddenly started to move again. What looked like a photograph came into view and she sat up straighter in her seat. As they made their way closer, she could see the height of the bridge in front of her and the incredible metal structure that connected the eastern shore of Maryland to the mainland of the state.

"Wow," she said with awe in her voice.

"Yep. Pretty cool huh?" Jacob asked. "It is over four miles long. Just wait til we get to the highest point. It's amazing. I have read about it but never crossed it." His voice was full of wonder and awe, like meeting your idol for the first time. He began to babble on about the features, but Ashley tuned him out.

She watched as they rose higher into the air and then looked out over Chesapeake Bay. Cargo ships dotted the water and there were a few sailboats out enjoying the sunny summer day. She watched as the bridge changed and high above them were trusses and suspension cables creating an amazing architectural structure that was both functional and beautiful to look at. The two bridge spans side by side were a wonder to look at.

Jacob slowed the car down at about the midpoint of the bridge. "This is the highest point. Can you imagine getting stuck up here? We are three hundred fifty-four feet above the water." The little boy's wonder was still in his voice.

Ashley watched as they continued to drive across the amazing bridge. As they passed the midpoint, she stared straight up at the steel like tunnel created by the beams above them. Jacob was right. This was worth waiting for. They slowly made their way closer to the other side of the bay and she found herself looking back at the cars still crossing.

"That was amazing," she said. "Let's do it again."

Jacob laughed next to her. "Yeah, if it was free maybe." He reached down and grabbed her hand. "It was pretty cool though, right?"

"Yes, it was," she agreed. She was awake now and this was the last part of the trip. She needed to stay awake and take in everything else about her new home for a little while. So far it hadn't disappointed.

Chapter 5

"Well, what do you think?" The professor's voice pulled Ashley from her thoughts as she watched a few students walk through the grassy space in front of her, *the square it's called, I guess,* she thought.

They were sitting on the steps of the building, looking out. The campus was pretty empty of students since he had told her the second summer session wasn't starting until the following week. And it was a Thursday. The trees lining the entire campus gave it a very calm and serene feeling, nothing like the University of Minnesota with its huge campus and multitudes of students all the time. U of M was also in the middle of the city, so there was always traffic adding to the hustle and bustle too.

Ashley nodded and turned to smile at the advisor who had given her the tour. "The campus is beautiful and small, just like I wanted. The intimacy of it all feels very comfortable and safe," she said, looking around again at the square. She glanced to her left and met Jacob's eyes.

"I agree. This place is amazing for such a small-town area." He smiled at Ashley, knowing the safety she was looking for was here.

Ashley smiled back and nodded. Turning to the advisor, she asked, "Can we walk around for a little while and then I can give you a call next week?"

Professor Roslin nodded and the three stood. "Absolutely. Take your time, Ashley. I don't think there will be any issue with admitting you, given the records you have sent us. You just let me know your plans and we will go from there. It was very nice to meet both of you and I hope to see you in the fall." He put his hand out for each of them to shake and then he turned to go back into the building, leaving Ashley and Jacob alone on the steps.

"Should we walk?" Jacob asked her, motioning with his hand.

Ashley moved down the steps and waited on the sidewalk for him to meet her. She looked around and shrugged. "Where should we go?"

Jacob chuckled. "Well, it's not like you could get lost here. I remember my first time at the U. I got lost so many times I couldn't even count." He looked to the left and then right. "I think he said there are just residence halls that way, so let's walk straight through here and see where we end up."

Ashley nodded and took his outstretched hand. She sighed. Jacob had to leave in two days. She was nervous about being alone, but the school had set her up nicely in an older couple's third floor apartment. Jacob and Ashley had talked to the couple, and they had agreed to let her continue to rent from them for a couple of months. Ashley hoped to be out and back in Minnesota by fall so they could have it back for student housing. But if she decided to stay and actually go to grad school here, she could stay there. The best part was it was only a short drive to the campus from their house.

They walked until they came to an arch, which looked like it led to a busier street. They walked through and found it was a sort of strip mall with restaurants and a gas station. The upper levels she wasn't sure about, but looked like they could be apartments or office space.

"Oh, there's Jimmy John's. Let's go there for lunch," Ashley said with excitement. "I can't believe we found something familiar!" She pulled a laughing Jacob behind her.

"Slow down, Ash. Geez, you would think you were in some foreign country or something. There are all kinds of things here that we have in Minnesota."

Ashley stopped and glared at him. "I'm not talking about fast food, Jake."

He continued to laugh at her as they walked into the small restaurant. The smell of fresh baked bread surrounded them as soon as the door opened. Ashley took a deep breath in. "Oh, I love that smell," she said dreamily.

"Sometimes I worry about you, Ash," Jacob said with a smile on his face. He ruffled the bun of braids on top of her head, earning him another glare.

After they ordered and got their sandwiches, they made their way to one of the three tables outside. The sun was hot, much warmer than either was used to in Minnesota, but there was a small breeze and shade to help a little bit.

Ashley unwrapped her sandwich and looked out at the street. "This is the main street through town, right? So, we are just on the end of campus basically?" She pointed across the street where the Salisbury University stadiums were—football, softball, and baseball that she could see.

"I think so. On the next corner I think is that food court-like place with the palm trees. We should check that out sometime too." Jacob pointed with his thumb over his shoulder.

"I think I am figuring this out. But everything seems to go in circles, not straight lines like I am used to. That will make it harder to learn my way around I think," Ashley said looking up and down the street.

This seemed to be a busier place than some of the other locations they had eaten at. It was probably because of the school though, she figured.

As they finished eating, Jacob leaned across the tiny table and took Ashley's hand in his. "Are you sure you are going to be ok while I'm gone?"

Ashley met his concerned blue eyes and tried to smile confidently. She honestly wasn't sure. She was still worried about being alone, but she also knew she had the older couple who were already looking after her.

Finally, she shrugged and looked at her hands on the table. "I don't have a choice. I have to figure this puzzle out." She met his eyes and added, "and you will be back soon, right?"

Jacob nodded. "As fast as I can. I am hoping it will be even less than the three weeks we planned on, but it depends on Papa Jasper's plans. We will FaceTime every day and if you ever need anything, I am a phone call and a plane ride, or two, away." He gripped her hand tightly in his and gave her a smile. "But we still have another day and an ocean to visit, so let's get to planning."

Ashley smiled broadly and pulling her hand from Jacob's, she rubbed her hands together. "Ok, so I looked at GPS and we can go to Ocean City, or we can go to Assateague. Gary and Sharon said the tourists are flooding Ocean City since it's summer, so if we want a quieter day at the beach, Assateague is the place to go."

"Ok, how about this?" Jacob leaned forward and tented his fingers in front of him. "Tomorrow, we go to Ocean City early. We can do all the touristy stuff before it gets too busy and then we can go to the other place in the afternoon."

Ashley melted. "You would suffer through two beaches just for me?" she asked softly.

"I would do just about anything for you Ash, just to see that gorgeous smile and those beautiful hazel eyes light up," Jacob said with his goofy, lopsided grin that she loved so much.

"Now you're just milking it, buddy," she said with her own grin. "But I'm going to take it!" She leaned in and kissed his lips lightly. "Let's go get our day figured out. I need to call Aja too, since she texted me about an hour ago when we were still on the tour." She stood and stretched while Jacob grabbed their trash.

Stepping into the bright sunlight and humid heat, Ashley pulled her sunglasses over her eyes and looked in both directions. "Uh, which way do we go again?"

Jacob looked as well and then pointed right. "I think we came from that way." They made their way to the edge of the building and found the archway they had walked through a little while ago. Breathing a sigh of relief, Ashley took Jacob's hand, and they made their way back across the campus. There was an abundance of shade from the trees and the buildings, so the heat was more tolerable than outside the campus where they ate lunch.

"I'm not sure I like this summer heat," Ashley commented as they walked through the grassy area toward the parking lot. "I mean Florida was bad, but this is stifling."

"I can't argue with you there," Jacob said with a shake of his head. "Maybe by the ocean will be cooler."

As they made their way to the car, Jacob clicked the key fob twice to unlock it. Before sliding in, Ashley opened all the doors and told Jacob to start it so she could open the windows and turn the air conditioning on to hopefully cool it off quickly. Thankfully her seats were cloth so they wouldn't get burned sitting on them while they were hot. They had only parked a little over two hours ago and it was already incredibly hot in the car.

Jacob slid in and started the car, turning on the AC full blast. He quickly moved back out and turned toward Ashley, looking at her over the roof of the vehicle. "So where to, when this beastly heat is removed from the car?"

"Let's go back to the apartment and figure out a plan. I want to talk to Gary and Sharon anyway. She said something about taking us to dinner before you have to leave too." Ashley couldn't hide the hint of sadness in her voice.

Jacob nodded. "Ok. Let's go then and see if I can avoid getting lost."

They settled into the now much cooler car and buckled their seatbelts. Ashley pulled out her phone to use the GPS. She didn't know how long it would take for her to get familiar with everything here. She had Jacob drive so she could look around more and start to make connections with different places and street names. She always preferred to know streets rather than landmarks. The problem was some of the street signs were hidden behind trees, so she found she had to do a little of both.

The house wasn't far from campus, and she was actually proud of herself. She'd mentally said the streets and turns before the navigation did and she was right all but one time. As they pulled up to the large three-story house, Ashley saw Sharon outside watering some flowers on her front step. Jacob parked around the back of the house, and they jumped out. Gary had told him the best spot to park Ashley's car earlier when they moved her stuff in.

They reached Sharon at the same time. She straightened and pressed her hand on her lower back, the other holding the watering can.

"Well, how was the tour?" she asked, setting the spouted can down next to her.

Ashley smiled. Sharon had shared that she had attended Salisbury University when it was a much smaller school and solely for educating teachers so many years ago. "It is a beautiful campus!"

"Yes, it sure is. And it is so much more diverse than in the past." Sharon nodded and picked up the can again, walking toward the front door. She glanced over her shoulder at them and asked, "What are your dinner plans? Gary and I were thinking about taking you to a restaurant downtown for some good seafood."

Ashley and Jacob locked their eyes and nodded. They hadn't made plans yet so it would be perfect. Then they could spend as long as they wanted tomorrow just the two of them—and a huge number of tourists as well she figured.

"Sounds great actually. I am not a huge seafood fan, but am willing to try just about anything," Jacob said with a smile.

Sharon smiled and nodded, moving to open the door now in front of her. "Ok. I'll just check in with Gary and we can get a time. When do you leave Jacob?"

"My flight is at three on Saturday. I suppose I will need to be at the airport at around one, right?" Jacob looked at Sharon.

She turned to completely face him and scrunched her eyebrows. "Are you flying out of Salisbury?"

Jacob nodded.

"Then no." She let out a snort. "This isn't like the big city, kids. Well, you will find out when you get there I suppose. Come on in out of the sun." She motioned with her hand, and they followed her into the cool house.

Ashley couldn't help but feel comfortable and welcome in their home. Aside from their different ethnicity, they could be her grandparents. She never had any, but she imagined this is what it would have been like. Jacob was used to having many family members around while he was growing up, but Ashley only had Aja and her uncle. Thinking of Aja, she remembered she was supposed to call her back.

"Hey, I was supposed to call Aja back. I'm going to go do that now," she said, as she headed for the back staircase that led to her third-floor apartment. She had an outside entrance as well, but they were working on making the stairs outside safer, so for now she was using the inside ones.

Jacob and Sharon nodded. Ashley appreciated the privacy Jacob was giving her by not following. She settled on the bed in the far corner of the small apartment and took out her phone. She looked around and could see herself staying here for a while, not that she wanted to be here that long. But it was a comfortable space.

The room or apartment was designed specifically for a student. It had a small kitchen with apartment size appliances, meaning they were tiny. The fridge was about half the size of a normal one and the stovetop had just two burners. There was a microwave on a stand in the corner and an oven that looked barely big enough for a pizza. There wasn't much for counter space, just one three-foot span. But she thought it would work for a pizza or toaster oven. She wasn't sure she trusted the actual oven.

There was a chair on one side of the space and a bed on the other. The bed was made up to look like a couch when it wasn't a bed creating a living room space within the bedroom space. The door for the bathroom was along the same wall as the bed. It was actually a decent size considering the rest of the space, which she was grateful for. She wasn't super tall, but at five-foot-six, she didn't really want to have to slouch to get a decent shower. There was a tiny table that barely fit two chairs, but for her it was perfect. Even with Jacob staying there with her, it worked ok. Maybe when he came back, they would know how much longer she needed to stay, and they could find a bigger place.

She leaned against the headboard of the bed and pressed on her sister's smiling face on her phone. It only took one ring for her twin to answer.

"Hey Ash! About time. Tell me everything!" Aja rushed out. They had just talked the day before and Ashley knew this was about the tour today. She was hesitant to say too much because she really wasn't sure if she was actually going to grad school. She kept the tour to keep the ruse up to her sister and uncle that this school was a good idea for her education. But now she struggled to answer. She hated lying to her sister.

Biting her lip, she said, "It was a beautiful campus, Aja. There were trees everywhere and the sidewalks were actually big enough to walk side by side with someone." She let out a little chuckle remembering some of the places they tried to walk around the University of Minnesota where the sidewalk provided barely enough room for one person let alone two and then to consider the people coming from the other direction. "And they were smooth! No ruts or cracks in the concrete. It was like a dream," she added with a silly dreamy tone.

Aja giggled on the other end. "So do you think it will be as good as you thought?"

Ashley sighed, not sure what to say. In all honesty, if she was going to seriously consider grad school, it would be a perfect place. It was peaceful and small, which surprised her how much she disliked the huge university setting of the U of MN. She was outgoing and loved to be in big groups of people. But even she had felt overwhelmed with the size.

She decided to go with as much truth as she could. "I think so. It's a tiny campus, but the advisor we met with said they pride themselves on their sense of community. They do a lot within the community as well, which would be good—creating students who are bigger than just their school or education. I actually loved it," Ashley said honestly.

Aja was quiet on the other end. A soft sigh escaped her. "Ok. It's most important that you are happy so I will be happy for you. But I miss you so much, Ash. We have never been apart for so long. Sam is being weird again, like last spring when he did that undercover thing. I'm worried he's doing that again. It was so stressful!"

Ashley had to agree. Sam was acting strange a few months ago when he was working on a big case. He never shared much but Aja had told her some of it. She had to admit it scared her. But both of them knew there was some deep personal connection between that case and their uncle. He wouldn't share what it was, but they hoped in time he would. Ashley also knew if he didn't want to, he never would.

"You know you can FaceTime anytime you want right? And I know Ryan will be there for you. He seems like the perfect big brother to you, Aja." She liked Ryan, and his sister had a special connection to him that felt like a brother-sister bond in some ways. They had always wished they had a big brother and Ashley was glad Aja found that at work. Ryan was a good guy, and his wife would do anything for anyone. They would make amazing parents someday, she thought.

Aja sighed on the other end. "I know, but it's not the same as having you here. But we will get through this. It's probably good for us anyway. We have always relied on each other. Maybe we need to break away a little and see what we can do on our own."

A slight pang of regret hit Ashley's heart. Aja thinks they need to try to be separated and this is a good thing. Oh, how she wished she could tell her the truth without both her sister and her uncle going crazy. *Soon*, she told herself. *Very soon.*

Ashley cleared her throat and told Aja about her tiny apartment and the couple she was staying with. She had already told her some of it, but she needed to change the subject before she felt more guilty.

A soft knock on the door interrupted Ashley as Jacob entered the space. He waved his finger as if to ask her if he should go but Ashley shook her head. He moved into the room as she finished her conversation and hung up with her sister. She laid her head on Jacob's shoulder and resisted the tears that threatened to fall from her eyes.

As if sensing her pain, Jacob turned and wrapped his arms around her. "Hey, it's going to be ok. You just need to get your answers and then you can go home."

"I know. I just hope I can find out what I need to," Ashley said with a sniffle.

"Let me see the letter again," he said, pulling away just slightly so he could look in her eyes.

Ashley moved from his embrace and opened her suitcase. She took out an envelope and moved back to sit beside Jacob.

Carefully, Jacob opened the envelope and removed the letter. It was getting worn from the many times Ashley had opened it, read it, and put it back in the envelope. He laid the paper flat against his thigh and smoothed it out as best he could without ripping it.

Ashley looked at the letterhead staring back at her for about the eight millionth time. She sighed and touched it gently with her finger as she read out loud, "DNA Results from your recently submitted sample."

Chapter 6

The day spent at the beach was just what Ashley needed with Jacob before he left. They walked the entire boardwalk twice, visited the shops along the way, and she bought a few things for him to take back for her sister. Some of the stores repeated further down the wooden walkway, but it was still a fun experience. Ashley wasn't sure if she would come back during the summer though. Even at nine am it was still busy. She couldn't imagine what it was like at one in the afternoon.

The time at Assateague did not disappoint. Sharon and Gary were right. Although there were people on the beach. It was just a beach. There wasn't any commercialism and no stores. It was quiet and peaceful, aside from the kids running and chasing each other around. There were wild horses wandering around too, which made it a little more exciting. Since it was a national park, the rangers had set up signs all over about respecting the wildlife, with warning signs about feeding the animals and keeping their distance from the horses. It was a little surreal, she thought.

The day was perfect for Ashley. The sun was hot, and the air was humid, but there were just enough clouds to give a tiny respite from the sun's heat now and then. They spent the afternoon sitting on the beach. Ashley was mesmerized by the waves lazily crashing against the sand. The ocean was beautiful just like she expected. The sunlight sparkled off the water, making it look like it was covered in glitter. Watching the children run back and forth chasing and then being chased by the waves made her laugh.

Ashley avoided the sad feelings that tried to creep in now and then, wishing her sister was here with her. It was Jacob's last day, and he would leave the next day. *At least they could have lunch together before he leaves,* she thought.

By nightfall, Jacob was sun-burnt but Ashley had just gained more "beautiful brown" as Jacob said. He complained nonstop about the unfairness of it all, but Ashley just laughed. It was a never-ending complaint of his and she couldn't help but find humor in his whiny little boy voice.

"At least you listened and put sunscreen on!" she told him with a laugh.

Jacob grumbled a reply. "Yeah, yeah. I'm still burnt though. I want skin that doesn't burn!" His cranky voice made Ashley laugh harder.

They were back in her apartment. The couple downstairs had offered to treat them to dinner, but they decided they would go out alone. Ashley was headed for the shower and Jacob had just finished. He had a towel wrapped around his waist as Ashley applied more aloe and after sun lotion to his shoulders.

"Let this sit for a while before you get dressed," she said as she moved toward the shower.

Still complaining, Jacob moved out of the bathroom and closed the door behind him. Ashley stood under the steady stream of water, trying not to think about this time tomorrow. They hadn't done any more work on her search, but she knew she had to start after the weekend. She found out that Sharon knew just about everyone in Salisbury, so hopefully she could get some information from her about where to start.

A light knock on the door pulled her from her thoughts. She turned off the water and called out.

Jacob's muffled voice came through the door. "Hey, are you gonna stay in there all night? I'm kinda hungry."

Ashley smiled. "On my way." As if on cue her stomach let out an angry growl.

They had decided to go to a local brewery for dinner. Jacob had discovered two for sure. This one was across from the hospital. The building was huge, but they discovered most of it was the brewery. There was a small bar area with tables right as you walk in. There was also a spacious outside dining area with large bulb lights strung around the perimeter of the space. They opted for eating outside since it was a little later in the evening now and the sun wasn't so hot. It was a nice atmosphere and surprisingly not very busy.

Ashley looked over the menu and decided to order a burger and fries. She wasn't a big seafood eater, but being here, she knew she would have to branch out a little bit. Sharon was always talking about the amazing crab cakes at an Italian restaurant in town. She was pretty sure Sharon would take her there at some point so she could try them. Ashley wasn't sure what to expect or what a crab cake actually was, but she would try just about anything once, except squid. That was a definite no-go.

After they ordered, Jacob took her hands in his and smiled at her. "So, are you ready to tackle this on your own now?"

"Not really, but I will figure it out." She looked at their joined hands and then gave him a small smile. "Sharon seems like a pretty outgoing person and since she has lived here her whole life, I am hopeful that she can help me." Ashley shrugged her shoulder slightly.

Jacob leaned in. "I will be back before you know it and then we can finish this together. Please don't do anything that would put yourself in danger, ok? I think your uncle would literally kill me if something happened to you."

"Oh, I have no doubt, but he would kill me first," Ashley said with a chuckle.

Their food came shortly after, and they ate in silence. The occasional ambulance drove by with its lights on and the traffic was constant but not disruptive. The warm night air was comforting as she leaned back in her chair taking everything in. Ashley decided the burgers were pretty good. There was tough competition with Minnesota burgers though. She wasn't a foodie like Jacob's sister, but she did have her favorites. And Minnesota had the best burgers, that she and Sally Jo could agree on wholeheartedly.

"So, what now?" Jacob asked as he leaned back in his chair, locking his fingers behind his head.

Ashley leaned back as well and wiped her mouth with her napkin before placing it over her empty plate. "I'm not sure. Just hang out and watch a movie?"

Jacob nodded. "That sounds good actually. Maybe we can just talk and come up with a better game plan for how you are going to move forward on this adventure." His statement was more of a question.

"Yeah. I need to figure out how to ask Sharon if she knows how to find someone without saying it exactly like that. I can't have anyone getting suspicious or asking too many questions." She leaned her chin into her palm, tipping her head to the side.

Jacob studied her and then just nodded. "Let's go then." He stood and held his hand to her. He left cash on the table for the bill and the tip. As they walked away, their waiter came out and Jacob nodded to him and pointed to the table to let him know where they put the money.

The waiter gave him a nod of acknowledgement and waved a "thank you" as they walked away.

Once back in the apartment, Ashley spread out on the bed/couch and put her hands together under her cheek. She watched Jacob move around and pack up his suitcase. Fighting the tears, she closed her eyes. *This is going to be harder than I thought.* For the first time since she left Minnesota, she was having second thoughts.

Jacob sat down next to her feet and picked one up. She opened her eyes as she watched him gently massage her foot. She gave him a sad smile.

"You know, Ash, this is all going to be ok, right? I won't be gone long, and you can do some investigating while I'm gone. We need to figure out what exactly the ancestry report says, since neither of us knows how to really read it. And I will be back by your side as you try to figure out who this person is and how they are related to you. You need to do this. We both know you will forever regret it if you don't."

Ashley nodded. She knew this. It was the same mantra she had been saying in her head since she got the letter to begin with. This person was somehow related to her, and she needed answers. It would eat away at her if she didn't.

"And we both know I don't want regrets," she said with a sad smile.

Jacob just smiled and gave her a nod.

Sitting up a little straighter, she reached for the remote. "Let's watch a movie, a comedy so I'm not thinking about you leaving me alone tomorrow," she said with a sly grin.

Jacob picked up a pillow and threw it at her. "You know I would stay if I could!"

Ashley giggled. "I know. Come on, let's watch something."

They decided on an old Eddie Murphy standup comedy movie. They could have watched an action movie, her favorite genre actually, but they couldn't decide on which one. Maybe they could start a binge of something when he came back to kill time while they tried to get answers. She knew she could use a good comedy to take the sadness from her heart and Eddie Murphy never disappointed, especially his older movies. Sam loved his eighties movies, so she and Aja had seen a number of them.

They fell asleep laying together on the couch. Ashley woke up early with a sore neck and slid out from under Jacob's arm. Thankfully she was on the outside and could easily move. Jacob grumbled in his sleep but shifted and was snoring softly again in no time.

Ashley stretched her arms high above her head trying to stretch out her shoulders. She glanced at the little microwave and saw the time was only six thirty. *Great,* she thought. *Too early to be up for the day but too bright to go back to sleep.* She silently hoped this wouldn't be a trend here. She never was a morning person.

She grabbed a clean pair of shorts and a tank top and went into the bathroom. She looked around, noticing most of Jacob's stuff was already removed and packed up. Most importantly, she saw his cologne was missing. With a sigh, she got dressed and brushed her teeth. She would need to find his cologne and hide it somewhere. Maybe it would help her sleep when he was gone if she could smell him still.

Quietly, Ashley opened the door. She was startled to see that Jacob was lying on his back with his eyes pinned on her. His arm was resting lazily above his head while the other was across his stomach. He smiled as she walked back into the small space.

"Hey, you," he said with his still sleepy voice.

Ashley grinned back. "Did I wake you? Sorry, I couldn't sleep."

Jacob shook his head. "No. Too many thoughts in my head to sleep. Should we got for a walk or something?" He pushed himself up and sat back against the wall.

"I would like that. And it shouldn't be too deathly hot yet, right?" Ashley glanced toward the window at the other end by the kitchen. There were three small windows in the space. One faced the back yard and the other two faced the side where the driveway was. One of those two had an air conditioning unit in it but wasn't hooked up yet. Gary had told her there was another unit in the garage he would get put in for her soon, too.

"Who knows. It seems to be scorching hot here all the time," Jacob said as he stretched his arms in front of him, turning slightly to crack his back.

"I'll make us something quick for breakfast and we can go." Ashley turned to the tiny stovetop and pulled out a pan from the cabinet underneath it. The small fridge was stocked with food now and she took out a few eggs and started to scramble them as Jacob headed to the bathroom with a nod.

She made simple scrambled eggs and toast for them. They had picked up some fruit at the store and she picked up an apple for each of them and set them on the small peninsula. There wasn't enough space for a table, but the countertop worked just as well. It all seemed so natural to be doing this with Jacob. It warmed her heart that they could be living like this soon. She poured them each a glass of orange juice and then sat down just as Jacob came out of the bathroom.

"I think I could get used to this," he said with a smile as he leaned on the door frame.

Ashley gave him a wide smile, "I was just thinking that. I just have to get through this and then we can do whatever we want—together." She lifted her glass in a toasting motion as Jacob made his way to the table.

They ate silently, each lost in their own thoughts. They cleaned up together and then moved to get their shoes on, quickly moving around each other. Ashley led the way downstairs as quietly as she could and was surprised to find that Sharon and Gary were both awake.

They were sitting at their table sipping coffee. Gary was reading the newspaper while Sharon was reading a book. They both looked up as Ashley and Jacob passed by the doorway.

"You two are up early," Sharon commented. "Where are you off to?"

Ashley leaned in and smiled at the couple. Maybe she should feel like they were intruding, but she didn't. She felt comfortable with them and was happy they were concerned. She would likely need that when she was here alone. "Couldn't sleep. We are just going for a walk. See you in a little bit."

"Ok. Have fun." She quickly went back to her book with an absent wave in their direction.

"You know, I am glad they will be looking out for you, but I think I would get annoyed with them always asking where you are going. It's like living with my parents," Jacob said quietly when they were safely outside with the door closed.

Ashley shrugged. "I guess I am glad they want to know. If I was here alone, and something happened, who would look for me?" She gave a slight shudder at the thought.

They walked the neighborhood for a while. It was a nice fairly upscale area of town, and the houses were pretty big. The lawns were well kept and a healthy green. It surprised her because with the heat and no one having sprinkler systems, she wondered how they stayed so lush and healthy. The houses were spread apart due to the large lot sizes, but everyone seemed friendly and waved as they walked by. She knew that Sharon seemed to know everyone in town, so maybe the neighbors already knew who Ashley was.

The morning flew by, and it seemed way too fast to Ashley. She wasn't ready for Jacob to leave. She wasn't sure if it was being alone or missing him that almost made her want to just go with him. *Almost*, she thought. *I still have to do this, as uncomfortable as it might be, I have to see this through.*

They drove to the airport, which was on the outskirts of town. When Jacob pulled it up on GPS, he was surprised to see how small the area was on the map. It looked like it only had a couple of runways, and the terminal building was tiny. After talking with Sharon and Gary a little more, they decided that he didn't need to be there too early since there were actually only two gates and security consisted of a single officer and only one line.

The nice thing was they could hang out at one of the three tables outside the security area and wait for the time Jacob had to leave. It was a little comical to both of them, being used to huge international airports that they could be this close to the gates and not through security. But today, Ashley didn't mind. She could spend as much time as possible with Jacob before he left.

When it was finally time for him to go through security and board the small plane, Ashley bit her lip to keep herself from crying. She was nervous and worried about being alone, but she also knew it was going to be hard being separated. She took a deep breath and closed her eyes as Jacob pulled her in for a tight hug.

"I'll be back before you even notice," he promised, as he kissed the side of her head.

Pulling back, Ashley nodded. "Be safe, Jacob." They shared a sweet kiss goodbye and then Jacob left. Ashley waited until he left for the plane and then went to her car. The airport was so small that she could wait in her car and see it actually take off too. She stayed there staring at the now blank sky no longer fighting the tears falling from her eyes.

After sitting for a long time, Ashley wiped her cheeks and closed her eyes tight. She took in a deep breath of air and let it out slowly. With Jacob now gone, she needed to focus on her goal. Their little vacation was over, and she needed to get serious.

At that moment her phone rang. The sound startled her, causing her to jump and nearly scream. She quickly adjusted the volume on her car's Bluetooth and then pressed the answer button, holding her chest trying to calm her breathing. She didn't even look at the caller id before she answered the call.

"Ash!" Her sister's voice sang throughout the car, making Ashley flinch again and turn the volume down a second time.

"Hey Aja. What's up?" She tried to keep her voice even as she was continuing to calm her wildly beating heart from the sudden loud noises.

Ashley heard her sister sigh on the other end. She sat up straighter and waited for Aja to talk.

"I just wanted to see how you are doing. It's been a couple days, and I know Jacob is leaving today." Aja's voice was quiet, and Ashley almost laughed at the irony of how she was scrambling to turn down the volume and now could hardly hear her twin.

Ashley smiled at her sister's thoughtfulness, then remembered how close they always had been. She didn't think Aja could feel her emotions this far away though. "I'm ok. Yeah, this is hard, but I will have a lot to keep me busy the next few weeks until he comes back," she said, again careful to not say too much. She still hated lying to Aja, but until she knew more, she had to. "I just watched his plane take off actually. I was just going to head back to the apartment."

"I'll ride with you then!" Aja said with excitement. "Turn on your video and face me toward the street." Her voice was so full of child-like joy, Ashley couldn't help but giggle at her.

"You're crazy, Aja," she said with a grin. "Hold on." She took her phone out of the cup holder and changed it to FaceTime. Then she moved the phone to the dash and stood it up, supported by her sunglasses case so it was straight up and down.

"Oh, this is so perfect!" Aja said with a laugh. "Now I can see everything you can see!"

Ashley swore she heard her sister clap her hands like a toddler waiting for a cookie. "What are you up to today, Aja? Nothing going on there?" It was Saturday, but she and her uncle were almost always working on a case.

A long silence followed, and Ashley almost turned her phone around to see her sister. Aja finally sighed and said, "Nothing at all. Sam is off somewhere—he wouldn't tell me where—and I am just sitting here missing you." Her voice was soft and sad.

Ashley picked up the phone and faced her sister. "Ok, so we are both bored and sad. So, let's do something fun."

Aja giggled nervously. "I know how your fun usually goes. I'm not sure I am *that* bored, Ash."

"Oh, don't be so dramatic! I was just thinking we could go to the ocean together, well, through my phone anyway." Ashley rolled her eyes even though her sister couldn't see her. She put the car in gear and started to drive out of the parking lot. She stopped to pay for parking and then quickly headed to Ocean Gateway or Highway 50, she learned was the main road taking you straight to the Atlantic ocean.

"Oooh, I can handle that, I think. How long of a drive is it?" Aja asked, the noises coming through her speaker sounded like she was getting comfortable on her bed or the couch.

Ashley thought for a second trying to remember how long it took last time, but she couldn't. "I honestly don't know. Maybe thirty minutes? But I can't remember."

Aja laughed. "Time has never been your strong suit, has it, Ash? But it's fine. I have nothing all day and would love to spend the day with you."

"Hey, what do you mean time is not my strong suit? I'm not late for everything. I always get up when I'm supposed to," Ashley complained, enjoying the time with her sister that she had been missing.

Aja snorted. "Yeah, you are always five minutes late to everything because you set your alarm for ten minutes later than it should be, so you run around like a crazy person trying to be on time!"

"Ok, ok," Ashley laughed. "I'll admit, I might need to trim back my sleeping time, but I like to sleep so much!"

Their banter carried Ashley down the highway to Ocean City. Once she was close again, she could remember where Sharon had told her to go. She made her way around the streets to the inlet parking lot. Ashley's favorite place so far has been the dark gray rocks on the shore. Just the day before she was sitting with Jacob for a long time on the rocks, just listening to the waves lightly crash into them. It was calming and relaxing and it drowned out everything around her, including her mind.

Aja had gotten quiet as she watched through the windshield. When the water came into view, Ashley heard Aja gasp. "Oh my god, it's gorgeous!"

Ashley just hummed her reply. She had no words for the view either. She parked close to the shoreline and then exited the vehicle holding her phone away from her.

She had grabbed her AirPods to use while she walked so, she could hear Aja while she continued to face her sister toward the water.

Making her way to the rocks, Ashley sat down close to the edge of where the waves lightly brushed the rocks. She put her earphones in and then smiled when she heard her sister's voice gushing about how perfect it was. Ashley glanced around. It was a busy day at the beach. It seemed as if every square inch of beach was covered when she looked out. There were a few people fishing off the rocks, but she didn't mind. She just liked this spot. There were some kids walking on the rocks, but they stayed away from her and those fishing.

The sky was clear with a few wispy clouds lazily drifting by. The water was perfectly reflecting the sun above with a million sparkles dancing on the surface like it was dotted with diamonds. There was nothing to compare it to and Ashley was mesmerized every time she came back here.

Turning the phone back to face her, Ashley smiled at Aja. "So, what do you think?"

"Ash, it's amazing! I want to come there too!" She gushed on and on about the beauty of the ocean and the rocks and everything. Ashley knew she would love to be here, and god knew she missed her sister, but she also knew Aja wasn't the one to just jump on a plane and come visit.

Ashley sighed. "I know. Hopefully you can come visit me before I come home." She was missing her sister and even though it was beautiful here on the Eastern Shore, she was already homesick.

"Of course, I'll come visit before you come back! I mean come on. You're going to be there for two years! I can't stay away from my other half for that long, Ash!"

Aja's emphatic voice startled Ashley from her thoughts. *That's right, two years is how long the grad program is*, she thought, reminding herself that her sister doesn't know her plans yet. "Right, of course," she stumbled. Taking a deep breath, she added, "You just have to get that crazy workaholic uncle of ours to give you some time off, sis. But I'll be home for Christmas and stuff." She breathed a quick sigh of relief when her sister agreed.

Changing the subject so she wouldn't get caught in some lie, she turned the phone back to the water and took in a deep breath of the salty air. She could live here, she thought. Right here on the beach where she could hear the waves hitting the rocks all day and night. It was a good thing her sister was on the phone because she could have easily fallen asleep here. But Aja's constant chatter kept her awake and focused, so she didn't slip up on something again.

Chapter 7

Ashley groaned as she kicked the covers off her sweating body. The single air conditioning unit didn't seem to be keeping up with the heat at all. She looked at the clock next to her head and saw that it was barely seven in the morning.

"How can it possibly be this uncomfortable so early in the day?" she complained. Maybe it was because she was on the third floor, but she was going to have to get a fan or something because no one in their right mind woke up this early for fun. Well, maybe Aja did, but that was her problem, Ashley thought. It was another thing that her and her identical twin were the exact opposites on.

She threw the rest of the covers aside and headed for the shower. She never really understood the whole cold shower thing, but the way her body was feeling, she knew a cooler than normal shower was all that would help her cool down. She turned on the water while she used the toilet and brushed her teeth. Since it was just her, she didn't worry too much about bringing in clean clothes and all that. She always made sure her blinds were pulled at night so no one could see in—if they happened to be climbing trees at crazy hours of the night. Maybe when Jacob came back, she would have to be more careful, though.

She braced herself stepping into the water's stream and was surprised to find she wasn't shivering. It actually felt good against her heated skin. She let the water run over her, calming and cooling as it made its way to the drain between her feet.

An alert on her phone brought her out of her daze. It was a single beep, so she knew it was a text message. Leaving the door slightly open had its benefits, she thought. Taking her time, she made her way out of the shower and dried off. Ashley took her time getting dressed, knowing it would likely just make her hot all over again. She picked out a tank top and shorts, her usual go to outfit here it seemed. She glanced at her phone and then decided to answer her sister's text later on.

She retied her hair up tightly on her head and twisted the extra strands around her hair tie. The braids were starting to loosen at her scalp, and she figured she should probably find someone here to rebraid them for her. There seemed to be a large population of African Americans and services, so she wasn't too worried about finding someone to set her up. She might have to ask Sharon though if she knows who to ask for a good referral.

Ashley made her way downstairs and was surprised to see it was already eight fifteen. The shower must have been more refreshing than she thought. She looked around the kitchen and didn't see anyone, so she headed to the back door to go for a walk. Since Jacob's last day, she had been getting in the habit of walking each morning—at least when it wasn't quite as hot and steamy in the morning, which this particular day might be considering how she woke up.

She stepped outside onto the brick patio. Ashley spotted Sharon off to the side of the garage watering plants. She smiled as she walked to the older woman.

"Good morning, Sharon," Ashley said as she got closer. "It's gonna be a hot one today, huh?"

Sharon looked up from her rose plants and smiled back. "I guess so. Just another July day I suppose." She leaned backwards slightly, stretching out her back. It seemed to be her signature stretch when she was watering plants. She put the watering can down and looked at her gardens with her hands on her hips. "What do you have planned today, Ashley?" Sharon looked back at her boarder with interest.

Ashley bit her lip. "I'm not really sure yet. I think the professor wanted to talk to me about enrolling for the fall again, but I haven't set anything up yet. I suppose I could go to the college. It's air conditioned anyway." She grinned and wiggled her eyebrows, making Sharon chuckle.

"Oh, it's not that bad," she said with a shake of her head. "But I guess when you are used to Minnesota cold, this is a little hot."

"A little? What's the temperature out here, Sharon? Like already at eight in the morning it's gotta be at least eighty-five!" Ashley looked around as if she might find a thermometer.

"Oh, psh," Sharon said with a wave of her hand and a teasing grin. "It is only about eighty, maybe eighty-one. You are a dramatic one, aren't you." She turned back to her watering can and looked over the bright red rose bushes. "These beauties love the weather." She shot a wink at Ashley and then moved to refill her watering can.

Ashley laughed. "I suppose I would be used to it if I was raised here too. I'll see you later, Sharon." She gave a small wave and headed for the road. She loved the neighborhood. It was quiet and with the houses spread out, she didn't feel like anyone really noticed her and she could relax and just take everything in. Maybe that was the false sense of security she felt in the small town, but she didn't care enough to worry about it.

She wasn't an overly paranoid person, but she did believe she had a healthy sense of safety. That likely came from being so little when Ashley was scared out of her mind. It stayed with her. She feared for her safety and her sister's when their uncle whisked them away shortly after her mom died. She still remembered being afraid the bad men were going to come take her and Aja away like they did her mom and dad. She was so young she didn't realize the extent of the danger they were in, but Sam had established himself as their savior and also trained them for self-defense at a young age. You can't teach a young child about self-protection without scaring them a little bit about why they might need to defend themselves.

She also had to learn that the "bad men" were actually the police officers who took her dad, not the mobster-type that Sam painted her dad's colleagues to be. Ashley never really worried about them, even if Sam seemed to always remind them. That was her sense of safety in Sam's care that allowed her to forget about those guys.

The street the house was on came to a dead end just a couple lots to the left of Sharon and Gary's house. So, Ashley always walked to her right out of the driveway. She had been able to establish a pattern in the few days since Jacob had left. It was already the fifteenth of July she realized, and she needed to get moving with her research. She thought being at a college might help so she could use the library resources there. She still wasn't sure how to go about her research, but she hoped someone there would be able to help her get started.

As she walked, Ashley tried to create a plan in her mind of how to get started. She decided to go back to the letter in her room. She would go talk to the professor and maybe even visit the library to get a lead on where to start looking for a person. She wasn't sure if it would be helpful, but she had to start somewhere. Once she had even a tiny lead, she could go to Sharon, who literally knew everyone. It was crazy to Ashley how many people she knew. But then again if you have lived in the same town your whole life it made sense. Ashley hoped she could use that to her advantage once she had a starting place.

Feeling better than she had since Jacob left, Ashley made her way back to the house. As she turned the last corner, she noticed a black car parked on the street. There weren't usually cars parked along the street because of how long the driveways were, and the houses being set back so far off the street. Maybe a stray Amazon or mail truck, but not cars.

Ashley intentionally moved to walk on the other side of the street as she passed the car. The windows were tinted so dark she couldn't tell if there was anyone in the car. She quickly looked away and tried to act unbothered. She didn't have her earbuds this morning, so she tried to listen carefully to see if she heard a door open or the engine start. She didn't look behind her, she just listened.

When Ashley was about three lots from the house, she turned to look back, acting as if she were just checking traffic to cross the street. At that moment, the car suddenly pulled away from the curb and drove off. Thankfully it was facing the other direction and was not heading toward her. She took a few deep breaths and continued on the side of the street to the house. She made a mental note to always have her earbuds on her when she walked so that she could listen while looking as though she wasn't paying attention.

When she entered through the gate to the back door, she noticed Sharon wasn't outside anymore. She resisted a chuckle, thinking that even with all her talk of the weather not being too bad, Sharon was likely overheated too. As expected, she found her in the house, sitting on the couch with her book and a tall glass of lemonade.

"Did it get too hot, Sharon?" Ashley couldn't help but ask with a grin.

Sharon turned toward her and smiled back. "Hey, I know when to be outside and when to be inside." She tapped her temple and turned back to her book.

Ashley laughed and headed upstairs. She wanted to pack a bag for the university and subconsciously knew she wanted the strange car to be gone longer than it had before she left again. She was grateful that it left before she got to the house, but obviously if it was watching her, it would already know where she was staying, she thought. She shook her head hard. *No one was watching me, stop being ridiculous!* she chastised herself.

She gathered the string backpack her sister got her for Christmas last year that said "Teachers make learning fun" written in bright letters across the front. It was perfect for today. She stuffed her binder with a notebook, the report in its original envelope, and an unopened letter that came a few days before graduation. Jacob knew it had come but he hadn't pressured her to open it. The return address was how she knew where to go.

Grabbing the bag and slinging it over her shoulder, Ashley made her way out of the house again. She noticed Sharon had moved again when she came downstairs. The woman never seemed to sit still for long, she thought with a grin.

After buckling her seatbelt, she leaned back and glanced around the yard. Sharon was nowhere to be found. She took a deep breath and started up her Rogue. Carefully and slowly, she made her way out of the driveway, glancing down the street before she left the driveway to double check that the car from earlier was gone. Ashley unknowingly let out a breath she was holding and closed her eyes for a split second before she moved out of the driveway and onto the street.

She drove slower than normal as she scanned the streets around the neighborhood. When she made it to the entrance of the development, she let out another breath and then turned onto the road heading toward the college. "Camden," she whispered out loud, trying to commit the road names to memory. Ashley relaxed as she drove through the tree covered street. It reminded her of an old town with huge trees close to the street creating a shady drive, even in the bright morning sun. The beauty of it struck her and she found herself smiling.

As Ashley turned into the parking lot of the university, she found a spot to park near the entrance and quickly made her way in to meet Professor Roslin. He had said she could come in anytime, so she hadn't called ahead. While Professor Roslin had a direct hand in admissions, he was also one of the top professors for the graduate program she was looking into. She just wanted to check in with him again so if she decided to enroll, he would remember her easily.

She hoped it was still ok that she just showed up. She locked the car door and then glanced around again.

"Why are you so paranoid?" she muttered, shaking her head. She huffed out a frustrated breath and shook her head sharply. She wasn't a paranoid person, she reminded herself. Ashley straightened her back and made her way to the building where the professor had told her his office was located. Even with her chastising, she still breathed out a sigh of relief when she was safely inside the building.

Professor Roslin was just locking his office door when Ashley came up to him. He turned and startled slightly when he saw her.

"A-ashley? Uh, hi. Can I help you," he asked. He looked like he was just caught in something, but she shook off the feeling. She *did* kind of just sneak up on him.

Ashley was surprised he remembered her name after such a brief encounter more than a week ago. She shrugged. "Sorry to barge in. I was just going to check in with you and maybe get more info about the program." She watched his eyes carefully. The last thing she wanted was to come across pushy. She could schedule an appointment if it would be better. She opened her mouth to say just that but stopped.

The professor shook his head and then looked at her. "Sorry I was just going to go to the cafeteria for a snack." He turned to fully face her. There was something in his eyes that looked a little off, but Ashley shook it off, thinking it was just because she startled him. "You are welcome to join me, if you'd like."

Ashley shrugged off her unease and nodded. "Sure. I was just coming to check in anyway. Nothing formal."

The professor gave her a quick tip of his head and dropped his eyes to the floor. "This way. I'm not sure if you know your way around very well yet," he said with a low voice.

What was going on with him today? she thought. "Uh, if it's a bad time, professor, I can come back another time." She stopped walking and turned to face the older man.

She had only met him briefly one other time, so maybe he just didn't recognize her at first. But he knew her name without her telling him again. They had only talked for a few minutes about the program and his classes. He had been very animated during their quick conversation before, obviously he loved his job and the content of his classes, even though he seemed distracted and in a hurry this time.

She looked him over as they stood in the hall. A few students walked by but for the most part it was quiet in the halls. Her mind drifted, wondering what kind of professors they had at the school. Professor Roslin was not your typical professor type. He had a short haircut and dressed neatly in a pair of dress pants and a nice shirt. Everyone has that crazy professor idea in their head, with the wild gray/white hair flying all over that doesn't seem to ever lay where it's supposed to. Maybe glasses that are too big for their face. A super casually dressed guy in baggy old jeans and a rainbow across his chest. Not a rainbow like today for Pride, but the rainbows the hippies wore in the seventies for love and peace, or whatever they used them for back then. She had a few of those professors at the University of Minnesota and they were the most fun teachers she ever remembered.

Prof Roslin stopped and met her eyes. He cleared his throat, pulling her from her thoughts, and gave her a small smile. "Sorry. I am a bit distracted today. We are fine to meet now. I have just been in my office too much lately and need to get out. Come on." He waved his arm in the direction they were headed. "So, what did you want to talk with me about, Ashley?"

Ashley nodded and followed. She didn't really have an agenda. She just wanted to get out and check out the library and maybe find a starting place for her research. "I guess I just wanted to check in."

A thoughtful look came over his face and then he suddenly stopped again. "You know, I was just thinking about a possible student teaching position you might be perfect for. Since you hadn't enrolled yet, I'm curious about what's holding you up and if I could help out at all." He turned slightly toward her and lifted his eyebrows.

This time Ashley cleared her throat. Did she want to stay here for school? Did she want to actually follow through with it? She looked away and tried to think of the right words to say.

The professor seemed to catch on to her unease and gently added, "There's no pressure. If you're not sure, that's ok. I can tell you about the position and you can see if that will sway you." This time his smile was genuine, and Ashley couldn't help but smile back.

"Ok, that's fair." She felt better that he wasn't pressuring her to make a decision at that moment.

She knew a lot depended on her ability to find answers to other questions, but his support felt good right now.

They arrived at the almost completely empty cafeteria in just a few minutes. Ashley had to remind herself that the campus was very small compared to what she was used to—also why she loved it so much.

The professor put his bag on a chair near the entrance. He glanced up at Ashley and asked, "Do you want anything?"

Ashley shook her head. "No thanks. I'll just sit here and wait, so no one takes the table." She grinned and looked around at the space.

Professor Roslin laughed and nodded. Ashley noticed he looked back at her a couple of times but looked away quickly when he saw she was looking back at him.

Ashley tried not to let it bother her, but it was weird that he kept looking at her. Maybe he was one of those professors who memorized his students' faces so he would remember them easily. She had a prof once who took a picture of each student—with their consent of course—and then by the second day he would know each person's name. It was actually nice to have professors who knew your name. It made her feel like more than a paycheck or just a number in their class. She took out her phone and noticed she missed a text from Aja. She sent a quick reply telling her she was meeting with a professor and would call later. She felt a little relief that she didn't have to lie about where she was.

Ashley glanced up to see that the professor had disappeared, so she sent a text to Jacob. He was planning on coming back in just another week and a half and she couldn't be more thrilled. She was doing fine here alone, but she would feel better when he was back with her. He replied quickly and they agreed to FaceTime later when she was done with the meeting.

Professor Roslin suddenly appeared at the same time a tray slammed down on the table next to Ashley. She jumped at the sudden noise, not knowing he was there.

"Sorry," he apologized. "I didn't mean to scare you. It kinda slipped out of my hand." He pulled the chair out and sat down in the spot next to her instead of across, which struck her as odd, but she didn't want to move and make him feel uncomfortable.

Ashley waved her hand dismissing his words. "It's all fine. I was lost in my phone and wasn't paying attention." She set her phone down and folded her hands on the table.

"So, what are you thinking about for the fall, if you don't mind me asking?" the professor asked. "I don't mean to pry, but you did come a long way from home to not be sure what you wanted to do."

He kept leaning into her. She wanted to believe it was an accident, but why did he have to sit right next to her to begin with? she wondered

Ashley tilted her head slightly and resisted a scowl. It really wasn't any of his business, was it? She realized she was starting to feel the pressure of everything. Maybe he was just trying to get to know her. She tried to shake off the irritation and shrugged her shoulder. "I wanted to take a break and thought I'd check out the school while I was here on vacation. I really wasn't planning on staying very long, unless I decided to attend school."

Professor Roslin just nodded his head and then turned his attention to the biggest Danish Ashley had ever seen. He smiled at her wide eyes. "Yeah, once in a while they bring in something special." He lifted it up and gave her a nod. "*This* is as good a reason as any to come here." He grinned and then took a bite out of it.

Ashley shook her head. "I guess the 'freshman 15' is a real thing here with those things around!"

"Oh, you would think, but we don't get these very often. When we do though, you don't skip breakfast." He winked and took another bite, offering it to her for a bite as well. But she shook her head. She wasn't about to share food with a stranger plus she wasn't hungry.

Changing the subject, she asked, "So what is the teaching position you mentioned?"

They spent about an hour talking about the school, the master's program, and the teaching assistant position he felt that she would be perfect for. Ashley had to admit that she was feeling more and more like a student at the school. She wasn't sure if that was a good thing or not yet. She did feel like Professor Roslin was getting just a tiny bit too comfortable with her and she wasn't sure if she liked it. It could just be an East Coast cultural thing, she thought.

When the professor stood and held his hand out to her to help her stand, she pretended like she didn't see it, turning to the opposite side to stand on her own. Ashley turned to face him and took a tiny step backwards. She nodded slightly and then started to move to the exit. Something was off and she suddenly felt uncomfortable.

"Thanks for the info, professor. I will let you know what I decide." As she started to move away, she felt his hand on her arm. She froze as she waited for him to talk but she didn't turn to look at him.

His hand dropped and he said quietly, "I just wanted to give you my phone number so you can reach me easily, you know, if you have any questions or anything."

Ashley looked over her shoulder and saw him reaching into his pocket. She was about to refuse when he pulled out a business card and held it out for her. She sighed quietly and took the card from him. He wasn't asking for her number, so it should be fine, right?

Giving him a smile and another nod, Ashley thanked him and left. She wasn't sure where she was in relation to her car, but she found the closest exit and figured she could walk. It wasn't a huge campus, so she shouldn't get lost. She didn't run, but she did move quickly through the paths outside. She didn't even notice the heat that had built since she had been here, just an hour or so earlier.

Once she was next to her car, she stopped and looked around. Her discomfort was unnerving. This is not who she was. She loved people and the more people she could meet the better. The feeling she was having though was not of excitement and intrigue. She was genuinely worried. Was the professor hitting on her? She didn't resist the slight shudder. Not only was she not interested, but he gave her a creepy feel when she thought about him trying to give her his number. *But maybe I'm just making a big deal out of nothing,* she thought.

Frustrated, she pulled out her phone. Leaning against the car, she opened her call log to find Jacob. She just needed to hear his voice and settle her nerves—without telling him why she was feeling off. Just as she was about to press on his smiling face, she yelped and jumped off the car. The heat had definitely built up, and her thin tank top didn't do anything to protect her skin from the hot metal. Ashley couldn't help the chuckle that left her lips as she heard Jacob's voice on the other end of the phone. Unfortunately, it was his voicemail, but it was enough to calm her nerves. She left a quick message and then unlocked her car. She didn't get in, but let the heat pour out of the closed-up vehicle. She leaned in to start it so she could open the windows, but stayed outside while it cooled a little. Ashley couldn't help the grin knowing "cooling" a car in this heat was not a reality without a fan on high, blowing cold AC throughout the vehicle.

As she scrolled her phone, she looked up to see the professor walking across the other side of the parking lot. She noticed he looked intently at his phone and had a scowl on his face. She couldn't help but wonder what was up with him today. Something was definitely off. She didn't think she was imagining it either. Ashley subconsciously strained her neck to see what kind of car he got into but couldn't quite see as he ducked out of sight behind a large truck. *Why do I care what kind of car he drives? There's no way he was near the house this am and still got here before me, was there?* Ashley shook her head and let out a chuckle.

She didn't have much time to worry about her crazy thoughts because her phone rang in her hand. She tapped the answer button, but the other line clicked ending the call before she could say anything. She looked again at the screen and the number wasn't one she recognized. Sighing, she decided to just head back to the house. She didn't feel like being outside and would use her laptop to start her search instead of the college library.

She was trying her best not to overthink these few weird things that have happened so far today.

Chapter 8

Ashley settled on her bed in the small apartment and pulled her computer up next to her. She had her notebook next to her on the opposite side and a pencil in her hand. The two envelopes were sitting on her legs which were stretched out and crossed at the ankles. Tapping her lips with the eraser of the pencil she stared out the small window without the AC unit yet. It overlooked the parking area of the yard, but she was up high enough that she saw only into the lush leafy tops of the tall trees.

She had stopped on her way home to get a couple of small fans to put in her space. Gary had told her he would get the second air conditioner unit out this weekend, but if she wanted it in sooner, he would do his best to accommodate her wish. Ashley didn't want to be a bother, so she just said it was fine whenever he had the time. She was wishing she hadn't been so easygoing about it now. But the fans were set up in two corners now so there was air movement at least. One unit was definitely not enough for even this small space with the heat.

Her attention was drawn to the sealed envelope on her lap. She picked it up and turned it over a couple of times, before settling it upside down in her hand. She had memorized the front since she had stared at it almost daily since it came in the mail a couple months ago now. "BK; Salisbury/Eastern Shore, Maryland." That's it.

Taking a deep breath, she ran her finger lightly through the semi-sealed fold, taking care not to get a paper cut. The high humidity must have somehow moistened the glue again. The flap jumped slightly when it was freed, but she didn't immediately take out the paper inside. Ashley turned the envelope over again and looked at the neat writing and sighed. It was addressed to her, but she didn't know what she would have told Aja or Sam about the sender. She was grateful she had gotten the mail that day so that no one discovered it first.

Gingerly, she pulled the paper out. The white lined paper, likely ripped from a notebook, had black ink that could be seen through the paper folds. Black ink was also used on the outside of the envelope, not that it mattered much, she figured. She set the envelope aside and as if handling an old letter from the 1800's, slowly opened the folded paper.

> "Hello. We don't know each other, obviously, but I think we are related somehow. I am very confused by what I have discovered and hopefully we can meet sometime. I have no idea how or when, since you live so far away, but I can hope anyway. I can't give you my address, but I can give you a post office box and if you want to meet or are here sometime, you can write me a note to this box number and I can get it. This is so weird, right? Obviously we don't know each other, so I am trying to be careful. Anyway, see ya hopefully sometime. BK"

Ashley stared at the writing. There was an address on the bottom of the page. It said they couldn't give her an address but gave her one anyway. Maybe it was just the post office or something, she thought. She reread it a few times before putting it back in the envelope. She set the paper aside and pulled out the report again. With a deep sigh, she looked over the DNA report from the ancestry site. She hadn't wanted to do the test, but one of her elective classes for her graduation required it. The professor said they could code the results if they wanted but it was important to the study of history and ancestry. Since the class was a history class around the development of Ellis Island in New York, it was a requirement—unless she could come up with a really good reason why she couldn't do it.

When the results came in, she was shocked to see what they showed, even though she really wasn't interested at the time. She had used her college address and kept it hidden from Aja. Sam had warned them both multiple times to be careful about what they disclosed in any kind of search they did. He told them it was because of the history of their father and his worry that someone still might come after them to gain something on their dad. But now, looking at this paper she wondered if it had something to do with this thing in her hand.

Well too late now, she thought. She put the papers aside and pulled out her notebook. There wasn't a lot of information on either paper. It could be a scam she mused, but how would someone tamper with these results? They would have had to know she was doing it to begin with and she hadn't told anyone. But after the fact, she supposed anyone could have sent the letter. That's why she didn't respond right away. That and she had no idea what to say.

Ashley was surprised when she received the letter though. She forgot when she put contact info down on the application form that she put her home address, not really thinking about it. What would Sam say if he knew what she was doing, especially after all the warnings he had given? Hopefully nothing happens while she's here or he might ground her for life—even if she was an adult.

She hadn't shown Jacob the letter, only that she received it and had a place to look for this relative. That is how she ended up on the Eastern Shore. She and Jacob had talked extensively about what to do and she decided soon after she received the letter that she had to meet this person. But she never reached out, terrified about what she might find. But now she was here and felt stuck. Ashley wished now that she had sent a letter right after she received hers.

Her ringtone sounded on her phone, bringing her attention out of her thoughts. Picking it up she smiled at Jacob's face smiling back at her. She pressed the answer button and put the phone to her ear.

"Hey, babe. How's it going?" His voice was loud and sweet, literally music to her ears.

"I'm doing alright. How's work? How's everyone?" she asked, pushing the papers aside and laying down on her pillow. The call was perfect timing since she was starting to think too much again.

Jacob sighed on the other end and Ashley felt herself stiffen. "Well, work is fine, but Papa Jasper needs me a little longer. One of the guys got hurt today, pulled something in his back and is out of commission for a little while. I'm sorry, Ash. I can't leave him short-handed."

Ashley didn't know what to say and if she did say something, she was worried it might come out wrong making him feel worse. She knew he wanted to come out there as much as she wanted him with her. And Papa Jasper was older and couldn't exactly pick up the slack from being down a man. She let out a soft sigh, as soft as she could muster. "It's ok, Jake. I am doing fine here, and Sharon is so wonderful. I will be ok for a while longer."

She almost mentioned the weird interaction with the professor but decided against it. She didn't want Jacob to worry about her being alone. She glanced at the papers next to her, just as Jacob asked about her search.

"Have you gotten anywhere with the leads?"

"No. I just don't even know where to start." She sighed a little deeper this time. Taking an immediate breath in, she added quietly, "Jacob, I need to show you something."

The line was quiet for a second before Jacob said, "Don't tell me you found someone else already, Ash. It's just barely been a couple weeks. Let me guess some hot beach dude with bleached blonde hair who surfs."

Ashley snorted. "Right. Like I have eyes for anyone but you, dummy." But his joking worked. She relaxed a little and then told him about the letter. "I can send you a picture if you want. I have an address, sort of, but it's not like I can go there and meet anyone."

Once again, Jacob was silent. Ashley hoped he wasn't upset with her for not opening it earlier. She held her breath as she waited for him to say something, anything.

"Well, I guess you really can only do one thing, Ash. You need to write a letter back." His voice was quiet, and she still wasn't sure if he was upset with her.

Taking a deep breath in, she whispered, "Are you upset with me for keeping it from you?"

"Of course not, Ashley. I know this whole thing has been hard. Don't worry about me. Aja maybe, but not me. I'm just here for support. And what you decide to share with me I will help you with. Now if there was some hot guy on the side, I think I would be upset if you kept *that* from me." She could tell by his voice he was smiling, and she breathed easier.

"Thank god. I'm so worried about this and I just don't know what to do to start. If I send a letter, it will be postmarked here. Do you think that's a good idea?"

Jacob seemed to think for a minute. "Maybe you're right. How about this? You write it and send it to me through email and I'll print it and send it from here. That will give them the impression that you are still here and give you some more time."

"That's a great idea actually. Thanks, Jacob. That will give me some more time to figure out how to find out more about this person." She started to think about what to say in her note back. She didn't want to give too much away since she still wasn't positive it was legit. And then there was the problem of whether it *was* legit. Who was this person and how were they connected to her?

"Ash? You there still?" Jacob's voice interrupted her thoughts.

"Yeah, I'm here. Just thinking too much lately I guess." She needed a subject change. "How long does Papa Jasper think he'll need you still?" She bit her lip waiting for an answer she wasn't sure she would like too much.

Jacob's hesitation confirmed her fears. "Um, I'm not positive. He said he was trying to get one of the other kids in for the rest of the summer and then I can go, but I have to make sure he is covered here. Even if he gets someone, I need to be here to train them in."

"I get it. It's really ok. I am going to go to the library on campus tomorrow and see if I can figure out a way to search for someone with the limited info I have. Heck, maybe my history class about Ellis Island will help me start. That was all about genealogy and stuff. If only I had a tiny bit more to go on—or if I had paid more attention in class." *Maybe my letter will get a response*, she thought silently.

Jacob let out a frustrated breath, making the phone crackle in her ear. "Have you talked to Aja lately? How's that going?"

"I talk to her almost every day. And honestly, it's getting harder and harder to lie to her. But I have been going into the college, so I'm not lying when we talk about that." Her lips lifted in a small smile as she thought about all the little white lies that she had accumulated to her sister. But then, white lies or not they are still lies, aren't they? Brushing those thoughts aside, she focused on Jacob again.

Their conversation was interrupted by a ding from her phone. She pulled it away from her ear and put the call on speaker so she could check her texts. Maybe it was Aja wanting to talk or something. Ashley furrowed her brows as she looked at her texts. There was only one unopened one and it was from an unknown number. Hesitantly she pressed on the alert and saw a blank text, like someone pressed the space bar and then sent it. Weird, she thought. Then suddenly there was a second one. This one confused her even more. It simple read "Mom? Are you home?"

She stared at the words and got lost in what it might mean. Shaking her head, she groaned internally. *Stop overthinking!* she scolded herself.

"Ash? Everything ok?" Jacob's voice startled her back to her phone call.

"Yeah, sorry, someone just sent me a text but it's a wrong number." She typed out as much and sent it to the sender. She didn't want them to be waiting for a response from the wrong number. She would feel horrible if it was an emergency and she just ignored it.

"That's weird," Jacob said. "Doesn't everyone have their numbers saved in their contacts? How do you send a text to a wrong number?"

Ashley wasn't sure either. "I'm not sure. Maybe it's a new phone or something. Anyway, I better get going. I have to figure out my game plan here. Call me later or tomorrow, ok? I miss you, Jacob." Her voice softened as she said the last words.

Jacob sighed. "Ok. I miss you too, Ash. Hopefully it won't be too much longer."

As she hung up with Jacob, Ashley sighed. She was here for a reason, and she needed to get focused on it. Tossing her phone to the side, she pushed herself up again and picked up the envelopes.

"Ok, where do I start?" she asked out loud. She picked up her phone again and typed the address at the bottom of the letter to see where it was. "UPS store. Great. No help at all." She knew that area, well, remembered a little about it. It was a strip mall near the campus. It could be this BK is a student or lives nearby or has a car and drives from just about anywhere to get there. "UGH!" She threw herself back against the pillows again.

Ashley sat up and pulled the envelope with the DNA results closer. She opened and removed the report. She studied it, trying to make sense of "familial match", "paternal match", and "maternal match." None of the words made sense, all she could focus on was the number. They were definitely related, but she couldn't figure out what the "close match" versus other things meant. But how? She didn't have any family that she knew of besides Sam and Aja. Her dad was in prison and her mom was dead. It had been just her and Aja for her whole life. She had pictures to prove it. And Sam never talked about cousins or other siblings he had. It was weird that there would be a close match to someone when no one ever told her she had more relatives. She did have to admit she didn't know much about her dad's side though.

A sudden thought occurred to her, making her stomach turn. Her father. He could have had an affair. She wouldn't put much past him anymore. What would she do if this person was a product of her father's affair with another woman betraying her mom? How would she be able to accept someone like that? She knew it wasn't their fault what her father had done, but it would be a constant reminder of him.

Taking a deep breath of air in and then letting it out slowly, she closed her eyes for a minute. *Focus,* she scolded herself. The first thing was to figure out what the numbers all meant and everything else she could get from the report. "Maybe Sharon knows someone who can help me," she mused quietly.

With renewed determination, she brushed aside the negative thoughts about her father before she traveled down that unending, and painful, road again. She tried hard to keep her father from her thoughts. It always led to the heartbreaking memories of her mother's death.

Ashley tossed her legs over the side of the bed and stood, stretching her tall frame, nearly touching the ceiling with her fingers high over her head. She twisted her shoulders one way and then the other, stretching the kinks out. She scooped up the envelopes and headed out the door, carefully locking it behind her.

She paused just outside the door of the kitchen and heard Sharon moving around. A random clink of dishes rubbing together told her she was likely emptying the dishwasher. Ashley made a habit of slowly entering the couple's space in case they were talking, and she didn't want to interrupt or have them think she was eavesdropping.

As Ashley slipped into through the doorway, Sharon looked up and smiled. "Hello, dear. How are things?"

"Good, actually. How are you doing? Anything I can help with?" Ashley glanced around the near spotless kitchen.

"Nah. I was just rinsing out some cups. What are you up to?" Sharon wiped her hands on the towel in front of her and turned to face Ashley. Her hip was resting against the counter as she studied Ashley.

Ashley shifted slightly on her feet. "Um, I was actually going to ask you something." She looked up and Sharon gave her a small smile and nod to continue. "Well, it seems like you know pretty much everyone in town. I was wondering if you knew someone who could read those ancestry website things. I had to do an assignment for one of my classes and submit to one of those sites. Now I don't know how to read the results."

Sharon lifted her brows. "If the teacher required it, didn't they go over the results in class? That's weird and irresponsible teaching if you ask me. As a teacher for over thirty years, I can't imagine leaving your students hanging like that." She chastised the invisible professor in front of her with a wave of her hand and a "tsk tsk" in her voice.

Ashley couldn't hide the smile that played on her lips. "Well, in his defense, I didn't get the results in time for the big class reveal and I didn't really listen when they covered it. So, it is kind of on me. I wasn't expecting anything, um, out of the ordinary so I didn't care. I just needed the passing grade." Ashley shrugged her shoulders and suddenly felt like she was going to be scolded like the invisible professor.

Sharon studied Ashley, like she wanted to say something but then shifted her gaze to her phone across the kitchen. "Well, you're in luck. I just so happen to have a good friend who is working on her family tree and if anyone would know anything about these things, she would." She grew thoughtful for a minute and looked outside the large glass doors that showed off their lot and pool in back. "You know since my kids were all adopted, I have thought about doing those for them. Maybe I should call Trish myself. Hmm." She tapped her lips thoughtfully, staring outside.

Ashley didn't want to interrupt her landlord's process, but the name and number of this Trish person would be nice. Sharon abruptly shifted and moved to get her phone. She scrolled through her phone and then poked at it.

"Here's her info. I'll send you the contact details if you'd like. Trish is a sweetheart. You'll love her! If you want, I can call her ahead of time and let her know I gave you her number." Her raised eyebrows and bright blue eyes stared at Ashley.

Ashley nodded. "I would appreciate that."

Sharon gave her a quick head tilt and said, "I should warn you though. Trish is old school. She likes phone calls. If you text her, she will not respond, like it's such an insult she won't even acknowledge it." Sharon rolled her eyes at her friend's behavior.

Ashley heard the familiar sound of her phone letting her know she got a text and then Sharon smiled. "I'll give her a call this afternoon. Will you be around for dinner tonight? I was thinking about teaching you a little about the food here." She had a twinkle in her eye that made Ashley almost run away.

Narrowing her eyes, Ashley lifted her chin with a question in her narrowed eyes. "What are you up to, Sharon?"

Sharon's smile widened. "Nothing, sweetheart. But if you are going to be here, you might as well learn what's good to eat."

"Ok, I guess you have a point," Ashley said. She knew that meant seafood was in her future, but she would try just about anything once.

Sharon clapped her hands together excitedly. "Great. I know the best place for crab cakes! Be ready at six." Then she picked up her phone and headed out to the deck.

Ashley shook her head and sighed. What was she in for? She glanced at her phone and saw that she had about two hours. She thought about going for a walk, but at this time of day she wouldn't make it outside without sweating. The thought made her cringe.

As if sparing her the decision, her phone rang. Seeing Aja, she smiled and headed back upstairs.

"Hey Aja! How's it going?" Silence on the other end made Ashley stop halfway up the stairs. "Aja?" then the line went dead.

Ashley pulled the phone away from her ear and stared at the blank screen. She bit her lip and tried not to panic. She snapped out of her fog and pulled up Aja's number.

Her sister answered after three rings, making Ashley's worry grow slightly. "Hey Ash, what's up?"

Ashley let out a relieved breath. "Well, you just called me, so I should ask you that."

The line was silent. "Uh, no I didn't," Aja said slowly. "I was just in a meeting with Sam and Ryan. I stepped out when you called."

"What?" Ashley asked. "I just got a call from you and then the line went dead. Your contact came up and everything. That's weird…" She didn't know what to think. Should she be worried about this? Was it just a fluke in the phone system? She did notice her coverage here wasn't as good as it was in the Twin Cities.

"Uh, Ash, I didn't call you. I swear. The phone company must have some glitch or something." Aja's voice was quiet on the other side, almost as if she were thinking about some other idea but trying to make Ashley feel better.

Ashley gulped. "Is that possible though? I mean what else could have happened. This is just weird." She tried to brush it off. But she knew that Aja was a wiz when it came to technology. If she was worried, Ashley would be too. If Aja thought it was possibly a glitch in the system, she would trust her sister.

"Ash, I can't lie to you. I am going to make sure that's all it was, ok? Is everything good there? Anything else going on that's weird?" Aja sounded like Sam when he went into operator mode. She was grateful her sister was able to check things out. She wasn't paranoid, but she knew when she had to be safe. Hopefully Aja could help her figure this out.

"Aja, please don't say anything to Sam. You know how he is. He'll insist on me coming back, saying some weird stuff about someone hacking into my phone or something." She knew she was pleading, but she couldn't let something as simple as this divert her plans.

Aja sighed on the other end. "Ok, but if I find out it's something else, I won't jeopardize your safety, sis."

"Wait, you think it could be some dangerous thing? No, Aja. It's a glitch. That's all." *At least that's what I am going with until proven otherwise. I don't have time for this.*

Chapter 9

Sitting across from the older couple, Ashley watched them interact. She felt a tiny pinch of pain as she thought about how much she didn't have when it came to family connections. She never had any grandparents and was a little jealous of Jacob and his big family. He had lost one set of grandparents a long time ago, but the other set was very close to the family. She had met them once, but they travel a lot now that they're both retired.

Resisting a sigh, she focused on her menu again. They were at an Italian restaurant where Sharon absolutely swore that they had the best crab cakes on the entire Eastern Shore. Ashley wasn't a food connoisseur, so she didn't know exactly what that meant, and she wasn't big on seafood. But she said she would try anything once, so she figured she would have to at least try them.

The prices hadn't gotten by Ashley either as she studied the menu. She hated spending so much on food, probably because she was still in college student mode and watching every penny. She also loved Italian food and hated to give up an opportunity to get something she loved on the off chance she would like the crab cakes Sharon wouldn't stop talking about.

Looking up at Sharon, she tilted her head slightly to the side. "Hey Sharon, I'm thinking I should order something safe since I may not like the crab cakes. Do you think I could try just a bite of yours?"

Sharon contemplated her idea. "Hmm. Maybe. I always get the order of three and never can finish them all, so I think that would be fine." She nodded her approval and turned to Gary who was still staring at the menu.

"Come on Gary. It's not like you won't order what you always do. Shrimp fettuccini with a crab cake on the side." Sharon smirked at her husband who just rolled his eyes. After a few minutes, he put his menu down with a deep sigh, just as the waiter came to take their orders.

"You know, someday I might want to change my mind, Sharon dear. You just never know when I might surprise you." He winked at Ashley and Sharon just snorted back.

Ashley loved their banter back and forth. She just smiled and leaned back in her chair.

"So, when is Jacob coming back, Ashley?" Gary asked. He and Jacob seemed to get along great while he was visiting.

Ashley smiled. "He was supposed to come back next week, but someone at his work got hurt so he's staying longer to help out his boss. So, I'm actually not sure when he will be here now." She tried to keep the sadness from her voice, but Sharon's sympathetic eyes gave her away.

She reached out and patted Ashley's arm. "It will go fast, sweetheart, I am sure. He's such a nice young fellow."

"He is," Ashley said with a smile. She was still getting used to the way everyone talked here with the "dears" and "sweethearts" from everyone, whether they knew you or not.

Their dinner came quickly, and Sharon went into a lesson about how to tell if the crab cakes are good or not.

Ashley half listened with amusement. Sharon was sure serious about her crab cakes, she thought.

"So, if they fall apart, then they don't have enough mayo. But if they have too much mayo that's not good either," Sharon finished with a forkful of her crab cake moving slowly to her mouth. "But the biggest thing that makes crab cakes the best is the meat. See the big chunks? This is perfect. None of that shredded stuff. Oh! And the seasoning is so important. It has to be Old Bay." She grinned and lifted her fork up in the air before it disappeared into her mouth. "Perfect," she said quietly with a soft moan. "Not too much filler, just enough to give it a nice crisp outside."

Ashley watched her with raised eyebrows and then glanced over at Gary, who was looking at her with a smirk.

"She is serious about these things, in case you didn't notice," Gary said, his eye twinkling. "So, Miss Ashley, how are you liking it here on the Eastern Shore?"

Ashley stalled, twirling her linguini noodles on her fork. She never really mastered the whole using a spoon as a guide for twirling the noodles neatly around the fork, but for some reason it caught her attention this time. Gently she picked up the large spoon and scooped a small forkful of noodles. Setting the fork tines into the curve of the spoon, she slowly twisted the fork.

"I never knew how people could do that trick," Sharon said as she watched Ashley with more interest than Ashley thought necessary.

Biting her lip, she carefully lifted the perfectly swirled pasta-filled fork to her mouth as if she was moving something extremely fragile and valuable. As soon as it was close enough, she stuffed it into her mouth and grinned with pride.

Gary chuckled and focused on his food again.

As she chewed her noodles, Ashley thought about his question. How *did* she like it there? Aside from the heat, of course, because that wasn't something she necessarily enjoyed. She swallowed the last bit and wiped her face with the linen napkin from her lap.

"I have a question," she started, looking between the two people in front of her. Both of them put their forks down and focused on Ashley, making her suddenly feel self-conscious. "Um, why is everything here say 'Delmarva'?" She had noticed it on the menu and multiple businesses had it in their name. It didn't really make sense to her.

Sharon let out a little laugh. "I suppose that would be weird. So, the Eastern Shore is on the peninsula, right? Well, to our direct north is Delaware—that's the Del. We are in the middle and m-a-r is for us and then Virginia is at the southern tip of the peninsula. So, the v-a is for that state. Make sense? I guess 'Delmarva' is easier than 'the DelawareMarylandVirgina peninsula'." She chuckled at her own joke and Gary just grinned and shook his head at her.

Focusing back on Ashley, Gary added, "The whole eastern coast of the Delmarva Peninsula is actually just referred to as the Eastern Shore. The Chesapeake side is called the Western Shore."

Ashley nodded thoughtfully and then turned back to her plate of pasta. If she wanted to finish her dinner today, she definitely wouldn't be able to do the twirl and stuff technique. With a slight sigh, she picked up her fork and began to eat again.

Her phone buzzed next to her alerting her to a text. She figured it would be rude to read it at the table, especially when her hosts were treating her to a nice dinner. She ignored it and looked up at the pair in front of her. "So, do you host students often? That apartment is perfect for one person and especially a student with how close you are to the college."

Sharon shared a look with Gary and Ashley didn't miss the slight shake of his head, causing her to wrinkle her forehead. *What was that about?* she thought. She watched the two with a renewed interest. What could these two sweet people be hiding?

Gary cleared his throat when Sharon looked back at her dinner. "We haven't had a student in a long time. We used to host them a lot, but then we got old and didn't want to be landlords so much anymore I guess." He reached over and squeezed Sharon's hand.

There was definitely a story there, Ashley thought. But even though she loved to talk to people and learn their stories, she also respected someone's right to keep it to themselves. Heck, she had enough of her own demons to keep hidden. She wouldn't push these two to tell her anything they didn't volunteer.

"So, what made you rent to me?" she asked, looking back at her dinner. She had only eaten about half and was already feeling stuffed. Leftovers would be a nice change from her typical sandwiches or microwaveable meals.

This time Sharon cleared her throat. "We just wanted to help out one more student I guess before we gave it up for good. And I heard there was someone coming in and may need a place for a little while. And since you were considering the college, we wanted to help out." She gave Ashley a smile and nod. "I attended SU, and it was a wonderful school forever ago when it was just considered a teaching college. It has grown so much since then. And with it being such a small town and all, it would be nice to have someone new around."

They spent the rest of dinner talking about nothing in particular. It was a nice relaxing dinner and Ashley began to really feel at ease around the older couple. They seemed genuine and grandparent-like with their interest in her. She had never known her grandparents, so it was a nice feeling. It made her think of Jacob and his family again and what she missed out on growing up. She had only ever had Sam and Aja. And she couldn't help but admit with a pang of sadness and jealousy that Sam and Aja definitely had a closer relationship than she had ever had with her uncle. She always felt a little more like the third wheel when the three of them were together. Ashley never felt like she could rely on anyone else besides Aja. Sam never really felt like a father to her, but rather a caregiver. Watching the couple in front of her, Ashley suddenly felt alone and wished she had parents she could have counted on growing up.

Sharon noticed Ashley's silence and reached across the table to touch her hand. "Are you ok, hon?" she asked gently.

Ashley nodded without looking up. "I guess I just am a little homesick," she admitted quietly. It wasn't a total lie, but it was definitely not the whole truth either.

"We can head out so you can call that gentleman of yours. That will help." Gary rubbed his belly and let out a sigh. "I'm stuffed like a turkey on Thanksgiving." He grinned at Sharon who rolled her eyes playfully at him.

The trio packed up their leftovers and made their way to the car. Ashley noticed the heat had subsided a little, but the humidity made it feel like she was in a damp cave. The air was thick with moisture and although she was warm, the air made her want a light jacket or something. It was the strangest feeling, she thought. She wondered if this is what the rainforest was like with the humidity as well.

No one talked on the way home. Ashley stared out her window, noticing even more now the number of buildings that had "Delmarva" printed or lit up on signs. She smiled. It all made sense now. The drive didn't take too long, and before she knew it, they were pulling into the long driveway of the large three-story home. It was beautiful, she noted, as they drove up to the house. She could imagine it all decorated like an old southern mansion for Christmas.

Ashley thanked Sharon and Gary for dinner and then hurried upstairs to the small apartment. After closing and locking the door, she leaned against it, suddenly feeling alone and sad. She missed Aja. Remembering the text alert, she pulled her phone out.

"Hey call me," Ashley read out loud. It was Aja, but Ashley furrowed her brow. Aja never texted like that. It was weird but she knew even through text that something was up with her sister. Maybe it was twin intuition, but she was suddenly nervous. What could Aja be upset or anxious about? Her thoughts drifted to the continued lie she was playing on repeat to Aja. Maybe she found out and was angry. Then again, Aja's go to when she was upset was to withdraw, not reach out for a fight. That was more Ashley's style.

Glancing at her alarm clock, she pressed Aja's face on her phone to call her. It only took one ring for her twin to answer.

"Is everything ok, Aja?" Ashley asked nervously when Aja's voice greeted her.

Aja cleared her throat and took a second before she said quietly, "I'm not sure. Ash, have you gotten any more calls? Like weird ones…" her voice trailed as Ashley remembered the strange calls.

"No. Just what I told you. Why? You sound nervous or something." Ashley settled on the edge of her bed waiting for Aja to answer. She was becoming more and more alarmed the longer it took for her sister to answer.

"Um, I guess it's nothing," Aja said quietly.

Ashley stood up and started pacing. "Uh no, Aja. What is going on? You sound like you had something to say and then changed your mind. Please tell me what is going on."

Aja remained quiet on the other end of the line and Ashley was about to burst. "Aja!" she nearly shouted into the phone.

A loud sigh and crackle from Aja's breath let Ashley know she was at least still on the line. "Ash, I can't talk right now. I'll call you later." The line went dead right after Aja's near whisper on the other end.

Ashley pulled the phone away from her ear and stared at it, willing her sister to call her back or something to give her some peace of mind. Something was going on with her twin and she wished she was there and not halfway across the country to help her figure it out. She threw her phone across the bed and laid down, staring at the ceiling. What did Aja find out and when would she call back? "UGH!"

As if on cue, her phone rang. Ashley scrambled to sit up and looked for her phone. Without looking at the screen she exclaimed, "Tell me what's going on right now!"

A soft chuckle on the other end made her pause and close her mouth tight.

"You ok, Ash?" the all-too-familiar voice asked.

Ashley smiled. "Hey Jacob. Sorry. Aja just called but was weird and then had to go suddenly and didn't even tell me why she called."

"Hm. That does sound weird. I'm sure she'll get back to you soon though. How are things going there? Anything new?" Jacob asked. She heard rustling in the background like he was getting comfortable.

"Nothing really. I went to dinner with Sharon and Gary tonight. Man, that woman is serious about her crab cakes." She laughed as she recounted the conversation from dinner. "Apparently Maryland has the best crab cakes because of the kinds of crabs they have here from the Chesapeake or something."

"Did you try any?" Jacob knew Ashley's aversion to seafood and Ashley just rolled her eyes at him, even though he couldn't see her. "Did you just roll your eyes at me?"

Ashley laughed. "Oh, you know me so well! Of course, I didn't try any." She actually felt bad when she remembered she hadn't. She hoped Sharon wasn't upset since she had wanted Ashley to try them so badly. "How are things going with Papa Jasper?" She didn't want to ask but wanted to know what was happening and since they had just talked earlier in the day, she cringed waiting for bad news.

Jacob sighed. "Well, he had a high school kid he thought would want to work more hours because he had asked earlier this summer. But then something happened today after I talked to you, and the dad showed up at the mill and told Jasper he couldn't work anymore. Something about grades or football or something. I don't know. So, he is back to square one. I'm sorry Ash. I am trying, I promise. But now he's down two guys."

"I get it. And there's nothing you can do anyway. Just keep helping until he gets the right person. I'm fine here and there's nothing new to report anyway. I'm going to meet with Sharon's friend about the report and see what she can tell me. I will send you an email with a letter attached so you can mail it for me. I am going to try to meet this person. I am curious where or she fits into my family tree for sure. I just need to find out a little more if I can before I walk into something blind. You know?"

Jacob was quiet for a minute. "I hope you will wait for me to be there to meet this person. Neither of us know what this is even about or if it's legit. I would hate for you to go into it alone."

"Have you been talking to your sister, Jacob?" Ashley asked with a chuckle. It was common knowledge that Jacob's sister Sally Jo had an incredible conspiracy theory brain. It's why she was such a huge asset to the FBI when she helped with a kidnapping case last year.

"Ha ha. No, I'm just a little weary of a stranger reaching out of the blue and wanting to meet you. That's all. It's not like you can call anyone if something happens. You don't know anyone out there." His voice was quiet and sounded worried.

Ashley couldn't help but feel a slight shudder as she thought about being alone out here if something did happen. Shaking it off, she tried to lighten the mood. "I won't do anything rash. I promise. Besides it will take a while for my letter to get here and this person's letter to get back to me. Now what do we need to do to get you out here, Jake? Do you know anyone who could help Papa Jasper out?"

"Not really," he sighed. "Now that I'm done with college, most of the people I know are out looking for careers, not labor jobs. But I'm sure he'll find someone. There are always high school kids around here who will do the job."

They talked for a little longer and Ashley was surprised to see it was almost ten. She suddenly felt sleepy and wanted to shower before she went to bed. As she was getting ready to end the conversation, her phone alerted her to a text.

"I'm going to head to bed, Jake. Will you keep me updated on what's going on there?" she asked him.

"Of course I will. And will you please not go meeting anyone alone until I can get out there?" She could tell he was smiling as he made the request. They both knew she was impulsive and would have a hard time waiting if new information came up. But she agreed to try anyway.

As she hung up with Jacob, she glanced at her texts. It wasn't Aja like she had hoped, but another random one like before with the blocked number.

Mom please call me as soon as possible. I'm in trouble.

Chapter 10

"OK, Trish is available to meet with you whenever it works for you, Ashley. I gave you her number yesterday, right? Just give her a call. Remember, she doesn't text, she's old school." Sharon smiled and shrugged her shoulders as she patted Ashley's arm. She picked up her half empty coffee mug and walked back to the pot to fill it.

Ashley was trying to figure out her plans for the day when Sharon walked back into the kitchen, having just finished talking to her friend. Ashley had wanted to talk to her about contacting Trish anyway, so the timing was perfect.

Ashley smiled back at Sharon and nodded. "Yes, I have her number, thank you. I was going to go to the library today and then maybe I'll give her a call." She picked up her phone and pushed away from the table. "I'll see you later. I'm off to brave the deadly heat outside!" She laughed at Sharon's wrinkled nose.

Ashley loved to tease the older woman about the summer heat. She was definitely not used to the humidity and realized she actually preferred the cooler temperatures. Even in Minnesota the temperatures were still warm into August. This heat was almost stifling. Ashley couldn't help but wonder if the heat carried all through the fall too. She realized she never really looked into the difference in the climate from Minnesota to the Eastern Shore of Maryland.

At least she wouldn't have to deal with the ridiculous cold of the Minnesota winter she hoped.

Catching her breath as she exited the cool temperature of the house, Ashley squinted her eyes against the bright sunshine. She made her way to the car, wishing she had brought her sunglasses in last night. Unconsciously, she glanced down the street. She still caught herself checking for the car she saw yesterday every time she left, even last night when she wasn't driving. Chuckling at herself, she unlocked her car and slid into the seat. Just as quickly, she jumped back out, rubbing the back of her thighs. Even with cloth seats, it was hot on her skin.

"Dang heat!" she mumbled as she reached in and started her car, turning on the air conditioning and opening her windows. She stood outside for a few minutes and then a bit more cautiously slid into her seat. When she didn't feel the burn, she smiled with relief. Glancing in the rearview mirror she rolled her eyes. "Who can enjoy summer when just walking outside makes your sweat?" she asked her reflection. She had never been big on makeup, but she definitely learned quickly not to bother with it until later in the evening if she wore it at all.

Ashley tossed her backpack in the seat behind her and readjusted her mirror. Making her way out of the driveway and onto the main street, she settled back in her seat and listened to the music coming from her radio. She noticed it was a country station, which she wasn't really a fan of, but didn't feel like changing it. It was an upbeat song, and she found herself tapping her steering wheel to the beat. She had no idea who was singing or what the song was called.

Before she knew it, she was pulling into the college's parking lot. She pulled into a spot close to the academic commons building. Ashley smiled as she realized she remembered the name of a campus building. She still wasn't sure about attending the school, but she was feeling more like one of the new students coming in as freshman. She had also learned this building housed the main student library. She couldn't pronounce the name on the building, but everyone called it GAC anyway. At least that's what Professor Roslin called it during her tour, so she was going with it.

The building was amazing. Ashley hadn't been inside yet, but the outside looked like it was fairly new. There was a wall on one side that looked like it was all a continuous window stretching from the ground floor all the way up to the fourth floor. She couldn't wait to get inside and take it all in. One thing she always loved about college was research. Maybe that was why she was excited to be here, even if she wasn't sure about her plans yet for grad school.

Ashley locked up her car and started toward the entrance to the building in front of her. A voice calling her name made her stop and turn back toward the parking lot. She saw Professor Roslin walking quickly toward her waving his hand in the air. After the last encounter they had, she wasn't sure if she should wait for him or continue to walk into the building and act like she didn't see him.

Before she could decide, he was almost to her. "Hey, Ashley. Thanks for waiting," he said, slightly out of breath. "I wanted to talk to you anyway, so it's a perfect coincidence that you are here now." His smile seemed forced, but she smiled back.

"I was just going to do some research in the library," she explained, hoping he would realize she was busy and wasn't there to see him.

The professor nodded and glanced over her shoulder at the building behind her. Moving his gaze back to her, he asked, "Do you have a few minutes before? Or maybe after?"

Ashley hesitated. She wasn't sure why this man gave her weird vibes and she wasn't sure if she wanted to be alone with him, especially in his office. It was still summer break and there weren't many students around. Maybe she was just channeling Jacob's sister too much.

Finally, she sighed and shrugged her shoulders. She said quietly, "I have a few minutes. I have to meet someone in about an hour or so though." Her lie came out easily and she hoped it would let him know if he had any strange ideas that someone was waiting for her. She chastised herself in her head. When did she get so paranoid about people?

The professor nodded and smiled excitedly making Ashley cringe slightly. "Great! I promise it will only take a minute. In fact, we can just go over to that bench, and I can show you. I just have to put some of this stuff down." He motioned with his head to a nearby bench and Ashley made her way over to it.

Professor Roslin had his hands full of files and Ashley creased her eyebrows. It didn't look like teacher-type files. It looked more like something her sister would bring home from work sometimes when they had a complicated case. She raised her eyes to meet his, trying not to show any expression.

He cleared his throat and set down a pile of papers and manila folders. One slipped and fell to the ground. A few things spilled out of it, and he quickly picked up the contents, stuffing it underneath the rest of the pile. But Ashley caught a glimpse of the 8x10 photo before he could grab it. The face looked oddly familiar, but she didn't get a good enough look at it. She racked her brain trying to place it, the eyes on the photo captivated her in the split second she saw it. The coldness in them gave her a shiver though, making her think it wasn't someone she would want to encounter again. She shook her head to clear her thoughts. It must have just been someone who had one of those faces that looked familiar. Brushing it aside, she looked back up to see the man pull out another folder and hand it to her—after thoroughly checking it.

Ashley hesitated and then slowly opened the folder. Inside was a single piece of paper with her name handwritten at the top and what looked like a job description. She furrowed her brows and raised her eyes to look at him. "What is this?" she asked, looking back at the paper again.

"It's the position I am posting, and I want you to apply for it." His smile looked genuine as he watched her carefully.

"But I'm not even registered as a student yet," she argued. Skimming through the rest of the paper, she had to admit it sounded like fun. It was a student teacher position for his undergrad teaching students. It was part-time and would require her to run one class on her own while also being his assistant teacher for one other class.

The professor waved his hand in the air. "I don't care so much about that. I know it says a student teaching position, but I am ok with it being a paid assistant position as well. I'm not picky." He was watching her intently and she felt a little uncomfortable with his eyes so focused on her. "My only requirement is a graduate with a teaching bachelor's."

She looked between him and the paper again, and then sighed. "Can I think about it?"

"Of course! Just let me know when you decide. I haven't posted it yet but would like to by next week. If you decide to enroll, then it will help to adjust your tuition as well."

Ashley nodded. "I will for sure let you know before next week if that's ok."

"That's just fine. You have my number now, so feel free to call, text, or email. I better be going, and I know you have someone to meet. Thanks Ashley. I hope you can do this. It would be great working with someone like you in this capacity." Professor Roslin stood and then held out his hand to her. She took it and gave him a firm shake.

"Thanks, Professor. I appreciate the thought." She stood as well and then made a move toward the building, almost forgetting why she had come there. She watched as the professor made his way to the building next door and then dropped her eyes to the still open folder in her hand. She wasn't sure what she thought about this whole situation, but she would talk to Jacob about it. She didn't want to commit to a job that would require her to stay longer than she planned, but then again, she didn't know how long she would have to stay here to get the answers she needed either. "Maybe a job would be a good idea though."

With a sigh, she picked up her bag and moved toward the sidewalk to the GAC. She held the folder in her hand while she moved through to doors. The building was just as beautiful as she imagined as she slowly made her way inside. The stark white walls and open layout made it look amazing. She found herself slowly walking forward while looking straight up to the fourth floor through the open atrium in the center of the space. The view was amazing. She almost spun around taking it all in. She would probably have to get a map to figure out where she was supposed to go for research looking at all the levels above her.

Just looking up, she saw rows of bookshelves two floors up, so that must be where she would go. She quickly found the slanted half walls of glass. It was literally a wall of staircases going up to each level. She glanced to her side and saw a desk for information and an older woman standing at the counter scanning materials. There weren't many people around, but she couldn't help but wonder what it was like here when classes were in full swing, especially around finals time with everyone scrambling to get their papers finished.

She decided to wander around by herself and see if she could figure things out. She made her way to the steps, walking around the tables set up throughout the main floor. As she moved slowly up the steps, she marveled at the view below and above her. It was so bright and airy, with huge windows and glass railings everywhere. It was a good thing no one was behind her because she was probably taking as long as a three-year-old learning how to walk up steps for the first time.

The second floor was made up of what looked like a bunch of private rooms, maybe classrooms. The center was open to below and there was a writing center in the corner. Ashley continued to the third floor grateful she wasn't afraid of heights given you could see the ground floor from almost anywhere up here. This floor looked like a more traditional library. Rows of shelves with books lined both sides of the open space overlooking below. There was a common area with computers and tables and bathrooms. There were a couple of rooms that could possibly be used for quiet study or conference calls. Along the glass walls of the open atrium, there were tables set up and plenty of quiet areas tucked in the back corners.

Ashley wandered through the entire area, glancing at the shelves and rows of reading materials. This is somewhere she could see spending a lot of time. She looked up to the next level and didn't see anything for studying, but she had heard there was a hall for rental where different events were held, private and public, and a couple of classrooms. Turning her attention back to the space around her, she chose a table that had a single chair at it in the far corner. She set her bag down on the table and moved around it to sit facing the area. She loved to watch people, and this was a good spot, even if it was tucked away.

Knowing she had to make a phone call, she felt comfortable talking in the corner and pulled out her phone. She also took out the letter and ancestry results. Slinging her backpack over the back of her chair, she looked at the documents in front of her. She had forgotten about the folder from Professor Roslin, but it now sat under the papers she had taken out. Biting her lip, she slid the folder out and opened it again.

Her thoughts drifted back to the folder that fell out of the professor's hands though. The image popped back into her mind as she stared blankly at the paper in front of her. The words of her uncle came back to her. The thought that people might still be looking for her and Aja struck her more than she expected. She looked around the empty space around her and suddenly felt cornered and exposed. Were there people actually looking for her and did they know she was here now?

The photo Professor Roslin had did not look like anyone she knew but did look somehow familiar. A sudden chill came over her as she remembered the eyes. Ashley quickly packed up her things. She moved to the stairs and looking constantly around her, she moved much faster than when she came in. Once she made it to the doors, she breathed a sigh of relief confident no one followed her. Keeping her eyes scanning around the campus and parking lot, she slid into her car and started the engine, forgetting the heat for a second until it hit her face at full force from the now hot air conditioning. She forgot to turn it down before she turned off her engine when she arrived on campus.

Ashley locked her doors and leaned her head against the headrest, closing her eyes tight. She tried to take a deep breath but found it difficult. She suddenly felt like Sam was in her head. He had always said people could be looking for her and Aja, but she never thought much of it. She had never felt her safety was at risk and maybe, as she thought about it now, a little naïve. She couldn't help but wonder if the photo Professor Roslin had was one of the people looking for her. Why would he have a picture of someone who was looking for her though—unless he was one of them too.

"Ugh!" she muttered, pounding her fist on the steering wheel. Her phone suddenly rang, making her scream. Looking at the screen she saw Jacob's smiling face. She couldn't help but chuckle at herself with her hand over her heart trying to calm it down.

"Hey, Jake," she said forcing her voice to sound calm, hoping she had succeeded. He might have been fooled, but there was no way Aja would have been.

"Wow, you answered quick. Are you sitting on your phone or something?" Jacob was in a good mood and didn't seem to notice, so she sighed with relief.

"I was actually just getting in my car, and it was right next to me. You sound happy, what's up?" She was grateful for the distraction from her conflicted thoughts.

She heard him switch his phone to speaker, or maybe blue tooth in his car, and then she heard him clap his hands together. "Good news, Ash. Papa Jasper got a couple high school kids to start next week. So that means I can head your way in about two weeks. I know it's longer than we planned, but at least we have a deadline, right?"

Ashley breathed out slowly. Two more weeks of the craziness her head was spinning. It was definitely better than a month, but she knew it was going to be a challenge these next few weeks keeping her wits about her and not letting things like today get out of control. For a second, she thought about having Sally Jo come too, but then again, she wasn't sure she would be able to keep her emotions in check with the things Jacob's sister would come up with.

"Ash? Is everything ok?" Jacob's voice startled her out of her thoughts. "I thought this would be good news."

Ashley shook her head to clear her brain. "Sorry. This is good news, great news actually. I just feel so out of sorts here. I'm alone and feeling a little homesick I think." It wasn't a total lie, she tried to convince herself.

Jacob was quiet for a moment. "Are you sure? I'm a little worried about you."

Ashley smiled. She was so glad someone knew what she was really doing here. "I'm good Jake. Really. I'm actually about to call Sharon's friend about the DNA stuff. I think I will write that letter later today and then you can mail it for me. I want to get things rolling as soon as possible so I can decide what I am doing and if I have to stay longer."

"Ok, if you are sure you're ok." He didn't sound convinced, but he really didn't have a choice, she mused.

"Yep, all good. I'll let you know when I send the email so you can take care of that for me. I should go though. I want to catch this lady before it gets too late in the day. I hope everything works out with the new guys and I will actually be seeing you soon!" She smiled a genuine smile this time.

Jacob sighed on the other end. "Ok, but please tell me if things aren't ok. I do worry."

"I know and all is fine. I promise. Love you, Jake. Talk soon." They said their goodbyes and Ashley pressed the end call button and dropped her phone on the passenger seat.

She sighed again and then looked around her. The parking lot was pretty empty, and she noticed Professor Roslin walking to his car. She didn't want him to stop and talk to her again, so she put her seatbelt on and shifted the car into drive. She avoided his path and pretended not to see him as she pulled out of the lot and onto the busyness of highway 13.

Ashley drove for a while just looking around her. Salisbury wasn't a huge town, but it had a bigger than small town feel to it. There were two Walmart's—yep, two. It seemed a little excessive for a town of less than 35,000 people, but she also understood commercialism. And in their defense, whoever "they" were, the two stores were on completely opposite ends of town. There were plenty of fast-food chain restaurants and a few restaurants that weren't chains. There was a mall which housed the most popular stores. Overall, it was a smaller scale version of the suburbs Ashley had experienced in Minnesota and other places she'd lived.

The feel of the people who lived there was still pretty small town though she noticed. She was starting to notice the same folks at the gas stations, working, or hanging out. A new thing for her was the gas station food. Most had a small counter with chairs for folks to eat at or just sit and read, almost like a small café. Many of the gas stations had a counter to order hot food. They were a one stop shop for gas, snacks, and lunch.

Ashley pulled into a Royal Farms station to fill her tank. She hadn't realized she had driven as far as she did. She was out of town a little and had traveled toward the ocean, she at least knew that much. She remembered the college across the street. She filled her tank and then went inside to get a chicken sandwich. The other thing she had learned was the abundance of chicken. This place had better chicken than KFC in her opinion. She and Jacob had gotten it once on the way to the beach when he was still there.

She entered her order on the self-serve screen, grabbed a drink, and then moved to pay. She looked around and noticed a couple of people sitting at the counter reading a newspaper they seemed to be sharing. Once she paid, she waited for her sandwich at the kiosk. Just when her number was called, one of the people from the counter walked by. He had longer straight brown hair, graying on the sides. He looked to be in his early fifties. He had mesmerizing eyes, and she couldn't look away. They were a dark blue which was striking against his tanned skin.

The man tipped his head to her and winked, with a smirk on his face. Startled, Ashley just looked away and grabbed her sandwich. She hurried outside and once in her car she locked her doors again, but this time didn't sit in the lot. She quickly headed for the exit and made her way back to Sharon and Gary's. She just wanted to be in her room. Things were weird and she didn't want to be out and about anymore.

She pulled into the driveway in just a few short minutes. It was probably more like fifteen or twenty, but she didn't even notice the time that went by as she was constantly looking in her rearview mirror to make sure the people from the gas station didn't follow her. Ashley hurried upstairs and locked the door. Only then did she breathe.

She dropped her bag and sat on her bed to eat her sandwich. She realized she never called Trish, but she told herself she would after she finished eating. *What a weird day,* she thought. She wondered why she was suddenly suspicious of everyone around her but tried to brush it aside for now. She had to get on task with this ancestry stuff and hopefully get back home soon.

Brushing the crumbs off her lap, she pulled out her phone. She had entered Trish's info into her phone earlier, so she didn't lose the post it note from Sharon. She opened the contact for Trish and pressed the call button, remembering Sharon said she didn't like to text.

A loud and exasperated voice rang out after just one ring. "About time, young lady. I have been waiting all day and was about to start my dinner."

Ashley was shocked and couldn't find her voice. *Wha*t? Did she think it was someone else calling her? Deciding that had to be the case, she cleared her throat and said, "I'm sorry. This is Ashley. I am staying—"

"I know who you are," Trish cut her off. "Now where have you been and why are you just calling me now? I have been expecting your call since Sharon called me earlier." Her voice was clipped and annoyed.

Resisting the urge to flinch, Ashley took in a breath of air. "Oh, um, I'm sorry. I didn't know I was supposed to call right away. I was at the library and—"

Again, she was cut off. "Yeah, yeah. I know all that. Now when are you coming here so I can help you with this whole ancestry thing Sharon keeps bugging me about?"

"Uh, sorry, I can come whenever it is convenient for you," she stammered.

Trish scoffed. "Three hours ago was great. How about tomorrow at nine am sharp? I'm too tired now. Making me wait all day. Tsk." And then she just hung up without waiting for Ashley to respond.

Ashley stared at her phone. *What was that?* she thought. "I was wrong. *Now* it has been a weird day!" she said out loud. A thought occurred to her. She had no idea where Trish lived. Hopefully Sharon did because she was slightly terrified of this woman. People on the East Coast definitely did speak their minds and Trish was incredibly blunt. Ashley hoped she would be helpful and not just an angry and impatient woman.

With a sigh, Ashley pulled out the letter from the stranger again. She decided to just type something and try to arrange a meeting. It would probably take some time for the mail anyway, so she sat down trying to figure out what to write and then hoped Jacob could get it out in the mail the next day. She had two weeks to get some research done before he came out there, so she had to get something done. It was almost August already.

Chapter 11

The drive to Trish's house wasn't too bad. It was further out in the country than where Sharon and Gary lived. Ashley looked around her as she drove to an area she hadn't been to before. The houses were far apart, and most were on acres of land. She couldn't help but notice the number of chicken houses that were around here. She knew it was chicken country and a few of the major chicken companies were based here on the east coast. But it still surprised her. She was a city girl and didn't know much about living in the country or farming. This did seem like a good place to come and escape the city life though.

Ashley noticed there were a lot of houses that looked abandoned and many chicken houses as well. She found herself wondering what might have happened to those families as she drove by. She thought about the life of a farmer, or specifically a chicken farmer. She didn't know anything about the profession but thought it might be fun to learn—not that she needed to or wanted to know about the killing and chopping up of the chickens. She didn't think she could handle that part of the job.

She found the street sign that Sharon had told her to look for and slowed to turn. Thankfully there weren't many people on these country roads. She was going so slow, trying to read the signs she knew it would have backed up traffic anywhere else. *You would think they could make the signs bigger*, she thought with a frustrated sigh.

Turning onto a tree lined street that was barely a car width wide, Ashley slowly continued down the road. It was paved, but she worried if another car came from the other direction where they would go. The trees didn't let up as she drove down the road. In fact, it looked like the woods were getting thicker as she drove. A slight twinge of anxiety came across her as she looked side to side. Both sides of the road were completely engulfed in trees. The shoulder, if you could call it that, was so small a person walking along the side would have to move into the woods to escape an oncoming car.

Shaking her head, Ashley continued her slow pace, looking for the next turn. She spotted the clearing and abandoned chicken house on the corner that Sharon said to look for. Thankful for the break in the trees, she turned left down a gravel road. She wondered what made someone want to live way out here with very few other people around. What if something happened to her and it took the ambulance too long to get all the way out here?

She shivered as she tried to rid her mind of those thoughts. She leaned forward and turned down her radio, like it would help her see better or something. The road wasn't long, which she was grateful for. A sign caught her eye, which was the end of Trish's driveway. "Prepare to meet thy God," she read. "Ok, it's creepy in my head, but even worse out loud." She chuckled lightly and shook her head.

The driveway to the house was long, almost like another street. At least it was now lined with corn growing tall on either side of her car instead of trees. Ashley wondered if Trish owned the entire plot of land, including the vacant chicken house. When she finally made it to the house, her eyes widened. She wasn't sure what she expected, but it wasn't this.

It looked like a cottage from a horror movie. The shutters that were still on the house were faded and sitting cock-eyed as if they were barely holding on to the siding. About half the windows had only one shutter, the rest had both on either side of the windows. The siding looked like it needed a good cleaning or maybe even replacement. Ashley had learned that with the humidity here, many of the houses had green film covering most of the outside. Gary had said he had to have his house power washed every other year to keep it from looking like an earth home with the green film covering it.

The house itself looked cute and homey if it was a little better kept. There was a large front porch that was enclosed and a large dormer with a window above it. The front door and other front windows weren't visible due to the large porch out in front. It wasn't a huge house but looked perfect for one or two people. What used to be white was weathered and Ashley wondered if it actually was ever white. Maybe it was always a grayish color.

There were multiple glass bottles in different colors and shapes hanging in the huge weeping willow tree in the front yard. An array of different statues was strewn around the yard. All different sizes and shapes, from gnomes to a large one of the virgin Mary, at least that's what she guessed, from her limited exposure to religion. It was a woman in a faded and dirty blue dress with her hands folded and looking down. She vaguely remembered something similar when her mom used to take her and Aja to church. There were also random things like old tractor tires, one was being used as a flowerpot. Ashley spotted some rusted pieces as well scattered around. It seemed random, but she couldn't help but wonder if Trish had a plan in her head. She seemed to have that kind of personality from the brief conversation on the phone and what Sharon had shared.

She parked along the driveway, a little way back from the house. There wasn't a garage she noticed, but there was a shed sort of building behind the house, almost hidden in the overgrowth of the field and trees. She looked back at the house and hesitated. At least Sharon had prepared her for this part. She turned off the car and sat for a minute. She closed her eyes and took a deep breath. Ashley gathered her papers from the front seat and then moved toward the front porch. It was closed fully enclosed and from the outside you couldn't see what was waiting for you inside. Even with Sharon's prep, nothing could truly prepare her for walking inside the tiny space.

A million eyes seemed to turn and stare right through her. Ashley caught her breath and focused on the door to the house. Even so, she found her curiosity had her glancing to the side. The number of dolls Trish had collected was impressive, but creepy as hell too. There were small dolls not much bigger than her hand and huge dolls that were about three feet tall. They had hair that looked like something out of a horror movie, matted and full of fuzz. She chuckled to herself for the second horror film reference. She hoped it was all just an attempt to keep people away and not some sick and twisted trap she was being lured into.

Ashley was relieved when Trish appeared in front of her without needing to knock. It pulled her from her morbid thoughts. Between the creepy dolls and the sign out front, not to mention the look of the outside of the house, Ashley actually hesitated to enter the house. It could be a house of terror and here she was just willingly walking inside. She nearly chuckled out loud as she thought about how Trish was keeping people away, whether it was intentional or not. And if they made it to the porch, she could imagine even the most devout Jehovah's Witness would run away at the sight of all those staring eyes.

Trish's deep brown eyes squinted at Ashley. They were almost as dark as her skin, with her twisted white and black hair offering a stark contrast to both. Trish let out a slight grunt and waved her inside. Ashley followed the stout woman through the door, closing it tightly behind her.

* * * * *

"So, what does that mean?" Ashley asked Trish, staring down at her folded hands on the table. Her body felt like it was on fire as she thought about what Trish had told her.

Suddenly the older woman crinkled her forehead. "Are both of your genetic parents alive still?"

Ashley was slightly taken aback and wasn't sure what that had to do with anything. Trish looked up at her over her reading glasses and Ashley gulped slightly. Trish's eyes were so sharp, and she had such an impatient air about her. Maybe it was just the "no-nonsense east coast way of life, but Ashley dropped her own eyes, shaking her head lightly.

"No, my mom passed away when I was little." She swallowed, hoping there wouldn't be any more uncomfortable questions that she would have to answer to this stranger. She really didn't want to answer how or why her mom had died so long ago.

"Huh," was the only response as Trish continued to stare at the papers in front of her, her forehead creasing more.

Ashley looked up at her, confused. "Why is that important?" she asked nervously.

Trish looked up at her and then back at the papers. "Well usually when someone dies in your family tree, it is listed on your report—a death certificate usually. But there's nothing here about a biological parent. There is only this one, 'Cecilia Sulliman'." She pointed her wrinkled finger at the page where there was an empty space.

Ashley thought for a second. "I don't even know who that is. My dad had a sister? She must have died before we could meet her. I'm sure my mom didn't do a DNA test before she died though. There wouldn't have been any reason to." She found herself hoping that was all that meant. She couldn't even begin to wonder why that would be an issue. Did something happen to her mom after she died? Knowing her father, who knew what he would have pulled. Then again maybe Sam had prevented her death from being listed anywhere to protect her and Aja. She was sure there were other reasons why it wasn't in the report. There had to be an explanation.

Great, now I have two things to solve, I guess, she thought. But a death certificate would be easy enough to locate. It was a public record after all, unless Sam did something to prevent that from being public, which he was also capable of. Then again, she wasn't sure if she wanted to know. She was actually surprised to learn her dad had a sister.

Trish gave a grunt and pushed the papers back toward Ashley. "Well, all I can tell you is what I see here. And I already told you what *that* means." She pointed again to the words "close relative."

"I still don't understand. Aside from my mom, which I think is just a matter of this not being around when she was alive or having any reason to do it, this other thing I just don't get." Ashley furrowed her own brow at the papers now in front of her again.

A frustrated sigh from the woman across from her, drew Ashley's eyes back to her face. "I don't know how to say it any other way, child." Trish brushed a stray white twisted lock away from her face only to have it fall back again and pushed away from the table. She picked up her mug and moved toward her coffee machine, at least that's what Ashley thought the contraption was. It looked like some antique from the 1950's Ashley thought as she watched Trish pour a cup, add three sugar cubes, a splash of cream, and then milk. She couldn't help but wonder what the point of the coffee was with the number of sweet things Trish added.

Pushing her own chair away, Ashley moved to stand closer to the window. The glass was dirty like it hadn't been washed in decades. The kitchen faced the side yard, so the front porch didn't block the view, but the window's condition definitely provided Trish with privacy considering the layers of dirt on it.

Looking around the rest of the space, it was likely the case. The kitchen was small but the amount of clutter she had all over the counters covered every square inch of the tops. It was clean, no dirty dishes or trash around, but just full of stuff that Ashley couldn't even guess what it all was. It wasn't as bad as a hoarder's house since you could easily move around. But it was definitely cluttered.

There were stacks of papers on the side of the kitchen that looked like Trish used as a desk area. She had plants that covered any area where the tiniest bit of light came in.

Some were what Ashley remembered one of her roommates in college called a spider plant. She was amazed at the length those things grew. This one had likely been growing since the windows were cleaned last.

"But it isn't possible. I have my sister and my uncle. I don't have any other close relatives. I don't have any other siblings, and I don't have any cousins. At least that I am aware of." Although she had to wonder about cousins now that she knew she had an aunt. Ashley's voice was soft as she tried to make sense of having a close relative, likely a sibling according to Trish. Aja didn't even come up on the report, which made Ashley question whether it was a legit report or a scam to get to her by her father's enemies.

She was avoiding the reality that her father had cheated on her mom and had another child somewhere out in the world. The thought still made her sick.

"All I can tell you is that this report says you have a close relative that you know nothing about that is most likely a sibling. That's all I can tell you. The rest of the family stuff I don't know. But girly, you're going to have to figure it out because this person is going to have more answers for you than me. And since your parents aren't listed anywhere because they didn't make a submission themselves or whatever, it doesn't say which side the child came from. Now you need to go cuz I have to take a nap."

Trish abruptly turned and leaned against the sink, drinking her entire cup of coffee in one gulp, rinsed it out and then moved to the doorway to a dark hallway. Ashley was still staring out the window when the older woman cleared her throat. Ashley turned with a start and looked at her. Trish waved her hand at Ashley as if to tell her to move along. At that moment, Trish's phone rang, or rather

"*Sharon*" screeched from it, startling Ashley even more. It sounded like an injured cat.

Trish picked up her phone, sighed and waved again at Ashley. Taking the hint, Ashley moved toward the door. Trish moved to another room and Ashley heard her answer the phone.

"Yeah yeah, I know *Sharon*. I didn't tell her anything about any of that. Jesus, woman. Give me some credit. You want me to give her some but not all, so I did what I could. I'm going to take a nap now. Goodbye." A door closed in another part of the house with a loud thud.

Ashley froze at the words. She heard Trish mumbling under her breath in the other room, but she couldn't make it out. She quickly moved to the door and hurried to her car. She didn't want Trish to think she was eavesdropping. If she was in a better frame of mind, she would have laughed at the woman's short temper, even with her friend.

Her thoughts started to run a little wild as she thought about what Trish had said to Sharon. Were they talking about Ashley and not telling her something? But that didn't make any sense. Neither of them knew her so there wouldn't be anything to hide. How would Sharon know stuff about Ashley when they just met a short time ago. Unless it was something to do with Sharon that she didn't want Ashley to know. That had to be it. Nothing else made sense.

Ashley sat in her car with the air conditioning on trying to cool down the vehicle and her racing thoughts. She was numb as she thought back to Trish's analysis of the paperwork. How could she have another close relative? Especially a possible sibling! She knew her mom never had any other kids. She would have remembered her mom being pregnant, wouldn't she? Even if she was really young. And she was there when her mom died. So that leaves her father.

She already had strong feelings about her dad. She didn't know how this new information made her feel. She didn't believe she could think less of him, but at the moment, she despised the man. He was never a good father. He was abusive to her mom for as long as Ashley could recall. He was rarely home and when he was home, he would sit in his beat up old easy chair and demand her mom or his girls to bring him a beer or make him dinner. His feet would be on the table with his dirty boots dripping sand and mud all over it. Then he would complain about the filth of the house.

Her mom would lower her eyes and nod, getting him everything he wanted, knowing the best she could do was to avoid as much conflict as she could, for her and her daughters' safety. She would get him his dinner and drinks without a word. Then she would pick up a cleaning rag and wipe the table, careful not to disrupt him or even touch him while he ate.

At some point, lost in her thoughts, Ashley had begun to drive back to Sharon's. She looked around and noticed she had almost reached their house without even thinking about it or using GPS. As she parked the car in her designated spot, she sighed. She couldn't help but wonder if she had blocked out things from her past due to the trauma of what she witnessed with her mom's death.

"No, I know I never had another sibling," she muttered with a frustrated breath. Thinking for a second if she should talk to Aja, she slapped the steering wheel and groaned. "Not yet, Ashley. Not yet."

Ashley gathered her things from the front seat and slid out of her car. Locking it behind her, she quickly made her way up to the house. She hesitated, not wanting to run into Sharon. She wasn't sure what Trish and Sharon were discussing on the phone. It might have nothing to do with her, but she didn't have a good poker face, and she didn't want to risk saying something.

Sighing again, she decided to just rush through and get to her room as fast as possible, trying not to be rude in the process. But one thing she had learned in the short time she had been there was rude and short were different. The culture here was definitely different than anything else she had experienced. People were nice and generally welcoming, but if they were busy, they didn't feel it was rude to tell you to move along. She would just channel that and move through the house to her stairs quickly.

In spite of her self-talk, she still slowly opened the door and peered around the corner. No one was within eyesight, so she made her way to the stairs and ran up them as if she were being chased. Once inside the safety of her room, she closed and locked the door. She dropped her things on the small counter. Her head was spinning, and it wasn't from the heat. As she made her way to her bed to try to calm her brain, her stomach let out an angry growl, making her laugh out loud.

It had been a long day already and it was only eleven. Maybe she should have stopped to get lunch on the way home. She didn't have much in her apartment, but she didn't want to leave either just in case Sharon was there.

With a sigh, she pulled out a bowl and some cereal. That's always a safe bet. She filled her bowl, added milk, and then sat at the small counter. The paper stared back at her, and she sighed. The only way to figure this out was going to be to meet this mystery person who contacted her first. Ashley wasn't sure how to do that and since she didn't know yet when Jacob would be coming, she didn't want to jump on that just yet either.

She could ask Sam, but she also knew that would lead to her being sent home faster than she could get the question out. She lifted the report from the pile. She felt a pang in her chest as she remembered that Trish was surprised her mom wasn't listed on the report. She remembered from class that when a death certificate is issued it usually shows up on these reports. Trish had reiterated that too. So why wasn't her mom listed then?

Her thoughts drifted to the possibility that this was someone from her father's past playing a game with her feelings. She wouldn't put something like this past her father, but would finding her after so many years really benefit any of his enemies? It had been almost twenty years since her mom died and her dad was sent to prison. She didn't even know anymore when he would be able to get out or if he was even eligible. She realized she never asked those questions because she didn't want anything to do with him whether he was in prison or not.

Aja had a different opinion than Ashley did about their father. She always wished for a more normal family and hoped they could reconcile someday. But Ashley couldn't get the image of her mom out of her head, so she didn't think she could ever stomach a relationship with the man who took her away from Ashley. No amount of rehabilitation would fix that in her mind.

Finishing her food, Ashley rinsed her bowl and set it in the sink. With a deep sigh, she pushed the papers together and decided to leave it for now. Maybe she could talk to Jacob or Aja and see what if anything she should do from here. Obviously, she would have to be careful what she asked her sister, but Jacob might be able to help more. She hated lying to Aja and was feeling more and more like she needed to come clean with her twin about this. Maybe Aja's super hacking skills would be able to help her out with everything.

She shook her head. *Not yet, just not yet*, she told herself. She moved to her bed and laid down, draping her arm over her eyes. She had to figure this out. The questions were becoming too many, and the answers weren't there at all. It was frustrating and Ashley didn't know which way to turn now. She hoped a short nap would help clear her mind and help her refocus. *Maybe Trish was onto something with these naps*, she thought with a smile.

Chapter 12

Ashley looked at the cold strawberry treat with hesitation. They were breaking daddy's rules, but momma was so sure it was going to be ok. It was the first time their mom had let them taste ice cream from their dad's special stash, hidden deep in the freezer behind the girls' popsicles and chicken nuggets.

Aja sat next to her and giggled as she put her tiny spoon in her mouth. Her eyes got big, and she smiled. "Ash, it's so good!" she dragged out. Aja quickly picked up another spoonful and popped it in her mouth.

Ashley looked at her own bowl. There was just a small scoop in each of their bowls and their mom looked at them with so much love and encouragement.

"Go ahead, Ashley. Try it," she said with a nudge.

Taking a deep breath, Ashley dug her spoon into the creamy treat. Putting it up to her mouth she stuck her tongue out first to get a tiny taste. Deciding it was ok, she put the spoonful into her mouth and grinned at her mom. "Mm, it is good. Thank you, momma." She said with a smile. She took another small bit of ice cream on her spoon and ate it.

"Aren't you going to have some, Momma?" Aja asked.

Their mom shook her head. "No. Your daddy might notice if we take too much. So just eat up quickly so we can wash up the dishes before he gets home, ok?"

Ashley glanced over at her mom and hesitated again. She knew something bad would happen if their dad came home and saw what they were doing. Normally Aja would be the rule follower, but this time, Ashley suddenly felt very anxious. She pushed her bowl to the middle of the table and put her chin on her tiny, folded arms.

Her mom noticed and gently pushed it back toward her. "What's the matter sweetheart?" she lightly touched Ashley's arm, making the little girl look over at her.

"I don't want daddy to hurt you again. I don't want to eat it." Her small voice was quiet and shaky, and she put her head down, hiding her eyes.

"Oh Ashley. It's ok. Your daddy won't be home until late tonight. So, it's ok. Go ahead." She lowered her voice and whispered in Ashley's ear, "Who knows when we will get the chance again." She smiled and rubbed Ashley's head affectionately.

Ashley slowly raised her head and nodded. She pulled the bowl closer to her and began to eat the treat again. She had never had strawberry flavored anything before, and it was the best kind she decided. She giggled with Aja as they ate their sweet treat. Even though they knew they were being sneaky, they enjoyed the time with their mom.

Before they could push away from the table to put their dishes away, they heard their father's car door slam. Ashley was surprised they didn't hear the car pull up. It was an old car and was very loud. The three of them looked at each other and a look of fear crossed over their mom's face. She tried to stack the bowls quickly and get them out of sight before he could come in, but she was too late. She didn't have time to rinse out the evidence of their misdeed before he stumbled in.

Ashley thought they would be ok though because both she and Aja had finished their ice cream. There was just a little bit in the bottom of the bowl. Their mom had already put the container back in its hiding place. He wouldn't find out. He couldn't find out.

As he came through the door, the screen door slamming angrily behind him, he looked at the three of them. Ashley and Aja shrank under his scowl. As his eyes moved to look at their mom, she knew he knew. And it wasn't going to be good either.

"Dammit, Sissy! I told you not to give the little brats my stuff!" The loud booming voice of her father rang through the silent house. All three sets of eyes turned and stared at the man whose face was bright red with fury. "I only keep you around to watch them and keep them out of my stuff! What's wrong with you!"

He stalked over to their mom and grabbed her arm, pulling her roughly away from the sink. The dishes dropped from her hands, the metal of the spoons banging against the steel.

Ashley shrunk in her chair and felt Aja grab a hold of her tiny hand and squeeze. Ashley glanced over and met her sister's terrified eyes. Ashley pulled her sister close, and Aja buried her face in Ashley's stained shirt. Wrapping her small arms around her twin, Ashley glanced up at the two adults in the room. Neither had made eye contact with her and she stared at them trying to decide what to do.

It was only seven o'clock. Her father didn't usually come home until a lot later. Her mom had even said it was early. She couldn't help but wonder why he was home early. It wasn't normal. He was never home before they went to bed. She was suddenly scared that something else was really wrong. And she worried about her mom.

"It was just a tiny bit, Vern," her mom said quietly, turning slightly away from him to rinse the dishes. Ashley knew as well as her mom that the dirty dishes could be the next thing that sets his anger off. She wished she could help, but she was stuck in her own fear as she watched things unfold in front of her again. She wondered if other kids' parents fought as much as hers did. Or if there were daddies out there who were like the ones on tv shows. Somehow, she didn't think so.

An almost feral growl came from her father as he grabbed hold of her hair, pulling her backward. "I told you my name is Viper. Use it!" he yelled in her ear through clenched teeth.

Ashley's mom whimpered slightly, trying to hold in her pain as her little girls looked on in horror. It wasn't the first time they had fought in front of the twins, but this time the girls were frozen, glued to their seats as they watched, unable to move. Typically, their mom would usher them into their small bedroom, away from their angry father's wrath.

Her mom's eyes turned toward Ashley, her hair still firmly in the grip of her father's hand preventing her from turning completely. Somehow, she got the message and Ashley snapped out of her froze state and moved off her chair as quietly and slowly as she could. They all knew if something caught her father's eyes during these episodes, he would attack that movement no matter what it was.

He once flew into a tirade chasing a mouse that had made the terrible decision to come out of hiding during one of his angry fits.

Once off her chair, Ashley grabbed a hold of both of Aja's hands and pulled her down with her. Quietly and as stealthily as they could, the girls made their way to the bedroom and closed the door tightly. They each took their big comforter off the beds and covered themselves in the corner. Huddled together, they listened to the chaos outside their door. Things were flying across the small house against walls and breaking. Smashing and cursing was all they heard from their father.

Ashley couldn't help but wonder what was happening as she listened, terrified for her mom and her sister. She suddenly remembered her uncle. The last time her father had hurt her mom so bad she was in the hospital, Uncle Sam had come. He had told Ashley she could call him whenever she wanted or needed to. But she didn't have a cell phone to call him. She wondered where her mom put her phone and if she could somehow get to it. The only other phone in the house was on the wall in the kitchen and that wasn't an option.

Slowly lifting the blanket off her head, she glanced around her room. Outside her door was still loud and scary and she hesitated to move, as if her dad could see her. Taking a deep breath, she moved out from under the blanket. She needed to find the paper her uncle had written his number on. He had given it to her mom first, but she left it on the table beside the bed, not wanting to take it. She said if her dad found out, he would hurt her again. That's when Sam had snuck it to Ashley.

A tiny hand broke her out of her thoughts, and she turned to look at a terrified Aja. "Ash, you can't go. I'm scared. I need you." Her twin's eyes were filled with tears and her cheeks already stained with many that had already fallen. The hazel shone brightly against the reddened whites of her eyes. Aja quickly wiped her eyes on her sleeve.

"It's ok. I need to find Uncle's phone number. He said he would help, remember? I need to call him." Ashley patted her sister's hand as if she were an adult.

Aja's eyes began to tear up again. "But what if he gets you too? Ashley, I can't live without you!" She pulled Ashley back to her and hugged her tightly.

"I'm not leaving our room. I promise. I just need the paper, and I'll come right back." She hugged her sister back and then pulled herself from Aja's grasp. *Where did I put it?* she thought as she scanned her room again.

She knew she had hidden it and tried to think of where. Her eyes stopped at her school bag. A slow grin played on her lips as she remembered she put it in her favorite class folder. Being only in Kindergarten, Ashley only had two folders. One was for math, and one was for reading.

Crawling to her backpack, she grabbed it and quickly pulled it back into the blanket fort she and her sister had made far too many times. She noticed the noise outside had dulled a little bit. Her dad was still cursing and stomping around, but nothing was being thrown or crashing anymore. She could now hear her mom's sobs which meant it was almost over. They had been through this so many times now that they had learned the cycle. It was almost as if he was satisfied when she was crying, and he somehow calmed down.

Ashley opened the zipper of her Little Mermaid backpack. Carefully and quietly, she pulled out her reading folder and, in the very back of her papers, she pulled out a small sheet of paper about the size of a post it note. Ten numbers stared back at her, and she lifted it with pride as she showed her sister.

"I found it!" she whispered excitedly.

Aja stared at her. "But you don't have a phone." She wiped her cheeks, the tears falling much slower now. She also knew it was almost over.

Ashley deflated slightly at the comment, forgetting the biggest hurdle wasn't finding the number but actually figuring out how to call their uncle. She bit her lip thoughtfully.

Both girls jumped when they heard the door slam. They locked their eyes on each other and then waited a few more minutes until they thought it was all clear, as Mom used to say. Usually when their father left, it would be a few more minutes before she came in to say he was gone. This time though, Mom didn't come.

"Do you think she left too?" Aja asked nervously.

Ashley didn't respond. She just stared at the blanket in front of her as if she could see the door. She heard a car door slam and then an engine started. Breathing a sigh of relief, she looked back at Aja. "We can go. He's leaving."

They gingerly made their way out of the blankets, on high alert for any more noises. Aja hid behind Ashley as she opened the door slowly, peeking out. There wasn't any movement that they could see or hear. With Aja still behind her holding tightly onto her shirt, Ashley made her way to the kitchen.

Ashley gasped when she saw her mom on the floor, surrounded by broken dishes and glass. The kitchen looked like a tornado had gone through. Every cabinet door was open, and the contents strewn all over the space. It wasn't a large space and with everything all over, there wasn't much room to walk. She looked at her mom again and tried to wake her from where she was standing.

"Mom! Wake up!" Aja was nearly silent behind her, her soft sobs the only sound.

Suddenly their mom groaned. She rolled over and put her hand to her head.

"Mom!" Ashley shouted. "Be careful!" She didn't dare move since she wasn't sure where it was safe to even walk with her bare feet. She wished she had put something on them. Glancing back at Aja, she pulled her back to the hall. "Come on, let's put our slippers on."

They made their way back to their room and slipped on the puffy footwear. They were a Christmas gift from their uncle, matching bright pink fluffy slippers. Then, the girls made their way back to the kitchen. Their mom had moved to sit up and Ashley made her way over to her.

"Where is your father?" she asked quietly.

Aja whispered, "Don't know. He just left."

Their mom nodded. "I better clean this up before he comes back. You girls go back in your room." She slowly stood and looked around her. The tears in her eyes spilled out over her red cheeks. Her eye was starting to bruise, and she had some cuts on her arms.

Ashley looked over at Aja and then shrugged. Looking back into the space, Ashley spotted her mom's cell phone. They may not have to call their uncle now, but maybe she should keep the phone just in case. She carefully moved to the edge of the counter and grabbed the phone while her mom's back was to them. Then they hurried off to their room again.

Once back in the safety of their room, Ashley took the piece of paper from Sam and held it in her hand. She bit her cheek and looked at Aja. "Do you think I should call him?" she asked.

Aja shrugged. "He did say if we ever felt scared or if dad hurt mom again to call. This time was worse, Ash." Her tiny voice was quiet, and she was clearly still scared.

"Ok," Ashley said with a sigh. She looked at the paper again and turned her mom's phone on. She dialed the number and waited for her uncle to answer. It only took two rings.

"Sissy, what's up?" her uncle's low voice came over the line.

Ashley hesitated and then Aja said, "Tell him, Ash."

There was silence for a moment and then Sam's voice came over the line again, softer this time. "Girls? What's going on?"

Ashley sighed. "Hi Uncle Sam. Um, daddy was angry again. We ate some of his ice cream. He was so angry." She found herself struggling to explain what had happened just a short time ago. Guilt was also playing at her nerves. They never should have had it, even if their mom insisted. She knew it would be bad.

"Is your mom alright?" Sam's voice sounded far away. Ashley heard rustling around on the other end. "Ashley. Is your mom alright?" His voice was rising as she hesitated to talk.

"Yes, I think. She's cleaning up the mess dad made."

Aja suddenly went pale, and she looked at Ashley. "Dad's back! Ashley! Hide!" Her voice was full of panic.

"Girls, I'm on my way!" and then Sam hung up.

Ashley was stunned, staring at the phone. Aja was pulling on her arm, trying to get her under the blankets again.

"Ashley!" Aja yelled, finally snapping her out of her trance.

The yelling started again in the kitchen and Ashley heard her mom start to cry again. She huddled with her sister as they rode out the second storm. *Dad was really on a rampage tonight, over ice cream*, she thought. She vowed never to eat his strawberry ice cream again.

Aja jumped when her mom screamed, "No! Vern, No! Please!"

The girls looked at each other, wondering what was happening. A loud sound was heard, and they both jumped out of the blanket. Ashley ran for the door.

"Ashley! NO!" Aja screamed, but Ashley wasn't listening.

Aja stayed under the blankets, sobbing.

Ashley ran to the kitchen and saw her mom lying on the kitchen floor. She was crying and holding her stomach. Her eyes lifted to her father's ice-cold ones as he lifted them to look at her instead of her mom. He raised his hand, and she saw he was holding a gun, pointed right at Ashley.

"You ungrateful little brats are just as bad as she is!" As he was about to pull the trigger, Ashley dropped to her knees and held her mom's hand, not sure what else to do. She didn't think about her father standing over her. She could only focus on her mom who was hurt so bad this time.

"Ashley, hide," her mom whispered, all energy leaving her body quickly.

A tear slid from her mom's eye as she closed them tight. Ashley felt her own body start to shake.

"Mom, no, don't go!" she cried, as she cupped her small hands around her mom's face. The chocolate brown eyes that always held so much love for her and her sister were now hidden from Ashley's sight. She forgot everything else except her mom's slow breath, which seemed to be taking longer and longer for her to take another one in. What was happening? Her five-year-old brain was struggling to understand.

She barely noticed when the door was slammed open, and the ensuing chaos erupted. She just stared at her mom's face, scared she would never see it again. There were shouts and pounding as people rushed inside. But Ashley stayed focused on her mom, willing her to take another breath or to open her eyes. She couldn't find her voice though as she continued to stare at her now relaxed features. Did that mean…?

When she finally looked up, her uncle had her dad pinned to the floor with handcuffs on his wrists. Her father was still cursing at everyone around him. Her uncle looked up at Ashley and then toward the door. A few minutes later two or three police officers came in and picked up her father. At some point an ambulance came and took her mom away. Ashley just sat there staring after everyone, numb and lost. How did this happen? Was her mom ok? Where did they take her? And what would happen to her and Aja? They couldn't stay in their house anymore by themselves. Where would they go?

She felt her uncle take her hand and gently pull her up to him. He held her close and whispered, "It's going to be ok, Ashley. I got you. Both of you."

It was then that she noticed Aja was also in his arms, sobbing quietly. Ashley reached over and hugged her sister tightly to her side. They were all they had. Would her dad come back for them again? Was he going to jail? Was her mom dead?

She glanced over at the spot her father had stood staring at her moments ago. Then she looked at the blood-soaked floor where her mom had just been. No one told her anything, they just took both of her parents away. She looked up into her uncle's eyes. She saw sadness and something else. She wasn't sure what it was though. Maybe guilt? He couldn't have gotten here any sooner, though, could he?

As her uncle took the girls out of the house they had lived in for so long, Ashley turned and looked at it one more time. She wasn't sure if she would see it again and she wanted to remember it. There were scary memories there, but there were also good ones with her mom and Aja. She didn't notice the cold wind that whipped the fallen leaves around or the dusk sky that was painted a multitude of colors. Any other time she and Aja would pretend to take pictures of the colored streaks above them.

Turning back to her uncle, she looked up at him. "We shouldn't have eaten his ice cream. He hurt momma so bad because of us." Ashley blamed herself. She knew they would get in trouble with her dad if he found out. She should have stopped Aja from eating it too.

"No, honey. What your dad did is not even close to your fault. He made a choice. He will pay for it too. Little girls deserve to have treats and good things." He pulled her close in a tight hug.

"Where will we go now?" she asked in her quiet little voice, not really believing him.

Sam looked down at her and tried to smile. "I will take care of you, sweetheart. You will both be ok. I promise. Just like I promised your mama so long ago." He stopped walking and squatted down to her eye level. "Do you believe me, Ash? Can you trust me to take care of you and your sister?"

Ashley studied his face. She knew he came around a lot and always took care of them and her mom when her father was gone. He always made sure they were safe before he left their house. She looked over at Aja holding Sam's other hand. Their eyes met and Aja gave her a hesitant smile. Finally, Ashley nodded. "Ok," she said simply.

Sam's face lit up with a smile and he rubbed her head. "Good. Now let's go figure out what to do next."

Chapter 13

Ashley startled awake from her dream, or rather the flashback, from the worst day of her life. She looked around and gathered herself again. It had been a long time since she'd had that nightmare. All of what Trish had told her came rushing back, making her catch her breath. She had a sibling somewhere nearby. Her father cheated on her mom, after everything else he had done. She needed to talk to someone, but who could she call? Glancing at the clock next to her head she saw it was four in the afternoon. She slept most of the day. Jacob wouldn't be off yet for another hour or so with the time difference.

Deciding she couldn't wait she sat up and looked around for her phone. She spotted it on the counter where the rest of her paperwork was dropped when she came in. Ashley slid off the bed and moved to grab it when it suddenly dinged, letting her know she had a text. She hoped that it was her twin intuition and Aja was texting. Even if she couldn't talk about what she found out, she could talk to her sister again. That would help her a little.

She picked up her phone and opened her texting app. She let out a frustrated sigh when she saw it wasn't either of the two people she wanted to talk to. Opening the message Ashley saw it was from an unknown number again. These were getting annoying. It was obvious they had the wrong number. The person on the other end of the text was desperately trying to get a hold of their mom again. The text read, "Mom, where are you? Please call me back!"

A sudden chill went down her spine. This is the third or fourth message she had gotten from someone looking for their mom. Ashley wondered if the mom was missing or something. She had a sick feeling about this. Biting the corner of her lip, she decided she should at least let the other person know they had the wrong number again so they could get the right help. She obviously couldn't do anything, especially without a number or a name.

She typed back, "Hey I think you have the wrong number. I am not a mom." She added a smiley face emoji at the end and hit send. She waited a few minutes and when no reply came, she shrugged and looked at the stack of papers again. "What do I do now?" she muttered. She jumped when her phone sounded again in her hand. Glancing down, Ashley saw it was from Jacob.

Hey Ash. How are you doing? How did it go with Trish today? I'm driving home now, give me a call when you can. He always ends his texts with a heart emoji, making Ashley smile.

Quickly she hit the phone icon on her screen and settled back onto her bed, waiting for him to pick up.

"Well, that was fast," Jacob said with a chuckle.

"It's been a day," Ashley said with a sigh. "How are things back home?" She was suddenly feeling alone and homesick.

Jacob seemed to sense her mood and took a second to answer. "It's ok. I think these new kids are gonna work out for Papa Jasper. So that's good news. I can be out there soon." He paused then added, "Is everything ok?" The concern in his voice was clear and Ashley tried to brush her emotions aside.

She wanted to tell him about her dream, about the worst childhood memory she had. But how could she? Maybe when he came out there, she would tell him. She knew if she started to talk about that awful day she would likely cry. The last thing she wanted was for him to feel bad that he couldn't comfort her from so far away. Plus, the guilt was still there. If only she could have convinced her mom to put the ice cream away sooner. Or if she had just eaten it quickly like she asked. Maybe her mom would still be alive.

"It's going fine. I just miss everyone," she said quietly. Before things got awkward, she quickly added, "But I'm glad to hear things are good at the feed store. I'm so looking forward to not being alone!"

Jacob sighed lightly on the other end of the phone. When he spoke, his voice was quiet, and he sounded worried. "How did the meeting with Trish go? Did she give you anything to go off of?"

"Actually yes, but it is throwing me for a loop." Ashley took a deep breath in and slowly let it out, while Jacob remained quiet on the other end. "Jacob, she said the report says I have a sibling other than Aja." She waited for him to react, but he was silent. For a second, she thought the call disconnected. "Jacob?"

"Yeah, I'm here. Um, Ash, have you thought about if this could be a trick? Maybe what you told me about Sam's concerns and people maybe wanting to get a hold of you are faking this whole thing? Maybe it isn't a real report, and someone is up to something. It might not be a bad idea to get Sam in on this. Because I agree it sounds weird. Wouldn't you remember another kid? Or even if your mom was pregnant at one time. Was it supposedly an older or younger sibling?"

Ashley thought about his question. "I guess I don't know. But I would think if it was an older child, I would remember them. And I know we would remember a younger one. It just doesn't make sense. And I don't want to call Sam yet. I want to try to figure this out first. Let's send the letter and see where that gets us. Maybe we can arrange a meeting, and I can hide and see if someone shows up who looks legit before I meet them."

Her words were ringing in her ears. Just thinking about meeting a stranger was starting to sound like a crazy idea—even to her. She bit her thumb nail, waiting for a reaction from him.

Jacob let out a groan. "Sam is going to kill me if you go do something stupid and something happens. I should be there first. Please Ashley. Wait until I get there. I'll beg if I have to."

Ashley grinned in spite of herself. "Ok, Jake. I wouldn't want you to beg. Your pride, oh my gosh. I wouldn't be able to live with myself." She made a dramatic moan and then laughed.

"Yeah, laugh all you want! Neither one of us knows what's really going on and I am serious. I don't want you doing anything alone. I'll be there soon. Just hold on." She could hear the humor in his voice, but also a little fear.

She could understand it. She had to admit she felt a little of that fear as well, not knowing for sure what she might be blindly walking into.

"Yes, sir. I will obey you, sir," Ashley said mockingly, trying to lighten the mood and shake her own worries away. She could imagine Jacob shaking his head at her, which made her giggle harder.

She could tell Jacob was grinning, even though she was making fun of him. "Where are you at with the letter?"

"I kind of lost track of everything, so I haven't written it yet. I'll sit down right after this and send it to you. I'll also take a picture of this other letter so you can see it and then we both have the address. I was thinking though, it might be better to give this person an email address. The mail will be slow and since I am here now, I would hate for it to take so much longer just because we are waiting for a letter from the post office." The idea came to her when she was thinking about the length of time, she had been there already with little to no progress toward her goal. Unless she intended to stay for a lot longer, they would need a faster means of communicating. But she wasn't sure what Jacob would think.

The writer of the letter already knew her name, but she was surprised that she didn't know theirs. It was just initials on the paper matching the ones on the envelope, and she wasn't sure how they were able to do that. Her name was printed on the report, and she didn't remember having an option to change it. She didn't have any idea of gender either. Did she have a brother or sister out there? There was a tiny seed of doubt planted with these realizations. Maybe it was a scam after all.

Jacob had been silent for a long time and Ashley was again wondering if the call was dropped. The reception wasn't great on the Eastern Shore, at least not compared to the Twin Cities. But that was probably common. Big cities seemed to have better resources for most everything.

Finally, Jacob sighed. "I'm not going to lie the whole thing makes me nervous. I don't want some high-end hacker getting a hold of your info and somehow tracking you down. But it does make more sense to go through email instead of snail mail. What email addresses do you have? Maybe we should start a new one that we can both access until I can be out there with you? That would make me feel a little better."

Ashley thought for a second. "Actually, that's a good idea. Gmail is still free, right? Can you create a new one and get me the login info and I'll add it to the letter? Thanks, Jacob. I actually feel better knowing someone else out there is watching out for me."

"And if there's anything shady, I can take it to Sam," he warned gently, but firmly. Ashley hoped it wouldn't come to that, at least not until she found out who this person was and how they were connected.

Nodding as if he could see her, Ashley said, "Deal. I can handle that. But there has to be something to report to him, not just a hunch, ok? I really don't believe this is some secret CIA mission to get me or the crazies connected to my father."

Jacob chuckled on the other end. "I know, but still. You really need to be careful."

"I will. I promise. And if you could see me now, I would cross my heart too," she added with a smirk.

They talked for almost an hour about nothing at all. It felt good to just talk without worrying about a new problem or hurdle for her to conquer. Ashley sighed as she looked at her clock. She hadn't eaten dinner yet and was starting to feel a little weak and lightheaded. It was getting dark outside already, she noticed but somehow it seemed way too early. She found that she didn't feel as exhausted anymore. Talking to Jacob helped to calm her down, even if they didn't talk about the proverbial elephant in the room. At least the one hanging over her head.

Jacob still wasn't aware of everything weighing her down, but soon, she promised herself. She would tell him everything. She just needed to have him in the same room with her when she shared the sordid details of her family history. She hoped he didn't look at her differently knowing what her father had done to her mom, all because of her and Aja. They say blood is thicker than water. Would Jacob worry that she would be like her dad some day since they shared blood? In some ways she knew she was being ridiculous. But she couldn't help the doubt that crept in.

After they had hung up. Ashley stretched her arms straight above her head and tilted her head side to side. She felt the muscles tighten and then release as she did. For not doing much today, she felt like she had run a marathon. Maybe with her stress and use of brain power she had run a mental marathon. She laughed at herself as she stood and stretched her back out.

"Now what to eat for dinner," she said out loud. She still didn't have much in her kitchen but thought maybe she could go get some groceries tomorrow. Nodding, as if she were having a conversation with someone else, she moved to her backpack and pulled out a notebook and pencil. Making a list would be ideal since she didn't have a lot of storage space and didn't have a lot of money so she would need to plan things out carefully.

Ashley plugged her phone into her charger and then sat down to make her list. Her stomach growled and she just shook her head. Something simple tonight and tomorrow she would make a better meal. Grabbing a package of wheat thins and some pre-sliced cheese from the fridge, she sat back down again. Thinking of what to buy to make meals for just herself was harder than she thought it would be. Everything seemed to come in bigger quantities.

"Ugh," she moaned. "How do I do this?" Ashley couldn't believe she hadn't made herself decent meals since coming here. An idea started to form. If she made meals like she was still cooking for her and Aja, then she could save half or freeze it to have another day. Snapping her fingers, she grinned. "That's brilliant!" she exclaimed and then laughed at herself.

She finished her list and added containers that were both microwave and freezer safe, then she dropped her pencil from high above the table, satisfied with her success. "And, mic drop!" she said with a giggle.

Ashley looked over at the clock and then decided to watch a little TV. She hadn't even turned the TV on since she had moved in and wasn't sure what she would even get for channels, but she wasn't tired anymore after her long nap. If nothing was on TV, she could always scroll social media for funny videos to entertain her for a while.

It had taken her a long time to convince Sam that it would be ok to have social media if she kept the account private and only allowed people that she knew personally to have access. He was always against it and Aja still didn't have any accounts. Ashley didn't use hers often, but when she was bored, she found some of the videos entertaining. Her friends list was still very small.

Grabbing her snack and phone, she moved the few feet to the bed and turned the TV on across from her with the remote. She didn't have any cable or dish channels so she would have to rely on local TV. The TV she and Jacob had gotten before he left was compatible with her Netflix account so she could always stream something that way.

A text came through her phone breaking her channel surfing. Opening it up she smiled. Jacob had asked what she was doing. She answered quickly with "looking for something to watch."

Suddenly her phone rang.

"Hey, didn't I just talk to you?" she asked Jacob with a smile.

Jacob laughed. "Yep. I was just laying here in bed and thinking the same thing. What's on to watch. Then I thought 'I wonder what Ash is doing?' So, I was thinking maybe we could watch a series together or something and then when we get back together, we can *actually* watch it together."

"That sounds like a great idea! I wasn't sure what to watch anyway," she answered. "What are you thinking? Something like 'The Crown'?" She couldn't help the smirk that crossed her face and she wished they were on FaceTime instead of just a voice call. Jacob's face had to be hilarious.

"Ok. I am not even going to respond to that," Jacob scoffed. "I know you are just playing, and if you're not, you can watch that on your own. I was thinking something more like the 'What If…' series on Disney+." Ashley's smile widened.

She had the same love for the Avengers that Jacob did. They watched every new movie that came out on the first weekend. She had actually forgotten about this series and was excited about the reviews she had seen before. Jacob clearly agreed and figured she would say yes without an issue. The idea was such a fun one, she couldn't even pretend to mess with her boyfriend.

"I'm so in! When do we start?" she asked, looking through her app while they talked.

Jacob must have been scrolling too because he was quiet for a minute. "Well, it looks like it is only one season and a total of nine episodes. I thought there were more. But that should get us to the day I get out there if we only watch one a day. Then we can save the last one for when I get there. What do you think?"

"I'm game. You did see that it's animated right?" she asked. She usually preferred live action but wasn't opposed to anime either. "Then when you get out here, we are going to see 'Black Panther 2' right?" That movie had just come out in the theaters or was set to soon. It would be a perfect date idea when they finally were together again.

Jacob sighed. "I know, not ideal, but it should be good. We never watched Loki either. I know there is some controversy with that one, and we don't have to watch it, but I know how much you love Loki."

He was right. Ashley loved Loki. He was a great bad guy. She had heard there was some controversy around racism and that's why it was canceled after two seasons, but that's not why she hadn't watched it. She just never made the time.

"Let's watch this one and then decide. You said it might only be another week or two so we can decide after we finish this one. We could always watch a movie together after that too." Jacob's idea made sense.

"OK!" Ashley exclaimed. "Let's do this. When do we start?" She pulled up the synopsis and was reading it while she waited for Jacob to answer her.

Her all-time favorite character was Doctor Strange. She wasn't sure why though she just loved his movies. They were so out of the realm of normal life, and she guessed it allowed her to escape reality for a while when she watched his movies. She wasn't into romantic comedies all that much. She liked a movie to help her escape real life and just sit back and be entertained.

Complex psychological thrillers were too much work for her to keep track of, but she has seen many because Aja loved them. She did love trying to guess the ending before they revealed it. Ashley knew her sister's job was perfect for her for this same reason. Ashley didn't mind being scared but wasn't a huge fan of horror. She loved Halloween and dressing up as someone completely different than herself, but the blood and gore for no real reason she could do without. Now action, that was her favorite. Sure, sometimes there was blood and gore, especially with the Deadpool movies, but they were fun and exciting, and she completely felt entertained when she left.

"Ash?" Jacob's voice broke her from her thoughts. "Are you still there?"

Ashley grinned. "Yep, just thinking about what movies to watch. Hey, how about we skip the series and watch all the Marvel movies in chronological order?" They could watch a different movie every night, or part of one and then continue until they were through them all. There had to be almost twenty by now, she thought.

"Hm, I like that idea. Then we could top it off with the newest one when I get out there."

"Well, you know there have to be close to twenty, right? You better be out here in less than twenty days, Jake!" Ashley was joking, but there was a tiny hint of worry in her voice. She knew there would be days they wouldn't watch a whole movie, which meant potentially more than twenty days.

"Yeah, I do, but we can still watch them in order whether I am there or here together. If you can log into your TV apps to Disney+, then we can FaceTime on the phone. When I'm there, then you can cuddle up with me and watch them. Right?" Jacob's voice had dropped a little and he was quieter.

Ashley was just looking forward to not being here alone anymore. "Ok, you're right. I am wide awake because of my nap. Do you want to start now?"

"Let's do it. What's first?" Jacob asked. She could hear his voice fade a little as she figured he was getting settled on his bed.

"You look up the order, I am going to pop some popcorn. I know I have at least some of that here." She got up from the bed and moved to her small kitchen to pop a bag of microwave popcorn. When Jacob had been with her, they had gotten a small box and had only made one bag of it. It was her favorite go-to snack and since she hadn't eaten dinner, this would have to do for now. *Shopping tomorrow*, she thought. She put the cheese and crackers away while she waited for the popcorn to finish.

"Why haven't you eaten dinner yet?" Jacob suddenly asked.

Ashley waved her hand in the air. "I just have to go shopping tomorrow. My options are limited but I think I found a way around my struggle with how to cook for just me. I was so worried about wasting food because I don't know how to cook for just one person. It's always been me and Aja and sometimes Sam. But I figured out I can still cook for both of us and freeze part and have two meals. So smart, huh?" she laughed at herself.

Jacob was quiet for a minute and then he said quietly, "Well don't get too used to cooking for one because I will want to eat when I am there too."

"Yeah, yeah. I guess I can feed you too." Her microwave beeped signaling her snack was ready. "So, what's first?" she asked, settling back on her bed.

"Looks like 'Captain America' is number one," he said.

This wasn't her favorite one, but it was the perfect place to start. She set up her TV and sat back against the wall, sitting on her bed like it was a couch. She had prepared a bunch of her pillows from home along the long edge of the bed, against the wall, to act as a couch since the space was so small. It actually worked perfectly. The only downside was she had to make her bed every day to make it function more like a couch than a bed.

They did a ceremonious countdown and then Ashley started her movie. She heard Jacob's start on the other end of the line as well and smiled. She turned her phone to FaceTime and then propped Jacob's face on the pillow next to her. It was funny to hear the sound in stereo between the phone and her own sound. They had actually done a perfect job of coordinating the starting of the movies.

"This isn't ideal, but it is so much better than nothing," she said as she grinned at him.

The next two hours were filled with easy conversation and laughs. She knew she was missing home and Jacob, but she didn't realize how much. This was the perfect solution to her homesickness.

"I wonder if I could find a movie that Aja would watch with me like this," she mused out loud.

Jacob snorted. "Right. You guys have the complete opposite taste in movies. I would be shocked if you could find anything you would agree on, even a tiny bit. What kinds of TV shows did you watch when you were little?"

Ashley thought for a minute. "I guess all the girly stuff. Princesses and all that." She shuddered at the thought now. But every little girl seemed to go through that stage at some point in their childhood. Her favorite was still Merida with her carefree and wild personality. The outspoken characters were Ashley's favorites, while Aja was drawn more to the quiet and delicate ones like Cinderella and Snow White.

After Sam took them away that day, he tried to make their lives as normal as he could. He was the one who introduced them to TV and movies. They had never had a television or been to a theater before that. They were pretty isolated in their home with their mom almost all the time. Rarely did they even go to the store with her since she tended to go at night after they were asleep. They didn't have a car, except for her dad's and he was always off somewhere. So, they had to walk if they went anywhere.

Sam had taken them to see the Little Mermaid in the theater and since it was the only movie she had ever seen, Ashley latched onto it as her favorite. Sam had bought her the backpack for school after that.

There was a food pantry not far from the house that Ashley remembered walking to a few times. They couldn't carry too much but it was enough to have some lunches.

They could get some cans of soup and boxes of macaroni and cheese. Her mom would buy some milk and butter at the store. Ashley didn't have real meat until Sam took them in. She remembered the first time he made something called hamburger helper. Putting noodles with meat was such a novelty. Now she laughed about it. He was learning how to cook for kids and since it was always just him alone, he never really worried about cooking at all. Ashley and Aja had learned how to cook at a young age since it was so new and exciting for them. And since the environment Sam offered was safe, they felt they could try things they hadn't even thought about before.

After the movie finished, Ashley found she still wasn't tired, but she knew Jacob had to get up early for work the next morning. She figured she should try to get the letter done since she has been putting it off.

"I'm going to get this letter done, Jake. Are you going to sleep right away?" she asked. He was already yawning, and it was almost ten. They had talked through most of the movie, and she had to admit it felt good.

"I guess I should. Five comes way too soon some days." He chuckled and rubbed his hands down his face. "What are you going to do?"

Ashley sighed. "I have to get this letter done."

"You did just say that didn't you. I guess I am tired." His face held a little bit of concern as he watched her through the screen. "Is everything ok?"

"Yeah, it's all good. I am just trying to figure out what to say without saying too much. I mean he or she already knows more about me than I do about them. I don't even know gender. All I have are two initials, which may or may not even be the right ones. It's annoying." She huffed out her frustration and Jacob sighed.

"Well, just be vague back. Tell them you would be interested in meeting possibly before the end of the summer if they were open to it. Ask them for a first name. They can just ignore the question, but they might give it up." He shrugged on the screen. "What do you have to lose by asking, Ash? You don't have to give up anything else about yourself, just ask a few questions. See what happens."

Ashley thought for a moment. "I guess you're right. I don't have to give anything away about myself. I've been thinking this is like a pen pal situation where you are getting to know each other, but we don't have to right now, do we." She nodded absently to her empty space, which looked a little eerie with the glow of the TV filling it.

After a few minutes of silence, Ashley looked at Jacob. "Ok, I am going to write it as soon as we get off the phone. I promise this time. I don't have a lot of time anymore, so I have to do this. I also have to decide if I am going to go to school, Jacob. I still haven't decided."

"Well, how about we wait and see what this brings. You can always enroll later or maybe this will all be resolved sooner, and we can just come back here," Jacob suggested.

"Ok, I think I can do that for a little while longer, I guess. I know I said I was going to do this before, but I really will this time. I am sending you a copy of the letter, so you have the address. Send it out as soon as you can."

"Ok and I will set up the Gmail account and send you the login too," Jacob added.

"Is that everything?" She couldn't remember what else they had talked about.

Jacob chuckled. "Yeah, Ash. That was it. Now, I have to go to sleep. I'll talk to you again tomorrow, ok?"

Ashley looked back at him and smiled. "OK. Love you, Jacob." She blew him a kiss, making him laugh and blow one back.

"Love you too, Ash. Sleep well."

Chapter 14

A ding on her phone woke Ashley up. She rubbed her eyes and looked over at the clock next to her head. Seven thirteen. Am. "Ugh," she groaned. She still didn't understand what possessed people to get up this early.

She pulled the cord of her phone since she couldn't reach the phone itself. When it came unplugged and the phone dropped to the floor, she groaned louder. "Forget it. I'll look at it later," she mumbled and rolled back over. It didn't take long for Ashley to realize she wasn't going to fall back to sleep. Maybe it was curiosity about who texted her or just the brightness in the room. Either way, she huffed a frustrated breath and threw her covers off her body. She lay flat on her back staring at the ceiling, irritation rolling off her in waves; big frothy ones like the ocean sent inland when it was angry.

Another alert on her phone brought her attention back to the reason she was awake at this crazy hour. She leaned over the edge of the bed and picked up her phone from the floor. The screen was dark, but the little blue light was blinking reminding her of the unread message. With a sigh, she woke up her phone and then opened the texting app.

Ashley furrowed her brow when she read the first message. She read out loud, "What are you talking about?

MOM! Please pick up. I've called three times!" She looked at her call log and didn't see any missed calls. The second text was almost a copy and paste of the first one. Same unavailable number.

This was getting weird. Since she had sent a text to the number yesterday saying it was a wrong number and hadn't gotten a response until now, she had forgotten about it all together. She had hoped it meant they had figured out the right number and the issue was resolved. What was going on with the phone company? Was it even possible to get phone numbers mixed up or signals or something? Maybe it was time to clue Aja in—on these texts anyway. Aja could crack anything. If there was something there, she would be able to figure it out.

As if on cue, her phone rang, and Aja's face showed up. *Perfect timing*, she thought.

"Hey Aja. You have amazing timing, you know that?" Ashley said with a grin. She settled back on her bed, leaning against the headboard.

The other end of the line remained quiet. Aja didn't say anything. Ashley wasn't even sure she was still on the line. "Aja? What's going on?" Ashley pulled the phone from her ear and looked at the screen. It still showed Aja's face, and the time was still moving. So, the call wasn't disconnected.

"Hello?" Ashley asked, hesitantly. When no one answered again, she pressed the *end* button. *What the heck is going on?* she thought.

Ashley stared at her black screen again, wondering what to do next. It was now almost eight, but that meant it was only seven where Aja was. She knew her sister was an early riser and may even be on her way to work at the moment, but she wasn't sure if she would be alone, and she didn't want to risk her uncle hearing anything.

With a sigh, she woke up her phone again and found Aja's contact and Ashley opened her messages. She figured it was safer to send a text and make sure her sister was alone first.

Hey Aja. Can you call me when you get a chance? I have to talk to you about something. She attached a heart emoji and then sent it off into the abyss.

Almost immediately, her phone rang, Aja's smile lighting up her screen again. Ashley quickly pressed the answer button and took a breath. "Aja?" She knew it sounded like a question, but she had to be sure.

"Yeah it's me, what's up? You sound kinda weird," Aja's concerned voice quickly replied.

Ashley let out a breath of air, not realizing she had been holding it in. "Thank god," she whispered.

"Uh, Ash? What's wrong?" Aja's voice was full of worry, but Ashley couldn't dismiss it yet.

Shaking her head, she focused on her sister's voice. "Hey, can you switch to video or are you driving? Actually, are you alone right now?" Ashley was trying not to sound anxious, but she was also aware that her sister knew her very well and would know something was wrong.

Her screen beeped with the notification to turn on videochat and she pulled the phone away from her ear and waited for Aja's face to appear. When it did, she smiled, relieved that it was actually her sister this time.

"Ok, what's going on, Ashley? Something is up and you are kinda scaring me here," Aja said with her brows lifted in expectation. Ashley almost laughed at the look.

Aja looked like a mom expecting her child to reveal a lie or something.

Ashley breathed in again and then stared at her sister. "Um, remember when I thought you called me before, but it wasn't you?" When Aja nodded, Ashley continued, "Well it happened again just a little bit ago." She bit her cheek waiting for her sister's reaction.

To her surprise, Aja was quiet and looked like she was looking somewhere else, avoiding Ashley's eyes.

"Aja, what is it?" Ashley asked tentatively. "What's wrong?"

Aja's eyes moved back to the screen, and she sighed. "Has there been anything else? Like random texts or anything?"

Ashley's eyes widened. "Yes, but I sent a response yesterday telling them they had a wrong number. I thought it took care of it, but then I got two more messages this morning, but they basically said the same thing. Why? What do you think it is? It's just a misunderstanding, right?" She almost crossed her fingers in hopes that it was nothing.

"Ugh. I was hoping I was wrong, but I am a little worried now. Ash, I need you to turn off your location on your phone, ok?" Aja sounded nervous and Ashley noticed she kept glancing to the side. It looked like she was already at work and was sitting at her desk. Maybe she was watching for Sam to come by or something, Ashley thought.

"Why do I need to turn off my location? That seems random and weird, Aja," she replied. She wasn't understanding.

Aja took a deep breath and focused on Ashley again. "Ok, let me try to explain my theory. I am thinking someone is tracking you somehow. When you get a call or text, it triggers your phone and location and then records it. It's how we find people who are missing, or people we are just looking for, and then try to track their movements. If there is any communication on the phone, we can track it. Our stuff is a little more sophisticated than that and we can track a phone as long as it is turned on by the signal it sends, even without an interaction. So, if you turn off your location, then it can't be tracked."

Ashley was silent as she listened to Aja talk. Someone was tracking her? Who and more importantly why? Her thoughts were spinning. She tried to think of anyone who would do that here but came up empty. She didn't know anyone here. And the few people she did know, she trusted. Maybe she was too trusting though she thought.

Ashley tried to think of the people she did know. Sharon and Gary, but they knew where she was most of the time. She willingly told them, so they wouldn't have any reason to track her this way. Even if she didn't tell them where she was going, they wouldn't need to track her for anything. Trish didn't want her around even when she was invited, so she wouldn't have any reason either. The only other person she had contact with here was the professor.

Ashley let out a frustrated groan. "Who would need to track me, Aja? That just doesn't even add up. Unless…" Her thoughts spun as she actually started to get irritated. "Do you think Sam is?" That would make sense in his overprotective mindset. Then he wouldn't have to question her all the time.

Aja laughed. "No, Ash. He could track you without blinking if he wanted to. He wouldn't have to send weird texts or calls."

"Ugh! I guess. But I can't think of anyone here who would want or need to do that. Are you sure it isn't just a glitch in the phone company or something?"

Aja sighed. "No. One time maybe, but the texts are a whole other thing. That just seems like an easy way to check a location, especially if you respond. Once you open the message it triggers the location of the device. I just think the best thing to do is turn off your location."

"Ok, ok. There shouldn't be any reason to leave it on anyway. There is literally nothing going on here and I am pretty much either here at the apartment or the school." Her mind jumped to the car she noticed on the street by Sharon's house, but she hadn't seen it since. And then there was Professor Roslin, who was acting a little weird. But nothing stood out to her as threatening.

"Ash, I think we should tell Sam though. This is weird and you remember what he said about enemies of dad trying to get to us. He could pull some strings and maybe track something else or trace your phone somehow." Aja's eyes were flitting back and forth again.

Ashley resisted rolling her eyes. It seemed like everyone was paranoid. Jacob and now Aja, too. "No, Aja. This is all just some weird thing. No one is tracking me. There's no reason to! You and Jacob are nuts." She tried to sound convincing but even she had to admit it was strange. "Besides, if I turn off my location, problem solved, right? It's fine, Aja. I promise. And Sharon and Gary are watching out for me too. Jacob should be coming back in a week or two, so I won't be alone anymore. OK?"

"Jacob's worried too? Ashley, you have to be careful. You don't know anyone there! Maybe he's right and I'm right and we should talk to Sam," Aja said with a little more force in her voice.

"No, Aja. It's fine. You are overreacting. It's not like anything has even happened! How about this--if something else happens that's weird, I'll talk to Sam myself. Is that acceptable?" She knew Jacob was worried about something else, but she couldn't tell her twin that part yet.

She had to just keep them both at bay for a little while until she had a reason to invoke the wrath of her uncle. She had no doubt he would either come out here himself and drag her home or start his own investigation, taking the info out of her hands, probably forever. She would never find out if this person was real, or if they were actually a sibling of hers and Aja's.

"Ugh, fine!" Aja conceded. "You are so stubborn, you know that? But you have to promise if anything strange at all happens, you call me immediately. Got it?" Aja was on a roll and the worry for her sister was clear in her voice. It was all that kept Ashley from teasing her even more.

"I got it. And I do promise. But I just think it's a weird coincidence. I'll turn off my location to make you feel better though. Happy?" Ashley smiled as she watched her sister scowl at her through the phone.

Suddenly Sam's face appeared in the frame behind Aja. "Hey Sam!" Ashley grinned and waved at her uncle.

"Hi Ashley. Are you behaving yourself out there?" Sam leaned over Aja's shoulder with his eyebrows raised.

Ashley laughed. "Of course not! What fun would that be?"

Sam just nodded and grinned back at her. "Figures. When do classes start?" he asked.

Ashley swore she saw a look cross his face, as if he knew she was lying about school, but it quickly disappeared as he looked up. Ashley breathed a sigh of relief as Aja jumped in, her eyes also rising above the phone. Something was happening there, Ashley thought.

"Uh, Ash we gotta go. Talk to you soon and remember our deal!" Aja pointed her finger at the screen and Ashley snorted at her.

"Go work! Talk soon! Love you sis," she said with a smile and small wave as the line disconnected.

Ashley sat back and dropped her phone next to her. She'd managed to get lucky not having to tell Sam about classes, but she knew it would come again. There was something in his eyes, she remembered. Did he already know she was lying? She tried to brush that aside. If she had managed to get Aja to believe her, Sam should. After all, their twin connection was off the charts in tune. She could even sense Aja's unease with the phone thing, which is why she agreed to turn off her location. Remembering that, she picked up her phone and did just that.

She dropped it beside her again and stretched her back and shoulders out. She tried to think of what to do today. She had sent the letter to Jacob last night like she agreed. The new Gmail address was done. Thinking of her conversation with Aja, she decided to look at the new email again and see what name came up. She didn't want to give away too much info there either. She was relieved when it just came up with her first name and last initial like Jacob promised.

Ashley decided to get up and get ready for the day. Maybe go for a walk but given the time it was probably too hot already. With a sigh, she got up and got her stuff to take a shower. She still had to go grocery shopping, and she thought about going to the library again. If for no other reason than just to sit and read in a different environment. She remembered the last time she was there and saw the photo Professor Roslin had. Maybe she wouldn't go there today after all, she thought grimly. She was still a little freaked about the eyes in the photo. She saw them somewhere, she knew she did.

It didn't take her long to get ready for the day. She grabbed her list and keys and headed out the door, locking it behind her. She hadn't left her room since the morning before when she went to see Trish. Thoughts of that visit came back to her, and she thought about how Trish had spoken to Sharon. Then again, it might not even be the same Sharon, and they were probably talking about someone else anyway, even if the odds of that were slim. Ashley decided she was just getting paranoid and needed to snap out of it.

Quickly skipping down the steps, Ashley looked at her list. She nodded absently as she read through everything. Sam had given her a good chunk of cash to get through for a while until she could find a job or get started at school. She was grateful he was able to provide them with financial help for school, so they didn't have to worry about working a lot during school or taking out a ton of student loans.

Aja was able to subsidize her education with her internship with Sam, but Ashley wasn't able to find an internship that paid well in education. She did work a little bit at the coffee shop on campus, but it was barely enough to cover gas for the week. Luckily Aja didn't mind putting extra in, especially since she was making really good money as a student intern. Ashley had to admit though she felt a little guilty taking money from Sam right now since she wasn't going to school or working as she had led him to believe.

Ashley left Sharon a note saying she was going to the grocery store and then maybe the beach or something. As she made her way out of the house, she noticed how quiet it was. Sharon wasn't around and she knew that Gary usually went golfing or something in the mornings with friends and old colleagues from before retirement. She made sure to check the door when she left to make sure it was locked. They hadn't said anything, but then again, she wasn't around yesterday either.

Ashley was learning to start her car and open the windows before getting in. As she stood outside the car, waiting for it to cool a little bit, she leaned on the frame. She looked down the street where the car had parked days ago. The street was empty today, not even cars in the driveways. It was calm and quiet, she thought. The sun was shining brightly, and the sky didn't have a cloud in it.

Ashley got in her car and closed the windows again, noticing the air conditioning had cooled the inside down. The heat from outside, even at nine in the morning, was still too much to ride around with open windows. The humidity was the main issue. There was no cooling off when the moisture in the air was so stifling, even when the temperature wasn't half bad.

For some reason, she drove slowly out of the development. When she got to the corner to exit to the main road, she wondered if there was some subconscious reason she moved so slowly through the tree lined street. Was she still worried about the car being hidden somewhere?

Shaking the thought away, she looked around her. It was a beautiful day--if you could handle the heat. The bright sun and clear sky made it a good day to go to the beach, she thought. Maybe there was a reason she had put that on her note to Sharon. Being by the ocean with the waves and seagulls might be just what she needed to regroup and figure out what she should do next, while she waited for the mysterious relative to email her.

She pulled into the parking lot for Food Lion, the grocery store chain here. She walked through the aisles picking up the things she needed and just looking around. She had been here one other time with Jacob, but they had only bought a few things. She liked to look around and see the differences in food options compared to Minnesota.

By the time she made it to the checkout, she had spent nearly an hour in the store. She was surprised to see the time. She made her way to the self-checkout and quickly went through the process. The city had banned plastic bags, so she bought one of their reusable ones and paid for her things. She had only one bag of food but had some cold things she needed to get back to her place before it got too hot in the car, which she knew wouldn't take long at all.

Having made up her mind what to do today, Ashley made her way back to the house to put her food away and gather what she wanted for the beach. She made a mental note to get one of those beach chairs she saw others had when she went with Jacob. For now, she would use a beach towel instead.

As she neared the house, she thought she saw a car pull out of the driveway of Sharon and Gary's house. It was a dark color, but she wasn't sure if it was black or a really dark blue. As she slowed and pulled to the side to let it pass, she thought it was Professor Roslin driving. The man looked away at the last second, so she wasn't sure though. She was focused on the driver and forgot to look at the color of the car. Looking in her rearview mirror, she still couldn't decide if it was black. She did notice the emblem on the back indicating it was a Toyota. But with Professor Roslin in the driver's seat, she doubted it was the same one she saw on the street before. It did have four doors, but she didn't remember the kind of car she had seen then.

Ashley felt her pulse rising slightly as she continued slowly to the house. Sharon was outside watering her flowers and not looking the least bit different than she always did. Ashley sighed. She needed to stop being paranoid. Maybe the car had actually pulled out of the neighbor's driveway and not theirs.

She parked her car and got out, grabbing her bag. She waved at Sharon who waved back, but then quickly turned back to her flowers. Ashley shrugged and moved to put her food away. She changed upstairs and quickly grabbed her notebook and pencils. She threw them in a canvas bag she had along with a towel, the letter, and ancestry report. She was back downstairs in less than ten minutes.

When she got back outside, she noticed Sharon was gone, and so was her car. Weird, she thought. Then shrugged and got into her own vehicle and started to head out. She hadn't been inside long enough for it to get sauna hot yet, but the car had already lost its comfortable coolness. Ashley started up the car and wasted no time turning up the air conditioning again and then pulling out of the driveway. It was the middle of the week so she didn't anticipate a ton of traffic on the way to the coast, but she knew she would have to go to Assateague for some quiet beach time since it was still tourist season in Ocean City, which was fine with her anyway.

Ashley blasted her radio as she drove, wishing she could have the windows open blowing through her braids as she drove. She allowed her body to move with the music while she enjoyed the bright sunshine and attempted to block out any thoughts from the last couple days.

As she drove, she looked around her. The scenery was like driving through the country, but instead of cows and horses there were farmer's market stands on the sides of the road and fields. The fields slowly gave way to trees lining both sides of the highway, reminding her of driving up to the north shore in Minnesota.

Ashley got closer to the beach, and she started to see the more touristy things. There were hotels and motels offering cheap accommodations for easy and close access to the ocean, without the craziness of being right in the middle of it. Then there were the stores that were likely overpriced and catering to the tourist on vacation who didn't have room to pack things like sunscreen and flip flops, which allowed the owners to overcharge for them. Local attractions for families like mini golf and go cart tracks were scattered around as well.

She passed Berlin, a small town that had a charming feel to it. She made a mental note to come walk through the streets here. From the advertisements, it seemed like a quaint little place with a small-town feel. She stopped at the stoplight and looked around. She glanced to her side and was startled to see a car next to her with a driver who looked a lot like Professor Roslin—again.

The light turned green and the car behind her honked—something else she noticed here. In true East Coast fashion, or maybe stereotype, they loved their car horns. You had better pay attention when the light turned green, or you would be subjected to the infamous beep behind you urging you to move.

She pressed the gas a little too hard and looked sideways to see the car that was next to her, lagging slightly behind. She watched her rearview carefully as the car switched lanes to be behind her, with two cars in between them. She caught her breath in her throat as she tried to focus on the road in front of her and the car behind.

The car that honked at her was impatient and revved its engine to then speed past her—only to be stopped at the next red light, now next to her. Ashley chanced a glance to the side and made note of the bright red sports car. The driver looked over and scowled at her, which made her laugh, even with her unease about the car behind her.

She shook her head and turned back to her mirror. The light turned green in front of her, and she slowly made her way into the intersection, glancing behind her at the dark car trailing now with only one car between them. She changed lanes, trying to gauge if the car was truly following her. The car behind her, acting as a buffer for her, sped up and was by her side for an instant. The driver looked over and smirked, nodding his head and then pulled ahead of her.

Ashley watched as the car moved in front of her. The dark colored car with the professor look-alike driver pulled up but didn't go alongside her. It stayed back a little ways so she could have changed lanes if she wanted to. Instead, she looked ahead and saw a shopping mall ahead with various small shops. She pulled into the turn lane and watched as the car in the other lane slowed as well.

She tried to think of everything Sam had told her when he was teaching her and Aja how to drive and what to do in certain situations. She and Aja had laughed at his ideas of what to do if they were followed. Only Sam seemed to think it wasn't funny. Now she was grateful for the training. She watched the car carefully as she had come to a stop at the intersection, waiting for traffic to clear so she could make her left-hand turn.

Don't stop with someone following you, he would say. *Just keep driving and turning randomly until they either turn the other way or you are somewhere safe like a police station. And then you call me immediately if you drive in circles and they follow your ridiculous route.*

The car slowed next to her and then made an abrupt right-hand turn. The parking lot it turned into looked like it had two entrances, and one led the car back across the street—right into the place Ashley was trying to turn into. *Ok now what?* she thought.

She looked ahead of her and decided to make the turn and then if he followed, she would turn again and get back onto 50 and see what he did. So, Ashley turned into the lot and slowly drove through, watching to see what the car would do, pretending she was looking at the stores deciding where to stop.

A car suddenly pulled out of a spot in front of her, causing Ashley to slam on her brakes to avoid hitting the vehicle. But then it stopped, halfway out of the spot. Ashley glanced behind her and felt her pulse quicken. Maybe she watched too many movies, but it felt like she was being trapped and this was a setup. She watched as if in slow motion as the dark car pulled up behind her.

Ashley stared in her mirror waiting. She wasn't sure what she was waiting for, but she was sure something horrible would be happening soon. A beep cut into her thoughts, and she startled, looking ahead of her. The car that had pulled out had vanished. She glanced behind her again and saw the car was moving closer to her. She faced forward again and pulled ahead, moving toward the exit. She quickly pressed her gas pedal and as soon as she could, she turned back onto highway 50.

She avoided her mirror for a few minutes, afraid of what she might see. When Ashley finally looked behind her, she noticed the road was clear. There was no one behind her and the road stretched for a while with no other cars. It surprised her to see the road so empty, but she didn't care at the moment. She took in a deep breath of air and tried to calm her racing thoughts. She found she was still heading toward the beach. Instead of heading to the more isolated Assateague, she decided to move toward the people and hopefully feel a little safer with hundreds of people around her.

Chapter 15

Ashley found a parking spot squeezed in between two other vehicles. She wanted to try to hide or at least surround her own car with others—thankful for the white color now since it was pretty common. If someone was following her, she wanted it to be a little bit of a challenge to find her. It wasn't hard to hide her Rogue though. The lot was almost full.

Moving toward the pay station to pay for her parking, she hesitated, wondering if this was another way for someone to track her. She decided to use the emergency card Sam had given her so it would track back to him and not her just in case.

She gathered her things and quickly moved through the lot to the edge of the beach. Once on the sand, she moved toward the water, looking everywhere for the biggest group of people she could find. She would try to blend in with the crowds, making it difficult to find her. Sitting alone on the edge of the beach, which was her original intent, was no longer an option. Today she was glad she didn't have a lot to carry as she moved along the sand, as quickly as she could as her feet sunk into the hot granules pouring over her flip flops.

There was a group of girls, most African American, playing a game of volleyball, so Ashley set her things down

Brenda Benning

a just a little ways from theirs. She would look like she was just taking a break from the game if anyone noticed her at all. She laid out her towel and sat down, staring out at the ocean. Her thoughts were swirling in her mind as she tried to figure out if someone was actually following her or if she was just imagining things.

A loud "Heads up!" and a tsunami of sand covering her brought Ashley's attention back to her surroundings. She flinched with the sand flying everywhere and then saw a girl next to her laughing hysterically. Ashley couldn't help but smile at the girl who had dropped next to Ashley holding her stomach.

"Hey! Are you alright?" she asked between giggles. "I'm sorry. I tried to dive but saw you at the last minute and had to dodge instead." She sat up and brushed the sand off her thighs and rested her elbows on her knees, staring at Ashley.

Ashley brushed the sand off her as well and smiled. "I'm fine. Only a little sand, no harm done."

The girl nodded and glanced back at her group, waiting for her to join them again. She turned back to Ashley and grinned. "Wanna play?" She tipped her head to the waiting group.

"Um…" Ashley glanced at the girls and then back at the stranger next to her. "I guess so. I don't have anything else to do." She shrugged and moved to stand as the girl did the same.

"Cool! I'm Raelynn. Come meet everyone," she said with a little more enthusiasm than Ashley was prepared for. She held a hand out to Ashley and pulled her the rest of the way up. "Hey guys, I got an eighth! Now we can play four on four!"

"Great!" one yelled, while another yelled, "Rae! Get the ball!"

"Oops, sorry. Gotta grab the ball. Be right back!" and she disappeared down the beach to get the ball that had rolled almost all the way to the water.

Ashley waited for her to come back and then walked with her to the group. Raelynn chatted with Ashley while they walked to the group. All of the group were girls and five were African American or biracial, while two Ashley thought probably had Hispanic roots. Every one of them welcomed Ashley and were friendly.

Raelynn was the lightest skinned of all of them and with her light brown hair and bright blue eyes, Ashley was surprised when she called a woman who was significantly darker skinned than she was her mom, who was sitting a few yards from their game. She had a younger teenage girl and boy with her who were much darker than Raelynn. Seeming to notice Ashley's surprise, Raelynn smiled and just shrugged, her freckled nose wrinkling slightly with her smile.

"It's a long story," she said with an eye roll and swing of her arm. "I seemed to have inherited all my white mom's traits and only got my dad's wide nose and ability to tan easily. Honesty is my stepmom but has been my mom since I was little." She laughed and then waved Ashley to follow her.

Ashley felt bad for even making any judgements about Raelynn, someone she just met, but Raelynn didn't seemed bothered by it at all. Ashley wasn't one to judge anyway. She and Aja had a different skin tone than Sam, her mom, or dad. Sam was biracial but he was a little darker than her mom. Her dad was definitely white, but his skin was always tanned from working outside, not that she really even knew what he did for work. She only knew construction was sometimes what he did.

She remembered her mom had fairly pale skin as well, but Ashley always brushed it aside that she was never outside, so she just looked pale. Her father would actually forbid them from going outside most days. Ashley never understood why, and her mom rarely offered a reason and just found things to do inside. Being little kids, they wanted to go ride bikes or go to the park or something. But they never really did those things until Sam took them in.

An arm wrapping around Ashley's shoulder broke her from her thoughts. She looked over to see Raelynn with her arm around Ashley and pointing a finger at one of the other girls.

"I found her, she's on my team," she insisted. Then she leaned over and whispered in Ashley's ear, "Can you play? Please tell me you can play."

Ashley grinned at her. "I'm not gonna lie, I'm not great, but I think I can hold my own." She gathered from the looks of the group, they were picking teams, and Raelynn had just claimed her. She realized she may have just made her first friend since coming here. Volleyball wasn't her best sport, but she was athletic enough she could always hold her own in gym classes and intramurals. The point was to have a little fun and she needed that right now.

After teams were finally decided, Ashley was pulled to the other side of the net by Raelynn. She stood next to her new friend and Raelynn introduced the other two on their team. Valaria was a petite girl with straight jet-black hair and dark brown eyes. She had perfectly tanned skin, likely her Hispanic heritage, and a smile that Ashley was sure would soften anyone's heart. The other girl was built like Ashley. Skyler was tall and athletic, muscular but not in a masculine body builder type.

Ashley chuckled at their front row with the shortest and tallest next to each other. "Don't we need some more height up front, Raelynn?" she asked, pointing at the other two.

Raelynn laughed. "Nope, just wait. Val has some hops!" She threw the ball to the other side and yelled, "Jazz, you're up!"

Ashley quickly learned their names. Jasmine, aka Jazzy, was the tallest on the other side. She had braids a lot like Ashley's, tied neatly back. Serenity was slightly shorter but not nearly as thin. She laughed when they were introduced saying her mom had hoped her name would reflect her personality—spoiler, she was very wrong. Ashley couldn't wait to get to know her better. LaDasha and Fuschia behaved like siblings, but Ashley didn't think they were. Both were slightly shorter than Ashley and darker skin toned. LaDasha kept her hair loose and it laid nicely on her shoulders, while Fuschia had hers pulled up in a tight bun on top of her head.

It seemed they were all competitive, which Ashley found a little intimidating. She had never played competitively and wasn't sure she would be able to keep up. Raelynn came over at that point and put her arm across Ashley's shoulder.

"Don't worry. This is really for fun. They might get a little over the top when they aren't winning. But don't worry, We really just want to have fun. This team," she swung her hand indicating the team Ashley was now a part of, "is just in it for fun—and we happen to beat them most of the time because they start to bicker like old married people." She snickered and Ashley couldn't help but like her.

"Ok, let's go!" Fuschia yelled from the other side, her impatience blaringly obvious.

The waves made it hard to hear, but Ashley got the message as Raelynn backed off and moved to her spot on the makeshift court. It didn't take long for Ashley to realize how accurately Raelynn portrayed her friends. They must have known each other for a long time. She felt a pang in her heart, realizing what she had missed, not having friends like this growing up who knew everything about you.

The very first serve went right to Raelynn, who passed it with ease to Sky, who spiked it into the sand on the other side of the net as soon as she touched it. She skipped back to high-five her teammates and then turned back to the other team. She popped her hip, putting one hand on it and then swung her other hand up showing her forefinger. "That's one to zero, ladies!"

Jazzy grumbled from the other side and threw the ball back to them. Ashley served it barely clearing the net, making Serenity dive—and miss—as the ball fell to the ground.

Raelynn, Sky, and Valaria all crowded Ashley and cheered. Sky swung around again and yelled, "Two to zero!"

The other girls grumbled some more and Fuschia called back, "Did you pay her to show up, Rae?"

Ashley knew she was joking, but there was also a little bit of a bite to her words. "They *are* really competitive," she thought out loud.

The group played until they were covered in sweat and sand. Deciding to take a break and go for a quick swim to wash off, they raced to the edge of the surf. Just as they reached the water, Raelynn flew forward headfirst into the water. Ashley stopped and stared as her new friend stood up from the ankle-deep water, sputtering.

"Really, Sahara? Come back here!" The teenage girl who was sitting with Raelynn's mom earlier was running in the opposite direction laughing like a hyena.

Raelynn started to run after her but stopped after a few steps. Her face broke out in an evil grin as she stared, crossing her arms at her sister. Her eyes tracked slightly up on the beach though, causing Ashley to try to see what Raelynn saw. As Sahara was looking back at a planted and smirking Raelynn, she was tackled from behind by a tall and thin boy who looked to be about her age. Sand flew everywhere and Raelynn doubled over laughing.

Ashley grinned and walked to Raelynn's side. "Do you know him?" she asked.

Raelynn glanced back. "Yeah, that's her boyfriend Kiah. He shushed me when he saw her running his way." She shrugged. "Perfect payback." She gave him a mocking salute in thanks.

They moved toward the water again. It felt cold against Ashley's heated, sand-covered skin. But she welcomed the break from the heat. As the water lapped around her calves, she relaxed in the gentle waves. She wasn't brave enough to go too far in, but she enjoyed the coolness of the water against her skin. Raelynn sat down where she was and waved her hands gently across the surface of the water. Ashley copied her and gasped slightly when the cold water hit her stomach.

It didn't take long for the couple to come walking up hand in hand to Ashley and Raelynn. Sahara splashed her sister and scowled. "You could've warned me, you know."

Raelynn laughed loudly. "Right, because that wouldn't take all the fun out of it or anything. Besides you got what you deserved. Who am I to stop Kiah from doing my dirty work for me." She shrugged and blocked the sun with her hand to squint at Kiah. "Thanks, bro. Perfect timing."

Ashley giggled as they fist-bumped. Kiah's eyes shifted to Ashley, and he studied her.

"Do I know you? You look really familiar," he said slowly, narrowing his eyes.

Ashley shook her head. "I doubt it. I just moved here a couple of weeks ago and Raelynn is the first person I've met since I moved." She tipped her head in Raelynn's direction.

Kiah continued to stare at her, making her slightly uncomfortable. Eventually he shrugged and moved closer to Sahara. He mumbled something Ashley didn't quite hear, and she shifted her gaze to the waves. She usually didn't think much of people thinking she looked familiar. Since she and Aja were identical, they likely met her sister before they met her. It created a comical deja vu for people. For a moment she forgot Aja wasn't here too.

"So, what's going on later, Rae? We were gonna hit a movie or something. Probably after dinner though 'cause you know how mom is about missing dinner." Sahara rolled her eyes dramatically making the small group chuckle.

"Hm, I'm not sure. What are you up to Ashley? Wanna hang out for a while longer? You could get to know these idiots when their pride isn't on the line," she said with a grin, motioning to her friends now hip deep in the water splashing each other a little further away.

Ashley nodded. "I don't have anything except a date with my phone and boyfriend later."

"Where are you staying?" Sahara asked. "We can meet up later if we change our plans." She turned to her boyfriend, who was still looking at Ashley. Sahara elbowed him. "Too bad she has a boyfriend. She might be perfect for your idiot brother."

Kiah looked over at her and scowled. "I wouldn't do that to anyone. He's been so grumpy lately. He used to hang out like we do with Rae and now he's just a cranky old man." Kiah groaned and then swooped Sahara's petite body up in his arms and carried her out to the ocean, with her kicking and screaming to be put down.

Ashley and Raelynn laughed as they watched him drop her in about thigh deep water, making her go under. She came up swinging her arms crazily at him, splashing water everywhere around them.

"You guys get along really great for stepsiblings," Ashley commented.

Raelynn shrugged. "Yeah, I guess. I mean they are all I have ever known. My stepmom raised me, adopted me and all that. I have her, Sahara, and Jericho. Haven't seen my dad since I was like eight. For fourteen years it's just been the four of us." Her eyes were fixed on the couple still splashing in the water.

Ashley was silent, not sure if she should say anything. But Raelynn didn't seem sad, just matter of fact.

"What happened to your mom?" she asked quietly.

Raelynn looked over at Ashley and shrugged again. "I guess she died giving birth to me. My dad did what he could until he met Honesty. Then he disappeared. No trace, no forwarding address, nothing." Her voice had a little wistfulness to it when she talked about her dad. Ashley couldn't relate to missing her dad who has been out of her life for about the same amount of time as Raelynn's dad.

"I'm sorry," Ashley said, not really knowing what to say.

"It's ok. It is what it is. I can't do anything to change it. And I have a great mom. I don't know what would've happened to me if she didn't step up and keep me with her. She adopted me so the county wouldn't come after me. It was more of a formality on her end. She has always said I am her daughter regardless of blood. She still loves my dad. We just all wish we knew what happened to him."

Ashley nodded. "That has to be so hard not knowing. At least I know where my dad is, not that I really care though." She realized too late that what she had thought was actually said out loud.

Raelynn didn't look shocked though. She just nodded. "Yeah, that's not uncommon unfortunately. Sky, Fuschia, and Jazzy's dads are all in prison too. I think not knowing is the hardest part though. My dad was a good guy, from what I remember anyway. Hopefully one day we will know what happened to him."

Ashley stared at her with her mouth wide open. How did she know she meant her dad was in prison? *And she was so nonchalant about it*, she thought.

The rest of their group had made their way back to where Raelynn and Ashley were sitting and plopped down in the water in a circle, splashing water everywhere. Ashley covered her eyes blocking the water.

"So, Ashley, what are you doing here? I heard you just moved," Jazzy asked, pulling Ashley's attention next to her.

Ashley glanced around the group and noticed everyone was looking at her with interest. "I was looking at SU for grad school," she said simply, turning back to Jazzy.

"I went to SU for my psych degree," Raelynn said excitedly. "Are you living in Salisbury?"

"I am," Ashley said with a nod. "I am staying in an older couple's apartment on their third floor."

The group nodded. "That should make it easy to all get together then," Serenity offered. "We all live in Salisbury too." She motioned with her hand around the group.

Ashley was surprised they were all so close together. She was suddenly grateful for the last-minute decision to go to the beach today. She wouldn't have met this group if she hadn't. They all seemed to welcome her without much hesitation, and she was thankful for the company—and the distraction.

It didn't take long before Sahara and Kiah came splashing up to them and plop down in the water as well. Sahara had intentionally splashed Raelynn, causing her to squeal and splash her sister back.

Raelynn looked over at Ashley. "I have to go home for dinner, so I can meet up with you all later. Ashley, you wanna come with me? I don't live too far from campus, so we are probably close to each other anyway."

Ashley thought for a second. "I don't have anything to do, so sure!" She had to eat anyway, right? And it felt good to be around people her age again. She just had to make sure she made it back to talk to Jacob and watch their next movie. It had quickly become her new favorite thing—even though it had only been one night.

The group slowly got out of the water, and then scattered to clean up their things, including the net. Ashley went to where she left her things, surprised to see the water had almost reached her towel with the tide coming up. She realized it was later than she thought. She shook out her towel and folded it into her bag. She had slid her phone into the bag when she joined the volleyball game, and she was glad she got back before it was swept up in the rising surf. The heat, however, had caused it to shut down at some point.

Making her way back to the group, Ashley felt something tug at her heart. She felt like for once, she was right where she belonged. She had never had a group of friends, even though she was more of an extrovert than her sister. They had just moved around a lot and because of her fears and trauma so young, she found it was a little harder to trust new people. By the time she warmed up to people, Sam's assignment would change, and they would be moving again.

Maybe it was the people, or just being here, but she felt like she was at peace for a change. She wouldn't jump to calling it home just yet, but she just felt good.

Serenity and Jazzy were playfully pushing each other, trying to trip the other first in the deep sand. The rest of their little group was heading to the parking lot. Raelynn and Sahara were talking quietly off to the side and Ashley felt Kiah's eyes on her again. Ashley looked up to meet them and raised her eyebrows.

"Why do you keep looking at me like that?" she asked, feeling self-conscious under his gaze.

Kiah shrugged and dropped his eyes. "Sorry, You just look so familiar, and I can't figure out why. I don't mean to make you uncomfortable. It's just weird. I'm sorry, I really don't mean to be creepy." He smiled and shrugged.

Ashley just shook her head, not really knowing what to say. She did feel a little creeped out by his stares. She glanced back to Raelynn and her sister, who were separating now. Raelynn stepped over next to Ashley and threw her arm around her shoulders. It seemed to be her thing, Ashley thought with a grin.

"Ok, so we are going to go home and change and then meet up after dinner. You are welcome to come back to our place for dinner if you want, otherwise I can text you where to meet us," Raelynn said looking at the group and then Ashley.

Ashley shrugged. "I'm good with whatever. I just need to be back around eight. Here, let me put my number in your phone, or give me your number and I'll text you. My phone overheated so I need to cool it off." She smiled sheepishly. The rest of the group seemed to have taken precautions to prevent their phones from not working because they were all checking them now.

"Oh, yeah, that's something you learn quickly," Raelynn laughed. "Here." She handed her phone to Ashley after she unlocked it and opened a new contact.

After she handed it back to her new friend, Ashley gave a wave. "I'll see you all later, then! Thanks for inviting me to play and letting me hang with all of you."

The group waved and then everyone went their separate ways. Ashley smiled to herself as she walked to her car, barely remembering where she parked due to the events of the day. As she neared her car, she remembered the earlier concerns she had and looked around to see if anyone was following her or if any of the cars parked near hers was the same as the one following her before.

Grateful for the many people still around, she ducked into her steaming hot car, cursing herself for forgetting to cool it down first. She started the engine, opened her windows, and then turned on the air conditioner. The heat from the seat reminded her that her legs were still bare. Surprisingly her suit and shorts were already dry. *One benefit of the heat*, she mused.

Ashley started to pull out of her spot when a horn blared behind her. She swung around to see what happened because she hadn't even moved a foot. She laughed when she saw Sahara hanging out the passenger window waving with Kiah driving. They moved and Ashley couldn't help but notice the car Kiah was driving looked a lot like the one that she thought she saw Professor Roslin in before—and the one she thought followed her on the way here.

"That's crazy," she murmured out loud. "I'm sure there are a lot of cars similar to that." She shook her head violently to clear her racing thoughts.

She slowly pulled out of her spot and then watched to make sure she put a lot of space between the two cars, probably more intentionally than she meant to. Once she felt it was clear, she moved out onto the main roads and headed back to her apartment. She didn't relax the entire drive until she was parked in front of the house. She was surprised to see the parking spaces empty. She took a couple deep breaths and then headed into the house to shower and get ready to meet her new friends.

Chapter 16

After a quick shower, Ashley dressed in a purple cutoff tank top and jean shorts, showing off the belly button ring she and Aja had done right after their eighteenth birthday. It irritated Sam but he ended up paying for it as their gifts, grateful they at least waited until they were eighteen. She grabbed her phone, now thankfully cooled off, and her keys then headed back out. The texts with Raelynn were like talking to an old friend. It was strange, she thought, how easily and quickly they had connected and become friends. Ashley wasn't like her shy and introverted sister, and it seemed like Raelynn was similar in personality, making the connection even easier.

She couldn't wait to tell Jacob all about the day when she got home that night. Once she was secured in her seat belt, Ashley pulled up the text thread between her and Raelynn to get her address. She found it and pressed it to activate GPS. It wasn't too far from Sharon and Gary's and she was relieved to learn she wouldn't be driving on any backroads. She shivered thinking about driving to Trish's in the dark. Her thoughts drifted to what that house might look like at midnight and then she laughed out loud at the visuals her brain came up with.

The tinny voice of the GPS let her know that her journey had begun as she exited the driveway. She looked at the empty street. It was definitely an older established neighborhood with very few kids out and about. There were a couple people walking dogs, but not many even though they were in a development and not out in the country.

Ashley pulled into a single lane rocky driveway about seven minutes later but pulled back out. She didn't want to block anyone in or out of the driveway and parked on the street in front of the house instead. Raelynn's house was on the other side of the college in a community of smaller homes. Some didn't have garages, but then Ashley remembered some of her research showed it didn't get super cold or snowy here, so they didn't really need garages. She was surprised that she only needed to take a couple of turns from Sharon's to Raelynn's and they were streets she even recognized.

The house was cute. It was a deep red color with white shutters on the two windows flanking the bright yellow front door. There were two dormers with windows above the lower ones. A small porch just big enough for two lawn chairs on either side of the front door stood at the end of a short sidewalk.

The house was in fairly good repair, and she could tell it was well cared for. Ashley could see the wear at the edges of the siding where it met the foundation. The window screens looked a little dirty, and one window was missing its screen, but they were not nearly as bad as Trish's. The sidewalk leading to the porch was cracked in multiple places, showing its age, but the porch stood as if it were newer than the rest of the house.

The lawn, though small, was neatly cut and picked up. Many of the other houses had toys, bikes, and other random things strewn about. But Raelynn's was clear of everything except green grass. There were brightly colored flowers in boxes under the windows, making it look charming and welcoming.

Ashley had stopped on the side of the road, but she hadn't turned off the engine yet. She was contemplating where to park when Raelynn came bounding out the front door, skipping all three steps to the sidewalk. Grinning, Ashley turned off the engine and waited as Raelynn made her way to the car and opened the passenger door.

She leaned into the opening, propping her forearms on the frame. "Hey, girl! Glad you made it. You can stay here, no one cares where you park and there really isn't a good driveway anyway." Raelynn shrugged and then closed the door.

Getting out and making her way around the vehicle to Raelynn's side, Ashley smiled at her new friend. She was relieved to finally have a friend here. "Hey, Raelynn. Are you sure it's ok that I'm here though? I feel like I'm intruding on a family dinner." She felt a little out of place and wanted to make sure she would be welcome and not an intrusion since it was a family dinner after all.

"Ha!" Raelynn's head was thrown back and then she shook it hard. "No! My mom is a huge fan of big gatherings. If she had her way, and we had the space," she swung her arm back to the small house behind her, "she would have had a ton of kids. You know, like the old woman in a shoe kind of kids." She laughed at her own joke and then added, "I can see all the little monsters hanging out the windows everywhere!"

Still chuckling, she waited for Ashley to join her. Locking her car, Ashley smiled back. She didn't know what that was like, to have a mom who would want more kids or to even want other siblings besides her twin. She used to wish she had a brother, and now she wondered if that wish might be true.

"So, Ashley, I feel like I need to prepare you for my mom," Raelynn stated seriously, making Ashley slightly nervous. Noticing her demeanor change, Raelynn jumped back in waving her hands in front of Ashley, "No, no. It will be fine. I just want you to be aware that my mom is kind of nosey and might ask some awkward questions. Just go with it or tell her it's none of her business. Ok?"

Ashley was taken aback. She would never tell an adult, especially a friend's parent, to mind their own business. It seemed so rude.

Her hesitation caught Raelynn's attention, making her turn to face Ashley, grabbing both of her shoulders. "I'm serious. She's relentless. But I know you said you're from Minnesota and I know all about that 'Minnesota nice' stuff, but you're on the East Coast now. We tend to say it like it is." Raelynn shrugged and grinned.

Not really knowing how to respond to that, Ashley just nodded.

They quickly made their way to the front door, which was still open from Raelynn's dramatic exit. As they were about to enter the house, another car pulled up, making Ashley freeze. It looked like the same dark car she had been worried was following her. She felt her throat clog up and she literally felt frozen to her spot as she watched the car.

The passenger door opened, and Kiah started to get out, but Ashley saw him stop and look back at the driver. His eyes gradually went back to Ashley and his face had a look of confusion as his head turned to look at the driver again. He nodded and then moved to exit the vehicle.

Ashley watched the car roll away from the curb, but instead of driving past her, it turned suddenly into a driveway across the street and then sped off in the other direction. She wasn't able to get a look at the driver. Her eyes went back to Kiah who was also staring at the retreating vehicle. He shook his head and then moved toward Raelynn and Ashley.

"Hey Kiah," Raelynn shouted from the doorway. "I'll grab Sahara. Come on Ashley. I've got to introduce you to my mom." She waved Ashley toward the open door and then disappeared inside.

Ashley glanced back at Kiah and found he had not moved yet either and was watching her carefully. She suddenly felt very self-conscious around Kiah and the look he gave her made her slightly uncomfortable. She turned away quickly to make her way inside to find Raelynn.

A high-pitched shriek made Ashley jump back and barely get out of the way of an overly excited Sahara. She nearly knocked Ashley over as she flung herself down the steps at her boyfriend. One would have thought they hadn't seen each other in months, not hours. Ashley laughed as Kiah barely caught Sahara's airborne body. Thankful for the distraction, she quickly went inside.

The house was small and probably not much bigger than their condo back in Minnesota. Ashley felt that all too familiar pang of homesickness as she thought about Sam and Aja. Pushing it aside, she heard Raelynn's voice straight ahead of her, in what she figured was the kitchen.

Peeking around the corner, she saw Raelynn with a slightly overweight older woman with long silver twists rolled and tied in a large bun on top of her head. Raelynn's mom, whom she recognized from the beach, smacked the other's hand with a wooden spoon as Raelynn tried to take a piece of pasta out of a pot.

"Keep your fingers outta there, Rae!" Another smack sounded as the utensil hit her friend's hand again.

Ashley covered her mouth to keep her giggle from sneaking out. Raelynn heard her though and spun around to give her a scowl.

"Mom, this is Ashley. She's new here." Raelynn introduced them and then watched as her mom made her way over to Ashley and then smiled mischievously seeing her opportunity to sneak a noodle.

"Don't even think about it, Raelynn," her mother threatened, not taking her eyes off Ashley. Her face softened and she smiled at Ashley. "It is nice to meet you, Ashley. I am Honesty. But most of the kids around here just call me Mama H. Come in, child. Sit down." She turned and scowled at Raelynn again. "Come and get your friend something to drink so I can finish dinner."

Ashley realized that Honesty couldn't be all that much different in age than Sam, but her face held wear and wrinkles from stress and hard work. She didn't know their story yet, but she knew Raelynn's mom must have struggled knowing that Raelynn's dad wasn't around. She would be supporting the kids alone as well as trying to keep a roof over their heads. Her features softened when she smiled, and it was genuine and welcoming.

Raelynn grumbled but it seemed lighthearted as she reached into the fridge and grabbed a Coke for Ashley.

"Thanks," Ashley said and returned her friend's grin. She watched as the mother and daughter worked around each other in the small space. She glanced around and realized that even though the space wasn't big, it felt very homey and not cramped at all. Ashley was surprised at the minimalistic kitchen. She hated to admit when she drove up to the house that she had a preconceived idea similar to what she saw at Trish's house.

She wasn't sure why, but she expected a small house to be overrun with things scattered about, clutter and knick-knacks everywhere, taking up space. Ashley scolded herself for being judgmental. Raelynn's home was nothing like that and she felt bad for even thinking it. It was clear that Honesty kept a neat and clean home with few extras around, which spoke of their financial situation as well.

Her thoughts were interrupted by pounding feet and a loud boom as those feet landed as loudly as possible at the base of the steps just outside the kitchen doorway.

"I'm here! And I'm starving!" A boy who looked around twelve stood proudly in the doorway with his hands fisted on his hips, in a weird Superman-like pose.

Raelynn laughed and her mom joined in. "Of course, Jericho. The world revolves around you, doesn't it?" Raelynn joked with the boy, who ducked out of reach of her hand trying to tousle his hair. "This is Ashley, be nice." She gave the boy a look which he just smirked at and lifted his eyebrows.

His eyes squinted as he gazed at Ashley. "Where are you from? I haven't seen you around these parts before." He used a voice that sounded like something out of a

Western movie where the man sizes up the woman in a very suggestive way.

"Jericho! I told you to be nice!" Raelynn shouted and smacked his head. He ducked too late this time, and she grinned. She pointed her finger at him, taunting him. "Haha! Gotcha!"

Ashley watched the interactions with humor. Everyone seemed to get along so well and she quickly felt at ease with the new family.

"I was just asking, geez, Rae," Jericho grumbled rubbing his head. He moved around Ashley to his seat at the round table set in the corner of the small room.

Raelynn grinned at Ashley and then turned back to the cabinets to pull out more dishes. Glancing over at her mom, she said, "I guess Ki is here too."

Honesty's mouth quirked up. "Oh, sounds fantastic! I love all you kids being here." She paused and looked at Raelynn. "You know we all miss you here Rae. You can always come back." Her eyes seemed sad, and Ashley watched as Raelynn reached over and gave her a side hug.

"I know, Mom, but like I have said a million times, now a million and one, I am an adult, and you should be spending your money on the little monsters. I need to take care of myself now. But I won't ever turn down dinner!" She winked and gave her another squeeze.

Honesty sighed but turned back to her cooking on the stovetop. "I make plenty to go around. You shouldn't ever be worried about that," she grumbled. Her voice was quiet, but Ashley heard her.

Ashley felt slightly out of place, like she was intruding on someone's privacy as she watched the interaction between Honesty and Raelynn. Sam had always made a lot of money and they never had to worry about that. Even when it came to her move out here, Sam didn't hesitate to purchase the Rogue for her. She suddenly felt a little like a spoiled child, while the family in front of her struggled to make ends meet. From the way Raelynn sounded, she moved out to ease the financial strain on her mom and family. Ashley was learning a lot about her new friend and realized she was a very selfless person.

"OK!" Raelynn said loudly, breaking whatever tension was in the air. "Let's get this dinner started! I have my salad and bread rolls ready, and you have the sweet potatoes, noodles, and fried chicken ready right, mom?" Raelynn glanced over at Ashley and whispered loudly out of the corner of her mouth, "We eat a lot of chicken here on the Eastern Shore, in case you haven't figured that out yet."

Ashley just smiled. She knew about the seafood, especially crabs, but hadn't been aware of the chicken as well.

"Ha! I knew it!" Jericho shouted as he jumped up from his seat and pointed his finger at Raelynn. "I knew she wasn't from around here!" Then he dropped quickly back into his chair and ducked his head from the expected swing coming from his sister.

Raelynn just laughed and shook her head at him.

Sahara and Kiah had just entered the kitchen as well and moved to sit at the table. The area was tight, and Ashley found herself squeezed in between Raelynn and Kiah, as plates of food were set in the middle of the small table.

"This is cozy," Kiah commented with humor in his voice.

Sahara pointed her fork full of chicken at him and said, "Don't go getting any ideas. She's taken remember. And she's too old for you anyway." She shrugged and shoved the food into her mouth.

Kiah laughed and put his arm around her. "I'm taken too, if I remember right." Then he turned to meet Ashley's eyes and added, "She just looks so familiar, but I can't figure out why."

Ashley didn't know how to respond. Kiah didn't look familiar to her at all. "I don't even know what to say, except that I am a little offended about being called 'old'," she said with a small smile.

"No kidding, right?" Raelynn said, rolling her eyes. "You're the same age as me, right? I'll be twenty-three in a few months." She looked at Ashley expectantly.

Ashley nodded. "Yeah, I'll be twenty-three in October." At that moment her phone alerted her to a text. Thinking it would be rude to look at her phone at dinner, she ignored it, making a mental note to check it after dinner. She had planned to tell Jacob where she was going, and she would call later but was rushing to leave so she forgot. She normally texts or calls him after he's finished working so he might be wondering why she didn't today.

The dinner went along with friendly banter and conversation. Ashley felt welcome as one of them and comfortable with everyone, even Kiah. The food was excellent, which she told Honesty multiple times. After dinner was finished, she stood to help Raelynn and Honesty clear the table of dirty dishes and planned to help wash. Honesty, however, put her hand on Ashley's arm and shook her head.

"You are a guest, honey. You sit back down and just relax." She then glanced over at Sahara with a sharp look and added, "But you can get up and help, missy."

Sahara groaned and Kiah laughed, earning both of them a frown from Honesty. "Really? Ok, smarty pants, you can help too. You get dish duty." She flung the towel in her hand at him and put her hands on her hips and waited.

Kiah jumped up and said, "yes, mam."

"Kiss up," Sahara grumbled as she stood as well.

"I can help too," Ashley argued, pushing her chair back from the table. "Consider it my way of showing appreciation for the wonderful meal."

Honesty seemed to have an idea and looked back at Ashley. "Ok, you kids go ahead and clear the table and clean up the kitchen. I think I'll take the night off!" She removed her apron and laid it over one of the chairs. As she moved to exit the kitchen, she stopped at the arched doorway, gave a little wave of her hand, and blew them all kisses. "Enjoy children!" and then she nearly skipped out of the room.

Ashley laughed while the others groaned. She turned back to the group and noticed Jericho had slipped away unnoticed. *Sneaky little kid*, she thought with a smile.

"So, what's the plan for tonight?" Raelynn asked her sister, as they stood side by side at the counter taking care of the leftovers. There actually wasn't much leftover, she noticed with surprise. Honesty had made a lot of food, and the group had finished almost all of it. She noticed Raelynn package it in a container with separate compartments and realized it was packed for a single serving. Honesty probably took it to work for her lunch.

Sahara shrugged. "I don't know. We could go down to OC and see what's going on at the beach," she suggested.

Raelynn shook her head. "Nah. You guys can go. I'm beached out today. Ashley, what do you have planned?"

"Not really anything," Ashley responded as she carried a stack of dishes to the sink and carefully dropped them in. Suddenly, her phone dinged again. She wiped her hands on a nearby towel and dug her phone out of her pocket. She didn't want Jacob to be worried, after their conversation last night about her being alone out here. But she suddenly didn't feel so alone anymore.

The first was just a text from him stating he had sent the letter, and the post office thought it would get there in about three to four days. Nodding to herself, she sent him a quick message thanking him and saying that she would call him later.

The second text was another of the random ones, since she could see it was an unknown number again. She felt her head spin slightly and had to sit down. She closed her eyes for a second. *What did Aja tell me to do?* Ashley opened her eyes and checked to make sure her location was turned off. Thankfully it was, so she took in a breath of air and closed her text app without opening the second text, pocketing her phone again.

"Hey, you ok?" Kiah asked, drawing the attention of the other two in the room.

Startled, Ashley looked up. Taking another deep breath, she tried to smile, but it was forced. "Yeah, I'm fine. I think I should probably head home soon." She looked up at Raelynn and added, "sorry. Something came up. Another time?"

Raelynn stepped away from the counter and pulled a chair out next to Ashley. "Hey, it's no big deal. Whenever you want to get together, you have my number. Are you sure you're ok though?" Her eyes held concern for her and it warmed Ashley's heart.

"I'm good. Thank you for dinner and everything," she smiled at all three of them and stood to go.

As she got to the doorway, she heard Sahara say, "Sure, she just didn't want to help clean up!"

Glancing back, she watched as Raelynn smacked her head and Sahara laughed. "Bro! I was just kidding! Besides I like her, even if my boyfriend can't keep his eyes off her."

Her words earned her a light smack on the butt from Kiah. "Are you jealous, girlfriend?" he mumbled as he pulled her in for a hug.

Ashley moved through the house quickly and didn't see Honesty anywhere. She wanted to say thank you again, but maybe next time. The air was still thick with moisture and heat, but she didn't care. She unlocked her car and slid into deathly air. *It wasn't even that long*, she grumbled to herself. She started the engine and opened her windows but didn't move. Her mind was racing now that she wasn't distracted. She struggled with whether she should call Aja about the text or if she should tell Jacob. But she didn't want anyone to worry either.

Her phone ringing pulled Ashley out of her spinning thoughts. She looked at the screen, her phone still frozen in her hand since she got the last text. The number was listed but wasn't saved in her contacts. The number showed it was a local number for Salisbury, according to the words under the number.

Ashley tried to think quickly who might be calling her and if this was someone, one of the few, she knew here.

Deciding it was safest to just let voicemail get it, she shifted her car and pulled away from the curb. She just wanted to be back safe in her apartment.

Trying to find her way without the GPS proved to be impossible. She had to stop at a parking lot and put Sharon's address in. She realized she must have taken a wrong turn because she didn't remember this area on the way to Raelynn's. Frustrated, Ashley looked around as the route was "calculated". She had pulled into a Dollar Store lot and there were quite a few people around. She had never lived in an area where she felt like she blended in with the general population so well. She had always lived in diverse neighborhoods, Sam always made sure she and Aja saw people with the same skin tones as theirs. But here she felt like there were many more people with darker complexions than lighter. She suddenly realized that in the home she just left, Raelynn had the lightest skin.

She wasn't sure why that struck her suddenly. Maybe it was that she never really felt like she belonged anywhere before. Or maybe it was how comfortable she was with Raelynn and her family. She felt a pang of guilt as she thought about Sam and Aja. It wasn't that she didn't feel comfortable with Sam. She just knew he was closer to Aja. Maybe she just missed the family connection her mom and dad would have, or should have, provided her.

"Follow the directed route," the voice on her phone called out, bringing her attention to the task at hand. She shifted the car into drive and started toward the route dictated to her. She had definitely gone the wrong way out of Raelynn's. But thankfully she didn't get far so it only added about five extra minutes to her trip.

Grateful to be back at the house, Ashley quickly parked and headed up to her apartment. She pressed the lock on her key fob twice to make sure the vehicle was locked before she headed inside. Ashley was surprised the house was completely dark when she went inside. Thankfully they had given her a key to get in since the stairs outside were still not even started. She usually didn't mind going through the house, but it was so dark, and she wasn't very familiar with it. After fumbling around a few times, she found the light switch for the stairs. She flipped it on and then ran upstairs quickly. Luckily there was another switch at the top of the steps to turn it off again.

She unlocked her door and then relocked it quickly after she was inside. She was never a paranoid or fearful person. Ashley had been a go with the flow kind of person for as long as she could remember. But lately, she was finding herself increasingly worried and afraid someone was watching her. She looked around the space and noticed the air conditioning unit had been put in and was surprised she didn't notice the cooler temperature.

Having the second unit would be so much nicer now. She also realized that the windows were almost completely covered now, except for a space above each unit that she knew she could fit through in an emergency. It somehow gave her comfort knowing no one could see inside her windows either, even though three floors up it would have been difficult to see much inside unless she stood right by the window.

Ashley moved further into her apartment and nearly screamed when her phone rang in her hand. Catching her breath, she looked at the screen and saw it was Jacob. She tried to slow her breathing, closing her eyes to help calm her nerves. She knew he would be worried if she answered the phone at that moment. He could read her almost as well as Aja.

Feeling her pulse slow, she opened her eyes and swiped on the answer button. "Hey Jacob," she said with as steady a voice as she could muster.

As the silence on the other end went on without anyone answering her, Ashley could feel her pulse start to speed up again. *Not again*, she thought, thinking this is what was happening with Aja's contact too. What was this person trying to do to her that they keep messing with her phone like this?

Before she could do anything more, the voice she loved so much came over the line. "Hey, babe. Sorry Sally Jo was going on about something with the wedding or something. I don't even know. But I couldn't get rid of her."

Ashley's voice was stuck in her throat, and she felt a wave of tears coming. She wasn't sure if it was fear or relief, but she knew she needed to tell Jacob what was going on. She really needed him to come out there as soon as he could because she was starting to really be afraid. But she still didn't know what it was, or who it was.

"Ash? Are you there?"

It was time to tell him what was going on. He needed to know and maybe he could help her calm down and be rational. She took a deep breath of air in and held it for a split second and then whispered, "Yeah, Jake. I'm here. Um, I think we need to talk."

Chapter 17

"Ash, I think you need to call your uncle into this," Jacob said quietly, after listening to the events of the last couple weeks since he left. "And I think I need to come out there sooner."

Ashley groaned. "I told you, Jacob. I'm not ready yet. Aja is on the weird calls and text thing, and I am still not sure this car is actually following me. I am just being paranoid because of the phone stuff. Nothing has even happened!" This was why she didn't want to tell him everything before, but now that it was out, she needed him to understand her point of view too. The strange number that had called didn't leave a message so she could easily assume it was a wrong number.

"Jacob, I still need time. You are coming out soon and I promise I won't do anything until we hear back from the letter you just sent out today. Ok?" She felt like she was begging, but she didn't want Sam to take this away. Not yet. Even with everything going on, she felt like they were making progress, and she would have answers soon, at least once the letter was delivered and an email could be sent. It could happen quickly now.

Silence was all she heard from the other end of the line. Ashley bit her lip, waiting for Jacob to speak again. Finally, he let out his own frustrated groan.

"Fine. But Ash, you have to promise me you will just stick around the apartment until I get there. I will try to speed up my departure from here and get there next week. That's only a week and then we can tackle this together. I would feel better about your badass uncle being in charge, but I know I can't get you to agree to that yet." Jacob's voice was low, and he spoke slowly.

He was clearly annoyed and frustrated, but Ashley took the win for now. She could lay low until he came out here and then they could hopefully get to the bottom of all this and move forward—whatever that looked like.

"Just a little while longer, ok, Jake? And I promise if things get even more weird, I will call Sam. Deal?" She knew she had already made this promise, but it felt a little more sincere this time. And with her own paranoia coming into play, she actually agreed that she might have to call him in.

His words of warning over the years about people possibly looking for her and Aja rang in her ears as she thought about all the things over the last few days. Maybe she *was* being watched and associates of her father were trying to get to her. *But why would they wait until now?* she wondered. That didn't make sense to her. They would have had many opportunities to find them over the years. Why now? Maybe that is what prevented her from believing someone was actually following her.

Looking over at her alarm clock, she noticed that it was now ten her time. A sudden disappointment came over her and she sighed. "I guess it's too late to watch the next movie, huh?"

Jacob let out a little laugh. "Seriously? Just like that this conversation is over and you want to watch a movie. Amazing."

"What? We have a plan, no reason to continue to beat it up. Plus, I want to end the night with something positive and fun with you." She knew her voice was almost whiny, but she didn't care. She was telling the truth. And there really wasn't anything more they could do at the moment.

"Ok, good point. But it is nine here. So how about we start and if we finish great, if not, we can watch the rest tomorrow and then watch the third one? We just need to start earlier," he suggested.

Ashley thought for a second and then nodding said, "Perfect! 'Captain Marvel' is next. But then it's 'Iron Man' and 'Iron Man 2' so maybe we should watch those two this weekend together."

"Ok, I can be good with that. Tomorrow is Thursday. We can watch them together then. I should only have a half day Friday because Papa Jasper has some inventory thing happening so the store will be closed. Let's see how far I can make it into this one first. I don't think I'll sleep tonight anyway after everything you told me."

He didn't sound upset but he did sound tired and worried. Maybe calling Aja wouldn't be a bad thing either, Ashley thought. If she could get Aja to promise to keep it between them and not tell Sam, then it would be ok. She made a mental note to call her twin tomorrow.

* * * * *

Ashley was surprised when they finished the movie. But looking at the clock and then back at Jacob, she felt a little guilty.

"You better get to sleep, Jake. It's going to be an early morning for you." She moved her phone to see him more clearly as she watched him rub his eyes like a tired toddler, making her smile.

Jacob's hair was messed up and standing on end in the front. He may have drifted off for a short time, she realized as he looked like he was either just waking up or falling asleep. He ran his fingers through his hair and looked at her with sleepy eyes. "I guess so," he said with a smile. "Love you, Ash. Please be safe."

Ashley smiled back. "I promise. Love you too Jake." She blew him a kiss and then the other end of the line disconnected.

With a deep sigh, she put her phone down on the nightstand and made sure it was plugged in. She laid back against her pillows and stared at the ceiling above her. The moon outside was so bright it was like having a streetlight shining in her window. She watched the shadows dance across the white ceiling, trying not to think too much. But it wasn't possible, she quickly realized.

Her phone suddenly let out an alert for a text. She told herself it was nothing and not to panic. It was a little after eleven at night and she thought about not even looking but she knew she wouldn't be able to do that. She didn't have that kind of self-control. Curiosity always won over her will. It took everything in her not to open the text from earlier with the unknown number. But Aja's warning was enough to win out.

Reluctantly, she reached for her phone, silently praying it was just Jacob saying goodnight. She closed her eyes before looking at the screen. Relief washed through her entire body as she saw it was a text from Raelynn asking to hang out tomorrow.

Ashley bit her cheek. She had told Jacob she would stay around the apartment. But she trusted Raelynn. Maybe she could have Raelynn pick her up so she wouldn't have to worry about being followed. *That should be ok then, right?* she tried to convince herself it would be fine.

She quickly typed back an answer and asked if Raelynn would be able to pick her up. The only downside was that she couldn't leave when she wanted to, but she figured she would be fine, having fun with her new friend.

Raelynn quickly responded and agreed to pick her up at nine the next morning. They were going to Rehoboth Beach to go shopping at an outlet center. Raelynn wanted a new swimsuit and some new shorts that were on sale at a couple of the stores. Ashley rarely turned down a shopping trip.

Feeling excited and happy for the first time since she had moved here, Ashley drifted off to sleep. She was looking forward to the trip and spending time with someone her age. She also thought it would be a good opportunity to ask about SU since Raelynn had gone there.

Her sleep was restless as her thoughts seemed to bleed into her dreams. She awoke several times throughout the night and each time the dreams were more terrifying. She had one about Jacob being kidnapped and held somewhere right when his plane landed. Then there was another that had Ashley and Aja standing in front of a man, who looked a lot like Professor Roslin. He was holding something in his hand and Kiah was there looking angry. She didn't hear words, just gestures and facial expressions, but they were all angry and dangerous looking. A third was just pictures that looked like an old silent movie, jumping from scene to scene and included Trish's house and a gang of men with guns.

The others she couldn't remember. Ashley finally gave up trying to sleep at seven in the morning, thinking a shower might help calm her nerves.

As she showered and let the water wash over her, hoping to have the anxieties left over from her disturbing dreams wash away as well, she tried to convince herself that this is just what she was thinking about while falling asleep. Having just told Jacob about everything that had been going on and thinking about calling Aja about it all had to be what prompted the dreams, right? That was what she had to believe anyway. The last thing she wanted was to put her boyfriend or sister in danger. Maybe calling Aja wasn't the right move today after all.

Ashley's stomach growled at the same time as a frustrated groan left her lips. Chuckling, she got out of the shower and dried off. She needed to remember to thank Gary for installing the air conditioner, the apartment was more comfortable. Shaking her thoughts away, she got herself ready for the day. Looking in the mirror she noticed her braids were starting to loosen at the roots. *Hm*, she thought, *I'll have to ask around and see who can rebraid them for me.* She decided to ask Raelynn later. She thought Jazzy had her hair braided similar to hers, so she might know someone. She tied them up and then threw her towel over the shower curtain.

She poured herself a bowl of cereal and milk and then grabbed her phone to scroll while she ate. She had to admit it was nice not having to rush around in the morning and just take her time. She still had almost an hour before Raelynn would be there to get her.

Thinking maybe she could catch Gary before he went about his day, she decided to go see what the couple was up to. It seemed like a long time since they had spoken. She still had a slight knot in her stomach about the phone call between Sharon and Trish, but she had to put that aside. It obviously didn't have anything to do with her or they would have said something. She must have misunderstood it all.

Ashley made her way downstairs and noticed there were others in the house. There was noise and conversation coming from the kitchen. Peeking around the corner, she paused. Sharon was standing at the stove making something and Gary was sitting in the small sitting area off to the side with a man she didn't recognize. There was another woman a little older than Ashley and a young child probably about five years old.

"Oh, Ashley! Come in!" Sharon's voice broke Ashley's spell and she jumped slightly.

Faking a smile, Ashley moved into the room. The woman came over to stand next to Sharon and held out her hand.

"Hey Ashley. It's nice to meet you. Mom has shared so much about you and how happy they are that they can help you out by staying here. I'm Ally." She sounded so cheerful and genuine that Ashley couldn't help but smile back.

"It's nice to meet you, too," she said, shaking her hand.

Ally motioned to the other two people in the room and said, "That's Shane, my husband, and my daughter Katie."

Katie looked up from her drawings and waved slightly before turning her attention back to the paper like she was solving some major world problem.

"What do you have planned for the day, Ashley?" Sharon asked, turning her attention back to the stove.

Ashley moved further into the kitchen and sat next to Katie. "I'm going to Rehoboth Beach with someone I met yesterday at the beach." She looked over at the drawing Katie was focused on. It looked vaguely like a unicorn and Ashley smiled.

When Sharon didn't respond, Ashley glanced over. She caught a look between Sharon and Gary, but Sharon recovered quickly and smiled at her with a nod. "I'm glad you are meeting people while you are here. That is wonderful."

Ashley didn't miss the slight change of tone in her voice, but she wasn't sure if it meant anything. She turned and looked at Gary, but he had already shifted his attention back to the newspaper in front of him. Trying not to get frustrated, she turned back to the little girl next to her.

"I love your drawing," she said softly.

Katie shifted her gaze to Ashley and her face lit up. "Thanks! It's a unicorn with purple wings and a sparkly pink horn. See?" she held it up closer for Ashley to look at.

"I do see that. Too bad you don't have any glitter. That would be beautiful." This is what Ashley loved about teaching, especially elementary age kids. Their imagination was so broad and open. She suddenly remembered she had brought along her paints and markers from her school lessons when she had to student teach. "You know what? I have something you can use. I'll be right back!"

She ran back up the steps and grabbed the bag she kept all her supplies in. She had brought them with her to keep up the ruse of going to school, but now she was glad she did. Ashley pulled out a few things she didn't want to get ruined and then brought the rest back downstairs with her.

Katie was waiting patiently when she came back. Sharon, Gary, Shane, and Ally had moved to the deck outside by the pool. Ashley set the bag down and started to take out the tools from the bag.

"I have some sparkly markers here and some pencils that have sparkles too. See?" she demonstrated the colors and Katie's eyes went wide.

"That is so cool! I'm going to show mommom. Can I use them too? I promise I'll be very careful." Her big eyes were wide, and she looked so cute, Ashley couldn't say no.

Ashley watched as Katie ran outside to show everyone. They made a big deal about her drawing and Ashley smiled sadly. It was another reminder of what she missed out on as a child Katie's age. She and Aja didn't bring things home from school often. When they did, her mom would look at them and fawn over the projects but then tuck them away so there wasn't "clutter" as her father called it.

Glancing at the microwave, she realized Raelynn would be there any minute. She moved toward the glass door and poked her head out.

"Hey Katie, you can use those if you want. I am about to leave though." She watched as Katie nodded and ran back into the house.

Sharon smiled at her. "That's sweet of you, Ashley. Thank you."

Ashley nodded and then moved back into the house. She went to the back door area and sat on the bench to put her shoes on. She grabbed her shoulder bag and made sure she remembered her phone and wallet. She waved to Katie and then went to wait outside.

Thankfully she didn't have to wait long as she was already feeling the heat building in the air. Raelynn pulled up in an older model four door bright red vehicle. Ashley didn't know the names of cars very well and didn't really worry much about it. Raelynn waved from the driver's seat and Ashley ran around to the passenger's side.

Cold air assaulted her as she opened the door and slid inside, grabbing her seat belt as she did. She noticed Sahara was in the back and Ashley was relieved that Kiah wasn't along for their shopping trip.

"Hey girl!" Raelynn said with a grin. "Ready? I hope you don't mind that I brought Sahara with me. She is looking for a homecoming dress, or at least that's her excuse since it is like three months away." She rolled her eyes and glanced back at her sister.

Sahara shrugged. "I don't care what you think. I know SU has homecoming and since I will be a student there in a few weeks, I need to be ready to impress. And besides, Ki needs to have someone impressive next to him or he'll replace me." She turned and looked out her window.

Ashley furrowed her brows. "Why do you think he needs someone who isn't you? He sure appears to be really into you," she said with a question hanging in the air.

Sahara looked at Ashley and the shock on her face was very clear. "Do you know who Kiah *is*? I mean, of course you don't, you're new here. He is the starting goalie for the lacrosse team! As a freshman!" She sighed. "Everyone already knows who he is, and I am just a nobody. Why keep me around if he can have anyone he wants." She turned then and gave Ashley a once over. "Like you. An older woman who is far more beautiful than me."

Ashley scoffed and gave her a shake of her head. "First off, Kiah is not into me. And secondly, I have a boyfriend who might have something to say about that as well. Jacob and I are pretty serious. Don't worry about me in this. I promise. And besides, Kiah looks at you like you are everything to him."

Sahara just looked out the window and mumbled something about how he looks at Ashley.

"Sahara, he thinks I look familiar. That's all." Ashley was surprised this girl who seemed so confident other times was actually so insecure.

Raelynn watched her sister and friend, the car still idling in the driveway. "Hey Sahara, I am just going to say this one thing." She paused, and cleared her throat. "Kiah is not dad. Ok? Not all guys leave. Kiah is a good guy. Give him a chance, ok?" Their eyes met in the mirror and Sahara seemed to concede to her sister.

Ashley watched the interaction with interest. It didn't even occur to her what the effects of losing their father had been. She didn't think much about it with her own father. But she could suddenly understand where they were coming from and why Sahara was feeling insecure about her boyfriend—and she realized it wasn't just about her.

Raelynn finally put the car in reverse and pulled out of the driveway, heading out of the development. It was silent inside the vehicle as they were all lost in their own thoughts.

Sahara suddenly shouted from the backseat, "Hey how about some music?"

Ashley chuckled as Raelynn turned on some music. She wasn't sure what it was, but it was fast and upbeat, which they all seemed to need.

The drive to Rehoboth was a little longer than Ashley thought it would be, but after a short time, they began to talk and joke around again. Sahara's personality bubbled over, and Ashley found she was really a fun person to hang out with, even with the age difference. The two sisters were similar in their engaging personalities, and she felt like she had known them longer than just a day.

When they finally arrived at the outlet center, it was packed. The stores had only been opened a short time, but the lot was filled. Ashley quickly discovered that the outlets were spread out over several blocks, requiring them to drive to different sections and different stores. She wasn't really looking for anything, so she just let the other two decide where they would go.

"Hey, Ashley," Raelynn said suddenly as she waited for a car to pull into a spot ahead of her. "We are actually in Delaware now. So, if you want or need anything, buy it here. They don't have sales tax like we do in Maryland. That's probably why it's so busy. Back to school shopping and all that."

"Oh, thanks," Ashley said. She hadn't even realized how close they were to Delaware and forgot about the sales tax. She was used to Minnesota where they didn't tax food and clothes but had noticed that difference in Maryland when she went grocery shopping. She actually wasn't aware of the tax differences between the two states and was grateful Raelynn pointed it out.

As Raelynn found a spot to park, they all headed in the direction of an accessories store, toward the end of the building. Ashley smiled to herself. She quickly felt like she had people she connected with. They hadn't even talked about where to start and yet they seemed all on the same wavelength.

"I figure we could start at Claire's and then move down the way. I'm not in any hurry, are you Ashley?" Raelynn asked, as they continued the trek to the store.

Ashley looked around and then back at Raelynn, who had positioned herself between Ashley and Sahara. "Nope, I have all day. I'll follow you guys since I don't really have anything to look for."

She looked around her again and thought about all the people that were there shopping. She always wondered in a group like this if she knew anyone, but it was silly since she had never been there before and knew very few people. But it was always fascinating to her how many people were in the world that she didn't know. And then her mind started to wonder about the six degrees of separation where everyone was connected somehow.

Her thoughts were interrupted by a squeal from Sahara, stopping the trio in the middle of the sidewalk. Ashley looked around to see what prompted it. She heard Raelynn grumble next to her and had an idea of what happened.

"Why is he everywhere we go lately, Sahara?" Raelynn's voice was annoyed but Ashley still detected some humor there.

Sahara laughed at her sister and shrugged. "You're just jealous, sissy. I know." She flung her long braids over her shoulder and then ran to meet Kiah a few yards from where they were standing, now moved off a little to let others pass by.

Raelynn leaned against the pillar and crossed her arms over her chest. "Well, there goes the girls' day!" she said with a smirk, looking over at her sister.

Ashley shrugged. "We can just go walk around without them. Not that I don't want to hang out with Sahara and

Kiah, but just thinking out loud I guess." She suddenly felt bad for even suggesting it, like she wanted to ditch her new friend's sister just because Kiah showed up.

"Hmm, not a bad idea." Raelynn glanced over at her sister still attached to her boyfriend's side and grinned at Ashley. She waved her hand signaling for Ashley to follow her as she ducked behind the pillar and then ran down the opposite direction as her sister, laughing like a crazy person. She glanced back at Ashley and yelled, "Hurry up, before they notice!"

Ashley looked at Sahara, who had not moved at all and was still looking in the other direction and then she ran after Raelynn. She had a pretty good idea this was all in good fun, but she still had a nagging in her head that she shouldn't have suggested it. She didn't want to offend her new friends.

Once she caught up with Raelynn, who had parked herself on a bench waiting for Ashley to catch up, she tried to apologize. But Raelynn just waved her off.

"We do this all the time. This is just perfect. It's like you already know us so well, you know? It's kinda weird and creepy actually," Raelynn said, squinting up at Ashley.

For the first time since meeting Raelynn, Ashley felt self-conscious and slightly uncomfortable. Why *did* she feel so connected to them after so little time together?

The two of them wandered around, going in and out of different stores for over an hour before Sahara and Kiah caught up to them. They talked about the differences between Minnesota and Maryland and laughed at some of them. They had stopped at a snack shop and bought ice cream and bottles of water. Raelynn had just sat down at a small table outside and Sahara nearly knocked her off her chair as she grabbed a hold of her around the neck in a playful chokehold.

"You guys are mean! So mean!" she whined.

Raelynn laughed and pushed her away. Shrugging her shoulders she just put a spoonful of ice cream in her mouth. "Oh well. I see it took an hour for you to even realize we were gone." She glanced around Sahara to Kiah, who just smirked at her and tipped his head slightly.

Sahara huffed. "So what? This was supposed to be a girls' day! And you ditched me!" She tried to pout, but Raelynn just laughed at her.

Pointing her spoon, now full of more ice cream at her sister, Raelynn stated, "That was until this guy showed up." She paused and studied Kiah again. "Unless…Ki, are you still identifying as a male?" She smiled at his scowl and then shook her head. "Nope, still a guy. So technically, Sahara, honey, *you* ditched us first for a *boy*!" she dragged out boy in the sing song way a preschooler would.

Sahara opened and closed her mouth multiple times, but couldn't come up with anything to say, making everyone in the little group laugh.

"Kiah, I am going to take Beau to the Nike store on the other side. Are you going to stay here with Sahara?" The voice came from behind him, and Ashley couldn't see who it was. But the voice was familiar. She knew that voice from somewhere, but where?

Ashley strained to look around Kiah to see who the voice belonged to. But the woman quickly looked away and turned her body so Ashley couldn't see her face. All she could tell was that she was likely biracial with thick black curls all over her head. Her light brown skin showed on her arm from the sleeveless shirt she wore. Her avoidance of Ashley's eyes felt intentional and made Ashley wonder why.

"Hey Miss Anders. We can give him a ride to you guys later on if you want," Raelynn offered, oblivious to what was happening between Ashley and this woman.

"Ok, sounds good. I'll text you where we are," the woman said and then she hurried off.

Kiah turned back to the group and shrugged. "That was weird. Usually, she wants to talk to you guys. Anyway, Sahara, want some ice cream? I could use some water."

Sahara jumped up and joined him as the two made their way into the building.

"Hey are you ok?" Raelynn asked Ashley. "You look like you saw a ghost."

Ashley looked up and met her friend's concerned eyes. She smiled weakly. "I'm fine," but added *I think* in her mind.

Chapter 18

After their shopping trip, Ashley welcomed the quiet of her apartment. It had been an exhausting day with the heat and unknowns of who Kiah's mother was to Ashley. It didn't make sense, but she was beginning to wonder if she could be part of this whole DNA report. There was something so familiar about her, but Ashley didn't think she had ever met her before. Maybe the heat was doing something to her head.

It was almost five when she finally got back to the house. She made herself some noodles and then sat on her bed eating and staring into space. *Who was that mystery woman?* she asked herself.

Before she knew it her bowl was empty. She set it aside and she suddenly had a thought. Was the woman related to her father? He had kept them pretty isolated, and they never visited any family. She actually wasn't aware of any family aside from Sam. Since her mom was his sister, he was the only family she knew about.

Maybe this woman was her father's relative, maybe even sister, and she had visited when Ashley and Aja were very young. It was a long shot, but it was possible. But then, that made Kiah her cousin? There were questions she needed answers to, and they were piling up.

She wondered if she should fess up to Aja what was happening and why she was actually in Maryland. Ashley wondered if Aja might know about any other family that she had forgotten about or didn't even know about. Aja spent more time with Sam after all. Maybe he had said something about other family members.

Picking up her phone, Ashley pulled up her sister's contact. Her finger hovered over her twin's face briefly, wondering if this was a good idea. Would she have to tell Aja what she was really doing in Maryland? *Maybe, but this was important*, she thought conceding to the idea of coming clean.

Aja answered after just one ring, making Ashley smile. "Hey, sis! I was actually going to call you. I had a funny feeling and just wanted to hear your voice."

Ashley's grin widened. The twin thing worked across the country after all! "Hey Aja. What is your funny feeling about? Did something happen there?" She wanted to know if this was twin intuition or if something was going on there.

"Nothing is new here. Sam has been distracted so we haven't talked much, but I don't know if it is the case we are working on or that you are so far away and he can't control anything with you," she said with a laugh.

Ashley couldn't suppress her chuckle. She knew exactly what Aja was talking about. Sam wasn't overbearing or a hovering parent, but he did like to know where they were and who they were with. He always said it was for their safety, but they also knew his protective side came out when he wasn't able to be there for every little thing.

"So, Ash, tell me what's happening there. Because I feel like this has to do with you and me, not Sam. Can we switch to FaceTime? I want to see your face," Aja said with sadness in her voice that hit Ashley a little harder than she expected.

Pulling the phone away from her ear, Ashley hit the video button and then waited for Aja to do the same. When her sister's face came across the screen, Ashley felt a relief she hadn't felt in a long time. She hadn't realized how much having her other half nearby made her feel a sense of calm no one else could provide. She suddenly felt homesick.

Aja looked sad. Ashley noticed that she had propped her phone up and it looked like she was lying on her stomach on her bed with her phone in front of her. A thought suddenly came to Ashley, and she raised her brows at her sister.

"Hey, Aja, how come you're not at work?" Aja was never sick, and she never skipped work or school, not even if she hated the class. It was Friday, not yet the weekend, and Aja didn't take days off either to have a long weekend. This was strange.

Aja let out a deep sigh on the other end and rolled over, taking the phone with her. She shifted and held the phone high above her while she looked at Ashley.

"I don't know. I just feel off. Like something is wrong, but I can't put my finger on it. Ugh, I know it doesn't make sense, but I think it's because you are so far away." She bit her lip and added, "Is that stupid?"

"No, I know what you are feeling, I think. It's just weird that we can still do this from half a world away," Ashley said with complete understanding of what her sister was going through.

Once when they were about ten years old, Aja was really sick and spent multiple days home from school. Ashley continued to go to school without her and brought home hand-made cards from their classmates and any homework for Aja to complete that she missed. She had never told Aja about the feelings she had while she was at school and Aja was home. What her sister felt right now was probably pretty comparable to that.

"What do you mean, 'still'? I don't think I have felt this way before. Have you?" Aja's eyes held curiosity and a little concern.

Ashley shared her experience from grade school and how she had felt those days while Aja was ill. Aja agreed that it was likely the same thing. Without thinking, Ashley had just given away that she was feeling uneasy and now Aja wanted to know more. She could have kicked herself for letting at least part of the cat out of the bag so to speak.

"So, then what is going on Ash? Because if I am feeling this because of your feelings, what aren't you telling me?" Now Aja's eyes had shifted to almost accusatory.

Ugh, how am I going to get out of this? Ashley wished for someone to call or knock on her door to give her an out. Maybe even the random number to change the subject but was disappointed as she waited a few extra minutes to answer but nothing came to her rescue. *Great*, she mumbled in her head.

Taking an extra breath of air in, telling herself she wasn't stalling, not really, she closed her eyes. She didn't know where to start or what to tell her sister. How much was she willing to give away? If she told Aja everything, which she knew would feel good to get off her chest, would she help? Or would she run to Sam and tell him and let him put a stop to it?

Opening her eyes, she bit her cheek. Deciding to start easy, she asked Aja a simple question. "Hey, can I ask you something?"

Aja rolled her eyes. "You know you can ask me anything. And stop stalling. What is going on out there?"

"I'm getting there. But I need to ask you something. Do you know if dad had any siblings?" She waited on bated breath for her sister to answer.

Aja furrowed her brows. "Why would you be thinking about that? You never want to talk about dad." Her voice had gotten quiet as she likely felt the same sadness Ashley did at the loss of their mom, the reason their father wasn't in their lives now.

"I know. I-I was just thinking, I guess. I don't know," Ashley struggled to answer, not wanting to lie anymore.

Aja looked at the screen again, and Ashley could feel her gaze as if she were here, sitting in front of her. "I don't remember ever meeting any aunts and uncles. For that matter, I don't remember Sam having any either. Just Mom."

Silence on both ends created a quiet that Ashley couldn't sit with. She locked eyes with Aja. "Do you think Sam would know?" Her voice was quiet as she asked her question.

Surprise filled Aja's face. Sam avoided talking about their father as much as Ashley did, maybe even more. "Why?"

"Ugh, stop being so FBI-ish and asking so many questions. Do you think Sam knows?" Ashley was frustrated and still wasn't sure how much to tell Aja.

"I don't know. But maybe if you tell me why you want to know so bad, I can try to find out," Aja said with her eyes narrowed. Her voice was quiet but the meaning behind her tone was not missed on Ashley. Her sister knew something was up and that Ashley was keeping secrets.

"Ugh, fine. But you have to promise me you will not tell Sam. If you can't promise me, I mean pinkie swear, twin promise me, I won't tell you." She pointed her finger at her sister and narrowed her own eyes to make sure Aja knew she was serious. Ashley had always been better at keeping secrets than Aja was, even though she eventually caved too.

Aja was quiet for a few seconds and then she slowly nodded her head. "I will promise only because I am actually worried about you right now. I know what Sam would do if he knew something was up and I also know you are a stubborn woman and will try to do this, whatever it is, by yourself before you ask for help. So, if I can at least help, I will. Lay it on me."

Ashley couldn't help but chuckle at her sister's stern face. She suddenly realized she missed her so much. Taking a deep breath, she decided to start with now and work backwards.

"Ok, so I met someone here and we really hit it off right away. They invited me to play volleyball with them on the beach and I had dinner with their family and then today we went shopping in Rehoboth Beach." She paused and heard a slight gasp from her sister. Lifting her eyebrow, she asked, "What was that for?"

"Are you cheating on Jacob? Because I won't help you with that Ashley. I like Jacob and that's just not ok," Aja said with a hint of anger in her voice.

Ashley laughed. "NO! I would never do that! I met a girl, Aja!" she exclaimed.

But Aja didn't look convinced. She narrowed her eyes again and said, "Are you into girls now, Ash? I mean, it's ok, but you should really tell Jacob. It isn't fair—"

"Oh my god, Aja! No! I made a new *friend*, jeesh!" Ashley laughed at her sister. "Jacob and I are fine. I even told him about her yesterday. Can I get on with my story now?"

Aja looked a little sheepish as she nodded silently at Ashley. "Sorry," she mumbled.

"I guess someone needs a boyfriend—or a girlfriend," Ashley joked wiggling her eyebrows.

"Whatever. So…you met this amazing new *friend*," Aja said, waving her hand in a circle trying to prompt the conversation along.

Ashley snickered at her sister. "Yes, I met this new friend. And honestly Aja, you would love her. We are actually pretty similar. She's our age and just graduated too. She actually went to the college I was looking at." She stopped short, realizing what she just admitted and decided to plow ahead hoping Aja didn't catch her slip up. "And we went shopping today, they are just so much fun to be around. She has a sister and a brother and lives with her mom. Her dad is not in the picture but that's a whole other story I guess." She stopped to take a breath.

Aja took the opportunity to just say two words. "Looking at?"

"What?" Ashley tried to sound like she didn't know what Aja was asking, but the reality was, she knew very well what Aja caught in all that she just said.

Aja wrinkled her nose. "You know what I am talking about. I can read you better than anyone. Don't lie to me Ash. What do you mean the college you 'were looking at'?"

Ashley let out a defeated breath. She knew she would have to come clean to Aja now, but she hoped she could keep some of it hidden. She was losing her confidence though because she knew Aja was right. And with the weird feelings Aja had, she would not let this go easily. She was more stubborn than Ashley sometimes, and Ashley knew this was one of those times.

"Just hear me out and I will get back to that, ok? I need to focus on one thing at a time. So anyway, Raelynn's sister, Sahara, has a boyfriend named Kiah. When I first met him, he kept looking at me, like creepy. He kept saying I look familiar to him, but I have never met him before. He's like 18 I think, same age as Sahara. But today…" her voice trailed off remembering his mom's voice and how it felt familiar to her.

"Ash? Are you still there?" Aja's concerned voice broke through her thoughts.

"Yeah." She cleared her throat and continued, "Um, today his mom came over and was talking to him, but she turned away from me when I tried to see her face. Her voice, Aja, was so familiar to me. But I don't think I have ever met her before. I remember some of the stuff you told me about brain development and how trauma in a really young kid's life can affect them later. Like things they hear can stay with them even if they don't really remember. I was just thinking maybe she had some connection to us when we were babies or something. That made me start to think about our relatives and possible connections to Dad or Sam." Ashley finished her little monologue and was met with silence.

She looked at the screen. Aja was still there, but the look on her face was something Ashley had never seen before. What was she thinking about? She looked almost scared for a second.

"Aja, what is it? Do you know something?" Ashley couldn't hide the slight fear in her own voice.

Aja shook her head quickly. "I am kinda afraid that maybe this is someone from our dad's past. Sam has been saying weird stuff lately, like 'Ashley better be careful who she is friendly with' and 'that idiot is going to try something one of these days'. It's really creepy actually, like he is talking to thin air or hallucinating." Her eyes lifted to meet Ashley's again. "Ash, I'm scared actually. He said something yesterday to someone on the phone like 'keep an eye on her if I have to come out there myself I will' and then hung up. He saw me standing there and then literally bolted from the office and I didn't see him again until like eleven at night."

"There is definitely something someone is hiding from us," Ashley mused.

"What do you mean? Is there more?" Aja asked, sitting up suddenly.

Ashley laughed when she saw her sister pull out a notebook and pen, like she was about to take notes to solve some crazy crime. She was definitely well suited to her job at the FBI.

"I guess I should come clean. But before I do, would you maybe want to come out here for a little while? Do you have some vacation time you can take?"

"Hmm, maybe. I will check. But why?" Aja looked confused as she met Ashley's eyes.

Ashley hesitated. Was it right to have Aja out here too or was that selfish to want her twin by her side so she wasn't so homesick?

"Ok, I'll just tell you what's going on and you can decide if you want to come out." She took a deep breath and held it before she let it out slowly and said quietly, "I think we have a sibling, well half-sibling, out here and I came out here to find them." She leaned back against the wall and waited for the storm to hit.

A wide range of emotions flashed across Aja's face as she stared at Ashley. Their closeness allowed Ashley to feel each one as well. Anger, annoyance, and finally fear. She didn't know which one would strike first.

"I can't believe you lied to me Ash. To Sam. What were you thinking? How could you look me in the eye and tell me such a blatant lie?" The hurt was something Ashley expected but was surprised that's what came out first.

"I'm sorry. I really am. But we both know if I had told Sam he would have stopped me and then we would never find out the truth. You know that is true, Aja. And I couldn't take the chance that he would find out. So, I couldn't tell you either." She almost whispered the last sentence, shame filling her heart. She just admitted that she didn't trust the one person who knew and understood her better than anyone in the world. If the tables were turned, she would be hurt so badly by Aja saying this and the betrayal she felt would be difficult to overcome. Ashley closed her eyes tightly and tried to control her breathing.

The other end of the phone was quiet as Aja processed what she had said. Finally, Aja whispered, "You don't trust me, Ash?"

Ashley lifted her now open eyes to study the ceiling above her. She let out a groan, knowing how her sister felt. "I'm sorry Aja. It's not that I don't trust you. I just…you and Sam are so close, and I just didn't want him to find out. I'm sorry." She held her breath while she looked back at the screen to see sadness on her twin's face. "I really am sorry I lied, Aja."

Slowly Aja started nodding her head. "I guess I can see where you are coming from. But I never meant to make you feel like you couldn't trust me to keep something big from him if it was needed. I would have tried, Ash. But you didn't even give me the chance. My loyalty is with you. Always and only you. I appreciate Sam for all he has done for us, but you are my other half."

Ashley's eyes met a matching pair of bright hazel ones on the screen, and she didn't miss the tears building in them. She could feel the same pain her twin was feeling as she tried to avoid looking at her. But she knew this was her fault. She had made the decision to lie and be deceitful. Now she regretted it but didn't know how to make it up to Aja.

"Aja—" she started but was interrupted.

"Ashley, it's fine. I think I get it. But I am not going to lie to you and say it's ok. It's not. It hurts me more than you could ever know that you thought you couldn't trust me. But I think I understand. I guess I have always been a little closer to Sam than you were, but I didn't know you ever felt out of place or that you didn't belong with him, with us." Her voice was still sad, but there was a new strength in it now.

Aja's determination was coming through, and Ashley couldn't hide the smile it brought to her face.

Aja visibly straightened her shoulders, sitting up straight. "Now, tell me the rest and then I'll see what we can do. I promise I won't tell Sam unless it's something dangerous—or just plain stupid," she said as she gave Ashley a pointed look.

"Psh. Like I would do something blatantly stupid. Come on, give me some credit, Aja," she said with an even bigger smile. She knew she was the one who primarily got them in trouble when they were younger, but seeing her sister roll her eyes and smile made the teasing worth it.

"Right. You are the good twin and I'm the evil one. Nice try Ash, nice try," Aja shook her head and gave her sister a real smile. "I am sorry I made you feel like that, Ash. Please tell me next time. You are more important to me than anyone in this whole world."

Ashley nodded and gave her sister a smile back. "I promise I will."

"Ok, now that that's figured out, did you say we have a half-sibling somewhere? Like *what*?" Aja asked, her eyes big.

"I wasn't sure if you heard that," Ashley chuckled. "Yeah, so it's a long story, but I am guessing it's because of an affair dad had. Like I wasn't disgusted enough with him." She made a gagging noise and Aja laughed.

Aja quickly got serious again. "He really was a dirt bag huh? So, what do you know so far? Wait, how did you even find out about this potential sibling? You never said anything to me before."

"I know." Ashley sighed, realizing how many things she had kept from her sister. "Remember that history class I had to take for graduation credit? We were studying Ellis Island and talking about the immigrant documentation and all that. The prof required us to do the DNA submission to see if we could trace our own family tree to Ellis. It was supposed to be a fun thing he thought, and since I didn't expect anything to show up, I didn't really care."

Aja nodded and listened on the other end of the line as Ashley explained what she knew to this point, which really wasn't a lot. But it felt good to tell Aja everything and have it out in the open. As they finished their conversation, Aja assured Ashley that she wouldn't say anything to Sam. She wanted to find out more and agreed that he would definitely take over if he knew.

"Hey Ash?" Aja said tentatively. "Please be careful. I can't help but think that Sam's agitation right now has something to do with dad too and you being far away doesn't help his sanity."

Ashley smirked at her. "I know. He's a control freak like someone else I know."

Aja stuck her tongue out at Ashley, making them both fall over in a fit of giggles. Ashley was so relieved to have her sister back and be able to talk openly about all this. Hopefully together they could unravel this mess.

Chapter 19

Ashley spent the night tossing and turning, the voice sitting in her head. She wished she could place it, but it was all in vain. She had talked to Jacob after Aja and told him she had come clean to her twin about everything. Maybe the three of them would be able to think of what to do together. The only thing she didn't tell Aja was the login information for the email account they set up. She wasn't intentionally keeping it from her, she just forgot about it.

When she finally woke up from a fitful night's sleep, she stretched and turned to her side. For some odd reason the random texts she had been getting had stopped, at least she hadn't gotten one for a couple days. Maybe Aja's suggestion worked and by turning off her location, they gave up. But if Aja was right and they were trying to get her to use against their father, they would find another way.

She shivered thinking that someone was watching her, to worse trying to get to her. Ashley was typically the adventurer of the twins, and she was rarely afraid of anything. But she felt a sudden sort of dread thinking she was here alone, and no one would know she was missing if something happened until her nightly call with Jacob was missed.

Thinking of Jacob, she smiled. He was happy to hear that Aja was on board now and relieved for Ashley that she wasn't lying to her twin anymore. He knew the lying was taking a toll on her. She remembered their conversation last night as she lay on her side with her phone propped up next to her.

"I talked to Papa Jasper, Ash. He said I can head out there on Wednesday," Jacob had told her. "He just wants me here for a meeting on Tuesday and the last inventory of the summer to make sure we have everything. With the new kids starting, he doesn't want to have to train them on that as well."

Ashley was relieved to hear the news. "Wednesday isn't so bad. It's Friday now so that's just a few more days. Way better than another two weeks."

Her relief was clear as she watched Jacob smile and nod. "Now what are we watching tonight? 'Iron Man' and 'Iron Man 2'? Oh, I forgot I do have to work tomorrow for a few hours just to make sure we are set at the feed store for next week. So, I may not make it through both tonight."

They ended up watching both movies and despite that time spent with him, she still struggled to sleep. Remembering that he would be coming next week, Ashley jumped out of bed. She would need to get more food and should probably clean up the apartment. There wasn't a lot of space but if they were going to share it, she would need to make sure he had places to put his clothes and things.

There was a pretty large closet, so she decided to go get hangers when she got more groceries. She could hang almost all of her things, and the small shelf would be good enough for her shorts. She hadn't brought any winter clothes, just maybe a sweatshirt or two and a couple pairs of jeans and leggings. All of that could be hung too.

Ashley was excited for the second time since being here. She thought about seeing what Raelynn was doing today. Since they spent the whole day yesterday shopping, she figured they would want to have some down time today. She realized that she didn't know where Raelynn actually lived, not that it was any of her business either she guessed.

When she finally got out of bed, she was surprised to see it was after nine. She must have gotten some sleep last night if it was this late. She shook her head to clear the thoughts of Kiah's mom and decided to take a shower. She was once again grateful for the air conditioner unit that was now installed and realized she forgot to tell Gary thanks for doing that yesterday. Her thoughts then drifted to little Katie. She had forgotten about her supplies that were lent to the little girl. She hoped they were downstairs.

She got dressed and headed that way after her shower and morning routine. She had to let Sharon and Gary know that Jacob would be back next week, so they weren't surprised. It was quiet as she descended the stairs. It wasn't particularly odd, but she slowed down anyway. As she neared the doorway to the kitchen, Ashley noticed the lights were on, so she moved through the archway.

Expecting to find Sharon cooking something on the stove and Gary to be reading in his seating area off to the side, Ashley was surprised to see neither of these things. Instead, what she saw made her freeze.

Professor Roslin was sitting at the island and Sharon was sitting next to him looking at a file folder in front of them. She couldn't hold in the gasp that escaped, drawing their attention to her.

Sharon jumped up and Professor Roslin quickly closed the folder.

"Ashley, how are you this morning?" Sharon said, rushing to the coffee maker on the other side of the island. "You were so quiet I thought you were still sleeping. Here, let me get you some coffee." She busied herself with making a fresh pot and then grabbing a mug from the cabinet above.

Professor Roslin just stared at her and when their eyes met, he just shook his head and looked down at his now folded hands over the file folder.

Ashley didn't know what to say or do. She turned to look at Gary who seemed unbothered by everything going on, as he walked into the kitchen, paper under his arm.

"Good morning, everyone," Gary said with a grin. He looked around at everyone and then Ashley swore he let out a soft chuckle. "How is that unit working up there, Ashley? Is it staying cool?"

That broke Ashley from the shock of what was in front of her, and she smiled. "I'm sorry, I meant to say thank you yesterday, but I forgot. Yes, it is working perfectly, thank you again."

Since she found her voice, she looked over at the professor. "What are you doing here, Professor Roslin?" she asked. She was trying to keep her voice steady. She still suspected he was the one following her to Ocean City the other day and was wondering about the connection to Kiah as well. Now he appeared again in her safe place, at least she thought it was her safe place.

Professor Roslin looked up at her and smiled, but it looked forced because it didn't reach his eyes. "Sharon is helping me with a class I am doing in the fall. She is going to be a guest teacher for part of it, since she has so many years under her belt of teaching elementary kids."

Sharon set a cup of steaming hot coffee in front of Ashley and then moved to sit next to the professor again. "That's right. We will be teaching strategies to the new group of teaching students." She smiled at the professor and then back at Ashley.

Figuring it was believable enough, Ashley nodded. "Well, I'm off to get some things from the store. See you later." She decided to save the information about Jacob coming for now, since she wasn't sure if she should trust the professor. He gave her a weird vibe if she was honest, and she wasn't sure she fully believed the story they told her. But she decided she had other things to occupy her mind and time for now.

She started up her car and waited for it to cool. As usual, the heat from outside was stifling, even in the morning. She stood outside her vehicle and looked up and down the street. Professor Roslin's car caught her eye on the street. Looking closer at it, she realized it was the same Toyota from her Ocean City drive, at least she thought it was. She felt a cold chill run through her. Why was he following her? Could he be the one looking for her and trying to trace her location like Aja said through her phone? Maybe he was just acting as a professor to try to get info about her. She never asked how long he had been teaching at the college.

What did that mean for Sharon then if Professor Roslin wasn't really a professor after all? Her imagination started to spin theories. She tried to dismiss her worries. After all, Professor Roslin had access to everything on campus. He had to be an actual professor, right? *Ugh*, she thought with frustration. She needed another set of eyes and ears here she decided. *Just a few more days*.

Ashley looked at the car again and decided she needed to pay closer attention to details, starting with the car she thought was following her. She couldn't remember if that car had two or four doors now that she thought about it. She still couldn't be certain if it was black or a dark blue color either. Frustrated, she decided she had to be more vigilant about what was happening around her.

Trying to rationalize things out, that maybe this was all her imagination running wild, she told herself to just calm down and be more careful. She used to laugh at Aja for having a notebook with her everywhere she went but now was thinking it was a good idea. She couldn't shake the uneasy feeling that Professor Roslin possibly had a connection to Kiah as well. Shaking her head, she tried to focus.

Her thoughts started to drift to Sharon and Gary. Did Sharon know about it and was she in on it too? Ashley could feel her thoughts start to spiral again and not in a good way. She suddenly felt exposed and vulnerable. If Sharon was up to something with Professor Roslin, and Ashley was literally right under their noses, how safe was she really?

Ashley moved to sit in her car and buckle her seatbelt. She took a deep breath of air in and then put the car in reverse to make her way to the store. She had a sudden need to leave the house. She needed to get out of there. She hoped she had locked her door when she went downstairs because she had actually planned to go back up there before she saw the professor. Luckily, she had her phone and could use her cash app from her phone to pay for anything she needed.

Then she remembered Gary had gotten into her apartment anyway to put the new air conditioning unit in, so they could access her space whenever they wanted to. She felt a chill on her skin that was not from the car vents. She had to get her thoughts away from this train of thought, or she would go crazy.

Focusing on the road ahead of her, she decided to drive a little further to the Target store. She could distract herself with the longer drive and feel some distance between her and the house.

She wandered aimlessly through the aisles of Target, not really looking for anything in particular. She did remember to grab hangers for Jacob's arrival, but that was still all that was in her cart. Ashley was startled when a cart crashed into hers, drawing her attention to the person in front of her.

"Hey girl!" Raelynn said with surprise. "What are you doing over here?" She moved her cart to the side and then stood next to Ashley.

"Hey! What a surprise actually." She smiled at her new friend. Looking around her, Ashley asked, "Where's Sahara?"

Raelynn shrugged. "No clue. I came from my place, so I don't actually know what she is doing today." She narrowed her eyes at Ashley and added jokingly, "You know I might think you prefer my sister to me when you ask something like that."

Ashley waved her hands in front of her. "No! Not at all!" Then she sighed, She couldn't admit that she actually was more worried about running into Kiah again than Sahara. "You just seem to always be together. Sorry."

Raelynn laughed. "Hey no worries. She's probably out somewhere with Kiah since it's Saturday and they don't have anything else to do. What are you doing way out here though?"

Ashley just lifted her shoulders. "I guess still trying to find my way around. I guess I don't even know where you live to know if this is out of your way though."

"Nah I just like Target for some things. I live over by to the college too. I was staying in a student apartment complex, and they actually let me stay for an extra six months while I figure out what to do with my life." Raelynn smirked causing Ashley to laugh. "Hey wanna go get some lunch? I know it's early but I'm starving, and it is a really bad idea to go food shopping when you are hungry."

Ashley looked at her empty cart. "I guess so. I really only need these anyway." She lifted the pack of hangers up out of the cart with a smile.

Raelynn gave her a strange look but shrugged. "Ok, let's go."

They made their way to the self-checkout. Raelynn chose one and Ashley moved to another. She was actually surprised that it wasn't busier on a Saturday. Because Ashley only had one thing, she finished quicker than Raelynn and put her cart away, waiting for her friend.

Raelynn finally came over to her carrying three reusable bags and pushing her cart with her free hand. Ashley grabbed the cart from her and put it away, then they walked side by side out the automatic doors.

Ashley paused for a second to see where Raelynn was parked and when she walked straight ahead, Ashley followed and was surprised to find that they had parked only a couple of spots apart. Strange coincidence she thought, but with everything else going on, she had a twinge of doubt. Could Raelynn be part of this "spying on her" thing too? No way, she's just a student like Ashley was, she told herself, shaking her head at her paranoia.

"So, what are you hungry for?" Raelynn asked, breaking her of her thoughts. She looked around them and added, "There's pretty much everything not far from here."

Ashley looked around and shrugged. "I guess I don't care. Maybe Mexican?" She looked back at Raelynn who nodded.

"I can go for that." She closed her car's trunk and then walked to the driver's door. "Where's your car?"

Ashley turned and pointed to her car. "I'm right there. You lead, I'll follow." She swung her hand to signal her words and then headed to her own vehicle.

She threw the hangers in the back seat and then got in quickly to follow Raelynn's car. Her bright red car was hard to miss as she pulled out of her spot. The restaurant wasn't far from the store she realized, just through a parking lot and across one street. They parked outside a place called "Plaza Tapatia." The sign out front advertised authentic Mexican dishes, which suited Ashley well.

Aja wasn't a fan of Mexican food and preferred pasta and Italian dishes. Ashley wouldn't call it all bland per se, but she personally enjoyed some more spice in her food. She thought it also reflected their personalities. Aja always chose safe experiences while Ashley liked to literally spice things up. Although she didn't go over the top spicy, or dangerous, she even had to admit her restraint at times.

The duo were seated right away, and two menus were set at the end of the table. The host walked away, likely to fetch their complimentary chips and salsa. Ashley picked up the menu but knew what she would have anyway. She just checked to make sure they had it and what it came with, so she was prepared to order. She set it down quickly, folded her hands over the top of it, and looked at Raelynn. Her friend was studying the menu with her tongue sticking slightly out, making Ashley giggle.

Raelynn raised her eyes to meet her friend's and glared. "What?" she demanded.

Ashley shook her head. "Nothing. You just stick your tongue out when you are concentrating. It's cute," she said with a smile and a lift of her shoulder.

Raelynn roller her eyes. "I know, I know. It's a thing I guess I do when I am unsure of something. It must have been a thing my dad did because my mom laughs like that too and then a sad look comes over her face. And I know my brother and sister don't." She sighed and turned back to her menu.

Ashley felt bad for making light of it, or for making Raelynn feel bad or sad or whatever emotion that was that flitted across her face for a millisecond.

"I'm sorry. I didn't mean anything by it. My sister does it too, only she looks more like an over excited dog panting," she said with a laugh.

Raelynn chuckled and set down her menu. "That is quite the image. How old is your sister?" she asked.

Ashley didn't know if she should divulge too much information about Aja but in the end trusted Raelynn, and it was pretty clear that Raelynn trusted her. She was really open with her life and family, which surprised Ashley a little.

"Aja is my twin, although I am a few minutes older, and I never let her forget it," she said with a laugh.

"Whoa, that's cool. Surprisingly there aren't many twins that I know around here. Are you identical?" Raelynn leaned forward, looking very interested in what Ashley had to say.

Nodding, Ashley said, "To a fault, at least in appearances. We are pretty much opposites in personality, what we like to do and eat, and our interests." She sat back in the bench seat and stretched out her arms.

Raelynn's face it up. "That would be so amazing. Did you guys do the typical twin stuff like switch places and take each other's tests in school?" Her voice took on a wistful look and she turned her head as if staring off into space.

Ashley watched and could almost see the bubbles and cloud of Raelynn's mind playing a scene of two of her playing tricks on people.

"Yeah, we did a little bit, but Aja is a rule follower and didn't like to lie about anything. So, if a teacher asked her straight away if she was Ashley she would say no," Ashley laughed, remembering the exact thing happening when they were in ninth grade. Ashley was nearly failing biology and of course Aja was excelling at it, so Ashley convinced her to take her final and she would take Aja's English final. But the science teacher knew and asked Aja who couldn't lie to her. They didn't try again after that because Aja didn't want to get caught.

Raelynn wrinkled her nose. "Well, that takes the fun out of having someone who looks exactly like you, doesn't it?" She laughed as well. "I always wanted a twin. Growing up I always felt a little alone, not quite fitting in. My stepmom is great, don't get me wrong, but she's not my biological mom, you know?" She fiddled with her fingers, staring at them.

"Actually," Ashley started slowly, surprised she was about to admit this to a near stranger, "I have always felt like that too."

Raelynn's eyes snapped to Ashley's with shock. "How is that possible? You have literally another version of yourself right in front of you, like a built-in best friend."

Ashley chuckled at her surprise. "I guess Aja always had a connection with our uncle that I really didn't." she said with a shrug.

Leaning forward, Raelynn put her chin on her folded hands. "You were raised by your uncle?" Her voice was filled with interest and curiosity as she studied her friend.

Raelynn was about to say something else when someone approached their table.

"Miss Raelynn, how are you doing?" A man Ashley recognized stood at the end of their table, but she blanked on his name.

"Professor Blake!" Raelynn said and jumped up from her seat. She gave him a hug and then motioned at Ashley. "This is my friend, Ashley."

The professor looked at Ashley and then nodded. "This is Miss Ashley? Raelynn has told me about you. You are attending grad school in the fall, right? It sounds like the university would be lucky to have you." He smiled a friendly smile, and Ashley was actually surprised he knew who she was. She didn't know him.

He was very friendly and approachable, and, unlike Professor Roslin, she didn't get a weird feeling from him. She briefly wondered why she hadn't been introduced to him before.

"I am still deciding, but I am really running out of time." she said with a small smile.

"Oh nonsense," he said. "You have time. I am head of graduate admissions so I will make any concessions we may need to. Raelynn can give you my contact info. Just let me know if I can assist you in any way." He glanced behind him and then turned back to the girls. "I have to get going, I am meeting someone. I hope to see you later." He nodded at both Raelynn and Ashley, his eyes lingering on Ashley for a split second longer and then he moved to a far part of the restaurant, out of sight.

Raelynn turned back to Ashley and smiled. "He was my advisor my last semester." She leaned back just as the waiter approached to take their order and they focused their attention to him.

Thankfully Ashley had taken a little Spanish in high school because his accent was pretty thick, and she used the few words she did know to help him with her order. After he left, Raelynn looked at Ashley with a strange look.

"What?" Ashley asked. "You look like you have something on your mind."

Raelynn just smiled. "I hope I get to meet Aja someday. I bet the two of you together are a trip."

Ashley just laughed. "That would be fun for sure."

"You know it would be fun to study twins," Raelynn said suddenly. "I heard they can have the same DNA if they are identical, or very similar if they are fraternal. I bet they sound alike too, even if they are male and female twins. It is just so fascinating, you know?"

Ashley listened to her friend as something suddenly occurred to her. Maybe there is a closer connection to her ancestry report than she thought. She never found out where twins fit into her family tree. Sam never really talked about family, and they never met anyone growing up with him. But what if her dad actually had a twin. It might explain why this person who was trying to contact Ashley was a close relative. Maybe her dad was an identical twin like she and Aja, and this so-called sibling was actually a cousin but because their DNA was closely matched the system got it mixed up.

Her mind started spinning ideas when someone walked past her table. She looked up to see a side profile of a man that she had seen before, or at least a picture of him. She sucked in a breath and watched as he made his way to the back of the restaurant, where Professor Blake had gone. Suddenly things became much more confusing than before.

Chapter 20

When Ashley got back to the house, she locked herself in her apartment to think. The man at the restaurant was definitely the man in the photo that Professor Roslin had dropped in front of her a while ago, down to the same messy, grayish black hair. And the dark, almost black eyes she couldn't forget for some reason. She still wasn't sure why he looked familiar, but she knew there was some connection between him and the professor. She didn't know where in the restaurant he went after he walked by their table because they had gotten their food shortly after that and she and Raelynn continued to talk.

She didn't want to get Raelynn caught up in something if it was her father's doing, so she didn't say anything. She thought Raelynn suspected something though as their conversation lagged a little bit after that. Ashley was distracted and her mind was spinning all kinds of things. She had actually even thought about calling Jacob's sister and seeing what she spun out of all this craziness. But then she would have to explain to Jacob what was happening, and she didn't want him to worry more than he already was. He just needed to get his work done so he could be out here with her.

Ashley decided to stay close to her apartment over the rest of the weekend. She wasn't particularly scared, but she just couldn't make sense of the things happening around her. She was beginning to question who she could trust and who was actually being genuine with her. She trusted Raelynn, at least she thought she did.

"UGH!" she groaned as she fell back against the wall. This was too confusing, and she figured out she needed to get some answers fast. The problem was she didn't know who would give her honest ones. She wanted to believe that Sharon and Gary were honest and trustworthy people, but she just didn't know with the weird vibes Professor Roslin was giving her and then seeing him in Sharon's kitchen like they were old friends.

She was just finishing up a little lunch when her phone buzzed drawing her thoughts back to the present. She picked it up and saw a text from Sam. She furrowed her brow. He never texted her. Was this another random text to see if she would respond so they, whoever *they* were, could track her?

Biting her lip, she decided to call him instead of responding to the text, which she hadn't even opened. She hadn't talked to him in a few days anyway, so it wouldn't be super random. She quickly double checked to make sure her location was off and then pulled up his contact.

"Hey Ash! Did you get my text?" Her uncle's voice boomed over the line. He was always loud on the phone, like he forgot the speaker of the phone was right under his mouth.

She grinned. "Yes, but I didn't open it yet. I thought I would just call. So, what's up?"

Her uncle hesitated. "Well, I was just checking in. Seeing what you are up to. It's Sunday and I'm not working, so thought I would see how you are doing out there." He sounded a little fishy, like he wasn't being totally honest, as if there was a reason for his call that he didn't want to share.

Ashley's thoughts drifted to Aja. Had she told him something? She felt her face warm at the thought her sister had told him of her plans.

"I'm just hanging out at the apartment today. You sound like something is up, Sam. What's going on?" She decided to just hit it head on and see what he said. He didn't usually hide it when he caught them in a lie, so she thought it would be best to just get it out of the way.

Sam cleared his throat and laughed, although it seemed forced. "No nonsense, Ashley, huh? I was honestly just calling to check on you. Are you going out and meeting people? What have you been up to this weekend?"

Ashley narrowed her eyes. Was he actually tracking her? She hadn't left the apartment since lunch yesterday. If he was tracking her maybe he was concerned that she hadn't left. Or maybe he worried something happened to her since her phone hadn't moved.

"Sam," she drew out his name slowly. "Are you tracking me somehow?" She asked the question slowly, like she was almost afraid of the answer.

He chuckled again. "Of course not. Why would I do that? You're an adult, you are free to do what you want. I wouldn't infringe on your privacy by tracking your phone or your car." Sam had always been a terrible liar, a lot like Aja actually.

Ashley felt her body heat up. "Are you kidding me? Here I thought I was losing my mind, and it was just you the whole time? Sam! You freaked me out! If you want me to update you on where I am, just ask. I will gladly just share my location with you!" She tried not to yell at him, but for the last week or two she had been worried someone was tracking her phone and here it was just Sam. "Wait a second. You are tracking my car too? Is that why you insisted on buying it? So, you could put your FBI stuff on it to spy on me?"

The other end of the line was silent as Ashley tried to control her breathing. She was angry, but there was a tiny part of her that was relieved. It was just Sam, making sure she was safe. No one was after her and she was making a big deal of nothing.

Finally, Sam spoke. "Wait a second. Ashley, how did you find out someone was tracking you?"

"Are you not even going to apologize for 'infringing on my privacy' Sam?" She was trying not to sound too relieved because she did want to be independent, but she was glad he was watching out for her.

"I'm sorry, Ash. I am. But you are just too close to… never mind. Answer my question. How did you find out someone was tracking you?" His voice had dropped, and he sounded a little more hesitant.

At first Ashley thought he was just being overprotective, but now something in his voice actually scared her a little. "What do you mean, Sam? How did you track my phone? Aja said that was what the weird and random texts were. That someone was trying to get a location on me through my phone." She paused for a moment, hoping she was wrong. But Sam's continued silence proved that her thoughts might actually be right after all. Her relief a few moments ago was quickly seeping away. "That was you, wasn't it?"

"Ashley, I can track your phone through the phone company. And I can track your location through your vehicle GPS. I wouldn't have to get you to respond to a call or text to get your location." Sam spoke with a dangerous aura coming through his voice, and Ashley involuntarily shivered.

Her moment of relief was now completely gone, and she sucked in a breath.

"Ashley, what is going on there? You have to tell me because if I am right, you are actually in danger right now." Sam's voice shifted again to a concerned parent and not so much scary FBI guy, as she and Aja used to tease him when they were younger.

Taking in another deep breath and she closed her eyes. Aja hadn't told him anything after all it seemed. But how much was she going to tell him? Could she hold him off a little longer? She knew she had to try at least.

"Um, I don't really know. I guess Aja told me to be careful about answering texts because you guys use phones to track people. I guess I was just assuming something. Nothing has happened, Sam. But now you have me a little scared. Is someone following me? Do you know something that you're not telling me?"

Ashley had always been pretty good at turning the tables on Sam. She could pull out a few things and then have him feeling guilty before he even realized it, even if she was at fault for something he was trying to discipline her for. In the past, she had always found it funny, and Aja called it her superpower. But right now, she hoped he would bite because she had to admit she was a little freaked out too.

A long stretch of quiet greeted her. She was about to speak, maybe even come clean but then Sam spoke.

"I guess I am just worried. I promised your mom I would always take care of you and watch out for your safety, and I guess it is hard to do with you so far away. When do you think you will be back for a visit?" His voice was strained, and she didn't quite believe him, but at least she was off the hook for the text questions. "How are your hosts treating you? Shari, right?"

Ashley forced a smile. "Sharon. They are fine. They check up on me and make sure I am doing ok. They took me to dinner once, introduced me to seafood. I've gone to the ocean a few times. I even made a new friend. It's going fine here, Sam. You don't have to worry."

"A friend? What's her name?" She heard rustling in the background and had to stifle a laugh. No doubt he was going to write her name down and do a background check.

"Raelynn. She's pretty great, she has a personality that matches mine so perfectly," she said, earning a groan from Sam.

"Oh fantastic. Another one like you. I bet that's a treat to hang out with." She could almost see his eyes roll like a teenager, making her laugh out loud this time. At least he seemed to relax just a little bit.

Ashley felt herself smile a genuine smile. "I think you'd actually like her Sam. She's fun."

The sarcasm in his voice made her smile bigger as he said, "Oh, I am sure. Maybe someday." He paused and she heard the phone crackle as he let a breath out. "Please be careful Ashley. Promise me you will call me if anything, and I mean *anything* weird happens. I worry about you out by…out there."

Ashley noticed this was the second time he had stopped himself from saying something. She didn't want to think about it, but it was starting to nag at her. What did he know or what was he afraid of? And why wouldn't he tell her?

Deciding to move on for now, she said, "Well, I'm going to clean this place up a little bit. Jacob is coming back this week."

"Oh, that's right. Good. I feel better about you being there with him coming. Not that he's much of a fighter or anything, but at least you won't be alone. And then I don't have to track your every move because he will let me know if something happens—at least if he knows what's good for him he will." His last words were filled with an implied threat hidden by his dry sense of humor.

"Yeah, I know, Sam. You scare him a little bit. And I think you actually enjoy it, don't you?" If she were standing in front of her uncle right now, she would have her hand on her hip and raised eyebrows.

Sam chuckled darkly. "Oh, there is no denying that. I hope anyone who gets close to you girls knows that I will literally end them, and no one will ever find their body if they ever put you in danger or hurt you."

"This coming from the guy who puts my sister in danger every day," Ashley said with a chuckle of her own.

"That's different. She never goes in the field. And besides, I am right there, so nothing will happen to her. These boys that you girls pick out are nothing next to me." And there was the puffed-out chest and superman complex she knew so well coming through the line, making Ashley laugh.

"Maybe you should have matched Aja up with Ryan or Damon then, not leave her to her own devices to find someone worthy of your approval." For once, Ashley wasn't all that upset she didn't work with Sam. She shuddered at the thought that her uncle would have that much say in who she dated.

Sam laughed on the other end of the phone. "I don't think either of them ever had the balls to date anyone related to me. Besides, they are too old for her."

Ashley shook her head. He definitely thought highly of himself. He really didn't have any reason not to though. He was sought after for many special assignments, which is why they moved around so much. He could contract his services for more than what a full-time job with the FBI would pay him. Sam only settled in Minnesota with his current team because he wanted Ashley and Aja to be able to finish school and then decide for themselves where they wanted to go next.

"Seriously, Ashley girl. Please be careful and don't be so trusting. People are never who they seem. You have always been less careful than Aja about who to trust and hang out with. You are an adult now and I won't tell you who to be friends with or who to hang out with. Just be cautious and vigilant. Ok?" Sam said quietly.

Ashley found herself nodding, even though he couldn't see her. "I will, Sam. I promise. I really don't do that much anyway. And the only person I have made friends with is Raelynn. I doubt she is some super spy hunting me down though." She laughed at the idea. Raelynn had less of a filter than Ashley did and said what was on her mind easily.

Sam sighed. "Ok, just promise to let me know if anything strange happens. Especially this texting thing. I am going to ask Aja about it, so you better warn her that I already know through your weird twin telepathy. Otherwise, I know she will lie to me, and she is the absolute worst liar on the planet." He chuckled again, and Ashley knew he was right—next to him anyway. You didn't need a lie detector to tell if she was lying or not.

"Yes, sir. I will do as you say," Ashley said in her best robot voice, making fun of her uncle. "If I was there, I'd salute you too, but this will have to do." She giggled as he groaned.

"Why did your mother leave me with you two? I will take what I can get though. I have to get something done here. So, I will talk to you again soon. Be safe Ashley."

"I promise. Talk soon, Sam."

The call ended and Ashley sighed as she put her phone down. She couldn't help wondering what Sam was keeping from her. Then she thought about what she was keeping from him and couldn't blame him she guessed. She was doing the same thing after all, wasn't she?

Shaking off her unease, she picked up her phone and sent a text to Aja letting her know that Sam knew about the texts and if they found anything together to let her know. She honestly didn't think much of it. Thinking that since she turned her location off now, it wouldn't be a problem. She still wasn't sure though who would want or need to track her phone. She also hadn't gotten one of the texts in a while so maybe they gave up.

Ashley looked over her apartment space. She found that she really liked the small space. It would be a little tight once Jacob came, but hopefully they wouldn't be here too much longer. The longer she stayed and the weirder it got, the more she just wanted to go home.

Aja responded quickly and Ashley laughed a little when she asked if Ashley was ok. Yeah, she was ok. But she had to admit Aja was right about Sam. He was acting a little strange, like he was preoccupied or something.

She decided to put all that out of her mind while she focused on something else—like cleaning things up and getting ready for Jacob. She couldn't deny she was excited to see him again. It hadn't even been a month yet, but she was glad it was almost over.

Her phone dinged alerting her to another text, this one was from Raelynn. She smiled as she thought about her new friend. Raelynn asked if she wanted to hang out later. A group of them were going to a bowling alley down in Ocean City. That was something she hadn't done in a really long time, she thought. It might be fun. Plus, she felt like she needed to get out. Her head was still spinning from her conversation with Sam, and she just didn't want to worry about this stuff anymore.

The plan was to meet in a few hours, so she decided to finish her initial idea of cleaning up the space and then showering. She responded to Raelynn that she would love to tag along and then got to work. Ashley cleared out part of the large closet making room for Jacob to put some of his things. She wasn't sure how long he planned to stay, but she wanted to make sure there was plenty of space. The more they could put in the closet out of view, the better, since the space was small enough without added clutter, even if it was necessities.

After nearly three hours of cleaning and rearranging, Ashley stood back with her hands on her hips and surveyed her progress. The place looked lived in but neat and tidy. She hadn't brought much with her besides clothes and photos in frames, so it wasn't hard to clean. The biggest challenge was the closet and living space, if you could call it actual living space.

The space where her bed/couch and TV were there wasn't a huge amount of room, but it did take up about half of the apartment. She was grateful for the few cabinets in the kitchen to put her food in, so she didn't have to clutter up the small countertop. The tiny appliances were neatly tucked against the wall. Her dishes were clean and put away, leaving nothing in the little sink.

Satisfied, she nodded her head. "Looks pretty good if I do say so myself," she said out loud. Glancing at her alarm clock, she noticed the time. She had a little less than two hours before she had to leave. She had opted to drive herself, just in case something weird happened. Ashley realized she had started to become a little more worried about her personal safety lately, something that was uncomfortable and unfamiliar for her.

Typically, she let Aja do the worrying for both of them. Aja was a planner anyway, so she would make sure everything was covered before they did much of anything. It used to drive Ashley crazy, but at the moment she was thankful for her sister's careful nature. She had learned a little bit from her and knew that after talking to Sam, she had to be more vigilant.

She spent the rest of the afternoon showering and getting ready to meet her new friends. Raelynn had warned her to leave early. It was still busy in Ocean City at night, and they had decided to go later, after dinner, hoping most of the families would have gone back to their hotels for the night.

When she was ready, she looked at the clock again. There was just enough time to go and take her time driving, hopefully a little less stressful than her last trip to OC. She left the small lamp on in the apartment so she wouldn't be coming back into a dark space, something else she wouldn't have thought about before. She made sure to pull the door shut tightly and locked it, checking it twice.

The humid air outside assaulted her body like the bathroom after a steaming hot shower—but she didn't feel as refreshed as that experience. Ashley felt sweat almost immediately start to form on her skin. She was relieved to see no one was home. Both of the cars were gone, which she was a little surprised about, but tried not to think too much of it.

She hadn't driven her car since the day before and that was a short trip to Target. And since Raelynn had picked her up for their shopping adventure the day before that, she felt like she hadn't driven in a long time. The heat that poured out of her car almost made her gag. She stepped back from the sauna like air and stood away from her car. One thing she had learned was not to touch the metal of the car in this kind of heat. She reached in and turned on the engine after a few minutes, not because letting the air outside into the car would do any good, but it did release a little of the oven-like heat from inside.

Ashley let the car run for a while. She had to chuckle at the difference from Minnesota. In the winter there, you let your car warm a little before you get in. Here you had to cool it off first. The comparison was comical, as if they were on opposite sides of the world, not just halfway across the country.

When she could finally get inside without feeling like she was suffocating, she buckled and then pulled up her GPS. The bowling alley, called "Alley Oops" was about twenty-four minutes away. She had about an hour before they planned to meet, so she had plenty of time. She decided to make a stop at the gas station and grab a drink and snack for the way. She wasn't sure if they were going to eat there, but she didn't want to have to worry about it.

After filling her tank, Ashley went inside to grab something to drink. The store was pretty quiet, and she quickly made her way through and back to her car. She was back on the road in just a few minutes.

Her mind started to wander as she drove through the outskirts of downtown Salisbury. It was a nice area, with a small-town feel. The people were friendly, and she never really felt out of place here. It wasn't home, but it was still an ok place to live while she figured things out.

Ashley's thoughts drifted to the DNA report. With the other things going on, she actually kind of forgot about the whole reason she was here. Jacob mailed the letter Thursday or Friday, which means the person should get it Monday or Tuesday. So, she should hopefully have an email response by the time Jacob gets there. She hoped it all worked out that way and she could get some info from this person.

A sudden thought occurred to her. Why was she even here to meet this person? Did she want a relationship with someone who was possibly conceived as a result of her dad's infidelity? She hadn't even thought of those things before she set off on this journey. She was a naturally curious person and loved to meet new people. But was this something that she could see herself maintaining over time?

Before she even knew it, Ashley arrived at the meeting spot with her mind and body taking over as it followed GPS. She sighed as she looked at the packed parking lot. It was still light out, so she didn't think anything of parking on the street. She just made a mental note to have someone walk her to her car later—just in case.

She didn't finish that thought and found a spot that someone had just pulled out of. She parked and then watched for cars coming and going. The street was a side street, so it wasn't as busy as the main road through Ocean City, but people were clearly on vacation and didn't seem to remember driving rules as a stray car here and there would fly down the road without much thought for safety.

As she made her way to the main door, she heard her name called from behind. She turned to see Raelynn, Sahara, and Kiah walking toward her. She stopped and waved, watching as Kiah turned and locked his car. She looked carefully at the car and noticed it was the same one that dropped him off at Raelynn's. But this one was slightly different than Professor Roslin's she saw at Sharon's. This one only had two doors and was a really dark blue, not black.

She sighed as she felt a little better about Kiah, besides his obsession with how familiar she looked to him. At least he had stopped staring at her.

Ashley waited for them to meet up with her and then they walked inside together. Just as the heat assaulted her when she walked outside, the blasting air conditioning in the building was nearly as dramatic. They moved around inside with Raelynn showing Ashley everything. They eventually found a table to sit at. Ashley was amazed looking around. It was much more than a bowling alley. Sure, they had bowling lanes, but they also had an arcade and a restaurant. The sounds from the games and the general noise all around made it difficult to talk.

When Raelynn and Sahara went to grab some drinks, Ashley was left alone at the table with Kiah. He looked across the table at her and then suddenly snapped his fingers, startling her.

Ashley looked at him with her brows lifted. "What?" she asked, confused by his behavior.

Kiah grinned. "I figured out why you look so familiar! I found a framed photo of you and a file in my dad's desk with a different picture of you." Then he frowned and dropped his eyes. "But I have no idea why he would have pictures of you."

Stunned, Ashley stared at him, just as Raelynn and Sahara came back with their hands full of drinks, soft pretzels, and cheese dip.

Chapter 21

Ashley was quiet on the phone with Jacob. It was Sunday night, and it was late. She hated calling so late, but she had to talk to someone about the bomb Kiah just dropped. She was so stunned by the information he spilled to her that she couldn't even ask questions. But now she had a million swarming through her brain. They hadn't even gotten to watch "Hulk" as planned because of her need to process the new information.

She had worried that Kiah was connected to Professor Roslin somehow because of similar cars, but tonight she figured out they weren't the same car. The car at Sharon and Gary's when the professor was there was black. Kiah came tonight in a dark blue car. His had two doors, not four like the professor's. She was paying closer attention to details now and it was clear the vehicles were not the same, aside from both being Toyotas. So, it probably wasn't Professor Roslin following her before either, or who dropped Kiah off at Raelynn's dinner at her mom's house.

She decided she was being paranoid and was a little more annoyed that she now had no idea who was following her—if anyone even was. She couldn't remember details about the car that followed her to Ocean City or the one on Sharon's street now that she thought about that possibility too. She couldn't remember if the one on the street was also a Toyota.

"Why would his dad have a picture of me, Jake? I have never been here before; I don't know anyone here. It just doesn't make sense." She was tired and frustrated, and she had to admit a little freaked out. But the biggest struggle was wondering if she was actually being followed or if it was all just her imagination. Kiah didn't seem to have any guesses as to why his dad had her picture either.

Jacob sighed on the other end of the phone. "I don't know Ash. It doesn't make sense to me either."

The long silence was palpable as Ashley waited for him to say more. She could tell he had something on his mind, so she just gave him time. His brows furrowed and smoothed out multiple times as she watched him struggle with what to say. She was pretty sure he knew she wouldn't like what he had to say given how much he was struggling to get it out.

"Just say it, Jacob. I won't get mad, I promise," she nearly whispered trying to let him off the hook.

He raised his eyes on the screen to look at her and sighed deeply. "Ash, I am really starting to think Sam might be needed here. This sounds more and more like the warnings he's been giving you for years. Think about it. Who carries around folders or files of people with pictures? Not everyday dads." He left the unspoken answer hanging in the air between them.

She didn't want to think about who might be carrying around files with pictures of her. The professor had a file folder of pictures too, well one picture anyway. Maybe she has seen too many movies, but assassins and people looking for people did that. Sam did, and he wasn't your run of the mill dad either. She wondered if she should ask what Kiah's father did for work, but then again, she didn't really want to know. And if he was into some shady stuff, he wouldn't likely tell his family anyway, would he?

Ashley let out a soft groan. "I know. Sam kept catching himself this morning, like he wanted to say something, or he was holding himself back from saying something. It was weird and a little unnerving. Honestly, I felt more uneasy after talking to him than I did before." Her confession was laced with frustration and a little fear.

After a long pause, Ashley spoke again. "I'm sorry I called so late, Jake. I know you have to be up early tomorrow. I don't want anything to get in the way of your work and delay your trip out here. I'm going to sleep on this, and I'll talk to you tomorrow and we can decide what to do. Ok?" she suggested, as she watched him yawn and rub his face with the hand not holding the phone.

"Yeah, I think that's a good idea. I am beat and I don't want to delay either. I have to be rested to help Papa Jasper as much as I can. I love you, Ash. Please just stay there and don't go out unless you have to. I don't trust this Kiah kid and we don't even know who his father is yet to know who not to trust." Jacob's eyes met hers again and she could see the pain and worry in them.

It was clear he would rather be there, or better yet have her there with him instead of over a thousand miles away. Ashley couldn't deny she was feeling the same way. "Hey maybe Sally Jo wants to come out and have a little fun with us? I would love her perspective. I am sure she could come up with some amazing theory about everything and everyone!" Ashley joked. But she was really only half-joking as she watched Jacob roll his eyes.

"Yeah, no thanks. I'll talk to you tomorrow. Seriously, stay safe, Ash," he said and then they both hung up.

Ashley tossed her phone aside. She couldn't just lock herself up in the apartment. She would go stir crazy--*that* she was sure of. She suddenly realized she had forgotten to go to the grocery store for food after she met up with Raelynn the other day. *How many days ago was that even?* she mused. It had been a whirlwind of a week.

She got up and glanced at the clock, and noted it was after midnight. She had stayed with Raelynn and the group for only a little more than an hour, saying she was suddenly not feeling great. Klah had avoided her after that, but she couldn't shake the weird feelings she was having. Who was his dad? She never got her wits about her to even ask, kicking herself. But then why would she even know who his dad was?

Frustrated, she headed for the shower to try to wash away some of her stress. She decided to try some of the lavender body wash she had since lavender was supposed to have a calming effect. Thankfully with her hair all braided she didn't have to wash it. She was careful not to get it wet as she stood under the stream of water. She just closed her eyes and tried to think of anything but what was happening around her. She tried to think about being back at school in Minnesota, only a few short months ago. Before she got this report back, before she thought about going to Maryland, before she thought about leaving Aja.

After almost an hour, she got out of the shower and put on her flannel pajamas. It was a crazy thing she brought with her given it was sweltering hot outside, but she cranked up the AC and then cuddled under her covers. The cold actually reminded her of Minnesota, and she finally fell asleep feeling safe and comfortable.

* * * * *

A soft knocking woke Ashley. She rubbed her eyes and then looked around, trying to get her bearings. The noise sounded again, and she stretched her arms above her head and sighed.

"Just a second," she called to whoever was on the other side.

Sharon's voice came through the door then. "No worries, Ashley honey. I just wanted to give you back your art supplies from Katie. I'll just leave them outside the door. Thank you for letting her use them."

Ashley heard some rustling outside her door and then she said, "No problem. Thank you!"

A soft hum from Sharon was all she heard and then her soft footsteps moving away from the door.

With a groan and another stretch, she sat up and grabbed her phone from the nightstand. It was almost ten and she was shocked that she slept that late. She looked around the apartment and sighed. The air was cold as she rubbed her arms with a laugh. *Well, the winter air worked,* she thought. She got up to turn the units down to a normal temperature and then moved to her tiny kitchen.

Taking out some cereal and a bowl, she remembered she needed to go to the grocery store before Wednesday. *What day was it again?* she asked herself. Silently calculating in her head, she surmised it to be Monday.

Only two more days until Jacob came to her. Her feelings of warmth at her boyfriend finally being by her side quickly cooled down as she remembered their conversation the night before. She was supposed to make a decision about whether to talk to Sam or not today.

"Ugh," she groaned out loud. She really didn't want to talk to Sam again, but she promised both Jacob and Sam that she would. But did anything really happen? Not really, she thought. She found out some weird information, but nothing *happened*. Biting her lip and satisfied with her justification, she smiled lightly and finished her breakfast.

After Ashley finished rinsing her bowl, she pulled out a small pad of post-it notes and a pen to make a list of food to get for when Jacob comes. She wrote down everything she would need for a week's worth of dinners. She had containers from her last shopping trip and would only need a few more things to make dinner for a couple weeks in the small oven. They would probably eat out a lot too, just because it was easier.

Making a plan for the day, Ashley quickly got dressed and picked up the apartment. She made the bed and stacked the pillows to make it look like a couch again. Then she washed her bowl and spoon and finished her morning routine, brushing her teeth and oiling her scalp and braids. Looking in the mirror again, she remembered she needed to ask for a referral for her hair.

As she opened the door, her art supplies fell into the room. She had forgotten that's what woke her up that morning. Sharon had set the small package against the door so when she opened it she wouldn't step on anything. Ashley picked it up and closed her door again, surprised that Sharon had taken the extra effort to protect her things. Then again, Sharon used to be a teacher, so she probably knew how much these things meant to Ashley as well. Not wanting anything just left out, which she found amusing since Aja was the neat freak of the two, she moved to put them away. She wasn't a slob, but she definitely wasn't as concerned with everything always being picked up as her twin was.

Carefully, Ashley put the supplies back into the bag and then the bin of her teaching supplies and secured the cover. She slid it back under the bed and brushed her hands together as if she had just accomplished a monumental task.

An alert sounded on her phone, surprising her because it was different than her texts. Crinkling her eyebrows, she looked for her phone. Ashley finally found it sitting on the counter. She must have set it there when she moved to put her supplies away.

Shrugging, she picked it up to look at the alert. She was shocked to see it was from a Gmail account. Was it possible the person had already gotten her letter? Her fingers trembled slightly as she pressed on the alert and the email inbox came up. She almost laughed when she saw the amount of spam she had already received to the new account. But the one that caught her eye was one labeled only "B. R".

How was it possible that they had already replied? It wasn't even noon yet. Although she guessed that mail could have already come, she was still surprised to see a reply so quickly. She wondered for a second if she should wait and read it with Jacob, or if she should tell him to read it when he gets a break. That made more sense, she decided.

Ashley sent him a quick text saying there was a reply on the email he set up and then almost immediately after she sent it, he sent a response saying he would read it since he was about to go on his lunch break. He asked if she would wait so they could read it together in a little while.

She agreed and then sat down on her bed. She set her phone next to her so she wouldn't read the email first. Self-restraint wasn't her strongest feature. If the phone wasn't in her hand maybe she could avoid the thoughts, but instead she just stared at it, willing it to just open on its own, like that would be possible.

Maybe if she was a witch or something, but then she might already know what it said without having to read it. No, that's more like ESP or whatever that was called where she knew what things were without seeing it. She shook her head hard. Her thoughts were going a little crazy on her and she couldn't help but chuckle at herself.

"Patience, Ashley, patience," she said, chastising herself. She had to wait for Jacob. What could she do while she waited?

She looked around and saw her list on the counter next to her keys. Then she looked around the space. *What else will Jacob need to feel comfortable here*, she asked herself, trying to distract her mind.

Ashley added a couple of things that would require a trip to Target again. *Darn*, she thought with a smile. Another trip to the store to wander wasn't a bad thing, she figured.

Her phone ringing brought her out of her thoughts, and she picked it up to see Jacob's silly face. He had snapped it when they were playing with her phone contacts, trying to figure out how to add pictures to them. He thought it was hilarious. Now it just made her smile when he called.

"Hey, Jake," she said, still smiling. "Are you really on lunch? It seems a little early."

Jacob laughed. "It is, but I needed a break from lifting all these bags of feed. Can we switch to video? I want to see your face."

Ashley faked a gasp and said, "That sounds creepy. Ew!" She switched to video and Jacob's real life smiling face greeted hers.

"You're such a weirdo, Ash. That was not creepy at all," he said with a grin.

"Ah, but I am your weirdo." Her wink made him smile wider.

"Yes, you are, and I will keep you," Jacob just shook his head. "So, what about the email? What did you think?"

Ashley stared at him. "What do you mean what did I think? I was waiting for you to call so we could read it together. Did you already read it, Jake?"

Jacob smiled sheepishly. "In my defense, I didn't think you would be able to resist. I mean it really isn't a strong personality trait of yours to wait for anything."

"Fair," she said with a shrug. "But I did wait. So let me open it and read it now since you already did."

Ashley opened the email app on her phone again, keeping it upright so she could still see Jacob and he could see her.

The letter back was very brief, more like a quick note. It simply said they received Ashley's letter and wanted to reach out right away. They even suggested the possibility of meeting as soon as she was free and that they were available whenever she was.

Ashley just furrowed her brows as she stared at it. "There is literally nothing here to go off of either. It's annoying." Raising her eyes back to Jacob's concerned ones, she added, "What should I do?"

Jacob shrugged. "I guess we can set something up for when I get out there. I don't want you to meet him or her alone anyway. What do you think?"

Ashley bit her cheek. "I don't know. I want to get answers as soon as possible and go home."

"Ashley, you can't go meet this person alone. Especially if this is all a ploy to get to you. If you are alone, it would be too easy to do...something." Jacob's face was almost pleading with her. "And don't even say you weren't thinking about it. I know you better than that."

She knew he had a pretty good idea that she would want to meet as soon as she possibly could. But she also knew for safety's sake she had to wait and not go alone. But what if she could find someone who would go with her?

"Ok, I hear you, *but* what if Raelynn goes with me? She is trustworthy," she said, adding *I think* silently.

Jacob let out an exasperated breath. "Ash, it's literally two days. Can't you wait for just two days so I can go with you? You don't even know this person that well. You don't know if she is *really* trustworthy."

"But—" she started but Jacob interrupted her.

"Ash! Seriously. Please wait for me. Two days. We can send a reply and then see if this person can meet on Thursday. Heck, we can even meet for breakfast, the earlier the better. I don't care. But don't go without me." Jacob was pleading now, and Ashley couldn't help but smile.

"Ok, Jacob. I won't," she conceded. "I have to go get some food shopping done. Is there anything else you want me to have here for you?" She knew she was changing the subject, but she didn't want him to beg anymore. She didn't promise because he was right. She wasn't sure she could wait even two days. She would try, for Jacob and for her safety, but she just had to know who this person was.

Besides she didn't think these things were connected. It just didn't make sense why someone would fake a DNA report. If they wanted to get to her, they had much easier ways to do it. No, she believed this was real and she wanted to get to the bottom of it. Once she did, she could go home, and the other stuff would go away. Right?

"Ashley, I need your word. I need you to promise me that you will wait for any kind of in person meeting," Jacob said, with a stern voice.

She was quiet on the other end of the line, not meeting his eyes.

"Ashley! Please. I have to know you are going to be safe," he said, his voice rising with frustration.

Ashley sighed. "I will try, Jacob. I really will. But you know how hard that is for me. And I still think this is not connected to anything else. No one would use a DNA report to lure someone out here." She caught her breath as she thought about how she might actually be the only person crazy enough to go across the country for something like this. She still wasn't even sure why she was doing it.

"I hate to do this, but don't make me call Sam in. He would never forgive me if I let you do this. Even if I have a feeling you are going to do something alone is enough for him to come after me. Heck, he might even kill me, Ash," his voice now quiet and almost pouty.

Ashley looked up and met his eyes. "Well, that was a low blow, Jake," she huffed out. He knew her weak spot. "Fine. I won't go anywhere alone."

Jacob finally looked relieved. "Thank you, Ash. It's just two more days. Go ahead and respond if you want and we will meet on Thursday. Ok?"

Ashley nodded and then changed the subject again. "So, what do you need me to pick up for you while you are here. We'll be driving back so you don't have to worry about bringing extra stuff home on a plane."

"I'm not sure. We can go shopping once I get there if I need something. No reason to worry about it now. I have to get back to work. Please be careful, Ash. I love you," he said with a small smile.

"I love you too Jacob. Talk to you later." She waved and then hung up.

Dropping her phone on the bed next to her she wanted to scream. Jacob didn't play fair, she decided. Then an idea popped into her head. She only promised not to go alone. She didn't promise to wait. It was a technicality she knew, but it was a way out, or *around* her promise anyway.

With a satisfied smile, she gathered her things again to go to the grocery store. It was surprisingly not a stifling heat when she walked out of the house. She hadn't looked at the weather at all because it seemed to always be sunny and hot. Maybe there was a change coming with the humidity being lower than normal. She decided she didn't care and would just enjoy it.

As she got in and started her vehicle, she realized it was more pleasant outside, but still not nice enough to go without the air conditioning. She noticed it was a little cloudier today than other days. Maybe she should pay closer attention to the weather reports, she thought, as she made her way to the grocery store.

She first grabbed some fruit as she entered the cool store. She had a rough plan and a list of what she wanted to get for meal prep. She also liked to walk through the store to see if anything popped out at her. As she walked the aisles, Ashley tried to think of things she could make ahead. Jacob was a sucker for sweets, but she wasn't much of a baker. She would make brownies but was afraid they wouldn't even come close to Gran Marion's and then it would just be a disappointment instead of a fun treat.

She wandered through the baking supplies. Her mom never made much for sweets and the only thing she ever remembered was ice cream that her father ate most of and wouldn't allow anyone else to even touch. Maybe she could handle making cookies, she thought. As she looked around for the flour and sugar, she realized she wouldn't have enough storage to get everything she'd need and there wasn't a small enough size to use it all in one batch.

"Prebaked it is," she muttered, moving toward the bakery. She wandered through the baked goods. Cookies, different breads, cupcakes, cinnamon rolls, and doughnuts. Maybe she would come back the Wednesday and get some fresh pastries for Jacob's arrival, she thought. Then again there was Dunkin' not too far away and Krispy Kreme where she could just drive through with more options.

She picked up a couple of containers of different cookies. Setting them in her cart, she moved to frozen foods. She didn't need too much, just some pizzas and maybe vegetables. Ashley studied the pizza options. The brands were different than Minnesota's and she had to admit she missed the Lottza Mottza brand.

Deciding on some Red Baron's she grabbed two and decided to head back toward the front of the store. Her thoughts on cookies had her sidetracked. She headed for the pastas and then sauces. She would need some fresh meat--chicken and hamburger only—not yet trusting her choices or ability to cook seafood. Then she made her way to the taco supplies.

She paused for a minute to recheck her list. She checked things off mentally as she continued to decide what else to get for her meals. Ashley gathered the rest of her list and then made her way to the checkout. She opted for one with a cashier instead of self-checkout since she had a lot more than normal. She looked at her half full cart and frowned. She wasn't sure she had enough room for it all back in her small apartment. Shrugging, she decided she would figure it out. She didn't want to have to come back every other day for things.

The cashier greeted her with a smile as Ashley started to unload the cart on the conveyor belt. It was so satisfying to listen to the beeping as he ran all her groceries over the scanner. Ashley pushed the cart to the end of the lane and waited for him to bag her things. She had left her reusable bag in her car so she wouldn't forget it every time. As one was filled, she grabbed a second one from the nearby hanging display for the cashier to ring up and start to load as well.

It didn't take long before she had two very full bags of groceries. She set them back in the cart and then swiped her card to pay for everything. Ashley grabbed her receipt from the friendly man and nodded her thanks.

Ashley made her way out of the store and into the warmer air outside. She looked both ways and started to cross the street. A loud honk made her stop in her tracks. She looked to her right and saw a car stopped, waiting for her to cross. The driver had his window down and was waving frantically at her to move. But what she noticed as she stood frozen to her spot were the dark brown eyes of her father, full of anger.

Chapter 22

Ashley sat in her car for nearly thirty minutes staring at her steering wheel. Her hands were shaking. She didn't know how she made it to the car in the first place, or how she managed to get her bags into the back seat. She tried to breathe, taking in air slowly, but found herself gulping instead. She was completely frozen, trying to get her brain back online to be able to think properly.

Closing her eyes, she forced her hands into fists resting on her thighs. She focused again on breathing. She had to get herself together. There's no way that was her dad, she rationalized. But the anger, the scowl, the tone in his voice yelling at her while he waved his arms telling her to go. What did she do? Did she wave him on, or did she cross? She didn't even know what she did.

Slamming her head back against the headrest Ashley groaned. Her phone rang loudly, and she jumped, letting out a shriek. She looked around slightly embarrassed, hoping no one saw her. Then she searched for her phone.

"H-hello?" she stuttered into the speaker when she finally found it.

"Hey, girl! Where are you right now?" Raelynn's voice rang out over the line.

Ashley breathed deeply. "I'm just leaving the grocery store. What's up?" She tried to even out her voice but was still having difficulty. She welcomed her friend's chipper voice to help reground and distract her.

Raelynn was quiet for a half second, like she was talking to someone. "So, want to do something? I'm just about to leave and pick up Sahara. We were going to go to the outlet down in OC for a little bit before I have to go to work."

Ashley didn't even remember there was an outlet mall nearby. But she needed a distraction badly, and shopping was a welcome idea. "Um, sure but could you drive? I have to go back to the house and put my stuff away, but it shouldn't take too long." She didn't feel like she should drive, and if she was honest, she didn't really want to either. Her hands were still shaking as she pressed the button to start the engine.

Her phone switched over to Bluetooth and she turned the AC on while she finished her call with Raelynn.

"Yeah, I can drive. I'll meet you at Sharon's house in about twenty?" she asked.

Ashley nodded. "Perfect. Thanks!" She wondered for half of a second if she had told Raelynn whose house she was staying at but quickly brushed it off. Of course she must have. Raelynn had picked her up before after all.

She finally felt like she could breathe again and had her wits about her. She shifted into reverse and then slowly moved out of her spot, shifted into drive, and headed back to Sharon and Gary's.

She felt numb as she drove back and then absently carried her things upstairs. She put the cold things away and then left everything else out. When she went back downstairs, Sharon was in the kitchen.

"Hi Ashley. Are you running off?" she asked as she stood at the stove stirring something.

Ashley started, not realizing she was there at first. "Oh, yes. I am going to do a little shopping with Raelynn. I should be back soon though because she has to work."

Sharon nodded. "Ok. Have you thought anymore about attending SU?" she asked, barely looking up from her pot.

"Uh, not sure yet. Hopefully I will be making a decision this week. Oh, Jacob is coming back on Wednesday. Sorry I forgot to mention it. I hope it's ok." She raised her brows, asking the older woman.

"Oh sure, no problem at all dear. There is plenty of room up there isn't there? Or if you need to find another place, we do have a couple of other properties you might be interested in. We could drive out and look at a few if you would like anytime." Sharon had stopped stirring and was looking at Ashley expectantly.

The look in her eye made Ashley suddenly feel self-conscious and nervous. It wasn't threatening, she didn't think, but it was strange. Why would they need to look somewhere else? Did Sharon not want them here? Then just as suddenly her demeanor changed again, and she was back to facing her stovetop.

Ashley furrowed her brows at Sharon's sudden change. "Um, I'm not sure yet but I appreciate the offer." She quickly moved to the door and outside.

"Oh Ashley," Sharon called as she was almost out the door. "What is Raelynn's last name?"

A confused Ashley stopped and looked at Sharon. "Uh, I guess I don't know. Why?" She thought it was odd that Sharon would want her friend's last name. And now she wondered if she had told Raelynn who her landlord was after all. Did they know each other?

Sharon waved her hand dismissively. "Oh no reason. Just wondering if I know the family. I've lived here my whole life. That's all. Have fun."

Slowly making her way outside, Ashley couldn't help but wonder if that was true. She decided she wasn't going to worry about it. She had bigger things on her mind, like why did she lock eyes with someone who had her father's eyes.

Ashley tried to shake that feeling off. She could feel herself sinking into that fear state again. But her father's still in prison—at least she thought he was. Sam hadn't said anything about him getting out anytime soon, but then she didn't ask either. Aja would have said something, at least she thought she would.

Rationally, she knew it wasn't her dad. But those eyes were unmistakable. The anger present in them coupled with the scowl, it was just too coincidental. She had to find out who that person was. He had to have a connection to her father somehow. Was he the connection to her ancestry report? It would make sense for the person to look like her father, given what she was thinking or guessing about the report. She had always been told she and Aja look like their mom. She didn't remember and Sam didn't have many pictures of her or them together. He had some from when they were younger, and she did think they looked similar. Except their eyes. She remembered her mom once telling her she wished she had Ashley's eyes.

The honk of a car horn broke Ashley of her thoughts and she jumped. Raelynn waved from the driver's seat with a smile on her face. Ashley shook her head to clear her thoughts and laughed at herself for being startled.

Sliding into the front seat, Ashley grinned at her friend. "Was that necessary, Rae?" she asked.

Raelynn shrugged and smiled back. "You looked lost in your own world. So, yeah, it was necessary."

"Ha ha," Ashley shot back. She glanced in the backseat and noticed Sahara wasn't with them. "Hey, where's Sahara? I thought you were picking her up."

"Nah, Kiah decided to ruin another girls' day and is driving her." She rolled her eyes dramatically. "But I guess it's fine. I have to work anyway, and my job is closer to your place."

They talked about Raelynn's job and Ashley thought about getting a job there as well--if she stayed. Raelynn said it was a cute little coffee and doughnut shop. They catered to the college kids since it was right across the street. They had a lunch menu and a dinner menu, but they weren't open too late into the evening. Then again, not many restaurants around town were open after nine or ten at night.

The drive went quickly as the two of them talked about nothing. Raelynn pulled into a spot close to one of the stores. This outlet mall was smaller than the one in Rehoboth Beach and didn't have nearly as many stores. Ashley glanced around and only saw a few of the big names.

They started to walk to the Under Armor store and Ashley heard Sahara yell at them. She turned and froze, locking eyes with the same ones that haunted her nightmares.

Raelynn stopped walking and touched Ashley's arm. "Hey are you ok?" Her head bobbed between her sister and the two guys with her. "Ashley?"

Ashley looked back at her friend's concerned face and shook her head. "I-I'm not sure. W-who is that?" She pointed her shaking finger at the younger version of her father who had also frozen in his spot staring at Ashley.

"Uh, Beau?" Raelynn asked, looking between Ashley and the other person standing next to her sister. "That's Kiah's brother."

Ashley's eyes shot back to Raelynn. "What?"

"It looks like you might have been right, Sahara! Look at these two, not being able to take their eyes off each other." Kiah's joking voice broke into her thoughts.

Ashley stared back at him and shook her head violently. "No, it's definitely nothing like that, Kiah, I can promise you that." With one more look at Beau, she grabbed Raelynn's arm and dragged her into the store, feeling the air leave her chest and dizziness start to take over again.

Once inside, she grabbed her chest and bent at the waist, trying to breathe.

"Hey, what's going on?" Raelynn asked. "Do you know him? Did he do something to you? I'll seriously kill him." The concern and threat in her voice was evident--as well as a hint of panic.

Ashley shook her head, not really wanting to get into her history or who he reminded her of with Raelynn at the moment.

"Ashley, you have me really worried. What's going on?" Raelynn held onto Ashley's hand and squeezed it. "Talk to me? Beau's not a bad guy, but if he did something to you, I swear I can take him." She looked back outside where the other three had moved to stand outside the store, Sahara and Kiah having an animated conversation.

"No, I'm fine. He just reminds me of someone. I have never met him before though." Ashley looked back at Raelynn with a weak smile. "I'm ok." She closed her eyes and tried to calm her rapidly beating heart.

Raelynn didn't seem convinced. "Are you sure? I mean Beau's got his own issues, but I swear he's not evil or anything. Pretty much just doesn't say anything and keeps to himself. I'm not even sure why he's here honestly." Raelynn was staring intently at Ashley, making her laugh a little.

"What do you need here again? Let's just do what we came here for." Ashley tried to pull her friend further into the store and distract her.

The other three eventually made their way into the store and Kiah caught up to Ashley with Sahara and Beau following.

"Hey, Ashley, are you ok?" Kiah asked.

Ashley nodded. "Yeah, sorry. Just had to…um…get out of the heat." She glanced behind him and was startled to see Beau staring at her again.

Kiah furrowed his brows and then nodded. "Ok. This is my brother Beau. Beau, be nice. This is Ashley. She's new around here. Oh, and she has a boyfriend, so lay off the charm." Kiah laughed at his sarcasm, indicating his brother was anything but charming.

Beau rolled his eyes at his brother's comment, nodded at Ashley, and then suddenly turned in the opposite direction.

Ashley breathed out a sigh of relief and then headed off to find Raelynn. She wasn't sure what to do about Beau

yet, but she wanted a distraction. His eyes were intense and stoked painful memories for her. She needed to get home and look at her reports again and send an email to the person about a meeting. She had to know if Beau was the person contacting her. Was he her father's illegitimate son? Ashley snuck a glance at him from across the aisles and couldn't help but notice the lines of his face. He had to be her father's son. His skin was darker, but the eyes and lines of his face were unmistakable.

Catching her breath in her throat, Ashley moved closer to Raelynn. She hadn't even looked at anything to purchase, just continued to spin thoughts in her head. *This can't continue*, she thought. *I have to know.* With that thought, she pulled out her phone and opened the email app. Hovering over the "reply" button, she thought about what to write back. Her eyes looked around trying to find Raelynn. Maybe she would agree to go with her. *But how do I ask her something like that?* she asked herself.

"Hey girl!" Raelynn's chipper voice drew Ashley's attention behind her, causing her to almost drop her phone. She looked to see her friend smiling at her.

"I was looking for you. Are you done already?" Ashley asked, motioning toward her arm full of clothes. She turned her phone off to face Raelynn.

Raelynn shrugged. "It's easy when you love everything." She waved her hand, signaling Ashley to follow her. "Are you getting anything?"

"Not today. I don't really need any athletic wear," Ashley said with a snort. "Not really into working out in this god-forsaken heat. Just sitting around burns enough calories."

"Ha, yeah right," Raelynn said with grin and eye roll. "You really are something you know that? It's not nearly as bad as you make it sound. You're giving us a bad name."

Ashley laughed. "No, the weather does that all on its own!" She followed Raelynn and helped her remove the hangers from her pile of new clothes while the cashier started to ring things up.

Raelynn paid and then took her bag, giving the cashier a quick thank you. She glanced behind Ashley to look at her sister.

"Hey Sahara. I'm going to head out. You good?"

Sahara nodded and waved.

Ashley followed Raelynn outside and took in a deep breath of air. It was humid again and they were close to the ocean, which probably didn't help the humidity. But the heat wasn't as stifling as it was further away in Salisbury. Maybe the wind off the water helped, she thought absently.

She looked back at Raelynn, surprised she came all this way for just one store. "Is that all you needed, Raelynn?" Ashley asked, surprised that she was ready to leave already.

Raelynn looked over her shoulder at Ashley and shrugged. "I didn't need that much, but you seem uncomfortable, so I thought we could just go somewhere else. You can tell me what's up or not, but either way, it's obvious you aren't ok hanging out with the guys." She shrugged as she unlocked the door so Ashley could get in.

Feeling a little guilty and sheepish, Ashley gave her a weak smile. "I'm sorry. Beau reminds me of…someone." She raised her eyes to look into Raelynn's concerned ones. "Thanks for understanding. I appreciate it more than you could know." She was relieved but she also felt bad because she was getting in the way of Raelynn and Sahara's time together.

As if reading her mind, Raelynn reached out and patted Ashley's arm. "Don't worry about it. I can see Sahara whenever I want. I don't get much alone time with her anymore anyway with Kiah always around, but I'm fine going too. Besides, Beau is a major killjoy. Guy never smiles and always looks so angry at the world." Raelynn shrugged and turned back to start her car.

Ashley was silent for a few minutes, thinking about what to tell Raelynn, if anything. The email popped back into her head. She glanced over at her friend. Biting her cheek, she sighed.

"Hey how often do you work?" she asked, thinking of a way to ask her to be backup for this meeting.

Raelynn looked over and then behind her as she backed out of her spot. "I usually work full time but asked for a couple weeks off for…some stuff." She hesitated, drawing Ashley's eyes to hers. "Uh, I have some family stuff to do, so I just asked to be put on the emergency list in case they need someone last second. That way I don't have to have a full schedule right now."

Raelynn turned away from Ashley and she couldn't help but wonder why—and the possibility that Raelynn wasn't being honest with her. But then again, she thought, she was doing the same thing, wasn't she?

Ashley leaned back in her seat and looked out the window. She never had a hard time trusting people, but this trip had been testing that so much. She wasn't sure if she was being followed, she wasn't sure if she could trust Raelynn, or Sharon, or Trish, or anyone here.

"Want to go get ice cream?" Raelynn suddenly asked.

Ashley looked over at her. "Sure. I don't have anything to do today. Where do you go for good ice cream here?"

Raelynn looked at her with a fake shocked expression. "You mean no one has taken you to Dumser's yet? What a shame! Best ice cream on the shore!" She made a sudden turn to her left and headed toward the ocean, mumbling something under her breath about the tragedy or something.

"Where are we going?" Ashley asked.

Raelynn glanced over as she was changing lanes. "To the boardwalk. It's the best place to get anything around here. Have you had Thrasher's fries yet?" Raelynn's face almost dared Ashley to say no and Ashley couldn't help but chuckle at her friend.

Slowly, she shook her head side to side, waiting for Raelynn to freak out at her. She almost braced herself for another sharp turn.

"Who has been your tour guide here? Seriously lacking in their services." She looked over and winked. "You should fire them and hire me. I know everything there is to know about the Eastern Shore. Hmm, I should start a tour guide business, you know like they do in Hawaii." Raelynn lost herself in her thoughts and Ashley sat back and laughed.

The short drive to the inlet was quiet as they were both lost in their thoughts. Raelynn managed to find a parking spot on the street that would be cheaper than the lot. It was close to the boardwalk as well, so they got out and met in front of her car. She paid at the kiosk and then they made their way across the street to one of the alleys leading up to the old-fashioned wooden boardwalk.

Ashley loved coming here and she wasn't sure if it could ever get old. The old wooden boards creaked as they walked over them but the character it gave to the coastline was beautiful and charming. It was packed with people as they made their way to the main part of the walkway. She followed closely behind Raelynn, not knowing exactly where to go.

They came to a stop at the end of a long line. Ashley couldn't even see where it started as she shielded her eyes to try to see where the people were going.

"You stay here. I am going to get in another line for milkshakes. Any flavor you don't want or prefer?" Raelynn asked as she stood just outside of the line.

"Nothing with strawberry," Ashley said with a wrinkle of her nose.

Raelynn lifted her eyes. "Really? Ok. Stay in line. I'll be back. This one will take a lot longer than mine." And then she disappeared into the crowd. Ashley wasn't even sure where she went, she just disappeared.

She slowly moved forward in her line, watching people of all shapes and sizes, families and single people walk by. Ashley couldn't help but notice what some of the women had on, barely covering their bodies. She knew it was summer and hot and they were at the beach, but some of them could just as well of walked around naked. No one cared how big or small they were either. She tried not to judge but couldn't help but notice the girls who wore the smallest pieces of clothing could very well have had the largest bodies.

She tried not to stare. The last thing she wanted to do was body shame anyone. And she had to admit they must feel pretty confident in their skin to show that much of it. *Gotta give 'em credit, I suppose*, she thought silently.

Ashley suddenly felt like she was being watched. She looked around and didn't see anyone overtly looking at her. Raelynn was still nowhere to be found, and she shuffled a little bit, moving forward about an inch in her line. She stared straight ahead of her and tried to act as if she didn't notice anything. She could finally see where the line was leading, and the smell of grease hit her nose about the same time she realized where she was going. She could now see the sign for Thrasher's in bright yellow above a small building. There were still about ten people ahead of her and she felt like this line was never going to end.

Glancing around again, she still didn't see anyone looking in her direction. Suddenly Raelynn appeared and almost knocked her over. Ashley grunted as her friend bumped into her and then watched as Raelynn turned around and yelled at someone passing by on a bike. It was then that she realized Raelynn was nearly run over by the biker.

"Are you alright?" Ashley asked, as she steadied Raelynn.

Raelynn huffed. "I don't know why they allow bikes when it is so crowded here." She flung her hair to the side and handed Ashley a milkshake. "Chocolate. Is that ok? They have all kinds of stuff, but someone who doesn't like strawberry made me question everything I might choose."

Ashley laughed. "Yeah, I get that a lot. Long story." She held up her cup after taking a drink. "Wow, this is perfect for today!"

Raelynn nodded and grinned back. They had moved up in the line until there was just a family of three in front of them. Ashley was glad Raelynn made it back in time to order.

They got to the window and Ashley was surprised she just ordered a large basket of fries and nothing else. She thought it would be some gourmet thing since she insisted on this place specifically.

"I'll pay for this since you paid for the milkshakes," Ashley said. After she paid, they stepped to the side to wait for their fries. Ashley felt the same feeling of someone watching her and looked around again. Still nothing and she let out a sigh without realizing it.

"What's wrong?" Raelynn asked.

"What?" Ashley looked at her confused.

Raelynn narrowed her eyes. "You sighed. How come?"

Ashley's eyes widened. "Um, I guess I didn't know I did." She glanced around again and then looked back at Raelynn. "Ever get the feeling you are being watched but don't see anyone looking at you?"

"I do," Raelynn admitted slowly. Her face became really serious for a second and then she turned away from Ashley. "We'll just get our food and then walk back to the car."

As if on cue their name was called, and Raelynn grabbed it with a few packets of ketchup and then started back toward the direction of the car. Ashley had to nearly run to catch up with Raelynn.

"Hey, is everything ok?" Ashley asked Raelynn when she finally caught up.

Raelynn stopped. "Sorry. I just wanted to get out of here. For your sake, I mean." Her eyes shifted back and forth. She turned and looked at Ashley and tried to smile. "Sorry. Let's go."

Ashley walked alongside Raelynn, confused by her behavior. Something was up with her friend, and she wasn't sure it had anything to do with Ashley. She didn't say anything about it though. She would ask when they got to the car, as it seemed Raelynn wanted to get out of there as fast as possible.

Once they were secure in the car, Ashley turned to Raelynn and asked, "What's going on? Are you ok?"

Raelynn let out a breath and shook her head. "Not really. I've been asking questions about my dad, and I think I have some people pissed that I am."

Chapter 23

Ashley stared at her phone screen. *How soon? Like tomorrow? I can meet tomorrow around 3:00pm. I am done with work around 2 so I can be pretty much anywhere by 3. Name the place. Scratch that, you're not from here. How about Backstreet Grill? If that works, I'll send the address. Email is still probably the easiest way to communicate for now. I can give you my number after we meet.*

She had Raelynn help her form a response after she agreed to help Ashley out, all too eager for some excitement in her boring life—Raelynn's exact words. She suggested Ashley tell the person she was in town for a vacation and so meeting sooner rather than later was preferred.

They were sitting in Ashley's apartment talking when the response came through, barely fifteen minutes after she sent it. Ashley was starting to question if she did the right thing, but after meeting Beau, she had to know. The resemblance was too much to dismiss. Now she had to think about what came next. Maybe she shouldn't have even reached out and just left town. Did she want to open herself up to someone who seemed to have the same angry disposition as her father? What if he was just like her father. She shivered at the potential danger she was putting herself in. The PTSD reaction she had when she first saw him at the grocery store should have told her everything she needed to know.

But she wouldn't be alone if things went south. She knew she could lean on Raelynn, who was happily chatting away next to her. She wasn't even sure what Raelynn was talking about she realized as her own mind had wandered.

Her phone beeped with a text alert drawing her eyes back to the now dark screen.

She was surprised to see Aja's text and the anxiety she felt even over text as she read the words *Ashley, call me asap. Something is really wrong. Sam just left in a hurry.* Aja was normally calm, especially over text. She was short and didn't give much away. She must really be worried if she gave away as much as she did here.

Ashley glanced at Raelynn who was now looking at her with concern. "Everything ok?" she asked.

"I don't know," Ashley admitted. She pulled up Aja's contact and called her.

Her sister's usually cheerful voice was not who answered the FaceTime immediately. This Aja sounded a little scared and worried. "Ash, thank god! Is everything ok there?" she asked, her eyes wide.

Ashley hesitated, not sure what to say. "I thought so, but I guess now I don't know. What's going on there, Aja?" she asked, furrowing her brows.

"I don't know. Sam grabbed his 'go bag' and told me to call you right away and tell you not to go anywhere. He said something happened but wouldn't tell me what. Ash, I'm really worried." Aja's eyes filled with tears as she studied her twin's face.

Ashley took a deep breath and glanced at Raelynn next to her, who was staying out of the camera view. But the shift in her eyes caught Aja's attention.

"Who's there with you, Ash?" she asked, narrowing her eyes slightly.

Ashley turned the phone so Raelynn could wave and say hi. Relief flooded Aja's face. "Oh, good you're not alone."

"Why would that matter? Aja what is going on?" Ashley was beginning to get suspicious. "What did Sam say before he left?"

Aja sighed. "All he said was he had to go out east for a few days, maybe a week. He didn't say he was coming to you, but I found some stuff on his computer about someone out there 'looking for her' or 'found her' or something. The person was going to try to lure this person out in the open. I don't know if this is related to you or to some old case, but it sounded like this person has been working on finding someone for well over fifteen years, Ash. That's about the same amount of time that has passed since…" Her voice trailed off, but Ashley knew what she was talking about.

Ashley resisted the urge to laugh at her twin, because of course she hacked into their uncle's computer looking for information. The fear in her sister's eyes was enough to silence her humor.

Aja added, "So anyway, Ryan went with him so I know it must be a big deal."

Raelynn and Ashley looked at each other. Was it a coincidence that right after they get the response from this person, Sam gets notified about some old case? Was this connected or just a weird coincidence? Ashley knew Raelynn didn't know the extent of what it could mean for Ashley, but the strange timing could be on her mind as well.

"I'll be careful, Aja I promise. Who is there with you? Are you safe? I mean what if they are talking about you and not me?" She couldn't help but wonder if this was a redirect, to get Sam to leave Aja so she would be easier to grab. The thought made Ashley shiver.

"Damon is here with me with strict instructions to follow me everywhere." She dropped her voice and giggled. "I don't mind. I mean, have you seen him?"

Ashley grinned. Yes, she had seen Damon, and she knew what her sister meant. Raelynn had a confused look on her face and Ashley just smiled and mouthed, "Tell you later."

"I have to run. We are in the middle of a case here too that hopefully will be wrapped up after this…situation. So, love you, sis. Be safe!" Aja waved and then abruptly hung up.

Ashley figured they were going on a raid or something and Aja would be behind her computer screens giving directions to the team. She marveled at Aja's abilities and at the same time was glad it wasn't her life. She liked excitement and adventure, but not when lives were at stake or guns were involved.

"So…" Raelynn dragged out after Ashley hung up with her sister. "You gonna tell me the rest of this story? Because there has to be a story here. And who is Sam?"

Ashley chuckled. "Oh yeah there's definitely a story. I guess I should probably clue you in." She paused, not sure if this would change how Raelynn saw her or if she would continue to help her with the meeting. She fidgeted with her hands trying to find the right words.

Raelynn reached over and put her hand on Ashley's. "You don't have to if you don't want to. But it did look like your sister was worried about you. And by the way," she wiggled her eyebrows, "I have to say, when you said you were identical, oh my god, you are like looking in a mirror identical!" She laughed and shook her head. "I can't wait to meet her in person. I bet that's a trip!"

Smiling, Ashley nodded. "Oh yeah, we are that similar. Except in personality. Only on the outside do we match perfectly." She sighed. "I guess I should give you the opportunity to bow out of this whole meeting thing with me. It's a really long story and I'll be honest I haven't listened to much over the years. I honestly don't pay attention to anything about my father. So, I only try to get the important pieces out of everything Aja and Sam talk about."

"If I can help I will. I have made some contacts within the law enforcement community while I have been searching for my dad. They might be able to help too," Raelynn offered.

Ashley nodded and gave her a grateful smile. "Ok. First off, Sam is my uncle. He works for the FBI."

Raelynn giggled next to her. "So, you have a legit Uncle Sam? Working for the government no less! That's classic!" She threw herself backwards on the bed as if it was the funniest thing she had ever heard.

Ashley couldn't help but smile and shake her head. It wasn't the first time she heard it and that's why she usually just referred to him as Sam. "So, what I know is limited, like I said. But apparently my dad was into some shady stuff, aside from being just an all-around terrible person. I know he is in prison for murder and after he was arrested, it was discovered that he was involved in some extortion case related to human trafficking and money laundering through his construction company. I haven't seen him in about fifteen years. Aja has done some visits virtually, but I refuse to have any contact. I was the one...I watched..." she paused and took a deep breath and closed her eyes. "I was the one who held my mom until she died--by his hand."

Raelynn was silent next to her, and Ashley was surprised she didn't hear anything, not even a gasp. She slowly opened her eyes and met Raelynn's sympathetic ones. There was something else there, like she wasn't surprised about this information, causing Ashley to narrow her eyes.

"Why aren't you shocked?" Ashley slowly pulled herself away from Raelynn, confused about why this person wouldn't be shocked by her story. It was almost like she knew already. "Raelynn?"

Raelynn closed her eyes and took in a breath of air. She opened her eyes again and opened her mouth to say something but was interrupted by her phone ringing. She looked at the screen and then slowly stood, holding it tightly in her hand, making sure the screen was against her leg. "I'm sorry Ashley. I have to go. I can't explain right now but let me know when the meeting is tomorrow, and I will definitely be there. I promise. I just have to take care of something quick." And then she disappeared out the door so quickly that Ashley was still in shock.

"What just happened?" she asked out loud to the empty space. She stood and moved to lock her door, worried now that she was in fact trusting the wrong person. Who could she go to? Maybe meeting this person wasn't a good idea after all. Her thoughts went to Jacob's warning about it being a trap. And then there was the bigger question--was Sam coming here?

Ashley laid down on her bed and sunk her face into the pillow. If she couldn't trust Raelynn, should she meet this person at a different time than Raelynn knew?

Her thoughts drifted back to that horrible day so many years ago. She tried to think about what was happening back then to make someone come after her, and here in Salisbury of all places, so many years later. But she was just a little kid then. There was no way she could have had any idea what was happening to put her in danger now, she realized.

They had moved around a lot when they were younger. Her father would work odd jobs, or so she thought. She remembered Aja telling her some of these things a while ago. Apparently, he had owned a company that had filed for bankruptcy, but he had hidden money somewhere and had drawn the attention of some crime task force somewhere out east. *Where was that again?* she thought.

They were born in New Jersey, she remembered that part. She remembered some time spent in Delaware and Pennsylvania. But were they ever in Maryland? she asked herself.

She decided she needed to talk to Aja again. Her memories were too fragmented. She needed to put pieces together. She sent her twin a text asking her to call her when she gets a chance. Aja could hopefully help her fill in the blanks about their father and the possibility of what Sam was chasing—more specifically if it had anything to do with Ashley.

Ashley turned back to the email. She tapped her lips with her fingernail. *What to say, what to say*, she mused silently. She decided to just get the meeting over with as soon as possible. Once she met this person she could move forward and if Sam sent her home, she could do that and feel like she got some answers. The rest, any contact or anything else could be handled long distance. And if Sam was coming to her, she had to get this over with before he wouldn't let her go at all.

With that thought, she sent a brief reply. *How about tonight?* She hit "send" before she could change her mind. Staring at her phone, she questioned herself. But a reply came quickly, simply saying *ok, does Backstreet Grill work? On Snow Hill Rd in Salisbury 7:00?*

Ashley held her breath. Was she ready for this? She glanced at her alarm clock, and it showed four thirty. Seven would work. She sent a reply back and then dropped her phone. She couldn't help but wonder if she had made the right decision or not, but she wasn't going to back out now. Raelynn doesn't know about this either, so if she was up to something, at least Ashley would be somewhere else now. She had a tiny twinge of guilt and apprehension about going alone, but she had to brush it aside.

Deciding to try to calm her nerves a little while she waited for her sister to call her back, Ashley made her way to the small kitchen to see what she had for a snack. Her phone was in her hand in case Aja texted or called her back, which she didn't expect for a while if they were doing some sort of bust or arrest.

She looked through her stash of newly bought groceries and decided to make something warm, which made her chuckle since it was like four hundred degrees outside. But hot chocolate was always her go to drink when she was stressed. She pulled out the small container of milk and poured a mug full of it and then heated it up in the microwave.

Her thoughts drifted as she thought about everything. She jumped when her phone beeped, pulling her out of her mind's rabbit hole. Looking down she saw it was a text from Jacob. What would she tell him about what was going on, she thought grimly.

Before she could answer his text, her phone rang with Sharon's name lighting up. She crinkled her nose, wondering why Sharon would be calling.

"Hello?" she asked uncertainly.

"Oh, hi Ashley, dear," Sharon said, her voice cheerful. "I just wanted to let you know that Gary and I would be out tonight for dinner. Just in case anything comes up."

Ashley was confused. They didn't typically tell her when they would be gone. Why was tonight special? They only brought it up if they were inviting her along. *Weird,* she thought.

"Ok, no worries, I have plans as well," Ashley offered.

Sharon was silent for a moment before she responded with a barely audible sigh and chipper, "Great. Be safe, dear, and we'll see you later!" and the line went dead.

Ashley just stared at her phone. *What was going on with everyone?* she thought. She tried to shake the strange feelings she was having. She drank her now somewhat warm hot chocolate, gripping the cup with both hands. Letting out a frustrated sigh, she reached for her phone again. She was starting to question herself. Maybe she should wait for Jacob. It was just one more day anyway. But then her thoughts drifted to Sam. If Aja was right and he was on his way to her, he would be there within a few hours. He wouldn't let her go meet anyone alone, or maybe even at all.

With renewed resolve, she shook her head and straightened her shoulders. No, he wasn't going to take this away from her. She wanted answers. The only way to get those was to pull up her big girl panties and meet this person who was supposedly her sibling, or something. She still didn't believe she had a sibling, but once again her thoughts drifted to her loser dad who most likely cheated on her mom, among plenty of other bad things earning him that special adjective.

She opened Jacob's text and smiled as she read his words. *One more day, Ash. One more day! Can't wait to see your smiling face in person.* And he added his typical heart emoji at the end. She sent him a smiling emoji back with the simple message saying *I can't wait!* She waited a few minutes for his response and then set down her phone with a sigh. He wouldn't be there until late tomorrow afternoon, so she had plenty of time to decompress after this meeting.

A car on the driveway outside her window drew her attention to the window facing that direction. She stood on her tippy toes trying to see over the air conditioning unit and see who was there. She caught a glimpse of those familiar gray locks and watched as she saw Sharon approach Trish and give her a hug. She couldn't hear what they were saying, but she didn't miss the hand gesture from Sharon toward Ashley's window.

Unconsciously she ducked, but then let out a small laugh knowing they couldn't possibly see her. But the short phone conversation she'd overheard at Trish's came flooding back. Trish had said she didn't say something to Ashley, but what could that have been? She doubted the conversation before was about her but now she suddenly felt like it was. There was something going on with the two women that somehow had something to do with her too.

The warning from Aja came back to Ashley for like the millionth time. Was there something to do with Trish and Sharon that has drawn Sam out here? Were they the ones trying to get to her? That didn't make sense though. She may have been a little biased but would never suspect two women who didn't seem shady at all as being associated with her father. Then again, it would be a perfect disguise. But they would have had plenty of opportunities to take her during her stay here. So that didn't make sense either.

Ashley was starting to frustrate herself with the arguments back and forth inside her own head. Stepping back from the window, she sighed deeply. Ashley looked over at her clock again and saw that it was almost five thirty. Time sure flew when she was running crazy in her mind, she thought.

"Ugh, where did I lose so much time?" she muttered. Grabbing her phone, she pulled up her maps app to see how far away the restaurant was from her place. Ashley looked up the address first and saw that it was only 3 miles but would take 8 minutes to drive it. It made her laugh a little about how long it took to go such a short distance to places, but she figured she did have to go around downtown Salisbury too, which meant plenty of stoplights.

Her phone rang, startling her and she saw it was Aja. She bit her lower lip trying to think of what to say. She had forgotten that she asked her to call and had to get her thoughts together again.

"Hey Aja!" she said as cheerfully as she could. "I forgot I texted you."

"Hey Ash. Just finished up this…situation. What's up? Did you hear from Sam?" Aja's voice sounded distant and distracted.

"No, I haven't heard anything. Have you found out any more about his trip?" Ashley asked trying to figure out the right things to say. She was stalling and she knew she couldn't for very long before Aja caught on. But she wasn't sure what to even ask her twin now.

Aja sighed on the other end. "No. I haven't heard anything, from him or what his computer so willingly let me know." Her small giggle made Ashley smile. "Now what did you text me about if it wasn't Sam?"

There it is, Ashley thought with a grin. Her sister was nothing if not predictable. And so focused. Ashley would never be able to get Aja off topic and keep her on something else for long.

"Um, I guess I was just thinking about some things. Do you remember anything about where we lived before we went to stay with Sam? I know it sounds weird, but I can't remember where we were. I don't know if I blocked it because of mom or if I just didn't pay attention." She bit the inside of her cheek as she waited for Aja to talk. She felt kind of stupid asking because it had to be strange for her not to know where she lived when she was a child.

"Hm. That's actually a good question. I guess I have to think about it. Why are you asking though? Did something happen?" Aja's voice had a soft and concerning tone, and Ashley didn't feel judged which helped a little.

"No nothing happened. I was just trying to figure out if we ever lived out this way that would draw these crazies to watch for one of us to come back here. Like I said, I just don't remember if we ever lived here." After a second, she added, "That is if this trip of Sam's has anything to do with me at all."

Aja was silent. Some subtle shuffling on the other end made Ashley wrinkle her eyebrows.

"Aja, if you are busy, we can talk later. I know you said you just finished up with something. Nothing I have asked is pressing," Ashley said, trying to convince herself and her sister that everything was just weird coincidences.

"Hm, come to think of it, I don't think I've ever seen our birth certificates. Have you?" Aja asked thoughtfully. "Every time I had to submit one, Sam just sent it in and then locked it up again."

Ashley narrowed her eyes. "Huh. That's weird right? I mean who hasn't seen their birth certificates by this time in their lives? Do you even know where they are, Aja? I'm curious now. Not really sure what I would find out, but I'm curious." It was odd that they had never seen them. Now that her sister mentioned it, she was right. For sports or jobs, Sam always brought the document in and then took it again.

A notification came in her ear, drawing Ashley's attention away from her sister. She put the phone on speaker, since this was one of the few times Aja didn't call her through FaceTime, so she could still hear her talk while she checked her alerts.

"I'm going to see if I can find them. Let's see how well Sam has trained me, shall we?" Aja asked with a soft chuckle.

Ashley scrunched her nose as she read another text from the random number asking where the mom was again. She sighed deeply. She thought this was over and done with.

"Ash, what's up?"

"Ugh, sorry. I just got another random text like before." She closed the app and turned her attention back to her sister, turning off the speaker. "I haven't gotten one in a while, so I was hoping it was done."

Aja was quiet on the other end. When she finally spoke, her voice was quiet, and she sounded worried. "Ash, please don't go anywhere until we figure out where Sam went and what is going on there, ok? Please promise me."

Knowing she couldn't lie to her twin, Ashley tried to come up with a half-truth. She wasn't going to skip this meeting tonight. But could she lie to Aja again? *It would just be one last thing and after this then no more lying*, she told herself.

"Ashley! Promise me!" Aja's voice was trembling as she shouted into the phone.

Ashley pulled the phone away with a grimace. "Don't scream at me!" Ashley said sharply, like a mother scolding her child. She took in a deep breath of air and held it, trying to decide what to say. Finally, she just said, "Aja, I can't just stay locked up here in this apartment. I need to get food and toilet paper and stuff." She waited for Aja to say something, sucking her lips in between her teeth.

Aja snorted. "You need toilet paper? Seriously? Fine!" she dragged out. "But only for toilet paper, Ashley."

"Ok, baby sister," she said with a grin, even though Aja couldn't see her.

Her reaction didn't disappoint. "Ugh. You're such a pain!"

Chapter 24

Ashley stared at the small building in front of her, second guessing herself for the millionth time. She had arrived at the restaurant about ten minutes earlier and just sat in her car waiting. She wasn't sure what she was waiting for, but she knew her anxiety was rising the longer she sat in that spot.

A knock on her window startled her but she managed to muffle her scream. She turned to see who was outside her car and scowled seeing it was Kiah, who seemed to enjoy sneaking up on people.

"What are you doing here?" she asked, rolling down her window, scowling at his wide smile.

Kiah shrugged. "Meeting someone," he said, but looked away avoiding her eyes.

Ashley held up a finger to roll up her window and turned off the engine. She opened the door and slid out. Maybe it wouldn't be so awkward waiting with someone she knew. Then again, she was expecting Beau to show up. Why was Kiah here?

Once outside the vehicle, she closed the door and leaned her back against it. "Who are you meeting, Kiah?" She became more suspicious as she thought about it, but his response surprised her.

"I, uh, I believe I'm meeting you, Ashley," he said with a quiet voice, his hand tugging at the back of his neck nervously.

She turned her face slightly to the side and eyed him. "Ok," she dragged out. "What are you talking about?" Her arms were crossed in front of her as she watched his reaction. She shouldn't have been surprised by his response, but maybe by the abruptness of it, like he had known who she was the short time they had known each other. It would make sense then that he knew she was already here and could meet sooner.

Kiah sighed and motioned for the door. "I think we should go inside so I can explain." He kept his arm in the air, waiting for her to move ahead of him.

Ashley had to admit this was a better outcome than being alone with Beau, but she was still confused. If Kiah was the half sibling she was looking for, who was Beau? His similarities to her father were unmistakable. Maybe they were both his kids, and their mom is the one who he had an affair with so long ago. Kiah didn't look like she remembered her dad, but he could take after his mom she guessed.

They settled in a booth inside and placed orders for drinks. Ashley settled for water because her stomach was already in knots. She didn't need any help in feeling more nauseous. As the waiter walked away, a sudden thought made her blood pressure rise. Didn't Kiah say he recognized her from a picture his dad had? Was she really the "she" referred to in the emails Aja found; the reason why Sam had to suddenly leave? Had her father's gang of dangerous men included Kiah and Beau, and they really were there to grab her?

She felt hot and cold at the same time as her mind spun so many different scenarios about what was happening. She stared at the menu trying to act like she was just looking for something to eat. Inside she was starting to panic. Before her mind could spiral too far out of control, Kiah spoke quietly.

"Hey Ashley, I'm sorry about all this. I had suspicions after I found the picture my dad had, but the letter coming from Minnesota confused me. I seriously just put everything together yesterday, I promise," he said with a sigh. He leaned back in his seat and folded his hands in his lap.

His eyes didn't meet hers, making her worry that he had actually set her up. *Why did I have to come alone?* she chastised herself.

She looked around and didn't notice anyone watching her or even looking their way. There were people lining the entire length of the bar watching various shows on the multiple tv's hung on the back wall. The seat backs on the benches were high and she couldn't see or hear anyone around them aside from those at the bar.

Turning her attention back to Kiah, Ashley didn't say anything. He finally looked up and met her eyes. There was something there, but she couldn't decipher it. Was it guilt? She had to say something or get out of there before something happened. She was suddenly scared. Everything was coming to a head. Sam's abrupt trip, the random text again, Kiah acting strange, Aja's warning, and then Sharon and Trish suddenly meeting up for dinner plans minutes after she had set up this meeting.

Ashley shook her head. *This is crazy. I'm making stuff up that isn't there*, she chastised herself. Convincing herself that she was overthinking, she took a drink of the water that had just been set down in front of her. The cold glass and liquid helped to ground her a little. She closed her eyes and took in a deep breath of air, letting it out again slowly.

"Ok, explain, Kiah. I'm kinda confused right now," she said simply and waited for him to speak. She leaned back and crossed her arms over her chest trying her best to act as if she was in complete control of her emotions and unbothered by everything swirling in her brain.

Kiah groaned. "It wasn't supposed to go like this," he mumbled. Finally, he looked up and met her eyes. "Look, Ashley. I know this is weird. Hang with me and I'll explain it all. Ok?"

Ashley simply nodded and waited, watching Kiah struggle with his words.

"Ok, let me see if I can explain this as simply as possible," he said, straightening in his seat and stretching his arms over the table. "So, I am going to first assume we are here for the same reason." He lifted his eyebrows at her.

Ashley furrowed her brows and then it struck her that she had just assumed he was here about the DNA report. She felt her face flush as she realized they might be thinking their meeting was not for the same reason. "Ok, why are you here?" She asked the question slowly, trying to get a read on Kiah's face.

Kiah cleared his throat and looked behind Ashley and then his eyes flicked back to hers quickly. It was subtle but she noticed, making her feel uneasy and the need to leave stronger.

Ashley slid out of the booth and went to stand, but before she could, she felt a hand on her shoulder keeping her seated. With shaky eyes, she looked up and saw those stormy brown eyes again staring at her. The anger wasn't there this time, but the darkness was. It scared her, but she had nowhere to go. She was too late.

He slid into the booth, forcing Ashley to move back to her spot. She moved closer to the wall this time and tried to figure out what to do. She was alone here, as Jacob reminded her so many times. *This was so stupid,* she thought. She could just smack herself. Why couldn't she just listen to those who cared about her. Now what was going to happen to her? She closed her eyes, trying to regulate her breathing so she wouldn't hyperventilate.

"Why do you look so scared?" the person next to her asked carefully. "No one is going to hurt you. We just want some information."

Kiah cleared his throat across from her, but she didn't dare open her eyes as she continued to try to calm her racing heart and rapid breathing. What kind of information could she provide?

"Ashley, are you ok?" Kiah asked, his voice thick with worry. "Beau, give her the glass of water."

She heard the glass being slid across the table. Ashley slowly opened her eyes and stared at the beads of water slowly making their way down the glass, pooling at the bottom. She didn't trust herself to move and pick it up with how much her body was on edge. She felt like she would drop anything that she tried to pick up.

Slowly raising her eyes to meet Kiah concerned ones, she chanced a glance at the man sitting next to her. His eyes were concerned and had lacked the edge she saw before. He actually looked worried. Ashley moved her eyes back to Kiah and resisted a scowl.

"Kiah what is going on?" She looked back at Beau and then quickly back to Kiah again. Beau's resemblance to her father just gave her too much anxiety to hold his gaze for long.

Kiah nodded. "Ok, so just let me get this out, ok?" When she nodded, he continued, "So I submitted the ancestry thing on Beau's behalf. I was supposed to do it as part of my honors bio class, but I just felt weird about it." He looked at Beau and then back to Ashley. "Well, Beau's adopted, so we figured why not take the opportunity to do some research at the same time." He shrugged as if it was no big deal.

The table was silent as everyone absorbed the information. Ashley felt herself breath deeper as she calmed down. *This wasn't a set up after all*, she thought with a little bit of relief. This was an actual "meet your long-lost relatives" thing.

"Wait, so you were adopted?" Ashley asked, looking directly at Beau for the first time.

Beau looked away and nodded. "I don't have a lot of information. My birth mom is my mom, the one who raised me. But I have no idea who my birth father is. My dad, my adoptive dad, somehow knows who my birth father is but has only said that he almost killed me when I was an infant, so my mom ran with me. That is literally all I know."

Ashley studied his face. There was a sadness there, something that made her heart reach out to him. She gently touched his arm, and he looked over. The thought that her father was this man's biological father pained her as much as it did to admit he was also her father. He wasn't a good man, definitely not someone you would be proud to call your father. Her thoughts drifted to that terrible night when she held her mother in her arms.

It suddenly occurred to her what kind of monster her father was. She didn't want to think about what could have motivated him to do such a horrible thing to someone as completely helpless and innocent as a baby. Ashley found herself wondering if he was somehow trying to get rid of evidence of his affair by killing Beau. He hadn't ever hurt Ashley or Aja that she remembered, just their mom. It was strange, and a new ill feeling came over her at how terrible a person her father actually was.

She almost felt jealous of Beau for being able to get away from the man at such a young age. He didn't have to suffer through the beatings of her mother or the fights or having to hide with her terrified sister. "You are lucky you got away," she said almost in a whisper.

Kiah and Beau exchanged looks. "What do you mean?" Kiah asked. "You know who his birth father is Ashley?"

Looking up to meet first one and then the other's eyes, she nodded slowly. "Unfortunately, I think I do. The report I got back from the registry said that I had a sibling. My mother died when I was five and all her time was taken up with me and my sister. I know she didn't have an affair. But my father was, to put it mildly, a class A jerk and I assume he cheated on my mom multiple times. Especially now." She waved her hand to Beau and tried to smile, but it likely came out as a grimace instead. "Sorry," she mumbled.

"So," Beau started slowly, "you are my sister?" His statement was more like a question and drew Ashley's eyes to his.

She nodded slightly. "I believe so."

Kiah leaned back in his seat. "Well, damn. There goes having you as my sister-in-law. Oh, hell, definitely not even as my girlfriend anymore! Ew." He gave an exaggerated shudder.

In spite of herself, Ashley laughed. "Am I that bad?" she asked, teasing him.

"Oh no, but if you are his sibling, then you are also mine. We do share a mom remember," Kiah said, waving his hands between Beau and himself. "We may not necessarily share blood, but it would still be like a sibling thing."

"Ah. Yeah, that would be weird. Not to mention, I do have a boyfriend," Ashley shot back with a grin and a lift of her eyebrow. She finally felt herself relax.

Kiah smiled widely and waved his hands in front of him. "And I got Sahara. We are good. Besides I always wanted a sister."

"Thanks, bro," Beau said sarcastically, but his smile made it clear he was teasing his brother. It was the first one Ashley had seen on his face and she had to admit he looked less scary without the scowl. "Wait, you said before that you have a sister. What's she like?" He turned his body to the side, putting his arm along the edge of the cushion.

Ashley nodded. "Yeah. Aja is my twin. We have been each other's rock since our mom died. Our uncle took us in when we were five, and we've been with him ever since." She fiddled with her hands in her lap, not sure if she should tell him where their father was or not. But the option was taken out of her hands when Beau asked the question.

"So where is this biological father, or sperm donor, now?" She didn't miss the edge to his tone. He likely wanted to pay back some of the pain that had been inflicted on him and his mom years ago.

"He's been in prison for over fifteen years. So, if you are looking for payback, it will have to wait. I honestly don't keep up with anything about him either. That's Aja's department. I don't want anything to do with him. And given what you have told me about what he did to you, it just reaffirms that I don't need him in my life." Ashley leaned back and picked up her dripping glass and took a long drink of the cool liquid.

The waiter showed up at that moment to get their orders. Ashley wasn't really hungry after everything she was learning but knew she should eat something. She ordered an appetizer while the other two ordered burgers.

"So, tell me about you, Beau. I don't know anything, except that you and I unfortunately have the same human as a father," she said with a sad smile.

Beau snorted. "Yeah. You know, I never really wanted to find out anything more about him. What he put me and my mom through, he doesn't deserve my time. But looking at you now, I am glad we did this. I hope we can form some sort of relationship after all this. And I am sure you will love my mom. She is amazing and made up for not having my father in my life."

Kiah cleared his throat obnoxiously. "Uh, excuse me. Is my dad chopped liver or something? I'm pretty sure he's been in your life for most of it." He ran his hands up and down his torso and added, "I mean I am here after all and not that much younger than you!"

Ashley and Beau laughed. "True. Ok, *Dad*, the only one worthy of that title in my life, has been great—aside from giving me this annoying little brother." Beau reached across the table and flicked his finger in the middle of Kiah's forehead.

"Ouch! Dude! I'm an adult now. Stop with that shi-I mean stuff!" He glanced sheepishly at Ashley. "Mom always taught us to be respectful around girls, so no cussing."

Laughing, Ashley shook her head. He was acting as if they hadn't met before or spent any time together. "While I'm flattered, Kiah, I'm not offended with swearing."

The waiter showed up with their food and Ashley was amazed at how quickly it was brought out. It definitely wasn't the typical slow southern pace of doing things. She looked at the plates set in front of Beau and Kiah. Her mouth almost watered while looking at their burgers. She couldn't help herself and quickly ordered one too.

"Sorry, that just looks so good. I haven't been able to find a good burger out here yet." She could feel her cheeks burn with embarrassment.

Kiah nodded. He lifted his burger, using both hands because it was so thick. "This is the best burger around here, unless you go to the chain restaurants around. Still a seafood guy, but this is the go-to order here."

"Agreed," Beau said as he looked at his plate. He glanced over at Ashley and lifted his eyebrow. "Do you want mine? I can wait for yours if you want this one."

To say she was stunned would have been an understatement. The impression of him as being like her father vanished in a second, if there were any doubts left in her mind, that is. His tone was soft, and his eyes had a genuine warmth in them. She felt drawn into them. She didn't know what to say at that moment. His offer was something her father never would have done. He never cared about anyone except himself. She was actually annoyed with herself for thinking just because he looked like the man that he would somehow act like him too.

"Uh, no, it's ok. I can wait," she stuttered, looking at her glass.

Ashley could felt Beau's eyes on her, but she kept hers down. She suddenly felt bad making assumptions about his character based on how much he resembled her father. But then she knew that it was her body's way of protecting her from harm, keeping her vigilant. But this person next to her confused her. It wasn't what she expected when she first came across him in the parking lot and at the store with Raelynn. Maybe he wasn't like their father after all. She needed to brush aside her assumptions and give him a chance. It wasn't his fault that he looked so much like the man who haunted her dreams.

Raising her eyes finally to meet his, Ashley gave him a small smile. "I'm sorry. It was a really nice offer. But as fast as they are here, I shouldn't have to wait long. Plus I have this to hold me over for those five minutes." She gestured to her potato skins as they called them here. She glanced over at Kiah who somehow only had about a quarter of his burger left.

"I was going to ask if you wanted to share these, but it looks like you will be finished before mine even comes out. Hungry, Ki?" She grinned at him, and he shot her a glare.

Beau next to her laughed as he followed her eyes. He leaned close to her ear and said loud enough for Kiah to hear, "He's a pig. Nothing you can do about it." He chuckled and shrugged as Kiah looked between the two and then flipped his middle finger at his brother.

Ashley laughed. "Oh, so you can make obscene gestures, but can't say the words, huh? Kind of hypocritical, don't you think?" She set her elbow on the table and rested her chin in her hand.

By now Kiah finally had his mouth empty and he swung his finger between the two of them, still glaring. "First off, you gave me permission to cuss, and secondly, I was being polite since my mouth was full." He crossed his arms and sat back against the bench cushion as if he had just had a "mic drop" moment.

"You are such a gentleman, brother," Beau said with an exaggerated makeshift bow from his seat at the table. He leaned over again and said, "I'm sorry about him. He was born in a chicken house. What can you do?" He lifted his hands in the air in a shrug.

Ashley burst out laughing. "Is that like an Eastern Shore thing? Like in Minnesota we say born in a barn."

"I guess so," Beau said, tapping his finger on his turned-up lips.

At that moment the waiter reappeared and set down Ashley's burger. Her plate of potato skins was still mostly untouched. She was surprised how comfortable she felt with both guys and was actually enjoying herself. Conversation was easy and she felt more relaxed the longer they talked.

"Would you like me to bring you a box for the skins?" the waiter asked.

Ashley looked between the two guys at the table and then shrugged. "How about we wait a little bit. I have a feeling they won't last long. Thanks though." She turned her eyes to look at Kiah who looked away with a knowing grin on his face.

They sat and talked for almost another hour when Ashley's phone beeped with an alert. She lifted her phone to see that it was Jacob. She had so much to tell him, but it would have to wait. She sent him a quick response back and told him she was having dinner, but she had a lot to talk to him about. She promised to call him in a little while when she got back to her apartment. His response was quick, and he reminded her that he was coming tomorrow afternoon. She hadn't forgotten, but the reminder warmed her heart. She was looking forward to him being with her.

Setting her phone on the table, she found both of them looking at her. "What?" she asked, looking back and forth between them.

Kiah just grinned and shrugged. Beau reached across the table and smacked his arm. "Bro, leave her alone."

"What did I miss?" Ashley asked, confused about their reactions.

Beau just shook his head. "Ki is immature and stupid. Your cheeks are a little flushed, so we are assuming that was your boyfriend on the phone." He shot Kiah another glare.

Ashley just nodded, unbothered. "Yep, that was Jacob. He's coming into town tomorrow to stay with me while I figure out what to do about everything. Honestly, I wasn't planning on meeting you tonight. It's just that, well, something happened, and I am not sure how long I will be able to stay."

"What happened?" Beau asked, leaning back again.

Ashley bit her cheek. "I'm actually not sure yet. I will hopefully know that soon. But we have the email account now so if for some reason we get cut off, we can always use that."

"Can I put your number in my phone, Ashley?" Beau asked. "I'd love to meet Aja too. It is always nice to know there is more family out there, normal ones, even though we have the same monster for a father it seems." His voice still held a hint of anger and hostility when he talked about their father.

Ashley understood his feelings well, even though her father hadn't hurt her directly like he did to Beau. Plus, she had Sam's help to get through that, but she still felt angry at her father for taking her mom away. She was also able to see justice served as he was sent to jail for her mother's death. Beau didn't get that closure.

They exchanged numbers and then Beau took the check to pay, even though Ashley tried to insist on paying for her own. He grabbed it and was gone before she could even get out of the booth. They walked to the parking lot together and she watched as they stood at the entrance waiting until she was in her car and waved as she drove away. *Their mom did a good job with them*, she thought. They knew how to treat women without being overbearing or chauvinistic.

As she drove home, she realized she now had a brother that she knew nothing about. She couldn't wait to tell Aja and Jacob.

Chapter 25

"I know, it's amazing, right?" Ashley gushed to Aja. "I wish you could meet them. They are funny and sweet. I hope I can meet their mom. She did an amazing job raising them."

"So, Beau is our half-brother, but what is Kiah? Is he dad's kid too?"

Ashley could feel a little bit of disappointment in her sister's voice. She always did seem to give their father a little more credit than Ashley ever did. "No, he is Beau's half-brother. They share the same birth mom, but Kiah's dad is married to their mom. I guess he's been in Beau's life for a long time."

Aja sighed on the other end of the line. "I still wish you wouldn't have gone alone, Ash. You were lucky, but who knows what could have happened!"

Ashley knew she was going to have to deal with that from her sister and Jacob, but it was worth it. And nothing happened which made it even better.

"I know, I know. But it is over now, and I am fine." She dropped her voice and then asked, "Anything from Sam yet?"

"No and he still isn't answering his phone. I think he shut it off because he knew I'd call. But I'm a little worried. Even when he goes on some assignment, he will tell us what's going on and when he'll be back. He didn't say anything this time," her sister groaned.

Ashley glanced in her rearview mirror as she sat at a stoplight. A dark colored car pulled up behind her and stopped an unusual distance back from her car. *Weird*, she thought. Another car could almost fit between hers and that one. She tried to shake off the uneasiness in her chest as the light in front of her turned green.

She slowly inched forward and then made a right turn at the last second. She watched as the car did the same and followed behind her onto a residential street. Ashley hated these streets. They were so dark with very few streetlights. She needed to get back on the main road.

"Hey, Aja, I gotta go. I'll call you later, ok?" Ashley quickly said to her sister. "Love you!"

Without waiting for a reply, she hung up the phone and concentrated on her surroundings again. This was a new part of town that she didn't know at all. She looked at the houses and realized she was in an older part of town. She would have to try to turn around somehow.

Leaning forward, Ashley tried to read street signs to see if any looked familiar. Finally, she saw Camden. That was one she knew. She quickly turned left and watched as the black car followed. She noticed it still kept a fair distance behind her, as if it was expecting her to make sudden turns. Or maybe it was just following her to keep tabs on her for someone else? Her mind started to spin, and she pressed on the gas pedal a little harder trying not to panic.

She watched as the car also sped up, getting a little closer now. Her heart raced as she tried to decide what to do. She scanned the streets for other cars but didn't see anyone. It wasn't that late, and she found herself annoyed that the sleepy little town shut down so early. Frustrated, she hit her palm on the steering wheel.

She was trying to think of who she could call when her phone rang through the silent vehicle, making her scream out loud. She glanced behind her to see the car closer now than before. She pressed the call button on her car's screen, hoping it was someone who could help her out of this situation, although she honestly didn't have a clue how.

"Ashley? Where are you?" Raelynn's voice rang out over the line.

Confused, Ashley looked behind her and then ahead to see what streets she was passing. "Um, Camden. Why?" She knew her voice was likely shaking, but she couldn't do anything about it at the moment. She needed to get somewhere safe.

Raelynn's voice sounded a little panicked like hers and she furrowed her brow wondering what was up with her friend. "Ash, you need to get to my place as soon as possible. I'm going to text you the address so you can just press it into your map. Please hurry!" and then the line went dead. Ashley stared at her phone and then heard the text alert. She glanced up again into her mirror. The vehicle hadn't gotten closer, but it wasn't far behind either. There was no room for any other vehicle between them anymore.

As she passed one of the few streetlights, she saw two people in the front, but she couldn't make out anything specific. Her thoughts only went to two against one and she wouldn't have a chance to make a run for it very easily, if she could even find a place to stop and get out—which she concluded quickly probably wasn't even a good idea anyway.

Pressing the address like Raelynn told her, she set the GPS to speak so she could concentrate on not getting in an accident. She thought about calling Sam but then remembered he wasn't answering Aja's calls anyway. Then again, she wasn't sure what she would tell him. Jacob was out of the question as she thought about how worried he would be.

As the GPS' tinny voice told her where to turn, Ashley gripped the steering wheel like her life depended on it. She slowed down for a stoplight that had just turned red. She noticed there weren't any other cars around and was frustrated the light even changed. It was like the world was stacked against her.

She waited for the light to change, tapping the steering wheel anxiously. She glanced back to see that the passenger door of the car behind her had opened. Panicked, she looked at the light that was still stubbornly red. When a second look in her mirror saw a figure starting toward her car, Ashley pressed hard on the gas.

Ashley didn't see the van coming from the right until the last second and she swerved but it wasn't enough to avoid a collision. The hit was hard enough that she slammed her head into the window and could feel things blur a little around her. She tried to get to the side of the road, but felt her vehicle being guided on the same side and she gave in and let her car be pushed to the opposite side of the road.

Feeling woozy and disoriented, she laid her head back against the headrest and closed her eyes. She felt herself drifting and heard far away voices, but nothing registered. She heard someone say something like "We got her." She vaguely felt her door open and then being lifted. She hoped it was the police or paramedics and not the people following her. That was her last thought before darkness overtook her.

* * * * *

Loud voices arguing woke Ashley. She startled awake and looked around her. She was in a small bedroom, but she didn't recognize it. She was on a single bed and there was a small dresser on the wall across from her and a nightstand next to her. The single small window was completely covered with a thick shade and dark curtains covered that. She sat up suddenly and started to panic. Did the people that were following her take her? What were they going to do with her?

This was the only conclusion she could come up with. If it was the paramedics who took her from her car, wouldn't she be in the hospital? She wasn't tied to the bed and her hands were free. She could just run, right? The thought was quickly brushed aside when she heard the voices again, making her freeze.

"Roslin! I told you to watch her, not let this happen!" The first voice was unmistakable, and Ashley felt her fear quickly turn to anger.

"Listen Warren, I did what I had to. They were getting too close. I wasn't about to sacrifice my entire life for her." His voice dropped and he added, "I'm sorry. I had to take her." *Professor Roslin?* she thought.

"Hey, it could actually be better this way, boss," a third male voice chimed in.

"I agree. You both need to stop. We need a plan because when she wakes up, she's going to want answers. We can't keep her in the dark any longer." The only female in the group seemed to calm them down. And she was right. Ashley definitely wanted answers. She knew every single one of those voices, except one. But she had a pretty good idea who it belonged to.

Ashley made her way to the door and slowly opened it to find four people sitting at a table. It looked like something you would find in an office building for executives or something, not a dining room table. It was dark with only a few lamps lighting the area around the table, so she couldn't make out what the rest of the space looked like.

But that didn't matter. Her focus was on the four people sitting at the table. She almost wanted to fist pump herself for her guessing skills but decided to put her relief aside for the frustration that was slowly building inside. What was going on?

"You're right, *Sharon*. She does want answers," Ashley said with an edge to her voice, as she leaned against the door frame. "What the hell is going on, Sam!" She turned her anger toward him but didn't move.

Ryan chuckled from the other side of the table. When she shot a glare at him, he grinned and put his hands in the air. "Hey, I told him to tell you what was going on a long time ago."

Sam huffed at him and turned his attention to his niece. "Ashley girl, we need to talk. Come sit down."

As she moved to the seat next to his, Trish came through the door with a tray full of cups, a tea kettle, and some cookies. She looked at Ashley and smiled. "Oh, you're awake. Perfect." It was as if this was the most normal thing in the world. Ashley hadn't seen the woman smile before either. It was actually a little creepy she thought.

Ashley shook her head and slumped in the chair. "What is going on, Sam? You told me you weren't following me. Maybe if you had told me, none of this would have happened. I wouldn't have been trying to get away from you if I knew it was you last night! Or whatever day or time it is, I don't even know!" Frustrated, she slammed her hand on the table and then immediately put her other hand to her forehead. "Ouch. My head hurts."

Professor Roslin let out a small laugh but closed his mouth when she glared at him.

Sam cleared his throat and reached over to rub her back soothingly. "Ok, first off, it wasn't me following you. It wasn't *us* following you last night. It is almost seven, so you were asleep for a good eight or nine hours." She was surprised that it was this dark in the house, but it was morning. The few times she had woken up before eight it was very bright outside, and the sun was fully risen. She looked around and all the windows were covered with thick, dark curtains like the ones in the room she woke up in.

"Where are we?" she asked, looking at each person in the room.

No one said anything until Sam cleared his throat again, drawing her attention back to him. "We are at Trish's house. Well, actually, a safe house we have here. No one actually lives here, but I believe you were here once to meet Trish?" His eyes held a question, but it seemed he already knew the answer, so she just nodded.

He looked into her eyes and tipped his head. "You are in danger, Ash. The car following you last night had two of your father's closest associates in it, waiting for the opportunity to take you. They were his muscle, his enforcers if you will, when he was out and for some reason, they have stayed loyal to him. They were going to use you to lure… someone out."

He let that sink in while she stared at him with her mouth hanging open. Her thoughts went to Beau and Kiah. Did she inadvertently put them in danger? Who else would her father want to come out in the open than his own flesh and blood. "Beau," she whispered. *He tried to kill him once and probably found out he was still alive*, she thought.

Sam's eyes shot open wide, and he looked at Ryan. "Beau?"

Ashley watched as they exchanged some silent communication. Sam's eyes shifted back to her.

"Ash, what do you know about A-uh, Beau?" Sam stuttered over his name, making Ashley narrow her eyes at him.

"Sam," she began slowly. "You need to tell me the truth. What is going on?"

Sam sighed. "I will, but I need to know how much you know first."

Ashley shook her head, frustrated. "What do you mean how much I know? I don't know anything!" She pushed her chair back and stood. She walked to the nearest window and was about to push the shade aside when Trish was instantly next to her. Pushing it closed again.

"Don't touch the windows, Ashley. It's not safe." The short-tempered Trish she had met before returned suddenly, making Ashley bark out a laugh. She almost expected her hand to get slapped like she was a three-year-old about to touch a hot stove. The only thing she *knew* was that this Trish was normal.

"Sam, just rip the band aid off and tell her what's going on." Ryan's voice rang through the silence and Ashley was suddenly grateful for him being there. He was one of the few people who could talk to her uncle like that and get away with it. She knew why he would be here with Sam, but she was still not sure why the professor, Sharon, and Trish were here.

"What is everyone else doing here, Sam? I mean I get Ryan, but why everyone else." She swung her arm around gesturing to the others in the room.

Sam groaned. "Ugh. Ok, Let's just start at the beginning. Sharon is one of my associates from back in the day. She's retired now officially but agreed to help me out since you would be out here alone. Which by the way, I'm still mad about you going off on your own, young lady," he said trying to be stern.

Ashley just snickered at him. "You never could control me, could you? Always annoyed you. That's why you liked Aja better. She was the rule follower. Easier to control and keep close. But not me." She wasn't trying to sound bitter, but it must have come out that way because Sam's face soured.

"I didn't like either of you better than the other, Ashley. Although you are right, Aja is much better behaved. But I made a promise to my sister, and I wasn't going to fail at that. I loved you both like my own. And I wouldn't trade any of it for anything. I'm sorry you ever felt that I didn't love you as much as your sister. You are both my beautiful girls." His face had an unreadable expression and Ashley instantly felt bad. It had to have been difficult for him to raise two little girls on his own. She noticed he never married or really had a love interest. He just always said they were all he needed.

She and Sam were just so different, and her stubbornness likely made it harder on him than Aja's more compliant personality. "I'm sorry, Sam. I know you did your best. I just never felt like I belonged. You two are so similar and I'm just…different." She shrugged trying to brush it aside and changed the subject. "So, you are the one who arranged my stay with Sharon? You are the 'old friend' they were doing a favor for. To keep an eye on me?" She wasn't honestly sure if she was upset or not, but she wished she had known before now that Sharon was there for support.

Sam simply nodded his head.

"We can explore family dynamics another time," Trish interjected. "Right now, we have a bigger problem."

"Right." Ryan moved to the table and dropped a file on it. Then he moved to sit on the other side of Sam.

"Ashley, I need you to sit down please. We have a lot to go over before this afternoon." Sam motioned to the chair next to him where she sat before.

Reluctantly she dropped down into it. She wasn't sure if she wanted to hear what was going to be said, but she needed to know what was happening. Everything that had happened over the last few weeks started to flood her mind. How much of what she had been seeing and worrying about was actually connected to these people trying to get to her? She shivered at the thought that she had been followed for so long by very dangerous people.

Everyone was situated around the table before Sam opened the folder and started to speak. The first thing he pulled out was a photo. Ashley's breath caught in her throat. It was the same one Professor Roslin had when he accidentally dropped it the day at the university. She raised her eyes to meet his, but he quickly looked away.

"Ashley?" Sam looked at her with the question in his eyes. "Have you seen this man before?"

She looked around the table at all the eyes watching her. Dropping her own, she nodded ever so slightly. "I have seen him before, yes." Her voice was barely more than a whisper.

Her mind suddenly recalled a memory when the man was at their house one night with her father. Her mom, Aja, and Ashley were sitting in their room reading a story because her dad didn't want them to be there during his work meeting, he said. When they thought he had left, they went to the kitchen for a glass of milk before bed and he was still there. The man's eyes shifted to hers and he gave her a creepy smile, with missing teeth. His eyes were all she remembered, and they popped into her head now as she caught her breath.

The shuffling around the table made her raise her eyes again. Sam and Ryan were taking out more files that she hadn't even noticed before. Sharon and Trish were having a private conversation, but Professor Roslin was watching her carefully.

"Where did you see him, Ashley?" the professor asked.

Ashley shrugged, trying to shake the memory. "I saw him at a restaurant that Raelynn and I went to for lunch. Oh my gosh, I forgot about Raelynn. She called me upset last night, right before the accident. She wanted me to go to her place." She looked around the table and became annoyed when no one seemed concerned.

Sharon sighed. "Rae is fine Ashley. I've already talked to her."

Ashley stayed quiet but she was starting to get annoyed. *So, Raelynn and Sharon did know each other after all*, she thought. It seemed everyone was somehow connected and even Raelynn had a part in this. "Someone better start telling me what is going on because I'm starting to get really annoyed," she muttered to no one in particular.

Professor Roslin chuckled next to her. She heard him say something like "The resemblance in uncanny" with wonder in his voice.

She wasn't sure if she was supposed to hear it or not, but she did and she wasn't about to let it go. "Who do I resemble, professor?"

The table went quiet, and Professor Roslin looked around sheepishly, before finally meeting Sam's glare. He shrugged and mumbled, "Sorry, but it's true."

"Who!" Ashley said, raising her voice. "Someone please talk!" She was on the verge of losing her temper and even though she knew it wouldn't help anything, she didn't care.

Sam reached over and grabbed her hand. "Ash, calm down. We will explain everything. I promise. But we need to get through some things first." He squeezed her hand tightly and looked intently into her eyes.

Nodding, but not necessarily agreeing, she looked back to the professor, who looked down in his lap.

Sam and Ryan huddled back together again and pulled out a second photo. Ashley leaned over to see it and almost fell over when she saw it. "Seriously?" she asked, not realizing she said it out loud.

"Do you know him too? Ashley?" Ryan asked her gently.

Ashley nodded. "That's Professor Blake." She looked over at Professor Roslin. "Don't you know him? Raelynn said he was her advisor. He told me he knew all about me and school and that he would help me get in if I needed it. Ugh! I'm so confused." She slumped in her chair and held her head in her hands.

The day she saw him at the restaurant with Raelynn, he was friendly, not suspicious in any way. He did say he had heard about her, but would that have been from Raelynn? What was his connection to the creepy-eyed man?

"Uh, Ashley, he's not a professor at the college." Sam and Professor Roslin looked at each other.

"What? But Raelynn said…" she stopped. Nothing was adding up. "So, is Professor Blake, or whatever his name is, a bad guy? Does that mean Raelynn is working with him too? Ugh! Who can I even trust right now?"

Sharon reached over and put her arm around Ashley's shoulders. "You can trust everyone at this table, dear. And Raelynn too. I promise. It is going to best for you not to talk to Raelynn for a few days though. She is working on something for us. She knows you are safe and with us."

Ashley snorted. "Yeah, well, if Sam wasn't sitting here, I don't think I would trust any of you."

"Hey!" Ryan said with feigned hurt in his voice from across the table. "What did I do?"

Smiling lightly, she shook her head. "Ok, Ryan. I actually think I trust you more than Sam right now." She understood why Aja liked him so much. He was genuinely a nice guy, and his wife was incredibly lucky.

Ryan smacked Sam's arm and gave a small fist pump earning a glare from Sam.

Sam groaned. "I thought I brought you instead of Damon for a reason, Carter. Get it together!" Ashley remembered Aja talking about her team and Damon was the comic relief of the team. He always seemed to be joking around and lightening the mood in tough situations.

Ryan gave him a mock salute and then winked at Ashley, making her giggle, and earning another glare from her uncle.

"Ok, we need to get all the info we can about Blake and Jones here. Ashley, I am going to need to know where you saw them and when so I can get working on acquiring surveillance footage. Roslin, get your wife and kids here. We need to end this as quickly as possible, and I would feel better knowing they are where I can have eyes on them." Sam lifted his eyes to meet Ashley's.

"Ashley, we are going to be revealing a lot of things in the next few hours. I am going to need you to have a clear head. This isn't going to be easy, ok?" Sam's voice was soft but firm. "I definitely wish I had Aja's skills for all this now." The last sentence he mumbled under his breath.

"What about Jacob?" she asked quietly. "His flight is landing this afternoon."

"Damn, I forgot about him." Sam looked at Sharon. "He knows you, right? Will you pick him up at the airport and bring him here?"

"Absolutely. I'll get all the info," Sharon said with a nod.

Sam nodded and then a look crossed his face. "Wait, I have to talk to someone else first," he said to Sharon.

An alert sounded somewhere in the room and two TV screens Ashley hadn't noticed before lit up on the opposite side of the room. Each screen was split into six different squares. They looked like video cameras from somewhere outside. Ashley could make out a screen porch that was eerily familiar. Then she remembered they were at Trish's house. She hadn't seen any cameras before though. Where were they hidden?

Trish let out a chuckle, seeming to notice her question. She left the room and one of the screens shifted and tilted sideways. Trish appeared again and turned one of the creepiest dolls from her porch toward Ashley, making her gasp as she looked from the doll to the screen showing the group at the table in one of the squares.

"Yep, built in surveillance! Literally my eyes on the yard. That was just a deer running across the lawn that triggered the one in the yard." She directed the last comment to the rest of the room.

Ashley started to laugh. "Dang! I knew they were watching me! That's how you knew I was here before I knocked! Brilliant!" She was seriously amused by the creepiness and ingenuity of the whole thing. "So, the random things in the yard also have hidden cameras? Like the statue and gnomes?"

Trish waved her off. "Of course! I don't miss anything within 100 yards of this place."

"Ok, let's get to work," Sam said clapping his hands together. "We'll come back together once we have everyone here. Ryan you can start by getting everything you can from Ashley. I want to know everything you can remember from those random texts to the chance meeting with Blake and anyone following you before yesterday."

Chapter 26

"Ryan, how are things going?" Sam asked as he came back to the table from the kitchen area. He had a tray with drinks on it and a large bowl full of bagged snacks. They would order and pick up dinner later, he had told them earlier. He didn't want anyone to know they were here, and it was far enough outside of town that nothing would likely deliver anyway.

It was now almost four in the afternoon. Ryan and Ashley spent a good part of the day going over everything she could remember since she had been here. She tried to remember if the car following her last night was the one that was possibly following her when she went to Ocean City, when she had first met Raelynn on the beach.

They also had a doctor come in and evaluate her after the accident to make sure she was ok. It shouldn't have surprised her that they had one under contract specifically for them. She was, however, surprised to find out he had evaluated her the night before in case she had a concussion. Ashley must have slept through it or just forgot. Either way she decided it didn't matter. Her head didn't need bandaging, so she didn't think anything of it. She figured she just passed out from the fear or being overwhelmed, not necessarily because she was hurt.

Sam had left them alone early in the day to get some food and gather some more things, not specifying exactly what those things were though. Sharon had yet to arrive, and Professor Roslin hadn't returned yet either. She wasn't sure who he was bringing back with him though. Sam had said to bring his wife and kids.

Jacob had texted that he had landed about thirty minutes earlier, so Ashley was expecting him at any moment. She was trying to hold in her excitement. She needed him with her right now and she was so glad that the timing for his trip had worked out at the same time that everything else was happening. She had even managed to take a short nap, which was helpful after everything that had happened in the last twenty-four hours.

Ashley sat next to Ryan at the large table, waiting for everyone else to come back. The room was a bit lighter since some of the shades were now lifted. Sam didn't want all of them open and told Ryan to only open the ones that had cameras on those sides of the house. Ashley already knew that when the cameras were tripped the screens lit up so Sam must have felt better about no one being able to sneak up on them. She had to assume he had contingencies in the woods off to the side of the house as well.

Ryan looked up from his notebook where all the things he and Ashley had gone over earlier were written out. Glancing back down and tapping his pen on the paper, he looked up again to meet Sam's eyes and shrugged. "I have everything I can think of from Ashley. We just need to compare notes once Roslin gets back. He's been following Jones the last few months so he should have more to add."

Sam just nodded and tapped his chin thoughtfully with his finger. Eventually he turned to meet Ashley's worried eyes. He let out a deep sigh and moved to sit next to her.

She watched his movements carefully, wondering what he was going to say. She knew he was hiding something from her. After he sat down, he turned his body to face her and took her hand in his.

"Ashley girl. There are some things that are going to be revealed today that may be shocking to you. But I need you to hang on for me and we will get to the explanations. We have a job to do first and foremost and it involves your father and his potential release." Sam kept his voice soft and quiet, but not because he was worried about Ryan hearing. He was watching her reaction carefully.

Ashley caught her breath. "Release? He's being released? When? How?" She felt her face pale and her hands shake slightly as her uncle's grip tightened on the one he held. He grabbed her other hand when he noticed her breathing hitch. Fifteen years didn't seem close to long enough for someone who killed another person without remorse, especially since it was her mom that was taken from her. *Forever might not be long enough*, she thought.

"Breathe, baby girl. Breathe. I need you to stay calm. If I have anything to say about it, he won't be going anywhere for a very long time. But we have to be careful and do this right so we can make sure he stays there. Do you understand?" His eyes never left hers, but she couldn't focus on her uncle. All her fears of seeing her father again came rushing back and her mom's blood on her tiny hands invaded her thoughts.

All she could do was nod. Her hands felt clammy, and her ears were buzzing. She tried to focus on her uncle's voice as he tried to keep her calm. Ashley closed her eyes tight and tried to force out the memory that kept haunting her.

"Everything ok?" a new voice asked, making Ashley force her eyes open to make sure her ears weren't deceiving her.

Meeting Sharon's eyes, she looked behind her to see Jacob and an unexpected person behind him, making her eyes widen. She leapt from her chair and nearly knocked Aja over as she ran into her sister's waiting arms. Ashley tried to contain her tears, but she was so relieved to have her twin here with her while Sam just dropped a bombshell on her.

"Oh my god, Aja, I can't believe you are here! I have missed you so much!" she gushed as Aja hugged her back tightly.

Chuckling, Aja smiled and patted her sister's back. "Oh, I can imagine. I have missed you so much Ash!"

"How?" Ashley asked.

Aja shrugged. "Sam wanted both of us together after new information came to light." She looked around Ashley and made eye contact with Sam.

"So, what am I here for?" Jacob complained, but his voice was full of humor.

Ashley pulled away from Aja and wiped her unexpected tears with the back of her hand, turning to Jacob. He was standing against the wall with his arms crossed in front of his chest with a fake pout on his face. She reached up to cup his cheek and smiled.

"I missed you too, Jake," she whispered and pulled him in for a tight hug.

He returned it and whispered back, "I know."

Sam cleared his throat behind them, drawing the three pairs of eyes to him. "So now that you are here, let's get going. There is a lot to explain, and we don't have a lot of time. First and foremost is the safety of you two girls. I need you to trust me and just do what I tell you. I have to make sure you stay safe and hidden."

Ashley eyed Sam. She couldn't believe he wanted Aja here with Jacob and then she saw Damon come through the door with a smirk on his face. She looked between the two men and then just decided she probably didn't want to know what prompted her uncle to bring both Aja and Damon here. She was just glad they were all here together. Sam seemed to want his team here together as well.

"Damon, come sit with Ryan and get caught up on what he has so far. We are still waiting for Roslin and his wife and kids." He glanced over at Ashley but turned away quickly.

She assumed it was from their earlier conversation and brushed it off. Ashley felt Aja tug on her hand, and she turned to see what was up.

"Can we go somewhere and talk? I found something I need you to see." Aja's voice was low, and her eyes never left Sam, even though his attention was now on Ryan and Damon.

Ashley narrowed her eyes but then nodded and they moved to the small bedroom she had been in earlier. Jacob followed them and closed the door behind him.

"What's going on Aja?" Ashley asked, confused by her sister's secretive behavior.

Aja sat on the bed and pulled up a bag she had with her. She had a file folder and Ashley couldn't hold the giggle. When Aja shot her a questioning glance she shrugged.

Shared Blood

"What is it with everyone carrying around file folders?" she asked with another giggle.

Aja just rolled her eyes. "Ash, this is important. Stop messing around." She was clearly tired Ashley thought.

"Ok, ok. I just think it's funny." She shrugged and moved to sit next to her twin on the bed. "What's up that has you all worried?" She waved her hand toward the file now next to Aja's other side.

"I don't even know how to have this conversation." Aja's voice faltered as she tried to tell Ashley what she'd found. "Maybe it's just easier to see it. This is going to sound really weird. But do you remember Mom's first name?"

Ashley shook her head. "I guess I just remember Dad calling her Sissy. But now that I think of it, even Sam called her that. I assumed that was her name. Why?"

Aja's hand shook slightly as she opened her folder and picked up three papers. The first two looked identical. Ashley reached for them while Aja held on to the third. Ashley's eyes scanned the two documents. They were their birth certificates. But something was off. Suddenly she realized what she was looking at. Her last name was not Warten on the paper. It was her father's last name. She knew Sam had changed it when their father went to prison for their safety, even though he never formally adopted them. These were their original birth certificates.

She did remember him explaining once why he had changed their last name. But he didn't make it the same as his because it might be too obvious in case someone was looking for them, but close so they would still feel like they were family. His was Warren and he just changed one "r" to a "t". He must have had the court handle the change quietly too because Ashley didn't remember ever going to court or anything. They just started using the new name when they settled in with Sam.

"Where did you find these?" she asked, still staring at it. Her mother's name caught her eye. Shayanne. She never knew it before. Sam never talked about her using her name Ashley realized. Somehow, he had managed to keep his own sister's name out of his mouth for years. Ashley couldn't help but wonder why. Maybe it was too difficult to talk about her, just like it was so painful for Ashley to mention her father.

Aja looked down at her hands in her lap. She shook her head and whispered, "I kinda broke into Sam's safe." She slowly raised her eyes and gave her sister a sheepish smile.

Ashley started to laugh and then couldn't stop. Her sister had broken into Sam's safe of all things! She couldn't stop the giggles. It was just so crazy to her.

It didn't take long for Aja to join in her laughter and soon they were hugging, relief mixed with curiosity at what she had found starting to sink in. Ashley hadn't realized how much she had missed her twin, literally her second half.

A knock on the door had them both looking in that direction as Jacob moved slightly to open it, revealing Sam. He glanced into the room and saw the papers in Ashley's hand. She thought he would be angry, but to her surprise, he just sighed and shook his head.

Making eye contact with Aja, Sam smirked. "Seems to me I've trained you too well, huh? Unbelievable," he muttered. Straightening his back and waved them out. "Come on, let's get this thing over with and then we can talk about those." He turned and walked out, making Ashley and Aja look at each other with surprise.

"Why isn't he fuming mad, Ash?" Aja whispered when she came to stand next to her twin.

Ashley shrugged. She had gotten herself in enough trouble as a kid to know that something was definitely up. Either he expected Aja to do what she had done, or he knew there wasn't much he could do about it. When she got into trouble as a child, he didn't hold back his disappointment and issued a punishment quickly. His reaction definitely piqued her interest.

Ashley grabbed Jacob's hand as they walked out, still holding the birth certificates in her other hand. Aja plucked the papers out of her hand as she walked by and tucked it back into the folder, giving Ashley a knowing look.

They entered the large space again and there were now more people in the room. The screens on the wall were lit up and showed the multiple angles around the property. Ashley was still amazed by all of it. There were now three large whiteboards on wheels spread around with different writings on them and pictures taped in the corners. Ashley recognized two of the pictures--Professor Blake and the man they called Jones.

"How long were we gone?" Jacob mumbled next to her.

Aja laughed softly. "Oh, this is normal. They can whip this stuff out in minutes. It takes a little getting used to." She patted Jacob's hand like he was a tiny child and winked.

Jacob chucked and rolled his eyes. Ashley pulled closer to him and leaned into his side for support.

Sam stood in front of the screens and clapped his hands loudly. "Alrighty everyone. We are all gathered here to make sure that Vernon's, a.k.a. Viper's, parole hearing goes smoothly, and nothing deters the system from keeping him where he is for many more years. Understood?" He looked around at everyone in the room.

Ashley followed his eyes. She knew everyone here. Professor Roslin was still missing, but Sam had his team here in Damon, Ryan, and Aja. There was a woman on their team, but she was on vacation or maternity leave or something she vaguely remembered Aja telling her. Sharon and Trish were sitting on the far end of the table and Ashley pulled Jacob to move to the opposite end with Aja following her.

There were more drinks on the table than before Ashley noticed. There were now pitchers with ice water and what looked like lemonade. A stack of cups had been set next to the pitchers and another large bowl of snacks had been brought out.

Ashley grabbed a bag of snack mix and settled with a can of Pepsi and watched as Aja and Jacob did the same. She didn't even know what time it was anymore but realized she was hungry. She wished for pizza instead of snacks, but figured it wasn't quite dinner time yet. Aja always talked about how they would sometimes work through many meals and ended up getting takeout a lot. Sam had said they would get dinner later, but she wasn't sure who would go and when that would be. It was pretty isolated, definitely not Minneapolis, and would take a while for anyone to go pick something up and then get back.

The screens flashed across from Ashley and she watched as four people walked through the porch to the front door. She found it handy that she had been here before and knew at least that part of the house. Even with everything going on, she felt a little proud of herself for knowing this much information.

It didn't take too much longer for the four figures to make their way through the doorway from the kitchen and Ashley's heart stopped as she looked at the group.

Jacob's hand grabbed a tight hold of hers and he leaned over toward her. "Ash, are you ok?"

She looked over at him briefly and then back at the professor. She noticed with wide eyes Beau and Kiah walking behind him. They seemed calm, like they either knew this was going to happen or knew these people already. The fourth person with them she assumed was their mom. Ashley was surprised when she walked right up to Sam and hugged him tightly to her. He returned the hug and whispered in her ear, making her turn toward Ashley.

The gasp that escaped her lips caused Aja to turn to her. Ashley barely felt her sister's hand on her arm as she stared at the same hazel eyes that she saw when she looked in the mirror or at her twin. Her eyes shifted to Sam who was watching her carefully.

"Come, let's sit down and talk," Sam said slowly. He turned away from Ashley for a moment to put his hand on the small of the woman's back and gently push her to sit next to him.

After they sat, every seat at the table was filled. But Ashley couldn't tear her eyes away from the woman who had matching ones. Had Sam lied about having another sister, like she thought when she heard the woman's voice while shopping with Raelynn? It would make sense seeing how much she looked like him. Maybe they were twins too. But then why wouldn't they have met before? Why did Sam seem to be hiding her from them?

The questions swirled in her head as she waited for someone to speak and explain what was happening. She glanced over at Beau and noticed he hadn't taken his eyes off Aja. She saw them shift back to meet Ashley's then. Any other time she would have laughed. It was crazy that just yesterday they had discovered they had a common connection to their father. Suddenly remembering that, she looked back at the woman. Did her father really force himself on Sam's other sister as well? The thought made her sick, renewing her frustration that he could be released soon. Hopefully they could add more charges, especially if he raped someone. Maybe there were even more victims of her sick father.

Professor Roslin cleared his throat and Ashley noticed he was still staring at her. His eyes shifted to Aja as well, but he seemed focused on Ashley.

"Sam we are all here. Let's proceed because I think there are a lot of questions to be answered." He spoke to Sam but didn't move his eyes away from Ashley's still. He reminded her of when they were at the college, giving her the creepy vibes again.

Ashley squeezed Jacob's hand tightly in hers and he returned the pressure. She could feel his eyes on her, but she found herself staring at Professor Roslin's wife again. There was a mixture of curiosity and pity for her having to suffer from what her father did to her.

"Ok, let's get started we will do introductions after this, so we don't get off topic. Ryan and Damon, I need you to follow up with Roslin about Jones. I suspect we are dealing with more than just one guy. Sharon has Blake covered for now, but we will need to move quickly if he suspects anything." He looked over at Sharon who nodded.

"Raelynn is good for now, he doesn't suspect anything, but she has her device on the alert setting so she just has to push a button to get help fast. I have a few people nearby." Sharon's report was straight to the point and all who were used to this type of thing nodded in understanding and turned back to Sam.

Ashley was amazed at how authoritative Sharon sounded considering she had only known her as a nice landlord who liked to garden. This new version shocked her. And Raelynn was involved too? She had a feeling that even with the new revelations that there were more things to come, and she was already starting to feel overwhelmed.

Aja tapped her arm, drawing her attention off the woman she thought she knew for that last few weeks. The thought suddenly hit her that the chance meeting with Raelynn wasn't so chance after all. She wasn't sure how she felt about it though. She thought she had connected with Raelynn on more than a surface level, like they were actually friends. Now she doubted that and wondered what would happen now between them.

"Are you ok, Ash?" her sister asked quietly.

Ashley gave her a slight nod of her head and then turned back to Sam. She wasn't sure yet if she was ok. She found her eyes drifting back to the woman between Sam and Professor Roslin. She looked over and met Beau's eyes, but he quickly looked away. She looked back at his mom and noticed they didn't share many of the same characteristics. He definitely carried all her dad's, their dad's, looks. She had to admit it still freaked her out a little bit, but having spent a couple of hours with him, she knew he wasn't like her dad.

She had lost track of what everyone was talking about until she heard her father's name.

"The goal is to have enough to keep him away with no chance of parole. To accomplish that, we are going to need to play his game a little bit, but with a special twist he won't see coming," Sam was saying. The evil grin on his face made her almost pity the guy who was at the other end of his evil plan, but she reminded herself this guy didn't deserve anything from her and definitely not her pity or sympathy.

Her interest was piqued again, and she focused on Sam.

"Trish, I am going to need you to keep a close eye on everything from here and I am going to have Aja help you. She will learn a lot from you, although she has already picked so much up just being with my team for over a year," he said with a little humor in his voice and winked at Aja.

Aja looked away and blushed, knowing exactly what he was talking about. But Ashley noticed he wasn't upset, which she had to admit annoyed her. Aja had broken into his safe and she wasn't even going to get chastised for it? Deciding it wasn't worth worrying about, she just brushed it off. Her thoughts needed to be on this situation at hand.

Trish clapped her hands together. "Good. I have heard a lot about your little protégé, so this should be fun. Maybe she can teach me something too." She raised her eyebrows at Aja but Aja just grinned and lifted her shoulder shyly.

"Ok, Ryan take over what we have so far so we can get moving," Sam said, turning toward his right-hand man.

Ryan nodded and moved from his spot and went to one of the whiteboards. "Alright. We have two marks we are watching. Jones and Blake, which you already know. We have reason to believe there is a third and fourth along for the ride, the ones who attempted to take Ashley last night. I do not have names yet, but we have photos from the traffic cams. Aja and Trish can work on those identities as quickly as possible. Sam recognized them as Viper's former muscle and enforcers. We have a team watching over them as well, but they haven't moved from their hole since we took off with Ash last night. Sam and I aren't positive yet if they know who we are or if they think we are competition for getting Ashley. Sharon, you need to make sure Raelynn is not in any danger as well, so keep a close watch over her too please." Sharon nodded and Ryan gave her a quick nod back.

Ryan continued, "We know that Vernon has a plan to take Ashley since she is here and lure out Shay." He glanced over at Roslin's wife. "But we are going to be one step ahead of him. We will arrange for the meeting to happen between the two of you," he waved between Ashley and Roslin's wife, "but we will be in every possible position to make sure nothing happens. We will also have surveillance on the two of you with listening devices nearby to capture the words of Dumb and Dumber as they get close enough to you to tell you about their plan. I am pretty sure this is where the two idiots from last night will show their faces again."

Ashley stared at Ryan and gulped. She struggled to find her voice. When she finally could speak, after several sips of her drink to try to get through her dried-out throat, she croaked out, "Why? Why does he want me?"

Sam sighed across from her. "It's not you he wants, Ashley girl. He wants Shay. He's hoping to follow you to get her to come out of hiding so he can eliminate the only witness to his dealings and then win his appeal and get parole." He watched Ashley closely, making her slightly uncomfortable.

Ashley's eyes shifted to Roslin's wife. She had a soft and sad look on her face as she studied Ashley and then shifted her eyes to Aja. Ashley swore she saw a tiny tear in her eye, but she quickly wiped at her eye and looked back at Sam, straightening her back.

Kiah had been quiet throughout the exchange but suddenly jumped up and started to pace.

"Ki, please sit down," Sam said quietly.

"How am I supposed to be calm and sit through this? You are talking about setting my mom up to be taken or killed or anything! I can't just sit by and watch or not know anything." He stopped pacing and stared at Sam, who was now standing beside him.

"Kiah," Sam started, "You know I won't let anything happen to your mom. It's been far too long, and I want her to be back in my life. And the rest of your family should be part of yours. This is necessary to make sure she can finally come out of hiding and not live in fear of him coming after her again. With all of us supporting and keeping close watch, she will be ok. Trust me nephew. I will do whatever I have to in order to keep her safe."

Ashley looked over at Aja as her twin met her eyes. Sam had another sister who was supposedly in hiding for many years because of their father. This was an opportunity to finally free her to be able to live without fear.

Beau stood up next to his brother and grabbed him around the shoulders. "Come on, bro. You know she has been struggling lately and we need to do what we can to help free her of this burden."

Kiah leaned into his brother and dropped his head. He nodded slightly and then sat back in his seat. He dropped his head in his hands.

Sam looked over at Ashley and Aja and then sighed. "I think we need to get the biggest elephant in the room taken care of." He moved to stand behind Professor Roslin's wife and put his hands on her shoulders. She reached up and put her hands over his.

"Girls, this is my sister. Shayanne Anders, or as you would know her as—"

Aja gasped next to Ashley as she said as if in a trance, "Y-you're our m-mom, aren't you?"

Chapter 27

"I don't understand," Ashley mumbled for the millionth time. She was sitting on the bed in the small room again with Aja and Sam. "I watched her die, Sam! In my five-year-old arms!"

"I'm so sorry Ashley. It took a lot longer than we anticipated. It should never have happened like that; she shouldn't have ever been put in that situation. *You* should not have had to suffer like that at such a young age either. And I blame myself for that every damn day." Sam looked at Ashley trying to reach out to her.

But Ashley pulled away and stood, moving to the other side of the room. She wrapped her arms tightly around her stomach and felt her eyes burn with unshed tears. This was too much. None of it made sense. Who was the woman she thought was her mother if not her mom? The one she called mom and cried for after she died?

Aja stood and put her arms around Ashley. "I don't understand either Ash, but we have to figure this out and Sam has the answers. Please sit and hear him out." Her sister's pleading and watery eyes looked back into Ashley's eyes. The same ones she had always wondered where they came from, and now she knew. No one else had the same hazel eyes she and Aja had. She gave her sister a small nod but didn't move from her place.

Staying at her sister's side, Aja spoke to Sam. "Please just go on, Sam. Explain what happened."

Ashley marveled at the calmness her sister was able to muster in this situation. She couldn't do it. Her thoughts were running crazy, and she started to feel anger and resentment toward Sam and whoever the woman was outside the door. How could either of them lead her and her twin to believe someone was their mother and then put them in a situation to watch her die? How could anyone do that and then continue to lie for nearly two decades?

"Ashley, I know this is a lot. And believe me when I say there isn't anything we can do to change what happened that terrible night. But it is also important to understand what happened before that and why we had to do what we did way back then." He pleaded with her to understand and give him the chance to explain, but she couldn't say anything.

"It's ok, Sam. Just tell her. Tell us everything. From the very beginning, our birth even, if necessary," Aja said with a sigh.

Ashley looked at her sister. "How can you be so calm about this, Aja? What do you know already know that I don't?"

Letting out a deep sigh, Aja moved from Ashley's side and took the file folder she had before with the birth certificates and opened it. She stood in front of Ashley now and looked at her, taking out a single sheet of paper. She held it close to her as she met Ashley's confused eyes.

"I found this paper last night with our birth certificates and was up thinking for a long time after we hung up. Here, see for yourself." She gave the paper to Ashley. "I guess I knew something was up but had no idea it was this much."

Gingerly, Ashley took it and felt her knees buckle as she looked at it. She read out loud, "Confirmation of multiple live births. Three." She met Aja's now tear-filled eyes and opened her mouth, but nothing came out.

Aja nodded and then looked at Sam. "Beau is our triplet, isn't he?"

"What?" Ashley suspected for that brief second but hearing Aja say it out loud was just too much. She fell to the floor and held her knees like she was five years old again. The paper flitted gently to the floor in front of her. "What is happening," she mumbled.

Sam's voice was shocked and quiet at the same time. He shook his head and marveled at Aja. "You really are getting good at this," he mumbled. A little louder he confirmed what she had said. "Yes, Beau is your triplet. His birth name was Asher. Shay changed it when she ran with him."

Ashley shook her head violently. "No, this isn't happening. This doesn't make any sense. Sam, what are you talking about?" Maybe she did hit her head harder than she thought yesterday because she was starting to feel lightheaded.

"I think we should let Jacob in to help her, Sam. Is that, ok?" Aja asked quietly. "And maybe Shay as well," she added even quieter.

"You may be right," Sam said with a frustrated breath.

Aja moved to the door, but Ashley stopped her. "Wait." She looked at her uncle and whispered, "Tell me what happened and who did I hold while she died."

Sam moved from the bed and sat on the floor next to his niece. "Cece was your aunt, your dad's sister. After we arranged for your mom, well, Shay, to take Beau and leave, we had her come to take care of you girls. She never had any kids and was thrilled to be there for you. We thought it would only be a few months and you would have been back with your biological mom. But it took years to get enough evidence of all your father's dealings. Shay helped us with everything she had taken before she ran."

Ashley looked at Aja. "Cece? I always thought her name was Sissy," she said quietly.

"Vernon called her Sissy. It is a term many call their sisters. I sometimes call Shay that too." Sam's voice was sad and full of emotion as he talked about their aunt.

Ashley nodded absently. "I guess I have heard Raelynn and Sahara use that term too now that I think about it." She wasn't talking to anyone in particular. She looked at Aja and then at Sam. Both had unshed tears in their eyes like hers as they watched her carefully.

"She's really our mom?" Ashley asked softly, tears now streaming freely down her cheeks.

Sam wiped her cheek and nodded. "Yes, baby girl. Shay is my sister, my only family besides you two." He paused and then added, "Well and two annoying boys now, too." He chuckled, making both girls smile through their tears.

"Why did she run and take Beau and not us, Sam?" Aja asked, sitting on the floor next to him like they used to when they were little and afraid of going to bed.

Sam sighed. "Let me start from the beginning. When you three were about six months old, your father got really drunk and became angry with Asher's crying. He picked him up and threw him before Shay could get to him. He always hated Asher for some reason and anything nice he had to say was to you girls only—which was still not much. We didn't believe he would hurt you two.

"One night he beat Asher so badly he ended up in the hospital. Your mom called me, and we convinced the hospital not to file a report with child protective services because we were starting a federal investigation against him. We didn't want him to catch wind of anything so keeping everyone off his radar was important at the time. They agreed and then I worked out a deal with witness protection to keep Shay and Asher safe.

"Shay changed their last name to Anders and when she and Richard married, he adopted Beau and changed his last name to Roslin then. Shay decided to keep her last name as Anders, more for our records than anything else really.

"We managed to convince your father that Asher had died in the hospital that night. And in return, Shay helped us gather more and more evidence about your father. She still had access to everything remotely and he was so arrogant and honestly didn't realize how smart she is, that he never suspected she was doing it." He glanced over at Aja and smiled. "I guess that's where your hacking skills came from."

Silence filled the room as they all digested the information. Aja was the first to speak.

"Why now, Sam? Why does he want to get to us now? It's been nearly twenty years."

Ashley was thinking the same thing and looked to Sam for the explanation.

"I found out a couple of years ago that he was trying to find you girls. I know he has had visits with Aja virtually, but he thought you would be an easier target, Ash. Since you didn't seem to think about him at all, he figured you wouldn't even suspect anything." He chuckled to himself and added, "and he knows you love a good adventure I guess."

Ashley let out a small laugh in spite of herself and shrugged, knowing it was true. "If I didn't know Beau and Kiah already, I would think the DNA report was a setup by him to get me somewhere away from you guys." She sighed and looked at Sam. "I know why you were suspicious now and I'm sorry I didn't trust you."

Sam nodded. "I knew about the report and knew it was Kiah and Beau. You kids aren't as sneaky as you think," he said with a chuckle. "I'm still not sure I should've let you come out here, but maybe it is for the best now. I believe he found out about the report too and realized that he could potentially find Shay too and put an end to all this. Things have worked out so far, let's hope they continue to go in our favor. We suspect he would have tried anything to get Shay to reveal herself."

"So why now?" Aja asked again.

"His parole hearing is coming up and his lawyer is trying to get an appeal, something about new evidence. We suspect your father is trying to find Shay and have her killed before the hearing happens so there isn't a witness anymore, then in theory, our case would fall apart. We think he is getting desperate as the date is nearing and he still doesn't have your mother. He is getting reckless, or rather his cronies are." He chuckled darkly. "He never was very smart, that one," he muttered under his breath.

Aja and Ashley were quiet as they thought about everything he had said. Ashley's thoughts were still spiraling, but they were starting to make more sense. Beau had said he was almost beat to death by his biological father and Sam's story was the same. Could she really be a triplet? It had always just been her and Aja. What would it have been like with Beau growing up? What would it be like now?

A light knock on the door made her jump as Aja stood to open it. Sam pushed himself up from the floor leaving Ashley there alone. She watched as the person spoke to Sam and then after he nodded, Shay walked in. She looked at Ashley and Aja and her eyes filled with tears.

"Are you three ok if I step out to get things ready?" Sam asked, looking mostly at Ashley.

When both girls nodded, Sam stepped out, shutting the door behind him. They watched Shay stand awkwardly looking between them with no words being spoken.

Finally, Shay spoke first. Her voice was soft and full of sadness as she moved to sit on the bed. Aja sat back down next to Ashley on the floor and held her hand like they were little girls again, giving each other strength.

"He was right. The resemblance is uncanny," Shay said looking between them. Her matching eyes to theirs were filled with unshed tears as she watched them.

When both girls looked at her, she smiled. "Richard. My husband. He has a photo of me when I first met him almost twenty years ago and you girls look identical to me then. You are about the same age as I was then."

Ashley realized suddenly what Kiah was talking about. "That was the picture Kiah thought was me. In Professor Roslin's office?"

Shay nodded, realizing what she was talking about. "I would guess so, since I do not have any recent photos of you girls. Sam thought it best if we didn't communicate for a while until Vernon wasn't a threat anymore. But before that I did get photos of you two growing up, until about three or four years ago. Sam sent me a coded message a few months ago about what was happening and when I saw you at Rehoboth Beach, I panicked a little bit. I hadn't expected to see you there." She let out a long slow breath before speaking again. "I can't even begin to apologize to you both. There has not been a day that has passed that I have not wanted to go to you, hug you, tell you how much I love you both. I am so sorry for the pain you have had to carry and not having a mother by your side. I am so so proud of you both and what you have accomplished though. And if I can do anything to start to repair the relationship that your father destroyed, I will."

Silence enveloped them as they were all lost in their thoughts.

"Does Beau know everything?" Ashley asked finally, not sure if she wanted to know the answer. She didn't want to believe he knew and lied to her yesterday. But she would try to understand just like she is trying to understand everything now.

Shay nodded. "Before we came over, Sam and I met and discussed it all. We decided it was time for you to get to know each other and be a family. Richard and I talked to both boys before we left. They are just as confused and hesitant as you are, but we will get there. We have to take care of your father first and then Sam is hopeful that we can come out of hiding and be a family. If you want that, that is." Her face held so much love and fear at the same time.

Ashley felt the urge to go to her and comfort her, even though she wasn't sure what to do. Being as connected as they were, Aja met her eyes, and they stood together moving to sit on either side of their biological mother and hugged her from both sides. Ashley knew there was a lot of healing to happen, but she knew in her heart Shay was her mother. The rest they could figure out. She now understood why Shay's voice was so familiar when they met while shopping. She was the first voice Ashley heard before she was even born. Maybe it was somehow imprinted on her soul. Whatever it was, she was glad to have another chance with her.

She had a strange feeling in her heart though. Her aunt, whom she had held as she passed away came to her mind. She always felt a different sort of connection to her and now she felt as if she could truly grieve her loss. Not that Shay would automatically take her place, because Ashley did think of CeCe as her mother. But she could properly grieve the woman who had selflessly given up her life to act in her mother's stead for her mom and brother's safety. Ashley was proud of her sacrifice and would forever remember her as a mother figure to her.

* * * * *

"How are you doing?" Jacob asked Ashley as they sat at the table to eat.

Ashley gave him a small smile. "Honestly, it's a lot. I thought everything existed one way and found out it was all upside down. At least my belief that my father is the bad guy still stands. I think if that weren't true, I might just lose my mind." She snickered at him, making him smile and shake his head.

"Leave it to you to be happy about the bad guy still being the bad guy." He pulled her close and hugged her to his side. "You are amazing, Ash."

Ashley reached up and kissed his cheek. "I know," she whispered, making him laugh again.

A throat cleared next to her, drawing Ashley's eyes to her side. Kiah stood next to her and had a look on his face she couldn't decipher.

"Hey, Kiah. You ok?" she asked him.

He nodded and motioned to the seat next to her, asking if he could sit. She nodded and looked over at Jacob.

"So, I just wanted to say, um, maybe we could all get together after this whole thing is over?" He gave a little shrug of his shoulder and added, "I guess it turns out I am actually your brother too and not just by proxy anymore." His smirk was small, but it was still there.

Ashley laughed and nudged him with her shoulder. "Are you trying to apologize for your clear infatuation with me, Kiah?" she teased.

A horrified look crossed his face as he looked around her at Jacob, whose expression made Ashley laugh harder.

"Oh my god. Boys. This is so silly. Jacob, meet my brand-new half-brother Kiah. My *little* brother at that!" She nudged Kiah again.

Kiah groaned. "Oh, great now there are two of you. How did I get such mean siblings?" He leaned in and whispered, "Is Aja just as mean as you two?"

Aja appeared out of nowhere and laughed. "No, I'm the nice one. Ashley is the mean one. I'm not sure yet about Beau, but only time will tell I guess." She shrugged and continued walking by.

Kiah jumped up and followed her. He called over his shoulder, "I'm going with my *nice* new sister." And gave a small finger wave to Ashley.

Ashley and Jacob laughed as he chased after Aja. She was right though, Ashley thought. Aja was definitely the milder of the two of them. Ashley looked across the table to meet Beau's eyes. He smiled almost shyly and looked away. She leaned over and told Jacob she would be right back and then stood to make her way to Beau.

"Hey," she said as she slid into the seat next to his. "Are you ok?"

Beau shrugged. "I guess. I mean I knew we were related and that you had a twin. But this whole triplet thing is weird. I don't know, I guess it's hard to explain. You and Aja knew you were twins growing up. I had no clue. And I don't know what it even is like or what it means to be a multiple. Heck I hardly know what it's like to have a sibling and now I have three. Maybe I'm overthinking it," he sighed, leaning back in his chair.

Ashley reached out and grabbed his hand on the table, drawing his attention to her. "I guess I always looked at it as having a sister, but we look alike and share a birthday. We can take this as slow as we want, Beau. There's no rush. And it really doesn't have to be any different than we thought it was yesterday." She squeezed his hand tightly in hers and was relieved when she felt him squeeze back.

Beau nodded. "I guess you are right. I'm glad Ki found you, Ashley. He's a royal pain in my ass, but I am glad he found you and we were able to meet before this bombshell was dropped. It made everything a little bit easier to process."

"Yeah, I guess it did. I think I will enjoy making up for lost time with Kiah. I always wanted a little brother to torment." Ashley laughed as her eyes drifted to Kiah with Aja across the room. Then she sighed, turning back to Beau, and added, "But I thought my mom had been dead for almost twenty years. That is a little much to take in,"

Ashley said. She was starting to get used to the idea and turned to see Shay and Sam close together talking quietly. She couldn't help but wonder how he felt all those years while she and Aja mourned their mother at the same time that he knew she was still alive, but unable to tell them the truth.

"For what it's worth, and I didn't know your aunt obviously, but you have gained an amazing mom. It must have taken a lot for her to leave you and Aja for me. I guess I have some making up to do, huh?" He gave her a lopsided grin and she laughed.

"She knew what she was doing. It's the same thing that made my aunt the amazing mom she was, even though we didn't directly share her blood. They both gave up so much for the three of us. They're both amazing women." Her voice had a longing to it that surprised even her.

Sam called to get everyone's attention as Damon and Ryan stood to move beside him. Sharon and Trish sat at the end of the table and Aja sat next to Kiah on the other end. Ashley glanced back at Jacob and then looked at Beau. She motioned for Jacob to move to her other side, and he quickly did.

Professor Roslin, or Richard, was standing off to the side, giving Sam his attention, while Shay moved to stand in front of him and leaned into his embrace. Ashley thought she looked relaxed and calm, and she felt a peace settle in her own heart. Was this the peace she had been missing for so long? She now understood why Richard always looked at her funny and she almost laughed at herself for thinking that it was a romantic interest. No, she just looked so much like his wife that it must have been weird.

A beeping sound went off and Ashley looked over where Sharon was sitting. She turned off something in her hand and then looked at Sam.

"Raelynn has been compromised. I have Baker and Chandler on their way to her. I will get an update soon. You go ahead, I am going to monitor this to make sure Rae is safe." She picked up her phone and whatever device was in her hand and left the room.

Ashley felt a pang of worry for her friend. She still considered Raelynn her friend but how Raelynn saw her was yet to be determined. She hoped she was ok, and was glad Sharon was watching out for her. Her attention was drawn back to Sam, Damon, and Ryan.

"Ok, so let's go over the plan for this meet and greet. Ashley, are you going to be ok moving ahead? I know this isn't something you have done before, but you will have a ton of people around to protect you and keep you safe." Ryan's concerned eyes met hers.

She was struggling to admit she was scared out of her mind. Yes, she was the adventurous twin, but this was literally life or death. Would she be able to do this without giving anything away? Would she be able to get the information they needed to keep her father behind bars?

"Sam, what if I go?" Aja's voice cut through her thoughts.

Ashley looked at her twin and raised her eyebrows. "You are needed here to monitor everything. It's what you do to keep everyone safe, Aja."

"Yes, but there are plenty of people here who are capable of that job. I have been training for this. Going out in the field has always scared me a little bit, but this would be a good opportunity to do two things at once. I can get some real-life experience while still being safe with all of you around in case things go bad. If they are sure they can keep you safe, Ash, with no training, I will be more than ok." She lifted her shoulders as if it was no big deal, but Ashley knew her sister too well. She knew inside Aja was scared.

Ashley looked at Sam to see if she could read his face but couldn't decide what he thought. Aja always stayed behind the computers at the office. Sometimes she would go out into the field in a van tucked far away and out of sight and danger. This was something completely different, but Ashley had to admit her sister had a point. Aja had a lot more training and knowledge about this than Ashley did, even if it wasn't an official FBI operation.

Ryan and Damon looked at each other and nodded. Sam let out a frustrated breath, running his hands through his hair.

"And the student outsmarts the teacher yet again," he muttered. He raised his eyes to meet Aja's and then nodded. "You are right, Aja. You would be better suited than Ashley for this. If everyone agrees, we will move forward. But these idiots have seen Ashley. So, we need to get your hair to look like hers and then we should be good. Ashley doesn't have the blue ends, Aja," he added when she scowled at him.

Ashley laughed. Aja loved her colored extensions, but Ashley had always been more natural. She needed a rebraid anyway, so they decided to have someone come and do both girls' hair to look the same, minus the colored hair. Shay had a friend who would be able to help out and would be discreet.

Aja let out an exaggerated sigh. "I guess I can take one for the team," she hung her head in fake dramatics, making everyone chuckle around the room.

"Alright. That's settled. We will set the meeting for tomorrow night for dinner. Roslin knows the communication lines to spill the beans and plant the seeds. We can't do anything about what has happened to this point, but we can all work together to make the future better for all of us. Get some sleep and we'll meet back here at eight am. Girls and Jacob, you come with me. Shay, Richard, see you tomorrow. If you want the boys to stay with my people, I'll make arrangements." Sam raised his brow at his sister who shook her head, along with Beau and Kiah.

"We want to be where you and Ashley and Aja are. This is a family, and we will work together to get through this; all of us together," Beau said with conviction, looking around everyone.

Ashley smiled. She couldn't be prouder of her newfound family. They definitely couldn't change the past, but they could change the future. And for that to happen, they had to come together and defeat a common enemy— their father.

Chapter 28

To keep up the pretense that Ashley was still alone, she went back to Sharon's. Her car was now towed and being looked at. They weren't sure what it would cost yet to fix, but it was hit hard enough that the airbags deployed making it undriveable for a while. When Sam had picked her up at the accident site, they had cleaned her car out so there wasn't any trance or evidence left behind of her full name or other identifying information.

Jacob and Aja had stayed at the safe house with Sam and Trish. Ashley tried to argue for Jacob to go back to the apartment with her, but Sam held firm that he didn't want anyone to back down. He figured the four people they had eyes on were the ones tracking her with the random texts and calls. She and Sam both acknowledged they started when Jacob left, which means they knew she was alone then. If they knew he was back, they might back off.

Reluctantly she agreed, only feeling ok with it knowing that Sharon was on her side, and she would make sure to keep Ashley safe for the next twenty-four to thirty-six hours. At least she hoped that's all it would be. Shay made plans for meeting back at the safe house with everyone except Ashley at eight am. Ashley would come later on the pretense she was meeting with Trish. If she were to be followed, it would appear as if she was alone.

Aja would already be there when Shay got to the house, and she would get her hair braided first. Then Ashley would meet Shay's friend at the salon she worked to get hers done the same way. This way their hair would be identical and being freshly done, no one would realize a difference. Ashley would then make her way back to Trish's around lunchtime. They figured two hours would be enough time to do something simple with their hair. As long as they matched, it didn't matter what was done. It was honestly the least of her worries anyway.

The last thing was matching outfits. The goal was to make it look like Ashley went into the house and left the house. If they looked identical no one would be the wiser, which included clothing. They hadn't matched clothes since they were little. They had a very different taste in clothes now, but Ashley figured it wouldn't be too hard since it was deathly hot out, hopefully she thought not a pun considering what was coming, and a simple pair of jean shorts and a tank top would suffice.

Raelynn had been picked up safely by Sharon's guys and she was waiting for Ashley when she got back to her apartment. They had a long talk, and Ashley was relieved to find out that meeting Raelynn at the beach was completely coincidental, and they were friends before Raelynn was asked to help Sharon out with Ashley's safety. Ashley still wasn't sure how that all came to be, but she didn't really care. She was glad to have a friend while she tried to unravel all this new information.

Raelynn was currently stretched out on Ashley's bed. "So, this is all weird, right? I mean who would have thought Beau was your long-lost triplet brother. No one, that's for sure!" She laughed.

Ashley grinned. "You're not wrong. But the weirdest part for me is that my mom is still alive. My aunt I guess will always be a mom to me as well, but to find out that she was my aunt is just—a lot."

"I hope I don't have some weird family somewhere in the world. That's just so much to sort out." Raelynn had a longing look on her face as she stared out into space.

Cocking her head at her new friend, Ashley softly asked, "Do you ever wonder what would happen if you found your dad?"

"Oh, all the time," she snorted. "But I am just not sure that will happen. It's been such a long time, and no one can even tell us what happened to him. I don't even know where he went when he left the house that day. Did he ever make it to work? Did something happen on the way home? At lunch? There are just so many unknowns and every time I think I have a lead, I hit a dead end." Raelynn groaned as she flung her arm over her eyes.

"You know, there's a whole network of people here now that might be able to help you, Rae," Ashley said softly.

Raelynn laughed. "You don't say! It's crazy, isn't it? I don't know though. Part of me does want to know and another part of me doesn't want to find out he's into something horrible and I lead the cops right to him. You know?" She rolled over onto her stomach and put her chin on her folded arms. "I am sure glad we met, Ashley. And I *cannot* wait to meet Aja tomorrow!"

Ashley laughed and threw a pillow at her. "She's a trip. Kiah already has latched onto her as his protector. He's so weird," she laughed.

"I know! But Sahara likes him so I gotta put up with him," Raelynn scoffed.

Ashley knew she was joking, and they both really did like Kiah, and he provided some comic relief the night before when everything was unraveling. If she was worried about anyone, it was Beau. He seemed to be a little more shell-shocked than even Ashley felt. But she understood and knew he would just need time. It seemed he was more like Aja than Ashley in personality; quieter and more introverted.

It was getting closer to the time Ashley needed to go meet Shay's friend to get her hair done. Sam was concerned about her being seen with Raelynn due to her situation yesterday, but Sharon assured him the situation with Raelynn last night had nothing to do with Ashley's. So, Raelynn had agreed to take Ashley to the hair salon, since she didn't have a car. Then Sharon would bring Ashley to Trish's. It would all look normal. Ashley hanging out with her friend and then going to visit someone she had already visited once before.

Her anxiety was still increasing with each minute that passed though. She knew that Sam's team would keep Aja safe, and that Aja did have training for what she was about to do. But she was still worried. She was so glad that Aja had sensed her fear the night before and stepped in in place of Ashley.

"I wonder if Beau will go back to his birth name," Raelynn mused suddenly.

"I doubt it. I mean he has been called Beau his whole life that he knows. My mother definitely wasn't creative when it came to naming us. I mean, come on. Asher, Ashley, and Aja?" She laughed and shook her head.

"Mm, for sure. Who's the oldest?"

Ashley laughed at her friend. "Seriously? You have more random thoughts than I do! *But* I don't know. I know I am a few minutes older than Aja, even though she acts like the older sister. I guess we'll have to ask that question, huh?"

"Absolutely. It is of utmost importance!" Raelynn said, sitting up suddenly and pointing her finger in the air as if making some weird declaration. They both toppled over in giggles.

A knock broke them of their random thoughts and Ashley told whoever it was to come in.

Sharon came through the door hesitantly. Her face softened when she saw Raelynn and Ashley laughing. "I'm glad you are handling all this ok, dear. We need to be getting you ready and heading out. Are you ready?"

Ashley nodded. "Yep. I want to stop and pick up another tank top to match this one I have on for Aja, and I already have two pairs of these shorts. I'm going to throw everything in my bag and then we will head out. I am meeting you back here after my hair, right?"

Sharon nodded. "That's right. Ok, have fun with your hair and we will see you back here in a couple of hours. I need to make some cookies since we are going to 'visit a dear friend'," she said with a smile, making air quotes with her fingers.

"Where do we have to stop for the tank, Ash?" Raelynn asked. "And do you have the address of the salon?"

Ashley nodded. "Yep. It is over by Target so I thought we could stop at the Old Navy store there. If they don't have this exact one, I will just grab two and change when I get back here. Ready?"

Raelynn nodded. "Oh yeah. Ready to kick some butt!" She did some funny karate chop thing with her arms as she stood from the bed, making all three of them laugh.

"Be safe girls. Please let me know if you are followed or anything happens. I still have the device from last night, Rae, so use it if you have to. Remember to get somewhere safe with a lot of people around. I can track your location so press the button and then go." Sharon's voice had lost her "nice old lady" persona and was in the operator mode that Ashley noticed Sam did often. It still surprised her though coming from Sharon.

Ashley hopped up off the floor to grab her flip flops as Sharon left. Raelynn slipped her feet in her sandals and stood at the open door.

"How long do you think you will be without your car, Ash?" Raelynn asked.

"No clue actually. Sam is handling all that," she said with a shrug.

Raelynn giggled. "I still can't believe you have an Uncle Sam."

Ashley just grinned and shook her head. They made their way downstairs and as they walked past Sharon, she called out to them.

"I checked the street cams, and no one is around. You two be careful."

Ashley stopped and looked at her. "You have cameras all over here too?"

"Of course I do!" Sharon said incredulously. "Why ever would I not?" The shocked expression on her face caught Ashley off guard.

"I guess I was just surprised is all," she mumbled.

Sharon's face softened and she moved closer to Ashley. "Sorry. I forgot this is all new to you. Yes, I have cameras covering the entire property and down the street in both directions. When you live in this life for long enough, you don't even trust your neighbors sometimes. And we have lived here forever!"

Ashley just nodded. She didn't know what it was like to always have to watch for people out to get you for one reason or another. Just the little taste of it she has had so far is plenty for a lifetime for her.

Sharon watched them walk out, holding the screen door open. Ashley felt as if she was being watched and cared for like a grandmother would and it warmed her heart that this woman had taken her in like she had. Sharon waved as they made their way out of the driveway and Ashley sighed.

"Everything ok?" Raelynn asked.

Ashley looked over at her. "Yeah. I was just thinking that this is what having extended family feels like. I never had grandparents in my life and just now, how Sharon was watching us leave and then waving. It made me think that must be what it's like."

"Mm, yeah it is. I only ever knew my mommom on my mom's side," Raelynn said.

Ashley looked over at Raelynn. "What is 'mommom'? I heard Sharon's granddaughter say it too."

Raelynn looked over and narrowed her eyes. "What do you mean?"

"Mommom. What is it?" Ashley repeated.

Raelynn scrunched her nose. "My mom's mom. What do you call it?" She spoke slowly like Ashley had grown two heads or something.

"Oh! Yeah, that's my grandma." Ashley let out a little laugh. "I guess mommom makes sense, just never heard it before."

"Weird," Raelynn muttered, making Ashley laugh again.

The trip to get a matching tank top was quick and they were back in Raelynn's car on their way to the hair salon in minutes. Ashley decided a light blue would be suitable for both her and Aja. Ashley tended to like brighter colors while Aja preferred lighter ones, which Ashley always found funny since Aja liked bright colors in her hair, and Ashley preferred natural ones.

The GPS let them know their destination was ahead and both girls focused on the road. Shay had told Ashley it was in a small strip mall with a nail salon next door. That didn't help much since there were multiple nail salons on Highway 13.

After driving by it once and having to make a U-turn, they finally arrived and moved quickly inside. It was a cute little shop with photos and posters of all different hair styles for African American men and women. There were two sinks for washing and two chairs for styling. There was a large screen tv in one corner set on some music videos. Music was playing that sounded like a mix of jazz and rap. There was a doorway at the back of the space that was covered with brightly colored beads.

A petite woman met them as they came through the door. Ashley noticed there wasn't a reception desk for check-in.

"You must be Ashley," the woman said with a soft and kind smile. She was dressed in a colorful top with large flowers all over it and a long flowy skirt that almost reached the floor. Her feet slid into flip flops exposing her brightly painted toenails. She had multiple strings of beads around her neck and wrists. Her hair was wrapped in a multicolored scarf.

Ashley nodded and smiled back. "I am. and this is my friend Raelynn." She gestured with her hand to her friend who was standing behind her.

"It is so nice to meet you. My name is Talia. Shayanne and I are old friends from way back. Come in and let's get started." She moved to the styling chair and motioned for Ashley to sit.

She suddenly remembered she hadn't taken her braids out before. "I'm sorry, I forgot to take my hair out before. Is it going to mess up our schedule?" She tugged at one to start to unravel it.

Talia turned and shook her head. "I think we will be fine. You don't have too many and we should be able to just unbraid them. Those are simple to remove. Your sister's, though, were a bit more difficult since the micros are just so time consuming." She picked up a few of Ashley's braids and nodded with a smile. "Yep, easy."

Ashley relaxed into the chair and looked at Raelynn, who had picked up a magazine to page through. Looking around, she realized that everything here was for the African American population. The photos on the walls were all black people. The colors were vibrant, not like the muted pastels she was used to in other salons. There were a few pieces hanging on the wall that looked like old African relics. Two masks painted black and a statue that looked like a woman carrying a basket on her head were situated on a shelf. There were also two animal silhouettes of an elephant and a lion hanging on another wall with a large shadow of a tree over them. It could have been something from the Lion King, she thought.

She felt very comfortable here. She hadn't realized that being surrounded by those cultural things would make her feel welcome and not out of place at all. It wasn't like the other places weren't welcoming, but there was something to being welcomed in a way that she could relate to instead of what others thought she should. Sam always made sure to take the girls to different places and meet different people, but this felt like where she belonged, surrounded by her culture, and faces and hair that looked like hers.

"I should do this with my hair," Raelynn suddenly said looking up from her magazine, which Ashley noticed also had a black model on the cover.

She leaned over to see what her friend was talking about. The photo showed a woman with long braids on one side of her head, as if the stylist had braided all of her hair intentionally to the one side.

"Then I could walk around like this, and no one would think I was weird because I had all this weight to one side!" Raelynn snickered, tipping her head almost to her shoulder.

Ashley laughed at her. "Shut up. That's actually a pretty style. You should do it, but don't walk like that." She pointed her finger at Raelynn and make a small spinning motion with it.

Raelynn scowled at her playfully. "Pfft. You're no fun." She fingered through her hair absently. Then she added, "Yeah, but I'm not sure my 'white' hair will make it work anyway."

"That's a beautiful style," Talia said, walking back into the space. Ashley didn't even realize she had left. "And your hair, as thick as it is, would look fantastic like that." She smiled and then nodded to Ashley to follow her.

Talia was very talented and fast. She had removed all of Ashley's braids, unbraided her actual hair, and had it washed and oiled in less than thirty minutes. In another forty-five minutes she had her hair braided in new box braids with dark brown hair added to the ends. She was grateful that Aja didn't talk them into a color knowing that Ashley wasn't a fan of that.

It wasn't quite two hours later, and they were walking out, thanking Talia for her work. Ashley rarely wore box braids, preferring her hair tied up, especially in the heat here. But it felt good to have her hair tightened and moving freely around her shoulders.

Sam had told Ashley to turn her location back on this morning so that if they were going to try to track her again, they would be led right into the trap Sam and his team set up. She would give her phone to Aja then when they left to meet Shay later on. Glancing down at her phone as they got back into Raelynn's car, she noticed she missed a text.

She hesitated to open anything from anyone she didn't know, but she was well aware this was for Sam now not herself. He needed the information. Trish had put some sort of tracker or cloning app on her phone as well so that whatever was texted to her, as long as she opened it, would be automatically sent to Trish's computer setup back at the safe house. Ashley had just shaken her head, it was above her head, but as long as she was safe, she would agree to whatever Sam asked at this point.

The text was from an unknown number again. Ashley opened it to see a different kind of message. This wasn't a girl looking for her mother. This was someone trying to meet up with her.

Your information is wrong. Be careful who you trust. Meet me at Winterplace Park at 8pm. Sand volleyball court. Alone.

Ashley caught her breath. She knew better than to agree to anything, but it did make her doubt everything that was happening. Pretty soon, her phone lit up with someone typing. Trish had set it up so she could use Ashley's phone to respond to anything, as if it were coming from Ashley herself. She had to admit it freaked her out a little bit.

She watched in awe as a message was sent telling the person she would meet them, but it had to be at six because she had plans at eight. Ashley let out a small laugh. It sounded like something a twenty-something girl would say.

A quick response came back agreeing and telling her that he or she would be wearing a purple bucket hat. *Weird,* she thought.

Ashley pocketed her phone and glanced at Raelynn who was studying her.

"Everything ok?" she asked.

Ashley just nodded. "I think so."

"OK, then, let's get the show on the road, shall we?" Raelynn grinned and winked at her.

Ashley gulped, wondering what she was missing now and who wasn't who they said they were. Was Sam walking into a trap that even he doesn't see coming?

Chapter 29

The drive to Trish's house was quiet. Sharon hummed along with the radio, while Ashley was lost in her thoughts. There wasn't any more correspondence on her phone after Trish sent her response. But something didn't sit right with Ashley. She was new to all this FBI stuff, and she had to assume they knew what they were doing. If she were alone, she would immediately think the worst. The person who texted her the warning would have made her think twice about doing anything or trusting anyone. She didn't say anything to Sharon, but she planned to talk to Aja about it. She wouldn't put her sister in danger for no reason.

When Sharon parked the car, Ashley waited for her, even though she wanted to run to her sister. They still had a part to play, and she had to make sure nothing jeopardized this. She followed Sharon to the door and Trish immediately opened it. Ashley looked around at all the dolls' eyes and realized that some of them actually did follow her movement, making her chuckle at herself. It freaked her out so much the first time. Now that she knew what it was, it was funny.

Once inside, they moved to the back part of the house again where the large table was still set up, the whiteboards lining the sides again. Almost everyone was back as if they never left. Ashley found Aja right away and pulled her into the small bedroom again. She waved Jacob to stay there and give them a second, as if they were just going to change clothes.

Ashley flopped on the bed as Aja closed the door.

"Is everything ok, Ash?" her sister asked with concern filled eyes.

Ashley shrugged. "I don't know. This whole thing has me all messed up. I don't want you to get hurt in all this, but I just have this creepy feeling and it's making me a little scared."

Aja sat on the bed next to Ashley and took her hand in hers. "I get it. This stuff is always the hardest part, knowing who the good guys are and who the bad guys are. But I trust the team out there. If they are sure of what is happening, then I am going to believe it too. It's the one thing that I have learned more than anything during my time working with Sam. He is very thorough and would do anything to ensure the safety of this team."

"I guess. There must be a reason that he is asked for all over the country right," Ashley said with a sigh. "It's still hard though."

"I know. But I also know that he brought me and Damon out here for a specific reason. Damon is his go-to guy for *enforcement* if you know what I mean." She wiggled her eyebrows with a grin. "Damon loves a good fight. Ryan is Sam's critical thinker. He makes Sam think differently on some of this stuff, which helps everyone stay on their toes and not get complacent. Trust me, Ash. This team is the best of the best. The only ones I don't know about are Richard, Sharon, and Trish. But so far, they have shown they are loyal to Sam and this mission."

Ashley thought back to her interactions over the last few weeks with Sharon and Trish. She did admit at first, she was suspicious of Sharon. But when she put the pieces together, she realized that a lot of her suspicion came from her interactions with Professor Roslin, who it turns out was her stepfather. So, she should trust them too, right?

She decided she had to trust her sister with all this. Aja knew everyone better than she did, and Aja also understood what they were all going to do. She was still apprehensive, but she needed to put that aside for the moment.

Aja pulled Ashley up from the bed and hugged her tightly. "We will be fine, Ash. I promise. And then after this and we make sure *Dad* continues to stay where he is, we will be able to get to know our new family. Ok?"

For the first time, Ashley heard a hit of anger and resentment in her twin's voice when she referred to their father.

Ashley gave her a weak smile and hugged her back. "Ok."

"Let's go see what we have to do now and talk to Sam. Maybe he has some insight into what these guys are trying to do, and it will set your mind at ease." She pulled away and gently pulled Ashley by the hand toward the door.

"Wait! You might as well change since that's what everyone thinks we are doing anyway." Ashley grabbed the bag she dropped when they first came into the bedroom.

Aja took the bag and quickly changed. Ashley finally looked at her sister's appearance and she was genuinely shocked at how similar they looked. Yes, they were identical twins, but they always had their differences, from clothing to hair to colors. Even she had to admit it was a little weird looking at herself standing in front of her, and it not being a mirror.

"Creepy, right?" Aja asked, obviously thinking the same thing. But she had a huge grin on her face as she looked at her twin.

Ashley nodded. "It is definitely weird! Ok, let's do this." She felt a renewed burst of determination.

They left the room, and Ashley was immediately swept up by Jacob's arms. "Are you doing ok, Ash?" he whispered in her ear.

She hugged him back and nodded, trying to give him a reassuring smile. "I think so. Aja trusts these people, so I need to try as well. I'm thankful I am not going out there though. I know I would alert anyone to my anxiousness and would give everything away."

Jacob nodded and returned her smile. "I can't say I'm not glad as well. I know you will be safe here. Besides this is what Aja is training for right?"

Both of their eyes trailed to where Aja was talking to Sharon and Sam quietly in a corner. She appeared confident and not at all worried as they went over the plans. Shay had left about forty minutes before Ashley and Sharon arrived to make sure there was no crossover time in case they were followed. Beau and Kiah had stayed at their house and would come to this one once Aja, Sam, and Sharon left to meet Shay. She wasn't sure where the professor was though.

"It seems like everything is all set," Ashley murmured to Jacob, watching everyone doing their thing in different parts of the room. She had only been to their offices in Minnesota once and it was only to pick Aja up. She wasn't sure if this was always how it was right before they went out on some assignment.

Trish walked into the space from the swinging kitchen door. "Sam! We have a problem." She walked over to Sam and pulled him away from Aja to a different and unoccupied corner.

Ryan lifted his eyes from what he and Damon were doing to watch and then he and Damon got up to move to where they were as well. Sam nodded as Trish talked and then when Ryan and Damon joined the group, they huddled together. Aja watched with a concerned look on her face and then moved to Ashley's side.

"What's going on, Aja?" Ashley asked, still watching the small group.

Aja shrugged. "I don't know but it likely isn't good. The only time I've seen them like this is when something unexpected happens to make the plan change last minute."

Her words worried Ashley. Was the text she received something more? She suddenly felt dizzy and moved to sit on one of the chairs by the table. Aja was instantly by her side.

"Ashley, what's wrong?" Aja sat next to her, and Jacob sat on the other side.

Ashley put her head in her hands. "I don't know. It might be nothing, but I got a text before. Trish responded to it for me, but I don't know, maybe it is something with that?"

"I don't think so. Trish told us about it as she responded to it. I think it is something else." Aja's eyes shifted to the group still huddled in the corner.

Sam suddenly moved from the corner and walked right to Ashley and Aja.

"Girls, we need to talk. Some new information has come to light, and we need to create a contingency plan, in case things don't go exactly as planned," Sam said, his voice serious and his posture rigid.

Aja nodded and squeezed Ashley's hand. "What's going on, Sam?"

He groaned and lowered his voice. "We just found out that one of the guys who was after Ash two nights ago is an undercover detective. They are trying to build a case against another guy and are concerned that we will compromise their investigation. We have to be very careful."

"Well, that shouldn't be a problem, should it? I mean we know which guy it is, right?" Aja asked.

Sam shook his head. "Unfortunately, the captain didn't want to tell us who it was for fear that we would treat him differently and then reveal who he is to the bad guys. If this goes sideways, they need to make sure his cover doesn't get blown." He let out a frustrated breath as he hung his head.

"What else is wrong, Sam?" Ryan asked quietly.

Sam let out a frustrated breath. "Richard is missing."

Everything stopped for a minute as the group processed his words.

Ashley looked between her sister and uncle. She wasn't sure what all that meant for the situation they were in, but since everyone was worried, she was too.

Sharon walked over to Sam. "I think we have a solution. Get your team and let's try to figure this out as quickly as possible. We still need to get to the park in a little over an hour to get set up there too. We have to move forward with our plans, but we also have to keep everyone safe."

Sam nodded and called Ryan and Damon over and then asked Aja to come as well. The group moved to the side of the room away from the table. Ryan pulled one of the whiteboards with him, making a sort of wall between them and the rest of the space. Trish joined them, leaving just Ashley and Jacob to wonder what was going on.

"I don't like this, Jake," Ashley whispered, leaning into him.

Jacob put his arm around her shoulders and pulled her close. "I know, but they do this for a living. We just need to trust that it is all ok. They'll figure it out."

"I sure hope so," she murmured staring at the group.

It felt like hours before everyone gathered around the table again. Sam stood while everyone else sat down. He leaned over the table on his fists and took a moment before he looked around at everyone.

"I am very concerned about what is happening right now and I want to go over a new plan with everyone here now, and only everyone here. It is vital we have this as a contingency plan only and I will give a signal in comms as needed to change tactics. This is not shared with anyone outside this group for now." He looked around and met everyone's eyes. Ashley noticed Sharon and Trish were now missing.

Sam went over the new plan with everyone. Ashley only half listened, not really knowing what it all meant, and she knew she wouldn't be going anywhere anyway. She instead watched the faces of the team and was relieved to see that no one was worried or showed any concern about the new plan. *They must be used to it*, she thought. Even Aja was intently watching and listening, with no fear crossing her features.

Ashley marveled at everyone gathered. This was never something she wanted to be a part of but was fascinated by those who chose this every day. Somehow teaching young children sounded so much more fun to her. She knew Aja would strongly disagree though, which was one of the many things they differed on. It was funny though, she thought. She liked the adventures and Aja preferred to play it safe. But she was the one going into the career of high adrenaline while Ashley took the safe route of teaching elementary kids.

Suddenly she remembered why she chose that major. She had always believed that was what her mother wanted to do before she had the twins. Now she wasn't sure if that was her aunt's dream or her mom's. Ashley thought for a minute about that and decided it didn't matter. She liked the choice she made and if it was her aunt's dream, she would forever share that with her. It was something she could learn about her biological mom now that they have reunited.

Ryan clapping his hands together broke her of her thoughts and she looked over at him. Sam was now sitting at the head of the table. Damon was sitting next to him, and Aja had sat down on the other side of Sam, next to Ashley.

"Ok, so we have our plan. Ashley and Jacob, you two will stay here with Trish. She will have the visuals on us at all times and can help you follow what's happening if you want. First stop is the park where Aja will meet whoever this person is that texted Ashley. We will leave shortly to set up our feeds in the trees or wherever we can get a high position. I have a local team helping with undercover surveillance." He looked around at everyone and then nodded to Sam.

Clearing his throat, Sam nodded back. "I have the equipment ready to go for the park. The plan for step two, the meeting with Shay will go as planned for now. The contingency is for this meeting at the restaurant only. Shay will meet at the restaurant after we give her the all-clear. We don't want her to run into any trouble on the way in. They could use the meeting as a way to grab her before she even gets inside. And we need to be extra careful, since we don't know where Richard is or what he's up to." He spit out the last words, clearly upset with the new developments.

Ashley didn't even think of the possibility that they could get to Shay before the meeting even happened, but now that he said that it would make the most sense. They could easily get to her before she made it inside the building. It also occurred to her that maybe she was wrong about Professor Roslin being trustworthy. Maybe he was the one who followed her after all. Is that why he pretended not to know Professor Blake worked at the college? Or are they working together, and he is working both sides, like some sort of double agent? She shuddered at the thought.

Damon rubbed his hands together. "Do I get to be Shay's bodyguard?" He had an evil glint in his eye, like he would love for them to try to get past him. Aja told Ashley he liked a good fight. Maybe he was itching for one tonight.

Ryan chuckled at him. "No, but you will be the closest to her. We want there to be no option for them to get far if they do manage to grab her."

"Sounds like a good time," Damon said with a smile, and then rubbed his hands together again as if excited for the opportunity.

"Alright. Are we good? Any questions?" Sam asked, standing again. He leaned on the table and looked at each person. When nobody asked a question, he nodded and then pushed his chair away. He looked at Ashley and Aja and told them he wanted to talk to them in the other room.

Once inside the small bedroom yet again, Ashley and Aja sat side by side on the bed. It reminded Ashley of the times when they had gotten in trouble or when Sam told them they would be moving again. As she thought about it none of those conversations were ever good ones.

Sam quietly shut the door and stood with his back to it. "I'm sorry this is getting complicated and that there is so much being thrown at you these last two days. I can't even imagine what you are thinking or feeling right now. We have time to get through that though, and we will. But right now, tonight, I need you to trust me and only me. Maybe Ryan and Damon as I trust them with my life as well as yours. But be careful. There may have been a breach in our group, and I need to make sure everyone is safe and on alert."

Aja nodded, but Ashley just looked stunned. "I'm assuming you mean Professor Roslin, right? There are only a few people involved in it as it is. And I thought you trusted him, Sam. I just don't understand how he can just switch sides without anyone suspecting anything." Ashley tipped her head back to look at the ceiling.

Aja wrapped her arm around her shoulder. "This happens, Ash. It's just a precaution."

"I know, Ashley. My concern is a little bit more complicated than that. I do trust Richard. He has been there through some really tough things with me and Shay. I need to be sure before I tag him as a traitor. I need to make an alternative plan just in case I am wrong, and it is better to be safe than sorry." Sam squeezed her shoulder, trying to reassure her.

This was a hard pill for her to swallow especially considering she had been sure he was following her and acting weird around her. But she didn't know him as well as Sam did.

"Ok, I'll trust you all." Ashley sighed. She had no choice really anyway.

They made their way out of the room and Ashley noticed it was almost four. That meant they would be going soon to set up in the park. She turned to Aja and pulled her in for a tight hug.

"Be careful, Aja. I know you know what you are doing, but please be careful." Her voice was barely above a whisper.

Aja hugged her back. "I will. We will be fine and then we can move forward with getting to know our mom again. I love you sis." She smiled, but Ashley noticed her eyes were teary.

"Alright! Let's head out," Ryan called.

They had one vehicle that they had hidden just beyond the chicken houses off Trish's, or the safe house's, property. It was invisible from the road, and you had to really look to see it. Everyone filed out of the house except Jacob, Ashley, and Trish. Sharon and Aja were going to drive in Sharon's car and then the rest would go in the opposite direction and set up in the park, a few minutes after Sharon was gone.

Once it was silent in the house, Ashley felt a sudden emptiness. She didn't even have her phone because Aja needed to have it.

Trish glanced over at her. "Do you want to watch?" She had put on reading glasses and Ashley thought she looked like a cranky old librarian, shushing everyone around her.

Swallowing her giggle at the visual, Ashley nodded and moved to the long table she just noticed was set up by the kitchen door. There were three screens set up with wires going in every direction. There was an open laptop in front of everything.

It took about fifteen minutes for the crew to show up on the screens in their black SUV. She watched in awe as they climbed trees and poles to put cameras everywhere. There was a decorative gate at the entrance that was a perfect spot for a broader view. How they managed to hide them in plain sight amazed Ashley as she was glued to the screens. It didn't even take the crew of eight ten minutes to have the entire park canvassed. She heard Ryan over the speaker next to Trish tell her to check each one. She and Ryan listed off numbers and a series of "checks" to see the screens light up from about twenty different camera views. Maybe even more.

Almost as quickly as they came in, they disappeared. Ashley knew her eyes were wide as she watched. "Amazing," she whispered.

Trish snickered next to her. "Pretty cool, right?" She wiggled her eyebrows above her glasses making Ashley laugh. This was a very different Trish than she met before. She seemed almost playful and fun.

Jacob stood from his spot still at the table and pointed at the larger screens on the wall. "Um, is that normal?"

Trish and Ashley looked at the screen and Ashley froze. Moving toward the house from the direction of the fields behind the house was a group of five dark clothed figures. They had guns drawn and were moving slowly toward the house.

"Nope," Trish said matter-of-factly then moved quickly. She pushed the table to the side and then the rug under it right after. Then she lifted a trap door that led to a set of steps going beneath the house.

She almost shoved the two of them down and Ashley nearly tripped in the darkness below. Jacob stepped behind her as Trish yelled down.

"There's a switch to the left, flip it up," she said and waited until the light lit up the space below. "Ok, now move toward the door. Once inside, flip that switch on then shut this light off. Lock the door behind you and stay there until one of us comes to get you."

Then she disappeared, closing the trap door. Ashley heard the table slide over the opening again and she gulped. Jacob gently touched her arm and pulled her toward the door.

"Come on Ash. We need to move." She followed him reluctantly, not knowing what was happening above and feeling like she was in a fog.

Jacob pulled her into the next room and ran back to turn the light off like Trish had instructed. Then he went back to Ashley and closed and locked the door behind him. He pulled her into his arms and rubbed her back.

They listened for any sounds from above them, but the basement they were in seemed to be soundproof. She hoped it was fire and bullet proof too. Suddenly she was worried. Was Aja ok? Was Sam? What about the rest of the team?

Ashley suddenly felt claustrophobic, but it wasn't because of the size of the room. It was actually a large space in what looked like a bunker but set up as a studio apartment. There were appliances, a small bathroom, a small living room with a couch and chair, and an area with a bed. The feeling she had was more about being stuck with nowhere to go.

She looked around the room and saw there was no door or anything to lead out except the way they came in. If that was the case, how would they get out if something happened upstairs and they couldn't move the table. She felt herself start to hyperventilate.

Jacob pulled her back into his embrace and slowly breathed, trying to help her slow her own breathing. "It's going to be ok, Ash. Sam and his team are the best."

"Yeah, but Sam made it sound like there was someone feeding information to the enemy, to my dad's people. Anything could happen now." Her voice was barely above a whisper. But holding on to Jacob helped. *How did we even get to this spot*, she thought grimly. Just a couple of days ago she was living a normal life. Now she was being chased by bad guys. Her father's bad guys.

After what seemed like hours, Ashley heard a beeping sound outside the door. She frantically moved to hide behind the bed, motioning for Jacob to come too. He moved, but not before the door was flung open and Sam was standing there, looking around for them.

"Oh my god, Sam!" Ashley ran to her uncle and flung herself into his arms.

"It's ok, Ashley girl. You're ok." He rubbed her back, holding her close.

Jacob spoke up first. "Everyone else? Is everyone ok?"

Sam nodded. "Yes, we got here just a Trish was taking out the first one with her shotgun." He chuckled. "She's so insistent on using that damn thing. There are so many other ones that are better and faster, but the cranky old woman won't use one."

Ashley pulled away from him and wiped her tears. "Is Aja ok?"

"I'm good," Aja called from the doorway, with a huge smile on her face. She opened her arms and Ashley ran to her sister, holding her tight.

After a few minutes, Sam cleared his throat. "Ok, we need to move forward with our plan. Now we know who the traitor is though, so it will make the rest easier. Come on."

Chapter 30

Ashley waited by the screens next to Trish watching the restaurant table where Aja and Shay were supposed to meet. They had changed the time and location once they found out who had leaked the information. Ashley was shocked to learn that Professor Roslin was the one working both sides. Sam had depended on him to get the information out so they could successfully trap the men after Ashley and Shay. But they didn't ever think it was actually Richard they were trying to set up. Ashley was hurting for Beau and Kiah, who opted to stay at their house after the discovery, despite Sam not wanting them alone.

Ashley learned from Trish that the five men who were ascending on the house when she and Jacob were rushed to the basement bunker included Professor Roslin, or Richard, and four of the men that Ashley and Aja's dad sent to try to get to Shay. Sam and his team had shown up just as the group had almost reached the sides of the house. For some reason they didn't try to get in through the back, they went to the side windows and front instead.

Considering Richard knew where all the cameras were placed, she thought it was an odd strategy. The front cameras were intended to identify people since there were so many of them facing so many different directions. He had to have known he would be identified quickly. But maybe he had thought Ashley would have been there alone and would be an easy grab and go.

Trish had shot one of the men just before he and the rest were taken out by Sam, Damon, and Ryan. Damon was complaining for an hour about not being able to interrogate anyone, while Trish chastised him about not wanting blood on the floors. Damon huffed around the rest of the time they prepared for the next stage of the operation, making the changes they needed to now that they knew about the traitor in their group.

Richard had disappeared in the action and Shay was completely distraught that he had deceived the whole team. She had decided to go ahead with the plan since it was probably the only way she would be able to get away now. They could hopefully catch Richard as well as the last two who were after Ashley at the accident scene, ensuring everyone's future safety. She didn't feel like she had another option anymore.

The rest of the team was moving along as if nothing had happened. Sam was upset because he had entrusted Richard with Shay's safety years ago when he had her in witness protection. They had fallen in love and Sam was reluctant to bless the union. He was worried being married to Shay would make it more difficult for Richard to be objective in her safety. He struggled knowing he left her in the care of his friend for so many years only to find out he was on the opposite side.

Ashley sat next to Jacob on the couch watching everyone get ready. She was trying to make sense of everything that had happened, particularly with Richard. Things didn't add up in her mind. But then maybe it was because everything in her own life had been turned upside down. But a thought suddenly occurred to her.

"Um, Sam?" she asked, slowly. She hesitated, not sure if she should say anything. It sounded so far-fetched to her, but the situation was nagging at her. Something wasn't right with Professor Roslin, but she couldn't believe after watching him with his wife and boys that he would just change sides, unless he was an amazing, Oscar-worthy actor on top of everything else.

When he looked over, she motioned for him to come to her so she could speak quietly. "What's up, Ash?" He sounded so upset or angry or *something*. She hadn't ever heard this emotion in his voice before that she could remember.

Ashley looked up into his eyes. "Why would Richard wait until now to take Shay? He had so much time while he was married to her and creating a life. Why would he jeopardize all that now? This could have been taken care of years ago, literally."

Sam sat on the coffee table across from her. "I don't know Ash. I don't know. I can't get past my own guilt here to try to figure out his motives."

Looking off to the side, she looked at her twin. "What if Richard had a relative who looked like him?" she said slowly, not sure why she would be defending this man. She remembered a case they worked on before with Jacob's sister where it was actually the brother of the suspect who did the crime.

Surprised, Sam looked at her. "Why would you think that? We saw him. It was Richard."

"But what do you know about him, his family?" She wasn't sure why she was doing this, but something didn't add up. She glanced over at Aja who gave her a slight nod and smiled, like she understood what Ashley was getting at.

Sam stood abruptly and called to Trish. "Aja, Trish, get me everything you can on Richard—" he looked back at Ashley and then turned back "—Preston." He sighed and looked back at Ashley. "I don't know why you are thinking this, but I have learned not to question gut feelings. We changed his name when they got married. He had to leave his family behind too."

He moved quickly back to where Trish was working, and Aja had set up a second laptop to look into the guys from the attack. They were running out of time though. Aja was supposed to be in the park in less than an hour. They had considered skipping the park meeting, not sure now if it would amount to anything, but for now would go as planned.

Ashley watched as everyone hovered around the two computers as the women's fingers ran over the keys and the screens switched and flashed.

"I got something, Sam!" Aja called, even though he was standing right behind her.

"Yep, me too. This isn't good actually," Trish said. Aja glanced over at Trish's screen and Ashley heard a small gasp as Aja turned back to her screen and typed something else, making another document pop up, then she switched back to the original screen.

They moved away from their computers to show the team what they found. Identical photos of Richard, one looked like it was a mug shot and the other was a drivers' license from Florida lit up the two screens.

"Ok, what did you two search?" Sam asked slowly, afraid of what he was going to be told. He leaned on the desk between them, seemingly for extra support.

Aja spoke first. "I did the search on Richard directly and Trish did the search on relatives." She moved a little further from the screen and added, "These are two different people, but look identical with different first names."

"Ok, but that could just be aliases," Ryan said, standing and crossing his arms across his chest. He wasn't challenging but being the critical thinker Aja talked about before. Looking at all possibilities before making a decision. "We see this all the time, Aja."

Aja moved back to her keyboard. "Yeah, I thought of that, so when Trish pulled up her photo, I did a second search on family births." She pulled up another screen and moved away again.

Ashley gasped when she moved closer to see what Aja found. "That's the same document you found…"

"Exactly. Richard was a multiple, a twin." Aja said with a small smile.

A sudden pounding was heard from the front door and everyone's attention moved to the security feeds. A slumped over figure was leaning on the door. Sam moved quickly toward the porch while everyone else was watching the screen.

Sam was almost carrying a man who was badly beaten. His hair was all over the place with what looked like twigs and leaves in it, and his clothing was bloodied and dirty. His face was swollen and bruised already. He could barely walk, and Ashley noticed his knee looked blown out and bloodied as well.

Ashley quickly moved from her chair and brought it over so Sam could set the man down.

"S-sa-m," the man mumbled. "Rod-er-ick…" then he passed out almost falling out of his chair.

Sam looked at the screen and saw the name Roderick. Richard's brother. "Dammit," he said under his breath.

The team moved Richard to the bedroom and Trish took over working on some of his wounds. He looked like he had been taken and beaten pretty badly. The team wasn't sure why they would have taken Richard unless their goal was to create deception and make everyone think it was Richard who had betrayed them. But how did he get free and what did that mean for the rest of Ashley's father's plan?

"We need to find out how long he had been held and how much of our plan has been jeopardized," Sam said as he walked back into the room. "Ryan, get Shay on the phone. I have to know when Richard left their house and if he left on his own or not."

Damon came over to his side as Ryan took out his phone. "He had to have left on his own, Sam. If they knew where he lived, they would have taken Shay already. And we know she was fine this morning. He's obviously been tortured for a while."

Sam nodded. "I hope so, but it still doesn't explain why. I need to talk to Shay."

Just then Ryan handed him the phone. Sam retreated to a corner of the room and talked to his sister for a few minutes then when he hung up, he clutched the phone tightly in his hand and stared at the ceiling.

"What happened, Sam?" Ryan asked.

"Shay isn't sure what time he left. We left here pretty late, but she said he didn't go to bed when she did, instead he had to get some paperwork done he said. He was gone when she woke up," Sam explained quietly. "He was likely gone right after she went to bed, but she didn't hear the car or anything."

The team was quiet for a few minutes before Damon spoke up. "Do you think he planned to go to them all along?"

"I do actually. He would give his life for Shay and the boys. There is no way he would lead them to his house where they would be sleeping and vulnerable." Sam let out a frustrated sigh. "If only he would have clued us in instead of going alone!" He dragged his fingers through his black and gray hair.

"He's safe now," Ryan said, moving to put his hand on his boss' shoulder. "Let's finish this for him and your sister."

Sam nodded. The team reassembled by the computers and Ashley tuned them out. She looked over at Jacob.

"I could never do this job. Too many emotional roller coasters. First, he's the guy you trust with your life then he's the traitor then he's the good guy again." She rolled her eyes. "It's so much."

Jacob chuckled at her. "I agree. Not the life for me. But I'm glad we have them on our side." He kissed the side of her head and pulled her back against him.

It was time to move forward. Aja and the rest of the team started getting ready. They were testing comms when Ashley noticed it was already past the time they were supposed to meet at the park, but they were all still at the house.

"Um, Sam?" she started. "Are you not going to the park?"

Sam glanced over and then motioned to the park cameras they had all over. "No. This is more pressing right now. We have been monitoring it constantly and nothing and no one has shown up to that spot or even walked in that direction. Their plan may have changed when Richard showed up to them. They didn't need you anymore. And right now, the restaurant is our focus. We don't need any more surprises." He gave her a smile and nod and went back to their equipment checks and last minutes plans.

Sharon was going to drop Aja off at the restaurant and then leave as if she were going somewhere else. Then she would come back in through a back door, in different clothes and a hat hiding her face. The rest of the team would be seated at the bar watching with Damon outside in case something happened there before Shay got inside. Trish had set up a small camera for Shay to wear that would look like a decorative pin. This also had a tracker on it in case things went sideways.

They had backup coming in to the situation with them, so the three guys decided to just take one vehicle. If anything came up and they had to separate, they had extra officers to assist with additional transport.

Soon Ashley was waiting and watching again. She opted to watch the screens next to Trish and felt her anxiety rising by the minute. Right before they all headed out, Beau and Kiah had burst through the swinging kitchen door. Beau looked around and Kiah looked frantic.

Standing from her spot, she went to them and gave them a soft smile and light hug.

"Mom said it wasn't him. Sam said he's here. Is he here, Ashley?" Beau asked urgently.

"Yes," she said softly. "Come on." She waved her hand and led them to the bedroom where Richard was resting. Trish had patched him up, but he had been unconscious since he passed out after Sam brought him in. They would have the doctor come once they were back to ensure safety for everyone.

Jacob followed her with two chairs and set them next to the bed. Kiah nodded to him in thanks, and both he and Beau sat down next to Richard.

Ashley and Jacob left to give them privacy.

"And to think I thought I was the one on a roller coaster yesterday!" Ashley mused.

Jacob chuckled next to her. "I have to agree. To go from your dad is an amazing guy to he's a traitor trying to kill your mom to he's a good guy again with an evil twin. Yeah, that's a lot!" He just shook his head, and they made their way back to where Trish was. "Too many roller coasters with no fun," he muttered, making Ashley smile.

"Ok, ready for the action?" Trish asked with a glint in her eye. She looked almost giddy.

Ashley just nodded, not sure how she found this so much fun. It seemed more life and death to her than fun.

Jacob pulled up a chair beside her and she immediately grabbed a tight hold of his hand.

Trish rubbed her hands together and cracked her knuckles. She locked her fingers together, inverted and stretched them, and then wiggled each one. Ashley laughed at her antics, drawing a frown from Trish.

"Don't knock the process little girl," Trisha said with narrowed eyes.

Ashley made a gesture as if zipping her lips shut but couldn't hide the smile while Jacob laughed, earning him a glare as well.

The screen shifted and Ryan's voice was heard over the comms. "Trish, all clear."

"Ten-four," she said. Then she started listing off numbers again, checking their cameras and comms.

After they checked everything, Ryan added, "Keep your eyes peeled. We still don't know how much they know of our plan."

"I gotcha," Trish said and then pressed a couple of buttons, so the screens shifted to a different view. She had three screens in front of her but then Ashley saw her shift the table and then hit a few more keys on her keyboard. She watched the large screen tv's light up with multiple camera views as well.

"What the—" Jacob said looking at all the views. "What happens if there is a breach here again though? We won't see it." There was a trace of anxiety in his voice, clearly remembering the situation a few short hours ago.

Trish chuckled. "Silly boy. Of course I have that covered. If someone gets to the cameras I have on the property, the screen will shift. It will all be fine."

Jacob leaned back in his chair, still holding Ashley's hand in his. "Ok, let's watch the show."

They watched the screens, but nothing seemed to be happening. Either the team wasn't there yet, or they were just blending in perfectly. Then they saw Sharon's car park in front of the restaurant.

"Showtime," Trish whispered.

Ashley held her breath as she watched her twin walk into the restaurant. The view shifted to the hostess stand and then the table as Aja was led to it by the host.

Trish pointed out the team members as they moved into the cameras' view. Ashley spotted Ryan and Sam talking as if they were strangers just meeting by chance at the bar. She still didn't see if Damon and Shay had arrived yet.

Aja sat with a menu, pretending to look at it, but also looking around her as if she were waiting for someone. *She's playing her part well*, Ashley thought with a little bit of pride watching her twin.

Shay still didn't show up. Ashley was starting to get worried. "Why isn't Shay here yet?" she asked Trish.

Trish pulled up the camera from Shay's scarf. Sam had it delivered from a courier so they wouldn't make contact at all. The view showed that she was outside the restaurant. She seemed to be walking at a normal pace which made Ashley feel better.

Just as she was breathing a sigh of relief everything changed. Aja was still sitting at the table waiting and Shay had just entered the building. She was walking toward Aja when everything happened at once. All Ashley saw before everything went blurry was Ryan and Sam suddenly moving out of the frame. It looked like someone set off a smoke bomb or something.

She gasped and stood, staring at the screens in front of her. *What happened?* she thought frantically. Her eyes shifted from screen to screen as Trish tried to clear the visuals for the team. Ryan's voice came over the comms asking Trish what she saw, trying to get clarity.

Ashley couldn't breathe, she couldn't think, her vision started to go blurry. She felt Jacob hold her tight, but she couldn't feel anything else.

"What's going on?" Beau asked from the doorway of the room. He quickly walked over and looked at the white screens. Every one of them was white.

Trish's fingers ran across the keys of her keyboard and just as quickly as it turned white, it cleared. Everyone stared at the screens. Trish's hands froze above her keyboard as she watched over her glasses, her face expressionless.

"Ryan, Damon, What is happening?" Sam's voice came over the speaker.

"No clue, Boss. Is everyone accounted for?" Ryan's voice responded right away.

Each team member did a quick check in, leaving only one unaccounted for.

"Where is Shay?" Sam yelled in his comm, making Trish cringe and turn down the volume.

"Volume, man," she grumbled. "Don't worry, I have a tracker on her. Just hang tight for a minute and then I'll get you a location. Go to your vehicle and wait for my directions." Trish pushed up her glasses and straightened her back in her seat. She wiggled her fingers and then started to type again. "I could use Aja here, Sam. If you can spare her that is." Her eyes never strayed from her screen, typing away. Ashley was impressed with how calm she was.

A few tense moments passed, and everything seemed to be frozen. Ashley couldn't breathe as she waited. At least she knew that her twin was safe for now. Ashley watched the cameras as Ryan, Damon, and Sam ran out of the building heading for their vehicle. It showed them putting Aja into a police cruiser and it speeding off quickly with lights on.

Beau and Kiah stood behind Ashley and Jacob, watching the screens with pale faces. No one moved or spoke, just waited in silence.

"Got it!" Trish shouted. "Sending link now. She appears to be in a vehicle moving fast. Head east on Snow Hill heading for 50. I'll keep you updated where the vehicle turns."

"Roger that," Ryan said. "Aja headed your way with one of the deputies from the sheriff's department a few minutes ago."

The screens showed the team starting their vehicle and taking off, following Trish's directions. Trish disconnected all the screens except the ones tracking Shay. One screen showed what the tiny camera was picking up and the voices in the vehicle with her, the other showed a map with the tracker blinking, accurately tracking her location.

While they waited for Aja to get back to the house, Trish focused on Shay's screens. The video showed clearly who had taken her and they could hear what the men were saying. Shay appeared calm and was sitting up in the vehicle, which was a good sign that they weren't going to hurt her, at least not yet. Her hands were not tied, and her camera showed her rubbing her wrists to show she was not restrained. It took about ten minutes for Aja to get back to the house and she immediately got to work with Trish. Ashley watched in amazement how they quickly worked together and had information to Sam and his team within minutes of sitting down.

By the time the vehicle with Shay stopped, Sam and his team had caught up and parked a short distance away. They moved slowly into position near the vehicle. It stopped at a vacant lot with an abandoned and broken-down chicken house. It was dark outside now and the light was sparce as Ashley continued to watch the action in front of her.

Trish had hit another button, and Ashley saw a red light on her screen. She pointed to it and asked what it was.

Trish grinned. "Voice recorder," she said simply.

Ashley nodded and continued to watch. It didn't take long for Sam, Ryan, and Damon to reach the vehicle and they double checked to make sure it was empty, but Trish had already told them that since she watched them all exit. They moved smoothly toward the chicken house, where Trish had told them Shay was taken.

There was a single light coming from a corner of the dilapidated building. Trish turned up the volume to listen and then relayed info to Sam. She pressed some more buttons, so the audio was then connected to Sam and the rest of the team's comms. The light was bad and there looked to be two shadows.

"I still don't understand why he got you," a voice grumbled. "He always does this; gets everything he wants. Well, time for the tables to turn. And I will finally get what I am owed. Bastard tried to cut me off, well thanks to your good for nothing ex, I finally will get paid back for all my brother's lies and everything he stole from me. Fifteen years he put me away for. His own flesh and blood!" A loud bang was heard, and Ashley jumped. The voice had thrown something against the wall of the building.

The camera view shifted when Shay turned, facing a scene that looked like a bedroom setup. Everyone looked on with confusion. What was this guy planning?

433

"Viper wanted you for himself, Richard wanted you for himself. Well, now you will make me some serious cash sweetheart." The camera finally showed the owner of the voice, and it looked exactly like Richard, which meant it had to be Roderick. He gripped Shay's chin tightly and she let out a small whimper at the force of it.

Ashley gasped as she realized what was happening. Roderick had picked up a video camera of some sort and then directed Shay to remove her clothes.

"You can either do it yourself or I will help. And I promise I won't be gentle," Roderick said with a sick chuckle.

"Oh, now that is no way to speak to a lady," Damon's voice came over the speaker.

Ashley nearly jumped for joy as she watched through Shay's camera. Damon stalked toward Roderick who had fumbled looking for his gun. Sam and Ryan were missing, but she figured they were taking care of the other two men they saw in the vehicle on Shay's camera. She looked at the other camera views but remembered the only two were Shay's. They didn't have any for outside the building.

As if reading her mind, Ryan's voice came over in stereo. "Targets one and two out. He's all yours, Damon." He even let out a laugh, knowing this is what Damon had been waiting for.

Damon laughed darkly. "You lookin' for this?" He held a gun up by the handle. "Tsk, tsk. Silly boy. You shouldn't be allowed to play with guns. These are for the big people. You should have just done what your boss wanted. Now you will have to deal with me." He cracked his knuckles after flinging the gun behind him. "And I am itching for a fight. Come on, tough guy. Let's play."

Chapter 31

It was late, well after midnight by the time everyone returned. Ashley and Aja had made some food for everyone so they could eat when they came back. They would need to focus on what to do next without worrying about dinner. They had finished just in time for everyone to show up and without speaking, everyone took plates of food and took seats around the house to eat and start their processing and planning their next steps.

The entire team gathered around the large table with Sam and his team at one end eating and quietly talking. Trish and Sharon joined them after a few minutes. The whiteboards were pushed aside, and a new one was set up. Shay was holding Richard, who had finally woken up. He was disoriented but he would be ok. The doctor had looked him over and did what he could for his healing. Beau and Kiah were sitting behind them, waiting to hear what was going to happen next.

Ashley and Aja sat side by side with Jacob holding Ashley's hand. Sam, Ryan, Damon, Sharon, and Trish were sitting at the end of the table going over documents and papers spread over the table in front of them after they finished eating. No one was speaking yet, which Aja explained was normal when they were processing. So, she and Aja cleaned up the table and then settled back down to listen.

"Ok, let's get this figured out so we can all go home." Sam looked out at everyone gathered, holding their intense attention. I have the sheriff taking care of our friend Roderick. Damon did a little number on him, in self-defense of course, but he will be pretty quiet for a few days. That will give us time to gather what we need on Vernon to keep him there."

"Sam, are we sure it was dad, or was it just Roderick going rogue?" Aja asked quietly.

Sam sighed. "Sorry Aja. Your father had orchestrated the kidnapping and killing of Shay. Roderick has been one of his guys for decades, even before you girls were born, well the three of you," he said, glancing at Beau. "But Roderick did go rogue on taking Shay for his own purposes. We believe he planned to disappear after he sold her. I guess he thought it would kill two birds with one stone. He would get Vernon off his back thinking he had killed Shay, and he could also have made some money in selling her into human trafficking." His eyes tracked to Shay.

"Jones and Blake, who we caught and neutralized outside the restaurant, caved pretty quickly in lieu of a lifetime of prison—preferably in Vernon's same accommodations. Once Roderick was brought in, they sang like canaries, I'm sure to stay out of Roderick's way. He's a pretty dangerous guy, connected to many different criminal activities, including sex trafficking, which is why we believe that was his plan for Shay." Ryan gave Shay a sympathetic nod. "Well and we figured out that Jonah Blake was the undercover detective once we got him in custody."

Ashley sat up straighter. "So, when I saw Professor Roslin following me all those times, it was probably Roderick?"

"That is what we are looking into. We know it wasn't Richard, but we need to investigate a little bit more to make sure it was in fact Roderick and not someone else," Sam confirmed. "It seems he was copying everything Richard did or had to make it look like Richard was after you and not Roderick."

Ashley shivered, thinking about what could have happened. Aja and Jacob put their arms around her from each side, calming her.

"Sharon, why don't you take the girls and Jacob back to your place for tonight," Sam said softly. He turned to Shay and Richard. "Maybe you should head home too. We will figure this out here and you guys need to get some rest. We will reconvene in the morning. Or maybe lunch time." He smirked, looking at his watch, noticing it was so late already.

Within a few minutes Sharon, Aja, Ashley, and Jacob were heading to Sharon's vehicle. Shay and her boys helped Richard get to their car as well. They agreed to come together the next day around lunch time.

Ashley settled into the back seat next to Jacob and Aja sat in the front. She tried to keep her eyes opened but it was difficult. The events of the past two days had been overwhelming, and she just wanted to sleep. It didn't take long for darkness to win, and she fell sound asleep.

* * * * *

Ashley stretched and quickly realized she wasn't alone. She looked over to see Jacob still asleep next to her. The events of the night before rushed back, and she sat up suddenly.

Jacob startled and sat up with her. "It's ok, Ash. Everyone is ok." He gently rubbed her back.

Nodding, she leaned into his side. "What time is it? When are we meeting Sam again? Wait, where's Aja?" She sat upright again and looked around frantically, knowing her apartment didn't have anywhere for her sister to sleep.

"Shh, it's ok. She's in one of Sharon's guest rooms. Let's get dressed and go see what they are doing, ok?" Jacob's voice was soft and calm, making Ashley nod and relax a little. Her nerves were still on edge though and she wanted to see her sister for herself.

Ashley opted for a quick shower to see if that would help settle her nerves. She needed to see everyone to make sure they were all ok like Jacob said. While she stood under the hot water, her thoughts drifted to the last few days. It was amazing to think that just a few days ago she was looking to find and meet a possible sibling to learning her biological mom was alive and her father was orchestrating an elaborate plan to kill that same person, which then turned into a completely different bizarre plan.

A knock on the door broke her of her thoughts as she shook her head. "Just a second!" she called and turned off the stream of water. She quickly wrapped herself in a towel and listened to see if the person, assuming it was Jacob, was still at the door.

"Hello?" she said loudly.

"Hey, Ash, Just me. You've been in there for almost a half hour. Just wanted to make sure you're ok." Jacob said from the other side of the door.

Ashley smiled as she thought about his concern. She was so glad he was here, and Aja was here. She was even happy Sam was here. She quickly dressed and opened the door, revealing Jacob fully dressed and leaning against the door frame.

"I'm glad you're ok, Ash," he said as he pulled her close for a tight hug. She knew he was talking about the events of the last couple days and not just the long shower she took.

"And I'm glad you are here, Jake. Let's go see Aja," she said with a smile.

They made their way downstairs and met Sharon, Gary, and Aja laughing about something.

"Well, look who decided to finally wake up," Aja said with a laugh as she met her sister's outstretched arms.

"How are you feeling, dear?" Sharon asked.

Ashley smiled. "I'm good. Glad that I have Jacob, Aja, and Sam here though."

"I'm sure you are!" she said with a chuckle. "What an amazing team he has too. Quite impressive." Sharon moved to the counter to pour herself a cup of coffee and motioned to Ashley and Jacob to help themselves as she set two more mugs on the counter.

"I sure wish I could have been there during the excitement," Gary said with a grin, and then quickly turned back to his newspaper.

Ashley couldn't help but wonder what he really thought of all this. He wasn't a part of anything the day before, so she wasn't sure what he did before he retired.

"Well, you guys grab some breakfast and then we can talk for a bit if you need to. We can head over to Trish's when you are ready. Sam let me know this morning they have everything set and we just need to wrap up." Sharon moved to the other side of the kitchen and sat next to her husband.

"Don't they ever sleep?" Ashley asked quietly, making Aja laugh.

Shaking her head, Aja said, "No they don't. Sally Jo asked the same thing when she helped us with that case last year. It gets in their blood, and they don't quit until it is completely taken care of."

Jacob grabbed their cups of coffee and Ashley noticed there was a plate of muffins on the island. She took the seat next to Aja and helped herself to a blueberry one, putting another in front of Jacob.

"So, what do we have to do today?" Ashley asked, looking at Sharon.

Sharon shrugged. "Not sure, but not too much. By the time we get there, everything will be done from a police/FBI standpoint. Then we will all just be there to help with processing and any lingering questions. My guess is they will have already talked to the proper authorities to make sure Vernon is taken care of."

Aja nodded. "Yeah, that sounds about right actually."

"Could we just meet here then? Or somewhere other than the house? It was a little traumatizing," Ashley asked quietly.

Aja and Sharon exchanged looks. Aja spoke first though. "Actually, it is better if we meet there. Sam has some photos to have you look at to see if you recognize anything and all their equipment is there," she explained.

Ashley met her eyes and just nodded. "Do they know why everything happened the way it did now?"

"I think so, Let's just finish up here and then we can go talk to them," Aja said, watching Ashley closely.

Ashley lifted her eyes to meet her sister's gaze. "You know you seem pretty relaxed Aja Doesn't this affect you?"

"Oh, it does, but I think I have been in this world for so long now that I have adjusted to the crazy," she said with a grin. "But the whole thing about our biological mother being alive? Yeah, that will take a little bit." She wrapped her arms around Ashley. "And we have brothers! *What?*"

The girls wrapped their arms around each other and hugged, laughing. Ashley was grateful once again to have her other half next to her.

They talked a little bit longer and then cleaned up the kitchen to go meet the rest of the group. Ashley felt a little anxious about going back to the house but decided with her sister and Jacob next to her she would be ok. And Sam was there too. *It would be fine*, she decided.

The small group drove up to the house and were greeted almost immediately by Trish. Stepping onto her porch would never get old, Ashley thought. And she felt safer once she got there knowing that cameras caught everything going on. They had even saved her and Jacob the day before when the property was breached.

She took a deep breath moving through the kitchen into the larger space they had spent so much time in the last twenty-four or thirty-six hours. Ashley noticed all the shades had been lifted and the room was flooded with light. It had been transformed and looked completely different with the natural light streaming in. The whiteboards were gone except for one that was now situated next to the screens on the wall. The table with all of Trish's gear was gone and a simple desk was in its place with just one computer and an extra screen. It all just looked so natural that Ashley was even wondering if it was all just a dream.

Trish followed them in and even she looked different. She had a soft smile on her face and was dressed casually in jeans and a t-shirt. Sam looked freshly showered and for the first time, Ashley wondered what else the house had in it. Were there other bedrooms? What other spaces were functional?

Her thoughts were interrupted by Sam's hand on her arm. "How are you holding up, Ashley?"

She turned to see his concerned eyes and raised eyebrows. She lightly touched his cheek.

"I'm ok, Sam. It was, well *is*, a lot to take in. But I think I understand. There is still some processing and shock to overcome, but we will be fine." She looked around him and then asked, "Where is Shay and the rest?"

"They are at home trying to heal and relax a little. I thought it would be best to finish this up and then we can all go to dinner or something. Let's go sit down and close this out, ok?" He nodded toward the table and Ashley grabbed Jacob's hand and pulled him with her.

"Alright everyone. We are going to give you a brief rundown of everything, so we are all on the same page and then answer any questions from there." Ryan started out as Sam, Aja, Ashley, and Jacob took seats around the table. Damon was absent she noticed. Sharon and Trish stood off to the side near the kitchen door.

Ryan ran through everything they had gathered and what they reported back to the courts in regard to Vernon's appeal and parole. His accomplices informed Sam and his team that they were given clear instructions to kill Shay and if they could get to Beau kill him as well. He had money hidden somewhere and used it to pay for the job. The money could be traced back to his crimes from before of money laundering and illegal trade, mostly guns and drugs Sam said. All the team's contacts within the courts and prison system were confident he would not be granted parole or a new trial given everything they had uncovered.

The team had managed to get everything from her father's lackeys recorded on video and audio and since they didn't get to Shay, she had all her previous evidence still stored and intact. Jonah Blake had also given evidence, anonymously, so he could continue his assignment undercover, supporting the activities and also had some additional evidence to connect Ashley's father to other crimes he had committed while in prison.

Ashley also learned that it was likely Roderick who was following her all the times that she thought it was Professor Roslin. He had apparently purchased a car that looked identical to the professor's as well, which was likely why Ashley couldn't tell them apart when she saw Kiah in Professor Roslin's car at Raelynn's. Roderick had developed the plan only a few weeks before when it was confirmed that Ashley was in Salisbury. It wasn't much before that when Vernon knew about the DNA report and Beau still being alive.

With her head spinning, Ashley started to tune things out. It was just so much to handle. She zoned out thinking about the evil of one person so intent on selling another human being into sexual slavery as they had uncovered the plan of selling her biological mother by Roderick. It turned out the other guys didn't want to participate in anything other than what Vernon had asked for—mostly because it was extra hassle and work that they wouldn't get paid for.

Her thoughts were interrupted by Damon entering the room with a huge grin on his face. He clapped his hands together and slapped Ryan on the back.

"That has to be the most fun I have had in a long time, brother," he said to Ryan, who rolled his eyes.

Ryan scoffed at him. "I am sure there have been more fun times, Damon. Like that guy we surprised who happened to have two little girls with him when we stormed in," Ryan said with a pointed look. "He was not prepared for you, let alone to be caught so soon after getting out."

Damon's face fell. "I forgot about that low life. Yes, that was more fun. I hate sex offenders, especially the ones who exploit kids." Then his grin returned, and he shrugged. "But the Rod-Man was so much fun." He rubbed his hands together and Ryan nodded his head at the group, making Damon stop talking and mumble an apology.

"Really? A nickname?" Sam asked, but his face was full of humor.

Ashley didn't understand the dynamic between them, but their interactions were comical. She leaned into Jacob and took in a deep breath of air.

"So, Sam, are we good?" Aja asked, looking between her twin and her uncle.

"We are good. Your father should be stuck where he is for a long time. And I am pretty sure we got the last two who have stayed loyal to him. The rest kind of fell off the face of the earth, likely in hiding waiting to start their own operation without Vernon at the helm." Sam looked at everyone at the table and nodded. "Thank you to everyone. This could not have happened without every single one of you."

Ryan stood taller and added, "Let's get out of here. I have to make a quick call home and let Lundyn know we are all good and will be home soon."

"Sounds good. You can call in the car. Let's go." Sam waved his hand to let everyone know they could leave. Trish stayed behind and said she would get everything locked up and meet up wherever they had planned.

Ashley walked out feeling lighter than she had since she left Minnesota not even two months ago.

Chapter 32

Aja had decided to stay with Ashley for a few days after the rest of her team left. They had planned to get to know their new family and then they would both decide what to do next. Raelynn had been missing from the events of the team, but she had texted Ashley that she wanted to meet Aja, so they had planned to meet up for dinner with Raelynn, Sahara, Jacob, Beau, and Kiah. Ashley had learned from their mom that she chose Kiah's name because it was an old African name meaning new beginning or new life. It seemed fitting.

Ashley still hadn't decided what to do about school, but she had told her sister she would make that decision before Aja left. She wanted to stay and get to know her brothers, but she had also started to take a liking to the Eastern Shore, despite the stifling heat and humidity. She loved being this close to the ocean and had yet to bring Aja.

"Aja, I think we should go visit CeCe's grave," Ashley said suddenly, as they were getting ready for dinner. She would have to find out exactly where it was when they talked to Sam again, but she felt strongly that she needed to thank her. She selflessly gave her life up for Ashley and her sister, figuratively and literally. Ashley felt like she deserved so much more than just a "thank you".

Aja nodded, thinking the same thing. "I agree. She deserves so much more than she got in life. I wish we could have known sooner, or that she could have had the chance to be our aunt now." Her voice was sad as she thought about what they had missed out on because of their father—primarily extended family and connection.

Aja's hair was still in her naturally colored braids. She said she liked them and would think about changing it when she needed it tightened up again.

Ashley was pulling hers up into a high and thick pony in front of the mirror in her apartment. Now that things were settled, Sharon and Gary offered to take her to one of their more spacious places if she stayed.

A light knock interrupted them, and Sharon stepped inside. "Ashley, dear, we are going to head out too. Make sure you lock up and we will touch base later, ok?" She gave them a nod and smiled.

"Ok, Sharon. Thanks again for everything! I wouldn't have been able to do this without you and Gary," Ashley said and gave her a hug.

"Oh, psh. You would have done just fine. But I am glad that Sam reached out and we could accomplish what we did. A few more bad guys off the streets and I can go back into retirement," she said and wiggled her eyebrows.

Ashley laughed. "Ok, enjoy your retirement! The flowers outside are amazing, so retirement must be going well."

Sharon nodded and then waved. "Have fun tonight!" And then she was gone.

"I'm so glad you had people here, Ash, even if it was Sam's doing," her sister said with a smirk.

"Yeah, I guess he's ok to have around, huh?" she grinned back.

"Of course I am nice to have around," Jacob joked, walking into the space Sharon just vacated. He brushed his chest and struck some weird pose, making both girls giggle at him.

Ashley walked over and gave him a kiss on the cheek and patted his chest. "Yeah, you're pretty ok."

"Are we ready?" Aja asked.

"Ready," Ashley said. She grabbed her keys, and they headed for the door.

Sam had made sure her car was ready to go before he left. He must have pulled some strings for it to get done that quickly, but she was glad to have it back good as new.

* * * * *

Once they were all seated at the long table, Aja asked what the plan was for the rest of the time she stayed.

Ashley shrugged. "I still have to take you to the ocean."

Everyone around the table had an idea of where they should go. Raelynn was over the moon gushing about Ashley and Aja being so similar and they couldn't help but compare them to Beau who looked completely different. It made everyone laugh, with Beau feigning offense saying he wouldn't want to look like a girl anyway.

Suddenly, Ashley clapped her hands. "I know!" All eyes turned to her. "Let's do a tour of Europe!"

"The heck are you talking about?" Raelynn asked, her nose wrinkled.

Ashley grinned. "So, this isn't a thing? Do you really not notice the names of your towns? Is that why there are like a million of them ending in 'ville'? No imagination?" she smirked at the locals around the table.

Everyone looked at her dumbfounded. She laughed harder and then waved it off. "Ok, let's do tours of Cambridge, Vienna, and Berlin. You know, England, Austria, and Germany."

Slowly realization dawned on everyone except Aja. Confused, she looked around. "Ok, I'm lost."

Raelyn laughed and turned to Aja, she added, "Those are small towns around here. Your sister is weird."

"Hey, it would be fun!" Ashley protested.

Everyone looked at each other and then shrugged.

"Ok, let's do it!" Raelynn said with a laugh. "A tour of Europe, Maryland style!"

Other works by this author

Bellbrook Springs Series
A Journey of the Heart
A Journey of the Mind
A Journey of the Soul
A Journey for Justice—in the works
A Journey for Peace—in the works

Coming Next
Bonded Blood, The Sense of Belonging, book 2
Mixed Blood, The Sense of Belonging, book 3

Following me on

Instagram at brendabenningauthor
TikTok @brendabenningauthor
And Facebook at Brenda B's Bellbrook Springs page

www.ingramcontent.com/pod-product-compliance
Lightning Source LLC
Chambersburg PA
CBHW030729230325
23750CB00001B/1